When the Harvest Moon Rises

Scott Welker

SLEEPING HOUSE, LLC

CHAPTER 1

Her Father's death was the last one. It happened in November before the first snow, which made her part easier. She had waited, anticipating how things would change after the last one was gone. And she was right, things did change, but not entirely in ways she expected. Bedroom doors could remain open now; that she expected. No more whispers in the halls; that she also expected. No more nameless strangers in every room, illuminated only by dim candlelight. No more long nights filled with secrets and cracking, calloused hands. Now, she would find her peace.

What she hadn't expected, though, was the silence. She expected its presence but not its temper. She expected its friendship, not its deviousness. She hadn't expected the relentless weight of it or the way it slithered through the corridors, up the winding staircase, down the long hallways and into every hollow space. She hadn't expected the way it would ring in her ears nor, as the years stole her sight, the way she feared it and welcomed it all at once.

She had always talked to herself. Her Father told her that, when she was a child, she would sit by herself and jabber endlessly. With him gone, there was no longer a reason to hide it. An occasional few words grew to strings of sentences until she no longer distinguished the voice in her head from the voice in her throat. She would mutter the words of the life she had thought she buried with her Father as she paced the floors of her empty home. She spent her days in conversations she had once had, snippets that had once been

whispered by the visitors, and the oft-repeated words of her Father's
rhyme he had taught to her like gospel:

When the harvest moon rises
O'er the briars and berms,
There is work to be done
Before daylight returns.
For soon come the cold nights,
The long winter chill,
The hard, frozen earth
That won't break under steel.
Soon comes the season
When no work can be done.
So, finish your chores.
Don't wait for the sun.

First, to the attic
Where the cobwebs have massed.
Dig through the remains
Of years that have passed.
For those still alive,
Find blankets and pelts.
Stash the belongings
Of everyone else.

Next, to the rooms
Where visitors sleep.
Make sure there is nothing
Unpleasant to see.
Scrub every surface
And hide every stain.
Every house has its secrets
That need not be explained.

Then to the woods,
Past the thick, clinging shadows,
For kindling and fuel
In the darkening hours.
Be sure that the fire

Is steady and hot.
Both clothing and bedding
Must burn down to naught.

Last, to the cellar
Where the dead things have lingered
While their flesh falls away
From their toes to their fingers.
Gather them up
And out to the yard.
Sharpen your shovels
For, the ground there is hard.
Turn over the dirt,
The grass and the stones
And bury the bones
And bury the bones.

1974

CHAPTER 2

Edith's Hollow wasn't like any town Jaime had ever seen. He caught his first glimpse of it as the long, wood-paneled car he was riding in came around a large hill and peeked over the tree line before descending gradually. The landscape surrounding them was speckled with yellow and orange and red as the first signs of autumn began to show amidst the green on the trees.

"There it is," his Mom said.

He looked out in front of him and a little to the east where a tiny bundle of homes lay in a small valley in the distance. He didn't bother to lift his head, which had been resting against the window of their station wagon in boredom for nearly an hour. The window had grown colder every day since he and his mom left Kingman. The small, foggy spot beneath his nostrils expanded abruptly as he huffed out a breath of disbelief.

'THIS is it?' he thought to himself.

He couldn't believe how tiny it was. Kingman might have been small but it was nothing like this. Besides, Kingman was home to all of his favorite things. There was a dirt trail that ran behind the junk yard which led to a spot where he and his friends hung out. It was by a river bed with shrubs and cottonwood trees that provided shade from the hot, Arizona sun. They called the place Glass Canyon because of all the bottles they would find in the dirt where the river once ran. They liked to collect them and pile them up in a corner under the giant tree with drooping, leafy branches that hung to the ground and created an outdoor shelter. They stashed their fireworks there, too and never worried about getting caught when they'd set them off at the bottom of the ravine.

There was a café on Route 66 where they would order a plate of French Fries and eat them with mayonnaise. The waitress never asked them where their parents were or scowled at them when they came in. There was an empty, dirt field close to Jaime's house with long rows of short hills that were perfect for jumping on his bike or riding up and over one after the other, after the other, after the other...

When his mom told him they were leaving Kingman for some tiny town in Massachusetts, he couldn't believe she could be so mean. What about his friends and Glass Canyon? Didn't she care that they didn't know anyone in Massachusetts? Couldn't she get a teaching job anywhere else? Or, why couldn't she just find some other kind of job? None of it made any sense. The school year had already started and she was ripping him away from everything he knew.

"These woods are so dark," his mom said, interrupting his thoughts. "How does anyone see in here?"

They had dipped back down beneath the tree line, into thick forest. His mom was right. It was early evening and the sun was low but still giving off a misty, colorful hue. You would hardly know it, though. The woods were so dense and the shadows so thick, they choked away hours of light from the sky. The narrow, winding road Jaime and his mom were on was crowded on each side by trees and shrubs.

Jaime gazed out the window at the landscape zooming by. There was almost a rhythm to the tall tree trunks passing swiftly, interrupted by an occasional mile post or a yellow or green sign. After two or three minutes of this, they passed something that caught his eye. A bald spot where the road met the woods stood out amidst the green. It passed quickly but he thought he saw a small, almost indistinguishable foot path that led straight into the heart of the dark forest. Something about the thought of walking that path and entering those woods made him squirm a little in his seat.

Suddenly Jaime could hear a voice in his head. "Are you scared?" it said tauntingly. It was his Dad's voice and he hated it.

"Don't be such a sissy," the voice said. Jaime knew it was right and that made him hate it even worse. He hated how easy fear came to him and he hated his Dad for always pointing it out. He hadn't seen his Dad at all since the divorce but, honestly, he didn't really care. He felt determined, though, not to be a scared little kid anymore the next time he saw him.

"Isn't it pretty here?" his mom interrupted his thoughts again.

Without moving his head, Jaime shifted his eyes to the front windshield. They were entering town now. There were a few cows in a small, grassy field to his right that backed up to a thick, imposing wall of bushy trees. A wooden sign just ahead said, "Entering Edith's Hollow." Small letters near the bottom said "est. 1896."

His mom had filled Jaime's head with dates and stories from Massachusetts history over the last few weeks, since getting her new teaching job. He couldn't tell if it was nerves or excitement that was making her so eager. Either way, he thought she was being a little over-ambitious. Although he wasn't in high school yet, he was pretty sure her students weren't any more enthusiastic about their history classes than he was about his.

Maybe a thing or two had stuck, though. The date on the sign seemed a little strange to him. From what his mom had told him, Massachusetts was way older than 1896. He expected this place to be older than that.

"These trees are breathtaking," his mom carried on. "Look how they are starting to change colors already. You don't get that in Arizona, do you?"

"Mmmm," he replied, still not moving his head from the window it was resting against.

After a brief moment of silence, his mom spoke again. This time, her tone sounded much more solemn.

"Jaime," she said, "I know you didn't want to leave Kingman. Trust me, this isn't easy for either of us. But, I think we can be happy here. Just don't give up on it before at least giving it a shot. Can you do that for me?"

He resisted the urge to just say "mmmm" again, knowing his Mom was hoping for something a little more thoughtful.

"Yeah, I guess," he said with a sigh.

———————————————

Edith's Hollow had just one of everything. There was one church with a tall, white steeple near the middle of town. There was one grocery store, one mechanic, and one school house where every kid of every age attended.

Nothing in town was new. The few roads that were paved were faded and cracking and the buildings were stuck in an era nearly 100 years passed. Things were kept up well enough with fresh coats of paint and cut grass in the yards but it was as if the townspeople felt that Edith's Hollow would be defiled if anything old were taken down or anything new added. The homes were no exception. The same houses had populated the land for as long as anyone could remember. No one added to them anymore. Strangers almost never moved in but if they did, it was only after someone left or died.

Jaime looked around his new home. The white paint on the outside was faded and inside it felt cramped and drafty. The creaky, wood floors didn't help. It had three small bedrooms, a small kitchen, one and a half small bathrooms, and a small living room with a small fireplace. The fireplace hogged up all the space right in the middle of the living-room wall where Jaime thought a TV should be instead. Apparently, nobody was thinking of that back when the house was built.

Outside was a raised porch that faced the narrow dirt road that led to the driveway. There were no fences or anything that marked off either a front or a back yard. There was no landscaping or grass other than that which sprung up naturally. Standing at the front door, Jaime looked around and saw nothing but trees. The nearest neighbor was back up the main road about a quarter mile and out of sight.

He was struck by the way the forest threatened to overtake the entire town. It was like a slow, creeping flood of brown and green poised to choke out the village and everything in it. He walked around to the back of the house and, looking west, gazed into the trees gradually becoming thicker and thicker until, a few hundred yards ahead, they formed a dense mass that swallowed the light.

Just then, the sound of tires on loose dirt caught his attention. He walked back around to the front of the house where his mom, who had also heard their visitor approaching, was coming out of the front door Jaime had left open. A white truck with police lights on top and decals that read "Sherriff" pulled up behind their car and came to a stop.

A short man with thinning, jet black hair, a receding hair line, and a thick mustache stepped out.

"You're the Ellingtons?" he said, standing next to his truck and leaning on the opened door.

"Hi." Jaime's mom replied. "That's right, we are. I'm Kat, this is Jaime."

The man nodded his head and closed the truck door. He took a few, meandering steps forward, looking around like he was casually investigating a crime scene.

"Is everything alright?" Jaime's mom asked.

His head popped up. "Oh yeah; sure, sure. Just came by to…" a quick pause like he needed a second to think "welcome you to Edith's Hollow."

"Well, thank you very much. Would you like to come in?"

He had made his way around the back of their station wagon where he nonchalantly peered into the windows while he moved around the car. "You've got a lot of stuff in here," he said.

"You can help us move it in, if you'd like," Jaime's mom said, only half joking.

The officer smiled and walked toward the porch where Jaime and his mom stood. He stopped short of the steps just in front of him. His full attention was now on the mother and son.

"They say you're from Arizona."

"Yep," Jaime's Mom said. "How about you? Have you always lived in Edith's Hollow?"

The officer snorted out an abrupt laugh like she had asked a stupid question. "Yeah, I've always lived in Edith's Hollow. Born and raised here," he said, "just like my dad and his dad before him. My great grandfather was one of the founders of Edith's Hollow." There was a clear sense of pride in his voice. "We were all born and raised here."

"You mean your whole family?"

"I mean the whole town," he said, staring at the two looking down at him. He turned his gaze to the open door behind Jaime's mom, straining his neck just a little so he could see inside. "Have you moved any of your stuff in?" he asked.

13

Jaime's mom shook her head. "We just got here about 30 minutes ago so, no. We haven't started. We could use an extra set of hands."

The officer shifted his feet in the dirt. "Wish I could," he said, tapping the badge on his chest "but I've got work to do. There's only one law enforcement officer around here and you're looking at him. But like I said, just wanted to stop by and welcome you to town." He started walking back to his truck. "Give me a holler if you need anything."

"Thank you. Good to meet you," Jaime's mom said.

He opened the truck door and paused before crawling inside, looking back up at the pair on the porch. "I hope you'll stay out of trouble." He smiled to soften his words but they certainly sounded serious.

Jaime and his mom watched the truck disappear into the trees.

"That was strange," she said.

"What do you mean?" Jaime asked.

She continued staring in the direction of the disappeared vehicle for a moment then she shook her head. "Nothing. Let's get these boxes inside."

CHAPTER 3

School was in an old, dingy building with a large, open-air courtyard in the middle that was surrounded by classrooms. The brick walls formed a square around the courtyard with several white, wooden classroom doors facing it. One wall of classrooms forming the square was for the youngest children from kindergarten through third grade, one for the elementary school students, one for the middle school students, and one for the high school students.

Jaime was eleven so his classroom was on the middle school wall. He walked several steps behind his mom while he searched the numbers on the doors for his. His mom found it first and turned around to tell him. "It's right here, Jaime," she called out. He nodded his head and quickened his pace to get inside, hoping nobody saw their exchange.

"Thanks," he muttered as he passed her.

"Jaime," she said before he could enter the classroom, "I forgot to tell you that I have to go up to Fall River this afternoon when I'm done teaching so I won't be here when you get out. I have to fill out some paperwork at the community college before classes start next week. It's about an hour away so, I'll try to get home before dark but I'm not sure I will."

"OK," he said, anxiously wishing the conversation would end before someone spotted him standing in the classroom doorway talking to his mom. He felt like such a baby with her classroom just three doors down from his.

She reached down and tussled his hair. Jaime quickly moved his head and squirmed a little. "Mom!" he said in annoyance.

She laughed. "It must be so rough having a mom that loves you."

She didn't see the subtle roll of his eyes.

"Be good. Make friends. I'll see you this evening."

"Bye," he muttered as he ducked into his classroom.

His teacher, Ms. Spencer, was tall and skinny with a face like a mouse. Her dark hair was pulled back firmly into a tight bun on the back of her head. Her nose was pointed and her mouth was small and looked like it had never seen a smile.

She wielded a sturdy yard stick which she loudly and aggressively rapped against the chalkboard when she needed to get her students' attention. "Quiet" she was saying as the yard stick hit the hard, black surface. Tiny particles of chalk dust flew. Silence swiftly fell over the room.

Jaime settled into his assigned seat in the front corner and looked around. The girl sitting next to him seemed friendly. She smiled at him as he sat down but neither said anything. A few rows back, two boys were laughing quietly and trying not to be spotted by Ms. Spencer. Jaime had noticed them earlier coming in with another boy who was now sitting on the opposite side of the room. They seemed cool.

His head snapped around to his teacher when he heard her say his name.

"And class, this is Jaime. He's new. He and his mom aren't from here."

Her introduction sounded more like a warning than a welcome. He expected her next words to be something like "say hi to him at the break," or, "we're glad to have you, Jaime." But she didn't say anything more. She simply moved on.

The first break was at 10:00. He had no idea where to go. He wandered into the courtyard where there were just a few kids hanging out. Out back was a larger outdoor area with some play equipment for the younger kids. He meandered around for a little before going back inside.

He felt like everyone was watching him so he did his best to look like he was walking with a purpose. He tried to hide the fact that really, he had no idea where to go. He was afraid of what everyone must be thinking of him.

There was a spacious area inside the school building with a basketball court and bleachers. He followed the noise to it and saw that that's where most of the kids were hanging out. He hadn't been there long when someone called out to him.

"Hey, new kid!"

He looked up to see one of the guys he had noticed earlier laughing in the back of the classroom.

"Hey," he said back.

"What's your name?"

"Jaime." One of the kids snickered when he said it. "But sometimes people call me James," he quickly added. It was a lie; no one ever called him James but it wasn't the first time it occurred to him that he had a girl's name. "What's about you? What's your name?" he asked.

"Mark. And that's Danny, and Joe."

"Look," Danny said, peering in another direction, "there's Paul Harrison. You know, I don't think he was around all summer. I didn't see him once." He nodded towards a short, pudgy kid with neatly parted and combed hair.

"I heard his folks shipped him off to stay with his grandparents in New York," another one chimed in. "I mean, can you blame them?"

The other boys laughed. Jaime did too because it just felt like the thing to do.

"We oughta get him back for getting us detention on the last day of school last year," Danny said, looking at Mark.

"Yeah right," Joe said, "his mom's a teacher."

"Yeah," Mark added. "He doesn't sneeze without his mom bringing him a Kleenex."

Again, everyone laughed, including Jaime.

"What are you laughing at, Jaime?" Mark said. "Your Ma's a teacher too."

"No she's not," he blurted out, instinctively.

"Come on," Danny joined in, "she's the new history teacher for the high school kids. What, she didn't tell you?"

Again, they laughed.

"How'd you know that?" he asked, surprised.

17

"What do you mean, how'd we know?" Mark sounded genuinely confused. "Everyone knows. You guys came up here from Arizona and moved into Mr. Harper's old place. Why wouldn't we know?"

Just then, the bell rang and everyone's attention shifted. The guys turned on their heels and started heading back to class. Jaime watched them for a moment before he followed.

By the time he walked home from school that afternoon, Jaime was fuming. In his mind, he had played back the conversation between him and Mark and the other guys over and over. Why did his mom have to be a teacher at his school? Why did they have to move to this stupid town? He hated it. He wanted to be back home in Kingman.

The next day his class took a field trip.

"One of the most important things I can teach you," Ms. Spencer said before they left, "is love and loyalty for Edith's Hollow. No doubt, you have been told that this town is special. Today, we are going to explore some of the things that make it special. Who knows what the Town's Heart is?"

Several hands were raised. "It's that book," a girl in the back said.

"Don't speak out of turn, Sarah" Ms. Spencer said firmly. "But, yes, you are correct. It is a book. Can you tell me what is in it?"

Sara shrugged her shoulders before continuing. "It's like history about our town I guess."

Ms. Spencer sighed a disappointed sigh. "Class, this is very important. The book we call the Town's Heart is more than just a history book. It is a living relic. Our forefathers who founded Edith's Hollow had the wisdom to compile their writings, pictures and stories into a volume and to pass the collection on to their children. Every generation that has lived in this place has added their voice to the book. One day, your generation will have its turn. What will the things you leave behind say about who you were? How will they add to our town's rich heritage? When we see the Town's Heart today, I want you to think about these things. We are not just going to see a book. We are going to honor the legacy of our ancestors.

A visit to a library to see a book? Jaime thought to himself. *What a lame field trip.*

"Now, everybody, line up!" Ms. Spencer said, loud and authoritatively. "We can leave as soon as you show me you are ready."

The class's neatly formed line quickly fell apart when they got beyond the school yard. As they walked across town, Jaime watched his peers form into groups of two or three or four. He felt like he was the only person walking by himself and he hoped he wasn't standing out. He imagined in his mind Ms. Spencer striking up a conversation with him in front of his classmates and he shuttered at the thought. Fortunately, Ms. Spencer didn't seem to care that he was walking by himself and, before he knew it, they arrived at the library.

The book they had come to see was displayed on a heavy wooden stand at the entrance with thick glass protecting it.

"No chattering, class," Ms. Spencer said as everybody entered. "Gather around."

As Jaime approached, he could see a bronze plaque fixed to the stand. He strained to see around the kids in front of him so he could read it. Just then, he heard a voice behind him.

"The Josiah L. Knightly Book of Remembrance," a girl said.

When Jaime looked to see who it was, he recognized the friendly face of the girl who sat next to him in class. He looked at her quizzically.

"That's what the plaque says," she said. "I could tell you were trying to read it."

"Not really," Jaime replied, unsure of why he lied.

"I'm Karen," she said.

"Hey."

"What's your name?"

"Jaime." He watched for any sign of laughter or surprise when he said his name but Karen didn't show any.

"So, do you want to know why it's called that?"

"Called what?"

"The book," she said, laughing a little. "Do you want to know why it's called the Josiah L. Knightly Book of Remembrance?"

"Oh. Sure, I guess."

"Well, you see, Josiah Knightly was this guy who lived in Edith's Hollow a long time ago, like when our grandparents were kids. He was the Sherriff – well, actually, my mom says he was a deputy Sherriff but he was the only officer in Edith's Hollow so it was kind of like he was the Sherriff."

"Oh. OK," said Jaime.

"I'm not done," Karen replied.

Just then, Ms. Spencer cleared her throat loudly, interrupting their conversation. Jaime looked up to see their tall teacher looking down, over her nose at him and Karen. They realized at the same time that no one was else was talking.

Karen whispered, "I'll tell you the rest later."

With everyone quiet, Ms. Spencer launched into a passionate monologue about heritage, loyalty, citizenship, and a bunch of names Jaime didn't recognize. He zoned out right away. He looked around at the other kids and spotted Mark and his friends. They were snickering at something – or probably someone. He missed his friends back home. He missed being in on the joke.

When it was time to leave, Jaime shuffled through the door in the middle of the crowd. He spotted Mark and his friends again up ahead and thought about trying to talk to them. He felt dumb approaching them, though. He didn't know what he would say. Before he could think it through any further, Karen found him again.

"I guess you don't need me to tell you about Josiah Knightly anymore," she said.

"What?" Jaime asked, thoroughly confused.

Karen laughed. "Josiah Knightly," she repeated. The guy Ms. Spencer just told us all about.

"Oh," Jaime said. He shrugged his shoulders, "I wasn't really listening."

Karen perked up. "Oh good!" she said. "Ms. Spencer left a lot of stuff out anyway."

Jaime usually preferred listening over talking so he didn't mind indulging Karen. He could tell she liked to talk and, truthfully, he kind of liked that.

"So where was I?" she asked, as if to herself. "Oh yeah – Josiah Knightly, the Sherriff. Or, actually, Deputy Sherriff, but whatever. You see, back then, Edith's Hollow was just a quiet, little, peaceful place, I guess kinda like it is now. And the Sherriff wasn't gonna let anyone mess that up. So this guy comes into town – a real rich fella' – I can't remember his name but it was something kinda different – like not a name you ever hear around here. Anyway, he thinks he's just gonna sort of do what he wants – and he sort of does for a while. He builds this big mansion kinda far out of town but still close enough that it's still sort of part of the town, you know? And then he starts this business – a big textile mill. Do you know what a textile mill is? I had to have my mom explain it to me."

Jaime shook his head, "no" but Karen wasn't waiting for his answer.

"You see, a textile mill is a place where they make fabric like for clothes and curtains and stuff. And I guess back in those days they would fill a big ol' building with these huge machines that people would stand there and operate and it could be real dangerous. Like, you could lose a hand or a whole arm if you weren't careful."

Jaime must have made a face because Karen felt the need to highlight this point a little further.

"No, really," she said, "a whole arm. The machine would just rip it clean off!"

Jaime wasn't sure how a machine that made cloth would rip a man's arm off – nor was he sure that Karen knew either, but on she went.

"So, anyway, this guy – I wish I could remember his name, it was something weird - he builds this big factory right here in Edith's Hollow – or actually, a little ways outside of it, but whatever – and he starts bringing in people from all around to work in his place. But something's not right and the Sherriff knows it. I mean, I guess everyone knew it but the Sherriff especially knew it. I mean, here this man was building this big, fancy house and this big, fancy business in the middle of town," Jaime furrowed his brow at this, to which Karen replied "you know what I mean – here he was building this stuff and bringing in folks from the outside and he couldn't have cared less about Edith's Hollow. He wouldn't even hire locals to work in his factory. He wasn't really patriotic, as they say. Do you know what I mean? A real loner actually. My mom says he kept to himself all the time and never let anyone around town know his business. So everyone knew something wasn't right.

The Sherriff was the opposite, probably one of the most patriotic people this town has ever seen. He was real loyal to Edith's

Hollow and he wasn't gonna let anyone disrespect her so he watched this man real close – and all the outsiders he was bringing in too but mostly this man with the big, fancy house.

So, in those days, the book – you know, the Town's Heart – used to get passed around different establishments and places in town so it would be there for people to see when they were out getting groceries, or going to church, or what have you. And the town decided it would be a good idea to place it out in the textile factory for a time - which I don't really understand seeing how everyone knew something was up with the owner and no one really liked the factory being there in the first place but I wasn't there so I can't say what went on. All I know is that they put the book out there for a time and one night, while the book's still out there, the factory catches fire. No doubt it was one of the town's folk who started it. It was the owner's own fault – whatever his name was - he wouldn't even hire any of the good, hard-working folks from Edith's Hollow and my ma says at that time a lot of people around town needed work and here he wouldn't hire a single one of them. So, naturally, someone's gonna burn the place down eventually. It was just too bad they did it when the book was still there. I mean, whoever did it must not have realized about the book.

Anyway, like I said, the factory was a ways out so it took a little while before everyone in town noticed the flames and when they did everyone went rushing out to see what was going on and probably just to watch the place burn I suppose. But when they got there, you'll never believe what they saw. The factory was about half gone by then and of course people remember that the book was in there and everyone starts to get real worried about it. But then someone sees the Sherriff and you'll never believe this – he's lying there on the ground passed out and covered in ash and clutching the book to his chest. He ran in there and saved it and risked his life doing it. And on top of that, lying there next to him is the factory owner and he's passed out and covered in ash too and not looking so good. Well, the factory owner died like that night or the next day or something but still, everyone agreed that was pretty nice of the Sherriff to drag him out too even though no one around town liked him.

So, the Sherriff became a real hero for saving the book the way he did. I mean, like I said, he was real patriotic and real good to the town so he was kind of a hero already but that just put him over the top, you know? So, from then on, they started calling the book the Josiah L. Knightly Book of Remembrance to honor his bravery."

"Hmm," Jaime said, nodding his head politely.

For a moment, there was finally silence between them and Jaime listened to the scraping sound their feet made on the gravel.

"That's cool, right?" Karen said.

Jaime shrugged. "Yeah."

Again, there was silence.

"So...." Karen said, searching for something to say. "What do you like to do after school?"

Jaime shrugged his shoulders again. "I don't know," he said. "I haven't really been here long enough to figure it out. My mom has to drive to Fall River as soon as she's done with work today. She's probably headed there already. So, I guess I'm just gonna hang out at my house."

"Fall River's kind of far," Karen said. "What does she have to go there for?"

"She's gonna be teaching a class up there this year. Some kind of night class a couple days a week.

"Well," Karen said, "you can come over to my house right now – I mean, as soon as we get back and Ms. Spencer lets us all go."

"Nah, that's alright," Jaime said.

"Come on, I'm serious. Come over."

Jaime hesitated for a second longer and then gave in. "OK," he said, brightening a little. Maybe it would be nice to have somewhere to go other than an empty house.

Karen's house was old and a little drafty like Jaime's. Jaime figured all the houses in Edith's Hollow were old and drafty. Karen's house, though, had a certain warmth to it. There was a small pile of warm, freshly baked oatmeal cookies sitting on a plate on the kitchen table when they walked in. The kitchen smelled like brown sugar and butter. It was a scent entirely foreign to Jaime's home.

Karen's mom was wearing an apron with a pattern of baby-blue flowers on a white background. She had dark hair that was styled like she had somewhere important to go.

23

"Hi, sweetheart," she said when the two came through the door. "Oh, and who is this?" She asked in a cheery voice.

Karen's mom was nothing like Jaime's. Jaime could only remember one time his mom had baked cookies. It was snickerdoodles and they weren't good. Jaime remembered sitting down across from her at the table as they each bit into one together. His was so hard he had to clutch it between his teeth and break a bite off with his hand. He tried faking a smile while the bitter taste of burnt sugar hit his tongue. She told him to shut up and stop lying when he said they were good. They both laughed as she chucked the whole batch into the garbage.

Jaime's mom liked adventures, outdoors, and guys with cool cars. Karen's mom liked baking and baby-blue aprons. They were different but Jaime liked Karen's mom. She was warm and friendly, even if she talked to him like he was a foreigner. The three of them sat in the kitchen and ate soft, chewy cookies while Karen's mom asked Jaime all about Arizona as if it was another planet.

Suddenly Karen jumped up, "wait right here, Jaime," she said. "I want to show you something."

Karen hurried down a short hallway and disappeared into a room. A little while later she emerged in a long, white dress that looked like it must be 100 years old. It was yellowing and droopy but still elegant in an outdated sort of way. It looked like something you might see in an old, black and white picture from the 1800's with a woman sitting still with her hands in her lap and gazing into the camera looking sad and a little eerie. It had a high neck, long, full sleeves, and a lacy hem that brushed the floor as Karen moved. A long, transparent veil also made of lace started at the top of Karen's head and ran all the way to the floor, draping her shoulders and falling down her back.

"Oh, Karen!" her mom exclaimed, "Why in the world are you wearing Grandma's old confirmation dress?"

"It's gonna be my Halloween costume, ma. I wanted to show Jaime."

"You are not wearing that on Halloween."

"But Grandma gave it to me! Look," she said, holding something out, "I even found this old, candle-lit lantern I can use instead of a flashlight."

"You'll ruin it if you go parading out in the streets in it. I'm sorry, Karen. The answer is no. What were you planning on going as, anyway? Your Grandmother?"

"No," Karen said defiantly, "I'm supposed to be Elizbeth Poole."

Jaime and Karen's mom both looked at Karen quizzically.

"Uh!" Karen said in the back of her throat. "Elizabeth Poole was the founder of Taunton."

Jaime still looked confused.

"Taunton, Massachusetts?" her mom asked.

"Of course," Karen said. "Did you know she was the first woman to ever found a town in America?"

"I didn't know that," her Mom said politely.

"Well, she was and I want to be her for Halloween."

Jaime thought this whole thing was very odd. "How do you know that's what she looked like?" he asked.

"Well...I don't," Karen said shyly. "The book I was reading didn't have any pictures. But I know she was very religious and pretty wealthy and I thought this looked like something a rich, religious woman like her might wear back in pilgrim times. You know, for special services or something."

"Yeah, definitely," Jaime said. "I mean, I think it looks great." He was just trying to be nice.

"See, Mom," Karen said. "People will like it."

Her mom just smiled a patient smile. "Go take it off, please. Halloween's still two months away. You have plenty of time to think of something else."

When Karen came back out, dressed in her normal clothes, Jaime decided it was time to leave. He thanked her mom for the cookies and headed home. When his mom got home a couple hours later, she came through the front door with a greasy bag of burgers and fries from a fast-food place she had stopped at on the drive home. They ate dinner on paper plates over their tiny, kitchen table then Jaime went to bed.

The next day at school, Karen took her seat next to Jaime before class started and was her normal, chatty self.

"So, did you really like my Halloween costume yesterday?" she asked.

"I thought your Mom wasn't going to let you wear it for Halloween," Jaime said, avoiding the question.

"Oh, we'll see," Karen said. "But did you really like it?"

"Ummm, yeah. It's great. I mean it's a little..." He wasn't sure how to finish his sentence. How could he tell her her costume was super weird and was sure to get her made fun of? Just the thought of Mark and his friends seeing her in that thing made his face flush with embarrassment.

"It's a little what?" she asked.

"Umm, a little old, I guess."

"Well, yeah. That's what I like about it! It's my Grandma's. Did you know my Grandma knew Josiah Knightly?" Suddenly her eyes brightened. "Oh! That reminds me, I was going to tell you something."

But before she could continue, Ms. Spencer stood at the front of the class and cleared her throat. "OK class, let's get started. I know it's Friday but the weekend has not begun yet."

"I'll tell you later," Karen whispered.

Her and Jaime didn't have another chance to talk until lunch time. She found him in the lunch line and picked up where she had left off. "Hey so I was going to tell you, after you left yesterday, my Mom reminded me of the name of the factory owner I was telling you all about. It was Mr. Fridman, which is kind of a funny name, right? At least around here it is. I mean, I've never met anyone with that name before."

Just then, Jaime heard Mark behind them.

"Karen and the new kid," he said. "What are you two love birds talking about?"

Mark's friends laughed.

A look of irritation crossed Karen's face. "I was just telling Jaime about Mr. Fridman," she said in a tone that made it clear she just wanted to be left alone.

Mark, Danny, and Joe returned blank stares.

"He's the guy who owned the factory that burned down a long time ago," she said impatiently, as if she could hardly believe their ignorance.

That sparked a light of recognition in each of their eyes.

26

"Oooh, did she tell you about the haunted house?" Danny asked, looking at Jaime. He sounded eager to launch into a story.

Karen rolled her eyes. "Don't be stupid," she said, "that's all made up."

"You didn't tell him about the haunted house?" Mark piped in. "What's the matter, Karen, is it too scary for you?"

The rest of the trio laughed again and, this time, Jaime joined in. Shocked by the betrayal, Karen shot him a look that made him feel an inch tall. Hoping to seize the opportunity with Mark and his friends, Jaime spoke up, "I want to hear about it. I love scary stuff."

Karen rolled her eyes again.

"Well," Danny started, "the factory owner lived with some lady that stayed locked up in his mansion on the outskirts of town. Nobody knows if it was his mom or his wife or what cause nobody ever saw her but people knew she was there."

"They say she was crazy," Joe interjected.

"Yeah, she was crazy," Danny said. "And that's why he kept her locked up. But, get this, you know how the factory owner died in the fire and stuff?"

Jaime nodded his head.

"Well," Danny continued, "after he died, the undertaker took his body to the morgue and, the next day, when they went to get it, it was gone."

Danny stopped for dramatic effect, giving Karen a chance to make a scoffing noise to reaffirm her disapproval.

"It's true!" Danny said. Ask Ms. Spencer – ask anyone. There's no grave for him anywhere. That's because nobody ever found his body."

Again, Danny paused for dramatic effect and the trio all looked at Jaime to see his reaction. He had a quizzical and slightly confused look on his face as if to say, "so what?"

"She took it." Danny said, in response to his unspoken question.

"That's stupid, why would she want his body?" Jaime asked. At this, Karen smiled a satisfied smile and made another, small noise just to make absolutely certain everybody knew how she felt.

"I don't know" Danny said, shrugging his shoulders, "but that's what happened.

"She took it because she was crazy," Joe said.

27

"And because she didn't want anyone else to have it," Mark said, taking over the story. "She took it to guard over it." Then he lowered his voice, "and after that, she never left. She lived the rest of her life in that mansion going crazier and crazier until the day she died. And, to this day, her ghost still haunts it."

Karen scoffed again. She couldn't help herself.

"If you think it's so stupid, Karen, let's go down to the mansion and see if you'll go in."

"I would if it even existed," she said defiantly. "It's not even around anymore. No one even knows for sure where it was."

"That's not true," Danny said excitedly. "I've been there with my older brother. It's out in the woods all by itself probably forty-five minutes from town. It's a creepy looking place."

"I know what you're talking about," Karen said, "but that's *not* it. That place isn't even a mansion. It's just some old cabin in the woods."

"How do you know?" Danny said. "Have you been there?"

"Well, no," she said, "but everyone knows it's just a cabin."

"She might be right," Joe said. "I've heard there's nothing out there but an old cabin." Mark nudged him with his elbow to shut him up.

"We'll take you there," Mark said. "You can see for yourself. In fact, you can go in and tell us what it's like."

Karen rolled her eyes.

"I'll go." Jaime said.

Everyone looked at him at once, a little surprised. Truthfully, he was surprised too.

Mark laughed. "Yeah right."

Jaime doubled down. "I'm serious," he said. "I'm not scared. Let's go out there and see what it is."

Mark's expression changed. "OK," he said, pleasantly surprised. "Danny can show us how to get there. We'll go tonight"

Jaime was suddenly feeling good as a shot of adrenaline rushed through him. "Awesome." He said. "Let's do it."

"Well I'm not going," Karen said defiantly.

Mark huffed. "Who said you were invited? Trust me, we don't want you there."

Mark's friends laughed. Karen looked hurt.

The trio decided they would meet at Danny's house and told Jaime how to get there. While the four of them made plans, Jaime looked back at Karen who looked annoyed and upset. He felt bad but she said herself she didn't want to go and there was no way he was going to back out. His stomach turned with excitement and nervousness at the thought of what they would be doing. He knew the hours would go by slowly while he waited for the evening to come. As the guys left, he swallowed a lump in his throat and reminded himself not to be afraid.

CHAPTER 4

When Jaime's mom got home from work, Jaime told her he was going to hang out with some friends that evening. She seemed happy with the news and didn't ask what they would be doing, which he was relieved about. If she had, he was prepared to lie. Somehow, it didn't seem like a good idea to tell her they were going into the woods to explore an old abandoned house and see if it really was haunted.

At 8:00, Jaime met Mark, Danny, and Joe outside of Danny's house. Danny confirmed that he had talked to his older brother and got directions. Everyone agreed that they should leave right away so Danny grabbed a flashlight and they headed out. It didn't take long for them to reach the edge of town.

Walking into the woods was a little intimidating for Jaime, who, coming from Arizona, had never experienced anything quite like it. The trees were thick and tall and a ghostly, evening fog hung between them. The ground was blanketed by soggy leaves, moss-covered sticks, and long, dark shadows. The path beneath their feet was barely distinguishable from the rest of the forest ground. Jaime strained his eyes to see in the gathering darkness and quietly wished the other boys would slow their pace.

"Are you sure you know where you're going?" Mark asked Danny.

"Yeah, I'm sure. I recognize all this."

Jaime was unsure how anyone could recognize anything here. All the trees looked the same, especially in the narrow, dim beam of light provided by Danny's flashlight which he had recently flicked on. Jaime did his best to keep the flashlight beam in view and avoid tripping over anything at his feet. After what felt like a lot of walking and a very long time, he found himself stepping in pace with Mark who had fallen behind the other two.

"So what's with you and Karen?" Mark asked him.

Jaime shrugged his shoulders. "Nothing. What do you mean?"

"I mean, why are you always with her? She's so weird. I don't know how you even talk to her."

Jaime forced a laugh. "Yeah, I guess she is kind of weird."

"She's *really* weird," Mark said. "And she never shuts up."

Jaime knew what Mark meant. Karen was a little quirky but he didn't mind. Her quirks made him laugh and he liked his conversations with her…even if they mostly consisted of her doing all the talking.

"You don't need to hang out with her, you know." Mark said. "You can hang out with us, instead." He sounded like he was giving Jaime permission instead of extending an invitation.

Jaime just smiled and nodded his head.

Just then, Danny called out from up ahead. "OK, here it is."

The group came to a stop and everyone looked around. "Here *what* is?" Joe asked, vocalizing what the rest of them were thinking. "I don't see anything."

"Danny, if you got us lost," Mark said, "I swear, I'm gonna kill you."

"No, no" Danny said, defensively, "this is it. Watch. This is why hardly anyone ever finds this place. You see how the trail curves to the right here?" He followed the bend in the trail with his flashlight beam. "Well, what no one realizes is that it's actually a fork in the trail. Look."

Danny pointed his flashlight to the left where the ground rose and was covered by a thick gathering of ferns. At first glance, it just looked like more, wild growth running along the side of the path. With his free hand, Danny pulled back some of the fern fronds and directed his beam to the ground. He was right, there appeared to be a trail that branched off from the one they were on and ran beneath the layer of ferns, extending up and over the hill in front of them.

"Come on," Danny said, following the hidden path with the rest of the boys on his heels. It took them another seven or eight minutes

31

of walking to reach the hill's crest. On the other side, it descended more steeply than it had risen. At the bottom of the hill, the forest suddenly opened up to a bald spot devoid of trees. It was mostly round and probably fifteen feet in diameter. The boys stood in the middle of the open circle while Danny scanned his flashlight beam back and forth across the wall of trees in front of them like he was looking for something. "There it is," he said, resting the beam on a wooden post sticking out of the ground. The post was man-made but it was old and nearly matched the trees around it, making it easy to miss.

The boys followed Danny to the post, at which point a path was clearly carved through the thick trees ahead. "It's right up here," Danny said. They walked just a few more minutes down the curvy path. It made a rounded turn to the left and suddenly, rising up in front of them, was a tall, black, wrought-iron double gate.

Danny shined his flashlight on it. "See, I told you" he said. "This is it!"

The gates were adorned with metal shafts that had been twisted and forged into an intricate design that looked like the entangled branches of a large, lively vine. One of the gates hung by only one hinge and, lying slightly ajar, had seized in place after years of non-use. The boys scrambled through the small opening created by the uneven gate. Beyond the gates stretched an enormous, spacious yard overrun by wild grass and weeds, each dying in the autumn chill.

An old, decaying horse carriage sat off to the right amid the untamed vegetation. Though rotting and falling to pieces, it looked like it had once been a fine piece of work. An unusually long chamber, about the length of a coffin, stretched behind the driver's cracked, leather seat and black curtains covered the windows. A solid, hand-carved, cherry wood trim ran along the base. Spider webs and a thick layer of dust covered every surface.

"Is that a hearse?" Joe asked as Danny shined his light over it.

"I think it is," Danny said in awe. He continued exploring the ground with his flashlight while the head of each boy swiveled back and forth, taking in the scene in front of them.

The boys stood on an old path worn by carriage wheels pushing at the ground. It curved from the gate to a front door, which was flanked by tall narrow windows on each side several feet ahead. They looked up at their looming destination.

The house in the woods was so old it looked like it belonged there. It was lifeless and still, weathered and faded and seemed to grow out of the ground. Moss speckled its surface and gnarled vines creeped up its walls. It was made of brick which had once been white but now bore a deathly ill color of greenish grey. Like the forest road that had led the boys to it, it had no name, number, or address.

It was tall but not as tall as the trees that shrouded it on every side and cast heavy shadows over it. It was big but Jaime wasn't sure he would call it a mansion. He imagined that this had been a home for the type of people that hosted guests and had servants, but not an abundance of either.

Mark urged the group on. "Come on," he said. "Are you guys scared, or what?"

"No!" the boys responded too quickly and too emphatically.

"Joe's about to pee his pants," Danny quipped.

"No, I'm not!" Joe said defensively. "Jaime's the one that's scared. Look at him shaking."

Jaime just shook his head. "Shut up, guys. Let's go inside." He sounded calmer than the others.

Mark got to the front door first and already had his hand on the handle when the rest of the group got there. It was large and iron with a thumb lever on top.

"Go ahead, man," Danny said.

"I was just waiting for you guys," Mark said, defensively. "Are you ready?"

"Yes! Come on! Open it," Joe prodded.

Mark drew in a breath and everyone stood still while his thumb pushed down on the lever. He pushed forward on the door but nothing happened.

"Locked!" he exclaimed.

Everyone relaxed a little.

"Let me try," Jaime said, pushing forward. He pushed down on the thumb lever and pushed the door back and forth two or three times. It didn't budge.

"Let's check the windows," Mark said.

The boys fanned out and began examining the windows in the front of the house but quickly found that they weren't designed to open.

"Over here!" Danny suddenly shouted. The other three turned their heads and realized Danny had wandered around the side of the house. They hurried over to see what he had found. When they rounded the corner, they saw him standing over a cellar entrance that stuck out of the ground and jutted out from the wall. A wide, trap door made of plywood and painted white sat on top of a wooden frame.

"How is that supposed to help us?" Mark asked. "It's locked."

He was right. A rusty padlock was fastened to a rusty metal piece on the front end of the door.

"I think it'll come off," Danny said as he began kicking at the lock, heel first.

The wooden door was weathered and rotting and after just three hard kicks from Danny, the padlock and the metal it was fastened to lifted from one side. One more hard kick and the entire locking system detached from the door and swung on the frame by a single nail.

Jaime's heart began to beat fast. They had found a way in. Everybody gathered around Danny as he reached down for the handle on top of the door. "Here," he said, handing his flashlight to Jaime. The rusted hinges creaked as Danny lifted the door and rested it against the wall of the house. Cold, stale air drifted out of the cavity below.

Jaime shined the flashlight into the darkness but it barely did anything. The dim, yellow light was swallowed up before reaching any surfaces. Dust particles swam in the beam.

"Wow, that's a deep cellar," Joe said. "Are you just supposed to jump?" he asked, glancing over at Danny.

"Don't ask me," Danny said. "Jaime's the one who's going in."

"Just me?" Jaime asked. "Are the rest of you chicken?" he said, shining the flashlight back at the other guys and looking from face to face. He thought he caught a subtle nod from Joe.

"I'll go," Mark said reflexively, although he didn't move a muscle. "But you go first, he said. Danny's right, you said you'd go inside. That was the deal."

Jaime again shined the flashlight into the cellar. He moved the beam toward the cellar wall near his feet and, when he did, he noticed the top rung of a ladder a few inches down. He looked at Danny and gestured with his head for him to take the flashlight. "Keep this shining right here," he said.

Danny grabbed the flashlight and Jaime crouched down to his knees, moving backwards into the dark opening. His feet found the ladder rung and he began to climb down. After a few steps, just as the crown of his head descended below the cellar opening, his foot reached for the next rung down but nothing was there. He positioned his hands on a lower rung and tried again, reaching his foot further down than before and swinging it back and forth in the air. Nothing.

"The ladder's broke." He called up. "It doesn't go all the way to the bottom."

"Are you chickening out, Jaime?" Danny called back.

"You're not coming back up until you've found a way inside," Mark said. "You told us you'd go inside."

"Yeah," Joe joined in, laughing a little. "Just drop down already."

Jaime reached down with his hands to the lowest rung he could grasp and then dropped both of his feet, letting them dangle. They swung from side to side. He pointed his toes hoping to feel dirt but still, there was nothing.

"Shine the light down here so I can see." He called up.

There was no response.

'*Whatever*,' he thought to himself. He peered down toward his feet into the darkness and his eyes began to adjust. He could make out the brick wall in front of him. Something small and quick darted across it. Following the wall down with his eyes, he thought he could see where it met the ground, just a little way beyond his feet.

He took a deep breath and let go of the ladder. He only fell for a brief moment before his feet hit solid ground. "Whew," he said in a whisper.

He yelled back up toward the top. "I'm at the bottom!"

Again, there was no response.

'*What are they doing up there?*' he thought to himself.

He began to look around. His eyes had finished adjusting and the light from the full moon shining through the open cellar door was helping. Looking up, he could see the broken ladder fastened to a red-brick wall. He heard something scurry on the dirt and looked down to see a small rat near him move into the shadows. He could see he was standing in a large cellar with a dirt floor but he couldn't tell exactly how large or how empty it was. The darkness was too deep; he couldn't see more than four or five feet in front of him.

He moved forward cautiously, instinctively putting his hand out in front of him to prevent himself from running into any unexpected objects. His eyes had to readjust as he stepped out of the moonlight and further into the darkness. When they did, he could see the outline of a staircase up ahead. The stairs were made of cold concrete and had no railing. He kept moving forward, straining his eyes to see what was at the top but it was too dark to tell. Suddenly, his foot unexpectedly hit the bottom step and he nearly fell over.

Regaining his balance, he began to climb. As he did, a door at the top of the staircase came into view. Reaching the top step, he could see a brass knob protruding from the door in front of him. He reached out his hand and grasped it. It was cold. His heart rate began to quicken and he could feel the metal dampen beneath his palm. He heard his Father's voice in his head; "don't be such a sissy," it said. With a deep breath, he twisted the knob. It turned a quarter of the way and stopped. *'Locked,'* he thought to himself. He tried twisting it in the opposite direction and pushing on the door but it didn't budge. If he was honest with himself, he felt relieved.

He walked back down the stairs and back to the ladder which now looked to be glowing in the moonlight. When he was directly below it, he yelled up at the opening above. "Guys, I'm coming back up. There's no way in."

There was just silence.

"Guys?"

Nothing.

Anger started to swell in Jaime's chest. He was pretty sure he had been abandoned. He looked for something to kick but there was nothing nearby. Had they really just left?

He looked up at the lowest rung of the ladder and, for the first time since dropping into the cellar, it occurred to him that he might not be able to reach it. He jumped from where he stood and didn't come close to touching it. Stepping back a few feet, he tried again with a short, running start. His reaching hand just swatted at empty air. His anger was beginning to turn to panic.

"Guys!" he yelled again, this time much louder.

He took several steps back and again attempted a running jump. He missed the rung and his body collided with the brick wall that the ladder was fastened to. This was getting him nowhere. Calming himself a little, he tried gathering his senses and using his mind. He gazed into the darkness and did his best to scan the cellar for anything that might help. He thought he saw something in the nearest corner to his left. As he got closer, he was encouraged to find a shovel propped against the wall with a small bucket lying next to it in the dirt.

"Perfect," he said out loud.

He bent down to pick up the bucket and, when he did, he noticed a long, narrow scrap of paper lying next to it. Curious, he picked it up. Carrying the bucket in one hand and the paper in the other, he walked back over to the spot beneath the ladder. When he reached it, he set the bucket down and moved the scrap of paper back and forth in the moonlight until he could see what was on it. It looked like it had been a list of some sort but almost all of the writing had faded beyond recognition. He thought he might barely be able to make out the last two lines, however.

Jaime brought the paper closer to his face and slowly read aloud the lines as they came into view;

And bury the bones
And bury the bones.

Just then, a noise at the top of the stairs behind him caused him to spin around. He couldn't see that far into the darkness but his senses were on high alert as he stood completely still. He heard the click of a door unlocking and the squeal of rusty hinges. His stomach lurched and his heart began to pound.

He spun back around, frantically moved the bucket into position and quickly stepped onto it. Without waiting to make sure he had his balance, he jumped for the lowest ladder rung, reaching both hands as high as he could. The tops of his fingers wrapped partially around the rung but they immediately moistened the metal and slipped off. He fell to the ground and tipped over the bucket. As he rushed to prop it back up, he heard movement at the top of the stairs behind him.

He stepped back onto the bucket as quickly as he could and, with everything he had, jumped again, reaching with just his right hand. His palm made contact and he grasped the rung firmly, immediately swinging his left arm into position and grasping the rung with his left hand. His kicking feet connected with the brick wall and he pushed with his legs, propelling himself up so that he was able to grab the next rung and then the next and the next again until he was climbing normally.

He quickly reached the top of the ladder and threw one of his arms over the edge of the cellar opening onto the ground above. As soon as he did, he felt a hand grab his wrist. He pulled it back and nearly fell over backwards before regaining his balance. Then he heard his name.

"Jaime, it's me."

Jaime pulled himself up and looked to see Karen standing above him. He nearly jumped out of the open cellar, and, before Karen could say anything else, he said loudly, "run!"

The two ran across the yard, past the old-fashioned hearse, through the gap between the tall, iron gates. They were still going full speed when they reached the open circle at the end of the trail, dashing past it and back into the thick of the woods. The old, decaying house was far behind them when Karen finally stopped running. Jaime went a few more feet before he stopped and turned around. "Come on!" he said, panting.

Karen's hands were on her knees as she panted too. "Why…are we…running?" she asked between breaths.

"Something's back there…something was in the house." Jaime explained. "I think it really is haunted."

Even in her exhaustion, Karen managed an eye-roll. "There's no such thing as ghosts, Jaime. You're running from nothing."

They took a moment to catch their breath. How could she be so matter-of-fact and unshaken? He felt extremely annoyed and he wasn't entirely sure why.

"Why are you here?" he asked, letting his irritation show.

"I followed you guys," Karen replied, again sounding matter-of-fact.

"Well you shouldn't have," Jaime said.

Karen furrowed her brow and drew in her chin. "Instead of being a jerk you could say thank you for sticking around and helping you out of the cellar."

"Sorry," Jaime said, calming down a little, "it's just…Where did Mark and them go? What happened to them?"

A subtle smile stole across Karen's face. "They heard a screech owl and got scared," she said, suppressing a laugh. "As soon as they heard it, they ran off. I mean, they took off fast."

Jaime returned a blank stare.

"Grant it," she continued, "it sounded a little like a person screaming or moaning or something but, if they had half a brain between them, they would have known it was just a screech owl. I was hiding a little ways off but when I heard you yelling from the cellar, I figured I better come over to make sure you were OK." She started to laugh, "you should have seen yourself coming out of that cellar like you had seen a ghost!"

Jaime was annoyed again and it showed on his face. Karen looked up and stopped laughing.

"What's your problem?" She asked. "Why do you care so much about what those guys think anyway? They're just a bunch of idiots."

"I don't have a problem." Jaime said defensively. "And who said I care about what they think? Besides, maybe if you were more normal you'd understand what normal people care about!"

Hurt, Karen immediately turned around and began walking briskly back towards town.

"Wait," Jaime said. "That's not what I meant."

Karen didn't respond. She kept walking.

"Karen, come on."

Still, she said nothing.

Jaime stopped trying but he began walking too. He didn't know what he could say to make her feel better and he wasn't sure he felt like trying. So, instead of catching up with her, he walked several steps behind her the rest of the way home.

CHAPTER 5

On Saturday morning, Jaime's mom came in his room before he was ready to get up.

"Up and at 'em!" she said, literally pushing him out of his bed. He tried ignoring her until she rolled him off one side. He fell to the floor still wrapped in his blanket and sheet.

"Mom!" he started to complain.

"Oh, you're fine," she said dismissively and with a bit of a laugh. "Get up. We're going on a hike."

Jaime groaned but he knew there was no point in resisting. He got up and started getting ready. When he came out to the kitchen, his mom had peanut butter and jelly sandwiches ready for the road. They climbed in the car and drove to a trail head about an hour outside of town.

All morning, Jaime's mind kept taking him back to the house in the woods he had visited the night before. His visit had filled him with unanswered questions. But, every time he thought he had a moment to dwell on it, his mom wanted to talk.

"So, are you making friends?" she asked him as they started their hike.

"I don't know," he said. "Sort of." He thought of Karen and then of the guys. It was complicated and he didn't feel like explaining.

"What does that mean?" she asked.

"I mean, yeah. There's some guys I've started to hang out with at school."

"Oh, good," she said. "Are they nice?"

Again he thought of Karen and immediately felt guilty. "I don't know, Mom. Can we talk about something else?"

She tussled his hair, knowing he hated when she did that. "Why do 11-year old boys never want to talk to their mothers?" she asked. "Anyway, knowing you, I'm sure they're nice. Just remember what I always tell you," Jaime finished her sentence before she could...

"Always be nice, even when it hurts," he said, as if he had repeated the phrase a thousand times.

She laughed a little. "Yes! Don't act like it's so hard to say! Those are words to live by."

"I know," Jaime said.

After a moment of silence, she started up again. "Hey, you're doing OK with me being gone so much, right? I mean, I'm sure it's not fun coming home to an empty house so often, but you're doing OK?"

Jaime nodded. "It's no big deal, Mom. Don't worry about it." He really was fine with it.

"OK, 'cause it won't be forever. I've gotta tell you, though, I'm going to have an overnighter coming up in a few weeks. They need all the new, part-time faculty at a meeting the morning after one of my teaching days so I'm just going to book a hotel that night. Are you alright with that?"

"Sure," Jaime said, shrugging his shoulders. "You've gotta do what you've gotta do."

"Thanks Jaime Bear."

He hated when she called him that but he tried not to let her know.

"You're a good kid," she said. "You'll never convince me otherwise."

Jaime looked up to see his Mom looking at him dotingly. He rolled his eyes. "Keep your eyes on the trail, Mom."

She laughed and tussled his hair again.

By Sunday, Jaime couldn't take it anymore. His curiosity was getting the best of him. He had to go back to the house in the woods. If he went during the day, there wouldn't be anything to be scared of. So, around 1 pm, he told his Mom he wanted to go

41

explore the woods and she told him to be safe and to be back by dinner.

He had a little trouble finding the head of the trail Danny had taken them down. Once he was on it, though, the rest was easy. Left at the fork, over the hill, through the circle in the trees and past the old, wooden post stuck in the ground. The journey felt shorter this time. Before he knew it, he was standing at the entrance, gazing up at the tall, wrought iron gates. He looked in both directions and saw that the gates were connected to a short, brick wall with a wrought iron fence on top that disappeared in the thick overgrowth on either side.

When he passed through the gates, the first thing he noticed was the house several yards ahead. It was shrouded in dark shadows cast by the trees that hugged it on every side. It hardly looked any different in daylight than it had at night. He noticed the tall, narrow windows shrouded by ornate, white drapes on both floors. One window, wider than the rest, sat on the second floor above the front door. It was the only one with the drapes drawn and tied back. It was large enough that he thought he might be able to catch a glimpse through it and see what the inside of the house looked like. He strained his eyes for a moment but he soon gave up. He was too far away.

He walked past the hearse parked near the garden wall and through the tall grass. His heart skipped a beat when, in front of him, he spotted the open cellar he had fled from a couple of nights before. The door was still propped open, leaning against a wall. Quickly calming himself, he steadied his nerves and approached the opening. Cold, stale air rose from the cavity like before. When its familiar smell reached him, it immediately brough him back to the cellar floor in his mind's eye. He could hear the creaking hinges of a door opening behind him in the darkness and feel his sweating hands desperately reaching for the ladder's bottom rung.

He shook his head, pushing the memory aside. "This is stupid," he said aloud. "Don't be a wimp." Decisively, he closed the cellar door and kept exploring.

The back of the house was largely unremarkable. Instead of a yard, there was just a narrow strip of land that ran between the house and the back gate. In the middle of the gate was an arched opening just large enough for a person to walk through. Jaime walked over to it and looked out. There was nothing to see but forest.

On each side of the back door was a tall, narrow window like the windows near the front door. He walked up to them to see if he could get a look inside but, again, found them shrouded by drapes. He checked the doorknob but it was locked.

Making his way to the other side of the house, he rounded the corner and was surprised to find a modest orchard stretched out in front of him. He counted five, long rows of trees. Each was some kind of nut tree but he didn't recognize the nut growing from the branches and lying scattered on the ground. It wasn't the trees themselves that were unusual, though; it was something else. Nailed to each trunk was a rusted, brass candleholder and above each candleholder was carved a set of two or three letters.

Jaime walked down one of the rows and examined the letters more closely. "JSW," one read, "CM" read another. Each set was different and each was stained by black marks made from a candle flame. Intrigued, he inspected every tree in his row until he reached the last one.

Then, walking out of the orchard, he nearly stepped on a wide, squatty green plant growing out of the ground. Furrowing his brow, he moved one of the broad leaves with his foot and saw an overgrown squash that was cracked and beginning to rot. Looking up, he saw more plants that he was sure hadn't grown naturally. There was cabbage, tomatoes, pumpkins, and others he didn't recognize. "A garden?" he thought to himself. He was fascinated to think it had lasted all these years.

At the end of the garden was a rusted well pump that stood about as tall as his waist. He examined it, circling part way around it. Then, looking up again, he noticed, several feet ahead, two trees standing by themselves near the front corner of the property, just inside the wall that enclosed it. They looked different than any other trees in the yard. He made his way to them and noticed a few shriveled pears hanging on their branches. One tree was taller and more mature than the other. Curiously, the older tree had a candleholder fastened to it and letters carved into the trunk just like those in the orchard but the smaller tree had neither. A small, shallow hole was at the foot of the smaller tree. The dirt looked freshly turned over like the hole was recently dug.

Suddenly, he had the uncomfortable feeling that he was being watched. "You're imagining things," he told himself. Still, he straightened his back and turned to look at the house and the grounds behind him. Everything was quiet and still. He peered up again at the wide window above the door with the curtains drawn back and noticed something he hadn't before. A long, lacey sheet of cloth, whiter and brighter than the curtains, extended from behind them. Then, almost as soon as he had notice it, the cloth shuttered as if from a breeze and whisked away out of sight.

Jaime's eyes widened. He thought about running. Instead, though, he took a deep breath and slowed down his mind. He told himself it was nothing – probably cobwebs or maybe even his imagination. Even so, he was starting to feel like it was time to go back home. He wasn't sure what he had hoped to accomplish by coming here.

Making his way to the double gates, he slipped through the opening between them. When the gate was eight or ten feet behind him, he suddenly slammed the lower part of his shin against something hard protruding out of the ground. The thick vegetation had kept the object hidden. After yelling out, grabbing his shin, and hopping on one foot until the pain finally subsided, he walked back to the spot to see what he had run into.

Moving the brush aside with his hand, he found a thick, rusted, flat piece of metal that was about a foot long and a little less than 6 inches wide. It was sticking out of the ground at an angle sloping upwards toward the house. A small track ran from the metal to the gates and, moving more brush, Jaime could see that a chain lay in the groove of the track.

"Weird," he said aloud as he grasped the metal and tried moving it. It had a little give but seemed to be fastened down to something. He pushed aside more vegetation and brushed away the dirt with his foot to find a flat, metal sheet that looked like the top of some kind of box.

He wondered if maybe he had found a lever of some sort attached to some kind of machinery in the ground. He propped one of his feet on it and tried pushing down. It moved ever so slightly. He tried again, this time with considerably more force. There was distinct movement and the chain in the track made a noise. Now determined, he jumped in the air and landed on the object with both his feet, pushing down as hard as he could. He landed awkwardly and nearly lost his balance. He could feel the scraping of rusted, seized up metal as the object moved at least two inches. It still had another couple of inches to go before it was level with the earth.

Jaime jumped again, again landing as hard as he could on the protruding metal piece. This time he succeeded at pushing it flat against the ground. Something crept and scraped in the metal box beneath the lever and the chain in the track tightened and began to move. Then the gates let out a long, shrilling creek.

Jaime looked up to see the one gate that was still fully intact slowly swing open. The other gate that hung askew on its broken hinges moved awkwardly but ultimately stayed in place. *'This is awesome,'* he thought. Following a hunch, he walked through the open gate and searched the ground eight or ten feet into the front yard. Sure enough, another metal lever that matched the one on the outside was protruding out of the ground. Jaime jumped on it until it was flush with the earth and the gate slowly swung closed. He played with the gate, opening and closing it a few more times before he was satisfied.

He felt his stomach rumble with hunger and decided it really was time to go. He walked home, arriving before his mom had begun boiling the water to start a pot of store-bought macaroni and cheese.

The next day at school, Karen was not her usual, cheery self when she took her seat next to Jaime. He said hi but she didn't respond. At lunch time, she left to the cafeteria in a hurry without giving him a chance to talk to her.

Mark, Danny, and Joe found him while he stood in line, said hi, then asked if they could cut. He let them and the four were soon laughing about something Danny said. Jaime still wasn't happy about being abandoned by the group a few days earlier but he didn't bring it up. Instead, when Mark asked about what had happened in the cellar, he told them all about the writing on the paper and the door opening, downplaying his anger at finding them gone and leaving out the fact that Karen had been there to help him out. They thought his story was pretty cool and he didn't see any reason to ruin that.

Jaime hung out with the guys every day after school the rest of the week. It felt good to have friends again. Mark and Danny liked to pick on other kids, which Jaime wasn't always comfortable with but, really, he was just happy he wasn't the one being picked on. Joe usually laughed and went along with it and Jaime did the same. Plus, he discovered he was pretty good at making the guys laugh behind others' backs.

One day after school, Jaime, Mark, Danny, and Joe stood in a huddle laughing at Jaime's description of a kid who had awkwardly tried his hand at basketball during PE earlier that day. When they were done and the group disbursed, Jaime heard a voice behind him.

"You're a coward."

He turned around to see Karen standing behind him with her arms folded and a stern, obstinate look on her face.

"What?" he said, taken aback.

"You only say those things to get a laugh but you would never be that mean to someone's face."

"Maybe I would." Jaime said defiantly.

Karen gave him a look as if to say "you and I both know that's not true."

"It's so cowardly, Jaime. You're not like those boys. I don't know why you have to pretend like you are."

Jaime's face got hot and anger swelled up inside his chest. He took a breath and bit his tongue. "Go home, Karen," he said, not wanting to say anything hurtful. Karen snorted and turned on her heel.

For the rest of the day, Jaime's irritation with Karen was the only thing he could feel or think about. Who did she think she was? What made her think she knew him so well? At home, his Mom asked him what was wrong but he told her he didn't feel like talking about it. When he went to bed that night, the word "coward" was still swimming in his mind.

The next morning, he woke up with an idea that helped cool his frustration and anger. That evening, his Mom would be gone for her night class in Fall River. It would be a perfect opportunity to go back to the house in the woods. He would go alone and this time he would find a way inside. He was determined. Then he would tell the guys all about it.

When he finally made it home after school, he searched the house until he found a flashlight. As he tested it to make sure it was working, he felt his stomach rumble. Not knowing when he would get a chance to eat again, he took a minute to grab a snack then walked out the door. He got away just before sunset. He noticed that the early, October days were starting to get shorter.

He made his way through the woods with ease, although the journey still wasn't particularly short. It took him a little less than an hour to reach his destination. It was dusk when he arrived. For fun, he stepped on the gate lever sticking out of the ground as he approached the house and the gate slowly swung open. The rusty levers were loosening and getting easier to push.

He walked through the open gate and pushed down the lever on the other side to close it. Just as he did, he heard a high-pitched scream nearby. He stopped, frozen in his tracks, and flicked on his flashlight. The beam was pointed at the ground as he strained his ears, waiting to hear it again. He couldn't tell where it had come from and he couldn't decide if it felt safer to shine his beam into the darkness ahead or to keep himself concealed.

He heard it again. This time it was a long scream followed by a strange cross between screams and groans. He furrowed his brow and felt his heart beating faster than normal. The screams seemed to be coming from up in the trees or maybe from the roof of the house. Suddenly, he remembered what Karen had said about Mark and the guys running from a screech owl the first time he had been there. He waited until the sound came again. When it did, he relaxed his shoulders and let out a short sigh of relief. The sound was eerily human but he was sure it was an animal. It had to be the owl Karen was talking about.

He pushed ahead and started his search for entry at the front door. He checked the door handle but it was still locked, which came as no surprise. He jiggled and shook it, pushing on the door but to no avail. Carefully, he examined the door and the area around it hoping for anything he hadn't noticed before that might give him a way inside but he found nothing.

He thought about breaking a window but they were so narrow that it wouldn't accomplish anything. Even if he could clear all the glass from the pane, he wouldn't be able to squeeze through the small opening. Giving up on the front of the house, he walked to the side of it.

Rounding the corner, he came to the cellar door he had descended beneath before. There were no first-floor windows on this part of the house. In fact, the only option worth considering was the cellar and Jaime didn't see any point in trying it again. He looked closely at the foundation as he walked along the house for anything helpful but there was nothing.

He made his way to the back, trying the back door and examining the area around it and then to the side with the orchard. He was getting nowhere and frustration started to mount. Soon, he found himself back at the front of the house. Feeling defeated, he folded his arms and leaned his head against the front door. Then, with a creek, the door moved.

Jaime stood up straight, nearly jumping in surprise. Cautiously, he pushed the door with his hand. It creaked some more and opened slowly. It was heavy and didn't swing easily on its hinges. He opened it just enough to fit through then put his shoulders in and peered inside.

All he saw was darkness. He raised his flashlight and shined it into the home. When he did, he was surprised to see a wall directly in front of him. Moving inside, he put his hand on the wall as if to make sure it was real. It was covered in worn out wallpaper that was brown with an old-fashioned design. With the aid of his flashlight, he looked to the left and to the right. Oddly, the wall ran the full length of the house. He was standing in the middle of a long hallway that seemed to be a dead end on both sides.

It was cold outside so he closed the door. The sound it made echoed up and down the corridor. He walked to his left, shining his flashlight in every direction. To his left, he passed windows with thick, yellowing drapes. The carpet beneath his feet matched the wallpaper with shades of brown and black. It was thin, faded badly, and balding in several spots. The wall to his right had no break or doors, only an occasional wall lantern covered in cobwebs and dust with glass stained by candle soot.

He reached the end and examined the walls surrounding him: a couple of spiders, a tear in the wallpaper, but no way in or out. He turned around and walked in the other direction, again examining the floor and the walls as he did. He didn't notice anything remarkable until he reached the corner at the other end of the hallway. Shining his flashlight on the wall, he could see the outline of a door. It had no door knob and was covered in wallpaper. It was only distinguishable by the cracks around its edges and a keyhole.

Jaime pushed on the door and it opened easily. Walking through it, he found himself inside a tiny, square room just large enough for a carpeted staircase that descended at his feet. Cautiously, he shined his flashlight down the stairs and strained his neck. All he could see were stairs and walls and wall lanterns so he took a step and began the descent.

The staircase was narrow and spiders moved on the walls on either side. Instinctively, he drew his arms in, holding them tight against his body. When he reached the bottom of the stairs, he stood in a small landing with a door in front of him and another one to his left. He tried the one in front of him but it was locked. The door to his left, however, was not. It opened into some kind of sitting room with stuffed chairs that were aged but elegant; a small, round, coffee table; and a large, oval mirror on one of the walls that was framed by an ornate design.

Jaime moved his flashlight beam around the room. It had the same wallpaper and wall lanterns he had seen in the other parts of the house. The room was covered in dust and cobwebs. When the beam hit the mirror, it spread around the walls, revealing two more doors in two different walls. He walked to the one directly in front of him and, finding it unlocked, pushed it open to reveal a short, dark hallway with more closed doors lining one of the walls. His beam just barely reached another door on a wall at the far end. He walked to it and swung it open. Another hallway stretched out in front of him but this one was much longer with doors lining both sides.

'This place is a maze!' he thought to himself.

Just then, the ceiling above him creaked. He froze, held his breath in his lungs, and listened. Another creak and then another. He shined his flashlight back at the door he had entered through and thought about going back. If someone – or something - was walking above him, he didn't want to be trapped with them in the labyrinth of staircases and hallways he was standing in.

His Father's voice rung in his head. "Stop being a pansy. Why are you scared of *everything*?"

"This is stupid," he told himself. "I'm not scared. There's nothing to be scared of."

He pushed ahead, walking into the long hallway in front of him. When he reached the end, it curved to the right and to the right again until he was in another long, dark hallway that ran parallel to the previous one. This happened two more times, the hallway snaking back and forth to create parallel corridors, each lined with closed doors. Jaime was beginning to feel like the maze was never going to end.

As he walked, he moved his flashlight beam from left to right, occasionally trying a door. He was surprised when he finally found one unlocked. He pushed it open and curiously peered inside. He found a bedroom with a simple bed in the middle of one wall, a simple dresser against the opposite wall near the foot of the bed, and an empty nightstand next to the bed. The emptiness of the room gave him a strange feeling. He closed the door and tried others. He found two more unlocked, each which opened to bedrooms that looked virtually identical to the first.

While peering into one, he suddenly heard something from somewhere in the house but he couldn't tell where. He pulled his head out from the doorway of the bedroom and stood still in the hallway so he could listen more intently. Then, he heard the distant but unmistakable sound of a human voice. It was too distant and muffled to discern what it said, if anything, but he was sure it was a voice. It continued in an indiscernible string of sounds or words which he could barely hear.

He shined his flashlight behind him but there was nothing but darkness and a long, empty hallway. He looked around as if he might see where the voice was coming from. The endlessly winding hallways, the narrow passages, the stairways, and the enclosed spaces were playing tricks on his senses. For a moment, he thought the sound was coming from the next hallway over, then he was sure it was coming from one of the bedrooms nearby, then he thought it was somewhere above him. It stopped before he could figure it out. He stood carefully in the silence long enough to be sure that the sound was gone before continuing. Then, unsettled, he reluctantly pushed ahead.

When he reached the end of the hall, it came to a dead end. An empty wall stood in front of him. He tried the doors to either side.

One was locked but the other opened into another sitting room. He entered the room and walked to the opposite side where two doors stood next to each other in a wall. Walking through one of them, he found himself in an enclosed, narrow staircase ascending up to another door. He began to climb and, as he did, he heard the voice again. It seemed closer than before. He felt almost certain it was beyond the door in front of him. He wanted to turn back but wouldn't let himself. When he reached the top of the stairs, he could still hear the voice – a muttering string of indiscernible words.

He turned the doorknob and opened the door slowly, trying not to make any noise. Everything was too old, though. The hinges let out a loud shrill which caused Jaime to wince. The voice stopped suddenly. Jaime's heart began to pound. Whoever or whatever it was knew he was there. He briefly caught a glimpse of a large, spacious room on the other side of the doorway as he quickly turned off his flashlight and waited. There was nothing but silence. Then, a creaking noise like the sound that wood makes when it's stepped on. It was close and seemed to come from the pitch-black room in front of him but he couldn't tell exactly where. He silently tried to tell himself that it was probably just the sound of an old house settling against itself.

He stood still in the dark, open doorway feeling exposed for what felt like a very long time. He heard nothing but his own breathing, which he realized was fast and which felt uncomfortably loud. "I'm not scared," he repeated to himself in his mind as he finally gathered the courage to move again. He put his free hand over his flashlight to obscure the beam and flicked it on. A reddish light glowed through his fingers and illuminated a small piece of floor near his feet. Where he stood, the flooring changed from carpet to stained, wooden planks.

With one hand still over the beam, he raised the flashlight. Suddenly, he gasped and nearly fell down the stairs behind him. A still, white figure in an old, white dress that draped to the ground stood in front of him, nearly close enough to touch. Her back was to him and a long, wispy veil made of lace hung from her head to the floor. Jaime's foot banged against the door frame as he struggled to regain his balance, breaking the silence. At this, the figure slowly turned her head until Jaime could see the outline of her face. She was old with deep wrinkles and wiry, white hair.

As quietly and carefully as he could, he backed down the stairs, hoping desperately not to make any more noise. His flashlight shook in his subtly quivering hands. He kept the dim, reddish beam in front of him. After a few steps, the woman turned her head back as if she had decided the noise wasn't worth exploring. When he arrived at the bottom of the stairs, he reached around his body and opened the door behind him without turning his back on the figure in white whom he could only assume still stood in the darkness at the top of the stairs.

He stepped backwards through the doorway, closed the door, and turned around, ready to run through the door at the other end of the room. Instead, he stopped in his tracks. On the opposite wall, there were *two* doors. He hadn't noticed the second door when he first entered the room a few moments earlier. He walked across the room and tried both doors. They were both unlocked and they both opened to long, dark hallways. His heart sunk.

Completely disoriented but desperate to keep moving, he took a guess and walked through the door on the left. He ran down the hall lined with doors which, at first, looked familiar. When he reached the end, though, the hallway turned to his left and he knew he had chosen wrong. He thought of turning back but decided against it. Maybe if he just kept moving, he would find a way out.

The hallway came to a dead end and, nearly in a panic, he hastily began turning the knobs of the doors around him. He found an open one which led to *another* staircase that ascended up. His heart sank again but he didn't hesitate. He ran up the stairs in a few leaping steps. At the top was a door in front of him and a door to his right. He opened the door in front of him and shined his flashlight beam into the darkness. He caught a glimpse of an old, cast-iron oven against one wall and a long, wooden table in the middle of the room before quickly deciding to try the other door.

When he opened the door to his right, he was hit by a cold draft and a stale smell of dirt. He shined his flashlight through the opening but couldn't see anything. Lowering the beam near his feet, he saw a familiar, concrete staircase descending in front of him. He had been here before. He had found the cellar.

Encouraged, he hurried down the stairs then raced across the dirt floor to the other side. He reached the brick wall and shined his flashlight upwards to make sure he knew exactly where the ladder was. Then, looking down, he saw the tin bucket still sitting where he had left it before. Stepping onto the bucket, he switched his flashlight off and stuffed it into his pants. He took a deep breath and, with everything he had in him, jumped for the ladder, reaching with one hand just as he had done before. He grasped the bottom rung, kicked against the wall with his legs, and made his way up.

At the top, he pushed the cellar door open with one arm and crawled out onto the ground which was cold and damp. Suddenly, he realized how fatigued he was. He needed to stop and catch his breath but he didn't want to. He began to run again but he couldn't manage to go as fast as before. He rounded the corner of the house and headed toward the front gate but, before he could get very far, he tripped and tumbled to the ground. As he got up, he twisted his neck to glance back at the front of the house and saw something that made him stop and stare.

In the wide, second-story window above the front door stood the old lady with a candle-lit lantern in her hand. She held the lantern out in front of her, illuminated by its soft light. It reflected off her white clothes and her veiled, white hair, causing her to glow in a way that looked inhuman. She stared absently into the night.

A shot of adrenalin shot through Jaime again, urging him to flee. He began to run and made it to the gate before Karen's words suddenly echoed in his head; "There's no such thing as ghosts, Jaime." He slowed down in order to scramble through the opening in front of him, turning his head again to see the figure still standing in the window. Before he could get through the gates, he heard his dad's voice in his mind calling him a sissy.

He hesitated and tried calming his breathing. *'Stop!'* he told himself. *'There's nothing to be scared of.'* He looked again at the house and took a deep breath. *'Don't be a sissy,'* he thought. *'Don't be a sissy.'*

He thought of Mark and the guys and the stories he could tell them next time he saw them. Then, exerting all the willpower he could muster, he turned his flashlight back on. *'You can do this,'* he told himself as he took a deep breath and began walking back to the front door. When he reached it, his hands were trembling. But, as calmly as he could, he turned the knob and pushed it open. Slowly and cautiously, he entered the house and followed his previous path through the maze of doors and hallways, carefully checking around every corner and behind every doorway before moving forward. Finally, he found himself back at the top of the stairs that led to the large, open room where he had encountered the figure in white. The elusive sounds of creaking floors and a distant murmur again echoed in the halls. His heart began beating faster. Perspiration was beading on his forehead as he slowly pushed open the door in front of him, forcing his reluctant muscles to move.

Then, without allowing himself to hesitate, he gathered his nerves and shined his light into the darkness. The beam revealed a vast, empty room with stained, wooden floors and a spiral staircase in the center that led up to an open second floor that overlooked the ground level. Relieved that nobody was there, he stepped inside. A few, ornate pieces of furniture were carefully placed around the room including chairs that looked uncomfortable and an elegant, hand-crafted table in the center of the wall behind the stairs.

Above him, he could hear a muttering voice and a faint glow emanated around the corner of a wall at the top of the staircase. Despite his fear, curiosity began to tug at him. *'Keep going!'* he had to tell himself. He continued forward to the winding stairs. When he reached the top, still trembling, he turned left, keeping his hand on the railing. To his right was a wall with two doors in it and to his left, beyond the railing he held to, was a drop to the open room he had just left, one story below. Up ahead, the walkway turned right, down a hallway lined, on one side, by a wall with windows that overlooked the front lawn. The lady stood at one end of the hall. Jaime couldn't see her but, from where he stood, he could see the glowing light of her candle-lit lantern escaping around the corner and he could hear her voice echoing off of the walls.

He continued moving forward. As he passed one of the hallway doors, though, he noticed it was opened wide. He couldn't help but look inside, welcoming the distraction. The room was considerably different than the others he had peered into earlier. This one looked much more used and lived in – or like it had been at one time. Dust and cobwebs still lay all around but there was a bookcase against one wall filled with books and other items. An empty lantern gathered dust atop a dresser, and the bed was made with thick bedding with a hand-quilted design.

Jaime took a quick detour and entered the room. He looked around for a moment then wandered over to the bookcase. He pulled one of the rickety doors open, causing the pane of glass in it to rattle. There were two shelves filled with books, all old with titles that were entirely unfamiliar. One book at the far end of one of the shelves caught his attention. It was wider than the rest and jutted out. He took it from its place and turned it over to see its cover. "Journal," it read.

He brushed the dust off of it with his hand then put it back on the shelf. As he did, he noticed his flashlight beam reflecting off of something the next shelf up. He looked closer to see an old-fashioned, bronze key which he took down and examined. Like everything else, it too was covered in dust and seemingly forgotten. He thought it might be a valuable find and stuffed it into his pocket.

'OK,' he thought to himself, *'no more procrastinating.'*

He walked out of the room and cautiously rounded the corner toward the sound of the muttering voice and the glow of the lantern, turning off his flashlight as he did. He could see the lady and her wispy white dress at the opposite end of the long hallway in front of him. His breathing grew heavier and faster. Immediately to his left, he recognized the wide, draped window at which she had stood when he saw her from the yard.

Jaime stopped where he was, not wanting to get any closer. The old lady, however, was moving slowly toward him from the other end of the hall stopping at each door. The light from her lantern flickered again and again, causing long, dark shadows to stretch and jump all along the walls. Jaime could hear the sound of her talking to herself and the subtle clank of small metal pieces bouncing off of each other. He realized she was locking each hallway door.

She got closer still and Jaime began discerning words and sentences in her muttering. Suddenly, like a deer in headlights, his feet felt glued to the floor. He wasn't sure he could run, even if he wanted to.

"Yes, he is gone but a new one has already taken his place...No, not until the harvest moon, just as you've told me to do...Yes, I heard the screams last night. They went on until morning."

She was getting closer and her voice was getting louder. Jaime tried desperately not to move, hoping the shadows were hiding him.

"Yes, I know," she continued her one-sided conversation, "scrub every surface and hide every stain; every house has its secrets that need not be explained."

Suddenly she stopped, turned her head, and went silent. Jaime was sure she was looking directly at him. He froze. The candlelight reflected off her pale, wrinkled face. Her long dress and lacey veil hung from her frail frame like curtains from a rod. It reminded him of Karen's Halloween costume, which might have made him laugh under different circumstances. Although the old lady's dress was also aged and yellowing, it was more elegant than Karen's.

He studied her face and drew in a quick breath of air when he noticed her eyes. They had no color or pupil but, instead were pale and cloudy. Slowly, he brought one trembling hand up in front of him and waved it back and forth. She had no reaction. Although she carried a lantern, she didn't seem to be relying on its light. She held it absently to one side instead of out in front of her. She moved from memory, not from sight. She was blind.

But just when Jaime thought he was undetected, she turned her head to the side and spoke.

"Is there a little boy in here?" she said.

He suddenly became still again, not wanting to move or breathe.

"Did he come through the cellar?" she continued. "I heard something in the cellar."

"But why is he here?" She asked, as if responding to a voice Jaime couldn't hear.

She was silent for probably a full minute before repositioning her head and seeming to look in Jaime's direction again. "Why are you here?" she said.

She waited. Jaime didn't know if she really knew he was there nor did he understand how she could. The silence felt too heavy, though and he felt like he couldn't stand speechless any longer. Then, just when he was about to respond, she continued her conversation.

"He belongs to one of the men, doesn't he? Do I need to prepare a bed, Father?"

Jaime furrowed his brow.

As if nothing had happened, she turned back towards the nearest door and continued the task of locking each one.

"It will be a cold winter this year, won't it?" She said. "Yes, Father, I'll make sure there's plenty of wood in store."

Jaime relaxed, feeling like he could breathe again. He wasn't sure if he should be more scared or less having confirmed that Karen was right; the figure was not a ghost. Whatever the case, he had seen enough. He wanted to get out of the house and away from the old lady. As quietly as he could, he snuck away, carefully following the path back to the front door so as not to get lost again.

When he reached the front yard, he sighed in relief. As he made his way through the woods back to his house, he put his hand in his pocket and felt the bronze key between his fingers. He felt good about what he had done. He couldn't wait to tell the guys about this.

CHAPTER 6

Jaime found Mark, Danny, and Joe huddled in front of their classroom door before school started the next day. As he approached, he could feel the weight of the bronze key he had slipped into his pocket before leaving home that morning. Showing them the key would add to the effect of his story. He couldn't wait to see their reactions.

They were laughing about something when he got to them. Danny was impersonating an old-voice; "you...you...delinquents!" he said, shaking a fist in the air. The others laughed harder. Jaime smiled awkwardly.

Mark nodded with his head to say hello. "Tell Jaime about it," he said to Danny. Then, looking at Jaime, he added "you've got to hear this."

With a broad smile and a fading hint of laughter still in his voice, Danny started his story. "So, on Saturday," he said, "we paid old man Miller a visit – I guess you could say."

The other two chuckled.

"He doesn't know who that is," Joe reminded everyone.

"Oh yeah," Danny said. "Old man Miller is just this crazy old man who seriously has lost his mind."

"My Dad says he's an outsider," Mark chimed in.

"It's because he is," Danny said. "My Dad says he was born in Edith's Hollow but then his family moved away for a long time and he's the only one who came back once he was older. So he didn't really grow up here or anything."

"Neither did Jaime," Joe said.

Mark shrugged his shoulders. "I know. That's why it's different with Jaime then it is with you guys," he said, looking at Joe and Danny.

"What's that supposed to mean?" Jaime asked, a little annoyed.

"No, you're cool and everything," Mark said defensively, "but...you know," he struggled for the right words. "You're just not really...It's just not the same, that's all."

Jaime furrowed his brow. Apparently, everyone understood what Mark was trying to say except for him.

"Anyway," Joe continued, "you know that brown house you pass on the corner just before turning down your street on your way home from school?" he asked.

Jaime tried brushing off Mark's comment, "you mean the one with the refrigerator on the front porch?" he asked.

Mark chuckled a little, "yeah, that's the one."

"That's his house," Joe said.

Jaime nodded his head.

"But seriously," Danny continued, "he's totally lost his mind. We've played so many pranks on him." Danny began laughing again and the others joined him. "You should see how confused he gets. So, on Saturday, we were just bored and decided to go doorbell ditch him. I did it the first time and we all hid behind some bushes by the corner of his house. The old man comes all the way out of his house and is looking back and forth over and over for like at least five minutes."

Mark and Joe laughed hard as Danny relayed the scene, partially acting it out. "Hello? … Hello?" Danny said, again impersonating an old man's voice. "He said it like ten times!"

Jaime forced a laugh. "No way," he said, trying to give them the reaction he knew they wanted.

"So then he goes back inside and Mark goes and rings his doorbell again and he does the *exact same thing*. I swear, he stood out there for at least another five minutes just going "hello? Hello?" When he finally went back inside, I rung the bell again but this time when he comes out, he's fired up. I barely made it behind the bushes when he came storming out the door. "You knock on my door one more time and I swear I'm gonna shoot you!" he yells. Well, I can't hold it in so I burst out laughing and we hear him coming towards us. Just then, Joe looks up and says, "guys, he's got a shotgun!" So we took off as fast as we could. But as we're running, we hear him yell at us "you...you...delinquents!"'"

The group laughed even harder. Apparently, that had been the punch line. Again, Jaime forced a laugh of his own.

When the laughter died, Mark changed the subject. "Speaking of pranks," he said, "has anyone thought about what we're gonna do to Karen this year?"

Jaime perked up, wondering what Mark was talking about. He noticed Danny shoot Mark a look and tilt his head toward Jaime as if to say, "why are you talking about this in front of him?" Mark brushed it off. "Jaime won't say anything," he said. "Actually, he can probably help us get her pretty good."

"What are you talking about?" Jaime asked.

"Well," Mark started with a mischievous smile, "every Halloween we pull a prank on Karen. We've been doing it since 3rd grade." There was a level of pride in his voice. "Every year has been better than the one before. Last year, we scared her so bad, she cried."

"And she doesn't know it's you?" Jaime asked.

Mark deflated a little at Jaime's question. "Actually, she does," he said. "Only because she figured it out last year. She made a big scene about it in class the next day. It was really stupid."

Jaime felt a pit in his stomach, suddenly understanding why Karen disliked these guys so much.

"You've totally got to help us pull off something huge this year," Mark said to Jaime. "She trusts you. We could come up with something awesome."

Jaime shook his head, "I don't think she really likes me now," he said.

"Oh, come on, I'm sure she does," Mark said. "We'll come up with something. You're in, right?"

Jaime forced a smile. "Yeah," he said. "Of course."

He stuck his hands in his pockets and felt the bronze key. He had forgotten about it for a moment. For some reason, though, he didn't feel like saying anything to the guys about the lady in the house in the woods. In fact, he started to feel a growing sense of curiosity about her. Who was she? How did she end up there? And

60

what was she doing there all alone? Standing there with the key at his fingertips, he suddenly realized that he kind of felt sorry for her.

"Hey," he said, "I've been thinking about that house we went to. Do you think there's anyone in town who knows more about the people who lived there? Like, who for sure was there besides the factory owner guy?"

All three shrugged their shoulders. "Why?" Danny asked.

"I don't know," Jaime said. "I'm just really curious about it."

"Old man Miller," Joe said.

Mark rolled his eyes. "He says all the time that he went there when he was a kid. He has some kind of crazy story about meeting the owner I guess. I mean, he's the only person old enough in town who could have been around back then but, like I said, he's crazy. Everyone knows you can't listen to what he says."

Jaime nodded his head without saying anything. Maybe he would have to see for himself how crazy Mr. Miller was.

Half an hour after school let out, Jaime found himself standing on an unkempt lawn in front of Mr. Miller's brown house with an old, broken down refrigerator on the front porch. He stood for a moment on one of the few patches of grass disbursed among the weeds questioning whether he really wanted to do this. Finally, he walked to the door and knocked. As soon as he did, he panicked, realizing that he had no idea what he was going to say when Mr. Miller came to the door. He quickly tried coming up with a script in his mind but, before he knew it, the door was opening.

Mr. Miller stood slightly hunched over with a cane in one hand. Even in his fragile, old age, he was a big man. His frame was withered but he was tall and his shoulders were broad. He was mostly bald with a little bit of white hair sticking out in every direction on the sides of his head like some sort of mad scientist.

His eyebrows were the defining feature of his face. They were grey and bushier than any eyebrows Jaime had ever seen. They weren't quite so messy as the hair on his head though. In fact, Jaime wondered if they had been combed. They stuck up, rising toward his forehead and forming a sharp v that nearly touched between his eyes. The result was a constant, angry scowl on Mr. Miller's face that was well matched by his fixed, unsmiling mouth and his 'I'm not-amused' eyes.

"Ummm, I'm..." Jaime started.

"I know who you are," Mr. Miller interrupted with a grumbling growl. "But I don't know why you're standing on my porch."

"Well, I was wondering if - I mean, I heard that you..."

"You're gonna have to speak up, son, if you expect me to hear you," Mr. Miller interrupted again loudly. "Just come inside. You're letting all the hot air out and I hate being cold."

Jaime followed Mr. Miller to a small, messy living room where a fire crackled inside a fireplace. Random items were scattered across the room with only a vague sense of order. A stack of cardboard boxes nearly covered the back wall and stacks of newspapers and magazines stood against another. A free-standing set of iron shelves was filled with old wooden toys, figurines, hand-crafted boxes, and World War II memorabilia.

A threadbare rocking chair with a blanket draped over it faced the fireplace. The fireplace mantle was also lined with knick-knacks and with a few framed pictures including one of a much younger Mr. Miller standing with his arm around an attractive girl, both of them smiling.

Mr. Miller sat down in the rocking chair and looked at Jaime. "Now don't stand there," he said, "you'll make me nervous. Grab one of those chairs from the kitchen and bring it in here. And sit down close to me so I can hear you."

Jaime went into the next room and took a wooden chair from around the kitchen table and brought it back into the living room where he set it near the fire, close to Mr. Miller's chair. Mr. Miller was staring into the flames as Jaime sat down. For a moment, there was only the crackling and popping of a lively, hot fire.

"So..." Jaime tentatively began, "I've heard that -"

"What's your name, son?" Mr. Miller asked abruptly, interrupting him again.

"Jaime," he replied.

"Jimmy?" the old man asked.

"No, Jaime."

"Jeremy?"

"Jaime," Jaime repeated, this time slower and quite loud.

"Jimmy," Mr. Miller said, nodding his head. "I thought I already said that," he added in a grumble beneath his breath. "You're that new kid, aren't you?"

Jaime looked at him, surprised and a little confused. He didn't expect that old man Miller would know who he was.

"Oh, don't be surprised," Mr. Miller said. "You can't pick your nose in this town without someone telling their neighbor about it. And these folks don't like newcomers." With just a slight move of his head, Mr. Miller looked at Jaime out of the corners of his eyes. After a moment of this, Jaime began to feel uncomfortable and wondered if he should say something. Before he could, though, Mr. Miller pointed to the picture on the mantle of him and a young woman.

"She's beautiful, isn't she?"

Jaime nodded his head. "Yeah," he said.

"Margaret and I met in Boston. I was born here in Edith's Hollow but, after Mom died, it was just me and Dad and he moved us out there." Mr. Miller looked at the fire again but seemed as though he was gazing far beyond it. "We were married for fifty-one years." Even though he was the only other person there, Jaime felt like Mr. Miller wasn't really talking to him. "She died in '61 and I moved back here the same year. I wanted to go somewhere peaceful." He chuckled quietly to himself at the word 'peaceful,' like it was a joke.

Then he turned his head and looked directly at Jaime. "They won't let you get away with it, you know. They won't let you be a stranger here. They'll run you and your mom off. They always do."

Jaime was taken aback. But, while he struggled to figure out how to respond, Mr. Miller's face suddenly changed from stern and grumpy to soft and confused. He looked at Jaime as if he wasn't sure how he had gotten there. "Now, you're Phyllis's boy, right?"

Perplexed, Jaime shook his head. "No," he said. "My Mom's name is Kat – or, Katherine, really, but she likes to go by Kat."

Mr. Miller furrowed his brow in deeper confusion. "I...I'm not sure," he said, shaking his head and looking at the ground. "We took the train from Beacon Hill yesterday but I don't know how I..." he trailed off. "It's nice up there. Margaret said she'd like to go back next weekend." He kept gazing at the ground.

After a minute or two of silence, Jaime cleared his throat. "Mr. Miller?" he said gently.

Mr. Miller looked up and seemed surprised to see Jaime sitting next to him. A surly expression returned to his face, which, strangely, brought Jaime a sense of relief. "I don't remember what we were talking about," he said with a grumble.

"Mr. Miller," Jaime said slowly and politely. "Can I ask you a question?"

Old man Miller cleared his throat. "Go on," he said, a little impatiently.

He seemed to be back in his right mind so Jaime continued. "That factory owner that used to live here a long time ago - Mr. Fridman – I heard that you went out there when you were a kid, that you met him and stuff."

Mr. Miller looked at Jaime with a touch of skepticism. "Why do you want to know?" he asked.

Jaime hesitated. For a moment, they studied each other, wondering if they could trust each other, trying to guess one another's motives.

"Because I've been to his house," Jaime finally said. "It's still there. And somebody lives in it. I've seen her."

Mr. Miller raised his eyebrows a little. "I wouldn't go out there if I was you," he said.

"Why?" Jaime asked. "Did you really go there when you were a kid?"

"I think you know the answer to that. I'm sure they've told you all about what crazy old Mr. Miller has to say about that place."

Jaime shook his head, "honestly," he said, "they haven't. Like you said, I'm an outsider here. People don't tell me stuff."

Mr. Miller's countenance changed a little. He took a deep breath, thought for a moment, and then started to speak. "When I was a young kid – probably seven or eight years old – Dad needed work and nobody in town was willing to give it to him. He wasn't very well liked around here. He went to the textile mill on the other side of town and offered his services out there but Mr. Fridman refused; he never hired locals, which nobody understood. Well, that didn't sit well with Dad and he was getting desperate so, one day, he put on his coat and he told me to put on mine and come with him.

I followed him to Mr. Fridman's place, which was a good ways outside of town – especially by foot. When we got there, there were these tall, iron gates out front keeping us out. So, Dad asked me to stay there while he tried to find a way in. Of course, I didn't listen, so I followed him around the back where we found an arched opening in the fence.

When we got on the property, Dad went straight to the front door. He knocked two or three times and even tried jiggling the handle – Dad was like that - but nobody answered and the place was locked. Meanwhile, I was looking all around and at some point I happened to look up and standing there in a window above the front door was this little girl – probably a year or two older than I was – and she was staring down at us. When I saw her, she quickly disappeared but just a few minutes later, Mr. Fridman showed up at the door. From the moment he swung the door open, he was flustered and angry. Instead of standing in the doorway, he stepped outside and closed the door behind him – the kind of thing you do when you have something to hide.

Immediately, he starts yelling at Dad, "What are you doing here?! Get off my property! How did you get in?!" Dad tried being polite at first and explaining that he came to ask Mr. Fridman to reconsider giving him work but Mr. Fridman wasn't letting up and Dad didn't like being yelled at so, before long, he started giving it back to him. And while they're yelling at each other, the door opens again and the same little girl I saw in the window comes out and stands behind her Dad. It took him a minute to notice but, when Mr. Fridman realized that she was there, his whole demeanor changed. He kind of turned white and looked at me and my Dad, like he was wondering if we noticed her, which is a silly thing because of course we noticed her.

He shewed her back inside really quickly and shut the door behind her, then, kind of quiet and subdued, he asks Dad, "you're from the other side of town, aren't you?" Dad said he was. Then Mr. Fridman took a deep breath and dropped his shoulders a little like he had been defeated. "Follow me," he said.

I straightened up like I was going to go with them but Mr. Fridman said I needed to stay where I was and Dad looked at me and nodded as if to say I needed to stay put. So, I let them go but when Mr. Fridman opened the door, I could see that the little girl was still standing there by the entrance, probably trying to eavesdrop on us. I heard her ask about me but the door closed before I could really hear anything else. I could hear her and her dad having some kind of conversation but I couldn't tell what they were saying.

Then, it went quiet on the other side of the door. I stood outside by myself for probably five minutes or more before the door opened again. I thought it might be Dad but it wasn't, it was that little girl. At first, she just stood in the doorway looking at me kind of awkwardly. Then she asked me who I was and what I was doing there. I didn't think she was very good at conversation. She didn't really seem shy just kind of unusual. I told her who I was but when I asked what her name was, she just didn't answer.

She stood in the doorway the whole time we talked and she kept checking behind her. So, I asked, "you're not supposed to be talking with me, are you?" She shook her head 'no.' I asked if Mr. Fridman was her dad and she said he was. I asked why I never saw her in school or in town and she said it was because she never went to those places. She said she never went anywhere.

About then, she thought she heard someone coming so she said she had to go and shut the door really quick. Dad came out a minute later. On the walk home, he was quiet. I could tell he was thinking about something really hard. Then, just as we got to our house, he told me we needed to start packing up our things because we were moving. Less than a week later, we were in Boston and we had a place to live and Dad had a job."

"Anyway," he said, with a wave of his hand, "that part's not important." Then he looked at Jaime. "This person you saw at the house, you said it was a woman?"

Jaime nodded his head. "She was really old," he said.

"I wouldn't go out there if I was you," Mr. Miller repeated.

"Why not?" Jaime asked.

"Do you know what happened to Mr. Fridman's little girl?"

Jaime shook his head.

"She grew up and went crazy. And when she couldn't handle being locked up inside that house anymore, she snapped and killed her own Father."

"But I thought Mr. Fridman died in a fire in his mill?" Jaime said.

Mr. Miller looked at Jaime somberly. "Who do you think started the fire?" he said.

A chill ran down Jaime's spine.

"Look, Jimmy," Mr. Miller said. He was looking at Jaime intently. The fire was crackling next to them and Jaime could see the flames reflecting in Mr. Miller's brown eyes. "Most people say that place is haunted but you and I know better. There's someone living there and she's not in her right mind. She's had all these years to stew in her craziness. She's killed before and she'd do it again. Don't go back. It's not safe."

CHAPTER 7

After speaking with Mr. Miller, Jaime was sure of two things; first, old man Miller's stories about Mr. Fridman's daughter were not crazy, and, second, Jaime was going back to the house in the woods as soon as he got the chance. He made his way there a few days later on a Saturday. He told his mom he was going to hang out with some friends and, by 11:00 in the morning, he was standing at the tall, black, iron gates. Just for fun, he found the lever in the ground that opened the gate when he stepped on it and, on the other end, closed it the same way.

When he got to the front door, he wasn't surprised to find it locked. He reached into his pocket and pulled out the heavy, bronze key he had made sure to bring along. Holding his breath, he pushed it into the keyhole and turned. To his delight, the door unlocked. He pushed it open, entered the hallway in front of him, and closed the door behind him.

For a moment, he stood still and listened but there was only silence. He moved down the hall to the hidden door in the wall. That, too, was locked and, again, he was happy to find that his key opened it. There was no light to illuminate the stairway on the other side so he pulled out his flashlight and followed the same path he had taken before.

As he wound through the hallways, he stopped occasionally to check a door to his left or right or to listen for signs of life. He found his key opened every door he tried. Each door along the hallway walls opened to a bedroom and every bedroom looked the same.

Each had the same, simple bed and the same, simple dresser. Each was equally barren and equally boring. After looking in on six or seven of them, he stopped unlocking doors.

Periodically, he thought he heard footsteps or clanking coming from some distant place in the house. Each time, a shot of adrenaline shot through him and then passed as he forged ahead. When he reached the door that led to the large room with wooden floors, he pushed it open slowly, knowing the woman in white was likely somewhere on the other side and not wanting to alert her of his presence. The hinges started to creak so he paused. He pulled up hard on the doorknob hoping to lift the door a little and relieve some of the pressure on the hinges then he pushed again. It worked. The creaking was much quieter. Once the door was open just wide enough, he slipped past it.

He could hear noises coming from another room up ahead. He walked across the floor, passing the winding staircase on his left and toward an opening at the far, right-side corner of the room he was in. The noises grew louder – the clanging of metal, the banging of something hard against a wooden surface, and the muttering voice of the old lady.

Jaime walked to the doorless entry and peered inside to see the woman shuffling around a nineteenth century kitchen that seemed to have frozen in time. A long, sturdy, wooden table stretched across the middle of the room. A large, black, cast-iron oven stood at one end with a chimney that ran out of its top and into the wall behind it. He could see a yellow flame dancing through the slats in the front.

One wall was filled with objects that hung from hooks and nails: copper cooking utensils, pots, pans, and small tin buckets. The opposite wall was almost entirely taken up by a large hutch that was both tall and wide. It had four long shelves and stood only a couple feet short of the ceiling. The bottom two shelves were lined with glass jars and bowls of all sizes. Some of the bowls looked like they were for preparing meals and others for serving. The top two shelves were divided into slats designed for holding plates. The slats in the top shelf were filled with porcelain plates but the lower shelf was mostly empty, only holding one.

The sun was shining through a window on the south wall, obscured by white, yellowing curtains. It filled the room with a hazy, orange hue. Particles of dust drifted lazily in its light.

The old lady was dressed in a white dress different from the one Jaime had seen her in before. This one was plain and unadorned. It was a working dress. She wore a bonnet on her head and an apron around her torso that tied in the back. She stood at the table with a cleaver in her hand. Lying on the table near her were two other knives, one small and one large. Each looked sharp and well cared for.

A rabbit carcass lay lifeless in front of her. Just beyond it were two wooden bowls, one larger than the other and each stained with old blood. The woman worked methodically, butchering the carcass. She chopped off each of the rabbit's paws with the cleaver and threw them in the larger bowl. Jaime was surprised and a little startled by the force she managed to exert wielding the knife. Next, she set the cleaver down and picked the rabbit up, holding it firmly in both hands. In one, swift motion, she snapped it in half, breaking its back. She then forced her thumb through the fragile skin, pressed her fingers into the hole, and, with remarkable strength, ripped the skin from the rabbit in every direction.

One long piece of hide came loose from the carcass. She tossed the skin in the bowl that held the paws and laid the rabbits' body back on the table. She then gripped the exposed entrails firmly in one hand near the rabbit's breasts, carefully pulled the heart and lungs from the chest cavity and then tore the rest free from top to bottom. She fingered through the soft, slippery clump she now held in her hands until she separated the liver, heart, and kidneys from the rest of the guts. "I'll save these for us; They'll make a special treat," she said as she threw the pieces she had picked out in the empty bowl and the rest of the parts into the larger bowl. She felt the rabbit's gut and the table for remaining pieces and threw those in the larger bowl as well.

Muttering inaudibly, she wiped her hands on her apron, smearing them with blood, and then picked the cleaver back up. With one strong and perfectly-placed strike, she chopped off the rabbit's head and threw it in the bowl that held the paws and the hide. Laying down the cleaver, she felt the carcass for any remaining pieces of skin, which she also tore off and tossed into the bowl.

Again, she wiped her hands on her apron, smearing it with a bit more blood, and carefully felt the table in front of her for the smallest of the three knives. She spent the next several minutes separating the rabbit meat from the bones and dividing the carcass into sections. The bones were thrown in the large bowl and the meat remained on the table.

When she was done, she had several carefully portioned pieces laid out in front of her. After washing her hands in a bucket of water, she took a large, copper container that resembled a cookie jar from the lowest shelf of the hutch and brought it to the table along with some glass jars of different sizes. Next, using a wooden scoop, she scooped generous portions of a salt mixture from the copper container and poured it over each piece of meat, using her hands to rub it into every crevice and fold. When she was finished, she unfastened the metal clasps that held down the lids of the glass jars and pushed one piece of rabbit meat into each jar. Finally, she filled the jars with enough salt mixture to cover the meat and then fastened the lids back down.

After washing her hands again, she lifted a frying pan from a hook on the wall, placed it on the stove, and poured oil into it from a small container. The pan sizzled loudly. "Careful now. Don't come over here," she said as she set the oil aside, found the wooden bowl holding the rabbit guts, and dropped them into the hot oil.

While the offal cooked, the old lady cleaned up the mess she had made. She washed the dishes and wiped the table clean. Finally, she picked up the large, wooden bowl that held the rabbit hide and other pieces and headed to a door at the back of the kitchen. When she opened it and disappeared into another room, Jaime decided to follow. He stepped carefully across the floor, doing his best not to make any noise. Beyond the door was a short staircase that descended just three steps into a small room with a door in each of the three walls. It looked familiar. He walked down the steps and saw that the woman had opened one of the doors, which he stepped through.

A cool draft and familiar smell hit him and he knew he was in the cellar. He pulled out his flashlight, and shined it into the darkness, knowing the woman wouldn't see it. He watched her descend the last stair to the cellar floor. Cautiously, he followed several steps behind. As he did, he could hear her muttering to herself words that sounded like the couplet of a poem:

"Last, to the cellar where the dead things have lingered
While their flesh falls away from their toes to their fingers."

She repeated these lines two more times while she walked across the dirt to the far corner. When she got there, she bent over and searched the space with her hands. She found a shovel that stood in the corner but continued looking for something that wasn't there. Jaime knew what she was looking for. In the same corner, several days before, he had found the tin bucket he used to reach the ladder that led out of the cellar. He shined his flashlight to the spot underneath the ladder and saw the bucket was still there.

Swiftly but as quietly as he could, he retrieved the bucket and walked it over to the corner where the woman was still searching. His heart began to beat faster as he got close enough to touch her. She unexpectedly swung in his direction, arms still searching the air, and nearly brushed his leg. He moved back and his feet made a quiet, subtle noise in the dirt. For just a second, she seemed to pause, wondering if she had heard something. He held his breath while a quizzical expression flashed across her face. It passed almost immediately, though.

When she rotated away from him, he again stepped close to her. He could smell the strong, rank smell of body odor drifting off of her skin. From this proximity, he could see that her silvery, white hair was matted and heavy with grease. Slowly and deliberately, he set the bucket down and then stepped backwards without making a noise. After just a few more moments of searching, her hand touched the bucket. She looked both confused and satisfied as she picked it up and examined it. She poured the contents of the wooden bowl into it, set it back down on the dirt, and headed back up the stairs with Jaime not far behind. She returned to the cellar with the jars she had filled with rabbit meat and salt. Jaime watched from the top of the stairs. "It's been a slow year for the traps," she said. "Let's save this meat until it's needed. Winter will be cold this year, don't you think?"

When she arrived back in the kitchen, she removed the frying pan from the heat and, with a set of tongs, transferred the fried rabbit parts from the pan to a cheesecloth that she took from a drawer and spread out. Walking to the hutch, she reached for the plate that sat on the next-to-highest shelf. She was tall enough that she should have been able to reach it with ease but she seemed to have difficulty stretching her body to its full length. She managed to pinch the plate between her fingers and pull it out from its slot until she could get a better grip. "Old age isn't fun, Father," she said as she pulled the plate from its shelf. "But don't you mind. The harvest moon is coming soon and I will complete the tasks."

She moved toward the stove and Jaime, who had been standing near the door frame that led to the stairs which led to the cellar, decided to go back to the kitchen entrance while the path was clear. However, as he passed the long, wooden table, he accidentally kicked one of the legs. The old lady immediately stopped, furrowed her brow, and turned in his direction. From the other end of the table, she peered toward him with her cloudy eyes, as if peering into a dark room, trying to see something she couldn't. She brought one hand down, feeling the tabletop in front of her for its contents.

Jaime noticed the set of knives near her. Her hand stopped when one of her fingers touched the cold, sharp blade of the largest knife. With her other hand, she slowly set the plate down, keeping her finger on the blade. Jaime's heart pounded. He watched her move her hand to the knife's handle which she gripped tightly. His palms began to sweat and he didn't know if he should run or remain quiet. Before he could make up his mind, he saw the plate she had unwittingly placed hanging off of the edge of table fall from its place and crash to the floor. Immediately, the old lady looked crestfallen and, all at once, seemed to entirely forget the noise Jaime had made.

She knelt down and felt the floor. A few large pieces of the plate remained. She picked one of them up and examined it in her hands, shaking her head in frustration and disappointment. "It was the last one," she said. "No, it's impossible," she continued, as if carrying on a conversation with somebody Jaime could neither see nor hear. She sighed heavily and stood up. "No need," she said, apparently still in conversation. "I'll make do. It's only a plate."

She took a broom and a dustpan from a corner of the room and, as best she could, swept up the scattered shards. When she was finished, she brought the cheese cloth with fried rabbit parts over to a tiny table with a single chair near the kitchen's entrance. Sitting on the chair, she sat and ate quietly without utensils. When she was finished, she stood, wiped her hands on her apron, and left the kitchen, walking past Jaime who was extra careful to stand perfectly still and quiet as she passed.

He followed from a distance as she walked into the large room with wooden floors, up the winding staircase, around the corner, and down the hallway to the last door. She muttered quietly as she walked but he was too far behind to hear what she was saying. He reached the door she had entered and looked inside. Of all the bedrooms in the house that Jaime had seen, this was the only one that looked lived in. The bed had been made but the thick comforter that was pulled over the top was ruffled and slightly askew.

A mostly-empty glass of water sat on a nightstand next to the bed. Another completely empty glass sat on a dresser on the other side of the room. A white wardrobe stood at an angle near one corner. One door was ajar and Jaime could see three other dresses hanging up just like the one the old lady was wearing. Her more elegant, white, lace-adorned dress and matching veil were draped over an object near the bed that resembled a headless mannequin.

The old lady yawned as she removed her apron and set it on a wooden rocking chair. "I'll go into the woods this afternoon," she said. "The harvest moon will be here soon and I believe there will be bones to bury. If we're lucky, we'll find beeswax to gather for the candle-lighting." She sat down on the bed without pulling the covers back then stretched out her feet and laid her head on one of the pillows. "But first, a nap," she said in a fading voice as she closed her eyes.

Jaime took this as his queue to leave. It felt like he had been there a long time and he was ready to go home. He walked quietly through the hallway and down the stairs. When he reached the bottom, though, he hesitated. A thought crossed his mind and he detoured back to the kitchen.

He walked to the hutch and looked up at the row of plates on the top shelf. Even hunched over, the old lady was taller than he was so, if she couldn't reach the plates, neither could he. But he had his youth and his sight. It was possible that she had forgotten the additional plates were even there. He picked up the chair the old lady had sat on earlier and carried it next to the hutch. Climbing on top of the chair, he took down a plate and set it on the small, dining table in the corner. Before moving the chair, he took down one more plate and placed it on the next shelf down.

Before leaving, he walked to the spot where the plate had broken and wasn't surprised to find several shards of porcelain that had escaped the old lady's broom. He swept them up and deposited them into a wooden bucket in the corner that served as a waste basket. Then, he returned the broom to its place and headed home.

Jaime couldn't stop thinking about the old lady the rest of the weekend and all through his classes the following Monday. Questions multiplied in his head. If Mr. Miller had been right about her existence, was he also right about the fate of her Father? Had she really murdered him?

The other rumors seemed to be true. She was crazy...at least as far as he could tell. She seemed to see things and hear things - and even talk to things – that weren't really there. He thought back; At times, it had seemed that she knew he was in the house with her but he was pretty sure that most of what she did and said were just reactions to figments of her imagination. He wondered if she could even distinguish between the noises he made and the noises in her head. Not that that thought was necessarily reassuring.

He kept thinking about something else he had noticed about her. She seemed to have surprising strength for a woman her age. The ways she had torn apart the rabbit carcass and wielded the cleaver were all remarkable.

After school, he decided to return to a place he wouldn't have anticipated wanting to see again: the town library. Perhaps, he thought, he might find something useful to help answer some of the questions in his mind or, at least, to feed his curiosity. When he walked through the front doors, his eyes first fell on the book of history his teacher insisted on calling the Town's Heart. He walked to the glass case that housed it and stared inside, suddenly filled with a feeling of intrigue that had been entirely absent last time he was here.

"Hi there," a friendly voice said. Jaime turned his head to see a short, plump man approaching him. He had brown hair that was neatly parted on the side, a mustache, spectacles, and a knitted sweater vest that buttoned down the middle. "Admiring the Town's Heart, I see," he said. "Isn't it wonderful?"

Jaime smiled politely but didn't offer any other response.

"*I* think it's wonderful," he said, pausing to stare at it for a moment. The silent staring and fawning made Jaime feel awkward.

"So, what can I help you find?" he finally asked.

It occurred to Jaime that he must be the librarian. "Um," he started, "I'm looking for some information on Mr. Fridman and the old mill that burned down way back when."

The librarian nodded his head. "And Josiah Knightly, no doubt?"

Jaime furrowed his brow to which the librarian cleared his throat in notable irritation. "The Sherriff – Josiah Knightly. Why do you want the information?" he asked, suddenly sounding suspicious and less friendly.

Jaime felt a little uncomfortable, not sure how to answer. He rubbed his neck, "I just...you know, there's a lot of rumors and..."

The librarian interrupted before he could finish. "Remind me who your parents are," he said, sounding even more suspicious and even less friendly.

"I'm Jaime Ellington. My mom's Kat. She's a teacher at the school."

To Jaime's surprise, a startled look flashed in the librarian's eyes. Then his face settled into a hardened, mistrustful expression. "I don't think we have what you're looking for here," he said.

Jaime was confused. "You mean, the library doesn't have *anything* about Mr. Fridman and his mill?"

The librarian shrugged his shoulders dismissively. "You can search the shelves if you want but I don't think you'll find what you need."

"Well, do you know anywhere else I can look for information about the mill and stuff?" Jaime asked.

"Why don't you ask your mom," he said with a tinge of sarcasm. "Apparently, she teaches history," he said, rolling his eyes.

Jaime was thoroughly perplexed. "Um, OK. I guess I'll look somewhere else," he said as he left.

The next day, he went back to the house in the woods after school. In fact, he returned every day for the next two weeks. It quickly became apparent to him that the lady in white was not idly wasting away in her solitude. Instead, every day was filled with the hard work of survival. It was fascinating to observe. She was incredibly resourceful and tough and knew how to do things Jaime had never even seen or heard of.

One day he watched her press oil from pumpkin seeds out of her garden. On another day, he watched her make a candle from animal fat and a candle wick she fashioned from threads of an old cloth. Several times, he followed her into the woods where she checked her traps every day and sometimes twice a day. One time, while hunched down over a trap, Jaime watched her suddenly stop and lift her head, straining her ears to hear something that had caught her attention.

Slowly, she walked toward a large tree, turning her ear toward it. The thick sound of buzzing bees could be heard all around it. The next day she returned with a gunny sack of supplies and several green branches. Jaime watched her carefully steal the bee's honeycomb after sedating them with a small fire that filled the hive with billowing smoke.

Afterward, she giggled in pure delight. "A good start to the day, indeed!" she said. "Shall we eat the honeycomb?" She paused as if listening to a voice Jaime couldn't hear. "Come on, just this once," she begged coyly. "No, you're right of course. We need it for candles. Oh, but it's delicious!" She immersed the tips of her fingers in the honey she had gathered in a pot. When she pulled them out, she brought them to her mouth and sucked on them. She smiled and giggled again.

Jaime, who was watching from a distance, couldn't help but laugh silently with her. He followed her back to the house and stayed until her final ritual that evening. After her work was done, she changed into her evening clothes – the elegant white dress and the long, lacy veil that occasionally caught a gust of air and moved like an apparition as she walked through the halls. Right on cue, at 9:00, she lit a lantern and stood at the second-story window that was above the front door, overlooking the front yard. As she did every night, she peered into the darkness with her sightless eyes, dimly illuminated by the flickering flame of a candle.

After a few minutes, she turned from the window and began her final job of the day. With a pair of bronze keys in her hand, starting with the upstairs bedrooms closest to her, she checked every door in the house, locking each one that she had unlocked during the day. "We'll have honey in the morning," she said. "But now it's time to sleep; time to sleep for everyone." Then, as she often did, she slipped into verse:

> "Next, to the rooms
> Where visitors sleep.
> Make sure there is nothing
> Unpleasant to see.
> Scrub every surface
> And hide every stain.
> Every house has its secrets
> That need not be explained."

Jaime knew that, when this ritual was finished, she would retire to her bedroom and sleep. Then, in the morning, the first thing she would do was unlock a few select doors including the door to the room with the bookcase where he had found the key that was currently resting in his pocket, the cellar door, and a line of doors that provided a path through the maze of halls to the front door. Until then, the doors would remain locked all night and anything inside would have no way out. Jaime, of course, had a key of his own but, rather than waiting until he was forced to use it, he quietly slipped through the halls, ahead of the old lady, and out the front door.

CHAPTER 8

Halloween was just a day away and Jaime could feel it in the air. The leaves were turning and the moon was almost full. Bulletins printed on Orange-colored construction paper hung on each classroom door, announcing the school-wide Halloween party and costume contest that would be held in the courtyard the next day.

Jaime stood against a brick wall with chipping, white paint on Tuesday morning, waiting for his teacher to unlock the door. He watched others of his classmates gathering nearby, everybody's breath showing when they exhaled, a few shivering in the sharp, Autumn chill. When he saw Mark, Danny, and Joe approaching from across the courtyard, he knew exactly what to expect.

"You're Mom let you out of your shackles for the day?" Mark said as the three got closer. Joe chuckled. This had become Mark's running joke ever since Jaime had discovered the house in the woods and began spending most of his free time there. He hadn't explained to his friends where he was going every day after school but it had become obvious that he had more or less stopped hanging out with them.

A few times, when he had needed an excuse, Jaime gave some version of "my Mom said I can't come over today. She said I've gotta do some chores first." Mark ran with this. Before Jaime knew it, Mark was automatically blaming Jaime's Mom every time Jaime bowed out of getting together with the guys. Jaime didn't encourage Mark, but he didn't resist either. He usually just shrugged his shoulders and played along.

The longer the joke went on, though, the further Mark pushed it. "Your mom needs to lighten up," he'd say. "I wouldn't put up with that if I was you." Recently, he had told Jaime, "your mom really sucks, man," to which Jaime responded swiftly and sharply, "shut up, Mark." Mark saw that Jaime wasn't joking so he punched him in the arm and laughed. "Come on man, it was just a joke." Jaime smiled but he didn't find it funny.

"Seriously," Mark said this time. "she's so annoying! Is she ever going to let you hang out again? It's been weeks!"

Jaime shot him a look, reminding him to be careful what he said. But Mark rolled his eyes. "You can't keep letting her tell you what to do! You have a right to hang out with your friends!"

Mark was right about one thing. It had been a long time since Jaime had spent any time after school with anyone other than the lady in the white dress. His excuses were running out and blaming it on his mom was starting to backfire.

"Actually," Jaime said, "My Mom's out of town today. She'll be gone until tomorrow. She has some overnight thing she's got to do for her college-teaching job in Fall River. So, I can hang out after school."

"Yes!" Mark said, pumping his fist. "'Cause we've got some planning to do."

Jaime looked at him, confused.

"For Halloween." Mark explained. "We've been talking about the prank on Karen. It's gonna be good," he said as an impish smile stole across his face.

Danny laughed. "It's gonna be awesome," he said.

"You're still gonna help us, right?" Mark asked Jaime.

Jaime felt a little bit of a pit in his stomach but he nodded his head and forced a smile. "Definitely," he said.

"Good," Mark said. "We really need your help to make it work. You're the only one of us she trusts."

Just then, the morning bell rang and Ms. Spencer unlocked the classroom door. Jaime found his assigned seat next to Karen's and she came in just a minute later. Jaime felt like the iciness that had developed between them was beginning to thaw. The last couple of weeks, they had been able to manage polite smiles and a little bit of small talk as they sat next to each other in class. This morning, though, Jaime couldn't bring himself to look her in the eye.

"Hello," Karen said warmly as she took her seat.

Jaime returned a closed-mouth smile and nodded his head without looking in her direction. To his relief, Ms. Spencer stood in front of the class and began her lesson before Karen could expect him to respond any further.

That afternoon, Ms. Spencer spoke to the class about some of the history of nearby Fall River. They talked about its booming textile mills in the late 1800s that earned it the nickname "Spindle City." "Of course," she added as an afterthought, "our very own Edith's Hollow had its own failed textile experiment, driven by outsiders trying to push an industry on us that simply wasn't right for our community."

As he listened to his teacher speaking, a notion took shape in Jaime's mind. Who knew the history of Edith's Hollow better than Ms. Spencer? He assumed nobody did. If anyone knew anything about the history of the house in the woods and the fate of the old lady's Father, he was sure she would.

After class, he made up his mind that he would talk to her. He lingered at his desk as his classmates slowly filtered out of the room, fidgeting awkwardly with his things. Mark, Danny, and Joe gathered at the back of the classroom.

"Are you coming, Jaime?" Mark called to him.

"I'll catch up," he replied. "Go ahead without me."

"OK, meet us at Joe's and don't take forever."

"I won't," he promised.

When everyone had finally left, Jaime made his way over to Ms. Spencer, who was sitting at her desk, head down, grading a stack of papers. The red pen in her hand hovered over each page, ready to pounce on every imperfect word or line. She made him nervous. He approached slowly and cleared his throat, unsure how to start.

"You're still here, Mr. Ellington?" she asked without looking up.

He cleared his throat again. "Yes, I am," he said.

"The question was rhetorical," she replied, still not looking up from her papers. "I presume you have something you would like to discuss. Perhaps your grades? Your past several assignments have been..." she paused and gave her writing hand a rest for a brief moment while she searched for the right word, "underwhelming," she said, resuming the work in front of her.

"No, it's not about that," Jaime said.

"Well, it should be," Ms. Spencer added.

Jaime continued undeterred. "It's actually about something from your lesson today – about the history of Edith's Hollow."

Ms. Spencer set down her pen and looked up from her stack of papers for the first time. "Go on," she said.

"Well, I guess I was just thinking about, umm, the textile industry and, like, how you said it affected the people here in Edith's Hollow. That was really interesting to me, you know?" He was searching for a way to ease into the topic of Mr. Fridman without being dismissed with an eye roll from Ms. Spencer.

"It was terrible for us," she said matter-of-factly. "Run your own communities to the ground if you wish but keep your businesses out of our borders. Our forefathers founded Edith's Hollow to preserve a better way of life, away from the sprawling cities. That outsider thought he could get rich at our expense by building a fancy home on our property and bringing his textile business with him. He was dead wrong. It nearly tore the fabric of our community apart."

"I've heard a lot of things about him." Jaime said,

"Who? Fridman?" Ms. Spencer asked.

Jaime nodded his head. "Is it true that nobody knows what happened to his body after he died?"

Ms. Spencer snorted loudly. Suddenly, she became noticeably irritated. "That's enough, Mr. Ellington. I'm not here to tell you ghost stories," she said sharply.

"I just..." he began, but Ms. Spencer interrupted him before he could finish.

"I don't think you're in a position to be asking these kinds of questions about our history, anyway. What are your intentions?" She narrowed her eyes as if she might discern his motives if she stared hard enough.

"I just...it's just interesting, that's all. I just like history, I guess. And, you know," he continued a little sheepishly, "after Mr. Fridman was saved by the deputy and stuff, don't you think it's weird that they never found his body."

"What are you implying?" she asked poignantly.

"Nothing really, it's just an interesting part of the story." There was a very brief moment of silence in which Jaime decided to try one more time. "So, it's true then, right? No one knows what happened to the body?"

Ms. Spencer became flustered. "Well, how would I know? *I've* never seen a grave for him but what does that matter? These silly tales you kids like to spin so you have something to do at slumber parties are quite dangerous, you know. The history is settled; it's written down. The last thing our townspeople need is for someone to fill their heads with some fiction about murders or ghosts or whatever it is you think you've heard." She spit the word "fiction" like it was a curse word. "They don't need it from anyone," she continued, "especially not from an outsider like yourself."

"I don't know what you have heard," she said, "but let me be clear. Mr. Fridman was a terrible, miserable man. He came to Edith's Hollow alone and he died alone. Josiah Knightly – bless his soul - tried saving him from that fire but he couldn't. But frankly, it was for the best and everybody knows it. You wanted a history lesson? There's your history lesson. Now, if there's nothing else, I have things to do. Good day!" With that, she picked her red pen back up and fixed her gaze back on the stack of papers on her desk.

Jaime was taken aback. He knew Ms. Spencer wasn't a particularly warm person but he was shocked to see her so agitated over a few, simple questions about Mr. Fridman. Clearly, he had struck a nerve but he wasn't sure why.

As he walked to Joe's, he replayed his conversation with Ms. Spencer in his mind. One thing that kept resurfacing in his thoughts; she had referred to "murder and ghosts" without any mention of either from him. She was so insistent that those things weren't part of the history, it almost felt like she was afraid she might be wrong.

The woman in white was real. She wasn't a ghost but everyone who insisted she was just a story – or that there wasn't even a house in the woods – had been wrong. Now, Ms. Spencer was insisting that Mr. Fridman hadn't been murdered. Yet, Jaime couldn't stop thinking about the old lady's strength, the way she wielded a knife, and the fact that she obviously wasn't in her right mind. He was more convinced than ever that maybe she had been responsible for her Father's death.

His heart rate quickened as he worked out the details in his mind. Whatever she had done to him, her plan was supposed to end with his body burning in the textile-mill fire. The townspeople would have assumed the fire was an accident – or started by a disgruntled member of the community. But Josiah Knightly had gotten in the way when he dragged the body out of the burning building. So, to ensure no evidence of her evil act would be discovered, she snuck into the morgue and stole the body in the middle of the night.

An image flashed in his mind of the shovel leaning against the wall of the old lady's cellar. He remembered the words that were printed on the slip of paper he had found on the cellar floor, "...and bury the bones, and bury the bones." It all fit together too neatly not to be true.

By the time he got to Joe's, he was completely distracted. When he knocked on the door, Joe let him in and the rest of the guys greeted him but he couldn't focus on any of the conversation going on around him. His mind was racing. He had to get back to the house in the woods.

"Jaime?" Danny's voice brought him out of his thoughts.

"Jaime!" Mark echoed. "Did you hear anything we said, man?"

Jaime shook his head as if waking up from a dream. "Sorry," he said, "say it again."

They were in Joe's bedroom with the door closed. Mark was sitting on the floor with his back against the wall. He rolled his eyes impatiently and made a noise in his throat. "Ugggh. Listen this time, OK? It starts with you. You've got to convince Karen to come trick-or-treating with you – which shouldn't be hard because it's not like she has any friends to go with." Danny laughed at this but Mark laughed harder. "She might not want to go out because she knows we're probably gonna prank her again. But that's why you're perfect for the job 'cause you can tell her that you know what we're planning and that you'll keep her away from us. Then, right at 8:00, walk her by my house. I'll be waiting outside with a hose and when you walk by, I'll spray her down really good. Then, right after that, Danny and Joe will jump out and dump theses all over her." Mark gestured to 4 bags of flour stacked on the floor next to him. He was beaming with delight.

"She'll be a Halloween ghost." Danny said. The other two laughed but Jaime didn't. He felt sick to his stomach.

"So, what do you think?" Mark asked.

Jaime smiled but everyone could tell it was forced. He couldn't hide his hesitation.

"I knew it!" Danny said. "You're gonna chicken out on us!"

"I didn't say that," Jaime shot back.

"Well, are you gonna do it then?" Danny pressed.

Jaime hesitated for another second, which was long enough to convince Danny he was right.

"See!" Danny said to Mark and Joe. "I told you we couldn't count on him. He's too chicken. He probably actually likes that freak."

Mark looked at Jaime hoping for some sign that Danny was wrong.

Jaime felt his face turn red. He shoved his hands in his pocket and shifted his weight from one foot to the other. He stared at the ground, not wanting to meet anyone's gaze.

"Come on," Danny continued. "Let's just plan it without him. We'll figure something out."

Jaime could feel Mark still staring at him in disappointment. "Wait!" he blurted out before he knew what he was saying. He looked up at Danny. "I'm not chicken," he said defensively. "It's not that." Suddenly, one of his fingers touched the heavy, bronze key that he had begun carrying in his pocket everywhere he went and an idea started to form in his head. "It's just - I had a different idea for Halloween this year." The other three looked at him with quizzical, skeptical expressions. He pulled out the key and held it up for everyone to see.

"What's that?" Joe asked.

Jaime smiled slyly. "This is a key to the house in the woods."

Joe's and Mark's eyes grew wide.

Danny scoffed. "No it's not." he said.

"Shut up, Danny!" Mark said, quieting him. "Where did you get it?"

"I went back after that night we were there and I found a way in. This was in one of the rooms. It unlocks every door in the house."

"No way!" Mark said, excited.

"What's inside?" Joe asked.

"You won't believe it," he responded. "It's crazy in there. It's a maze of hallways and like a hundred bedrooms. There's all this old furniture that looks like the kind rich people would've had back then and the kitchen has a wood burning stove and knives hanging on the wall." The others were hanging on his words. Even Danny seemed interested now.

"And..." Mark said in anticipation, waiting as if Jaime would know what he was thinking. But Jaime just stared at him blankly. "Have you seen the ghost?" he finally asked.

The room was quiet as the boys waited for Jaime to answer. Silently, he nodded his head. Joe's jaw literally fell open. The other two stared in excitement. "And the stories are true..." he said, pausing for dramatic effect. "She was a murderer and I can prove it. Come with me on Halloween night and I'll show you."

Jaime was surprised at how well his tactic was working. He could sense fear rising in the other boys. It shot a rush of adrenalin through his body.

"But what about Karen?" Joe asked innocently.

Danny and Mark looked at him expectantly.

"We'll bring her with us."

Danny furrowed his brow. "Why would we do that?" he asked.

He nodded toward the key in his hand. "To lock her inside."

An approving smile stole across Danny's face. "Yes!" he said. He began to laugh. "Make her stay the night!"

Mark nodded. "Alright," he said. "Sounds like we have a plan."

The sick feeling in Jaime's stomach was even worse than before but he tried to ignore it.

"Let's go and see it right now," Danny said.

Jaime shook his head. "No. We have to wait until Halloween. If you want me to prove to you the ghost's past, that's how we have to do it."

"That's fine," Mark said, looking from face to face. "We'll wait until Halloween." Everyone nodded in agreement. Then he looked at Jaime. "We're in," he said.

Jaime looked calm as he nodded back at Mark but his heart was starting to beat faster and his palms were beginning to sweat. He had one day to figure out how he was going to keep his promise and prove to the guys that the old lady was a murderer. He was convinced of it but how would he convince them? He needed proof. So, as soon as he left Joe's, he headed right to the house in the woods.

He stopped by his house on the way only briefly enough to grab a flashlight. Although it wasn't dark yet, he had learned from experience that several parts of the old lady's house were dark inside even in the middle of the day. His mom was gone until the next day so, when he got home, he was able to come and go quickly.

The sun was hovering just above the horizon when he reached his destination. Approaching the property, he could hear the sound of metal scraping against soil. As he got closer, he heard the familiar sound of the lady in white muttering indistinguishably to herself. He slipped through the gate quietly and snuck over to where she was. She was digging at the base of the small pear tree in the front corner of the property. The hole that Jaime had presumed was the work of an animal was, apparently, her doing. It was long and quite deep now and Jaime couldn't imagine what it was for. It seemed too large to be used for planting anything – even a tree. Perhaps, he thought, she had something she wanted to bury.

He stepped a little closer and his feet made a subtle noise as they brushed against some wild vegetation. The old lady paused with both hands on her shovel. She lifted her head and stared into space, seeming to sense Jaime's presence. He had been through this many times and still couldn't be sure whether she knew he was there or was caught in a delusion. This time, however, a subtle but sly, almost foxlike smile stretched across her mouth. Then she returned to her digging.

Jaime hadn't seen that look on the old lady's face before and it sent a chill down his spine. Remembering his goal, though, he shook it off. Before heading towards the house, he took a final look at the pear trees in front of him. The smaller one was still void of any carvings or attachments to its trunk. The larger one, though, still had a candleholder fastened to it. Jaime read the initials just above the candleholder, "JAF."

He turned to walk away and, as he did, he glanced at the grove of trees near the side of the house. He noticed again the initials and candleholder on each tree and furrowed his brow. He wished he understood why they were there or what they meant.

When he got to the front door, he found it unlocked. Walking inside, he pulled out his flashlight and followed the familiar maze of hallways and staircases that ultimately led to the old lady's room. A feeling of excitement rushed through him as he realized that, with her outside, this was the perfect chance to explore her room. He had never had that chance before. If he was going to find proof of her murderous past, this was his best opportunity.

He reached the final, second story hallway and could see her open bedroom door at the very end. He made his way to it but, before ducking inside, he glanced out the window that overlooked the property's front yard. The lady in her white, soiled working dress was still laboring with her shovel, slowly widening the hole at the base of the pear tree.

Walking into her room, he was struck by how tidy and clean it was. The bed was carefully made and no articles of clothing or any other needless items were left out other than an empty glass on the nightstand. He walked to the flowing, white dress that was draped over a headless mannequin torso that stood on a pole. He ran his hand along the lacey veil that hung to the floor. It felt aged and brittle. The intricate needlework, though, was incredible.

He turned to the nearby wardrobe and opened its double doors. There was nothing to see but white dresses on hangers. He opened each of the two drawers at the bottom of the wardrobe but only found more clothes including white bonnets and socks.

Next, he tried the dresser that stood near the foot of the bed. It had three rows of drawers. The top two drawers were empty except for cobwebs and so were the middle two. He crouched down to reach the bottom drawers which he expected to be empty as well. The first one was but when he opened the last drawer, he was pleasantly surprised to find a stack of old, black and white photographs.

The sun had set but a dim light was still coming through the window in the back wall of the bedroom. Jaime stood up and held the stack of pictures to the light. He nearly gasped when he saw the image on the top one. It was of a mangled leg that was severely twisted unnaturally beneath the knee. The leg was badly bruised and swollen to twice its normal size and the knee was hard to distinguish.

He shuffled the picture to the back and looked at the next one. This one was a close-up of a broken finger. The next three were each of different people sleeping, each by themselves on a bed; one was a child who was probably younger than Jaime and another was a balding man with a black eye and a cut across his forehead.

The next picture made Jaime feel lightheaded. It was of a bare arm and shoulder. The frame cut off any image of a face and captured just a sliver of the bare torso. The arm looked thin and frail and rested on what appeared to be a blanket soaked in blood. Just beneath the shoulder was a gash so wide and deep that it nearly severed the arm from the body. Jaime stared at the picture in awe for a moment then quickly shuffled it to the back when he began feeling sick.

The next four or five pictures were of more sleeping people, each by themselves, each resting on a bed with his or her head resting on a pillow. The beds and pillows all looked the same but the people were different. One of them had a swollen face and a disfigured nose. Jaime wondered why the old lady had these pictures. He was disturbed and intrigued and a little frightened by them all at once. An image of her wielding a cleaver in her kitchen and breaking the back of the rabbit carcass flashed in his mind. These pictures didn't exactly prove that she murdered her Father but they seemed to prove something.

There were several more photos to look through and Jaime wanted to explore the other second-story rooms before it got too late and before the old lady returned. So, he fanned the rest of the pictures with his thumb. Written in the bottom right corner of each one was a set of two or three letters. He read a few of them: "CM," "KLR," "MOA." He didn't know what they meant but, resolved to examine them more closely later, he shoved them into his coat pocket.

Looking around the bedroom, he decided there was nothing else to see there. He was a little disappointed he hadn't found anything more than the stack of photos but, still, he walked back into the hall and over to the next door. He tried the handle but it was locked. He pulled the bronze key from his pocket and slipped it into the keyhole. To his surprise, though, it wouldn't turn. "Hmm," he said out loud.

He assumed his key opened every door in the house but this was the first time he had tried it in this hallway. He moved to the next door. That one was locked too and, again, his key wouldn't open it. He moved down the line with the same result at every door.

Finally, he turned a corner and reached the bedroom where he had first found the key. The door was already open so he stepped inside. His eyes were immediately drawn to the bookcase in the corner. A memory flashed in his mind from the last time he had been there. He recalled a book he had pulled from the bookcase that said "Journal" on the front. Suddenly he was excited. That might be exactly what he was looking for.

He hurried over to the bookcase and found the journal with its spine jutting out a little from the other books. He pulled it down off the shelf and wiped a thin layer of dust from the cover with his hand. He flicked on his flashlight and opened to the first page, the spine cracking quietly as he did. In the middle of the page was printed, "This Journal Belongs To:" Beneath these words was a line on which was written "Edith Elizabeth Fridman."

"Edith," he whispered to himself after reading the name.

Jaime turned the page to the first entry and began to read.

June 3, 1899

I walked to the Ocean today. It took me most of the morning. Father asked me to take the journey in order to check the lobster traps. He instructed me to go alone and not to speak with anyone along the way. His instruction was easy to follow considering nobody was on the path nor at the seaside. The lobster traps were empty but I spent some time wading into the water up to my shins and searching for pretty shells. Perhaps that would not have pleased Father had he known but I do not intend to tell him. The water was cold. One shell I found was pink and orange. I brought it home and have placed it in my dresser drawer. I quite like seeing the ocean.

He sat down on the floor and flipped through the pages, stopping randomly near the middle,

December 2, 1900
Constant screaming from one of the guests downstairs made it impossible to sleep last night. This morning, Father was only concerned with whether the others heard it. I believe I took necessary measures to ensure they did not. I wonder sometimes whether Father's old kindness remains at all. At other times, he looks at me in such a way that I am sure it does somewhere inside of him. He perplexes me. He is under constant strain but so am I. I wish he could see that.

He flipped several more pages and began reading another passage.

September 19, 1901
I found a good spot for Father in the yard. It is close to the others but a little apart so he can be on his own. When it is his time, I think he will be comfortable there. One must have a plan for these things, whether or not they prefer it.

Jaime's breath stopped in his lungs and his eyes widened. He read the passage again. It was unmistakable; She was making plans to bury her Father. If the fire Mr. Fridman had died in was merely an accident, then why had she been making plans for his burial before it ever happened? He read the passage one more time but, this time, something else stuck out to him. "*It is close to the others...*" Who were the "others" she was referring to?

Looking back down at the journal in his lap, he noticed a piece of paper sticking out at the bottom. It had been folded and stuck between the last page and the back cover. He pulled it out and unfolded it. A poem was written down the left-hand side in Edith's handwriting:

When the harvest moon rises
O'er the briars and berms,
There is work to be done
Before daylight returns.
For soon come the cold nights,
The long winter chill,
The hard, frozen earth

When the Harvest Moon Rises

That won't break under steel.
Soon comes the season
When no work can be done.
So, finish your chores.
Don't wait for the sun.

First, to the attic
Where the cobwebs have massed.
Dig through the remains
Of years that have passed.
For those still alive,
Find blankets and pelts.
Stash the belongings
Of everyone else.

Next, to the rooms
Where visitors sleep.
Make sure there is nothing
Unpleasant to see.
Scrub every surface
And hide every stain.
Every house has its secrets
That need not be explained.

Then to the woods,
Past the thick, clinging shadows,
For kindling and fuel
In the darkening hours.
Be sure that the fire
Is steady and hot.
Both clothing and bedding
Must burn down to naught.

Last, to the cellar
Where the dead things have lingered
While their flesh falls away
From their toes to their fingers.
Gather them up
And out to the yard.

Sharpen your shovels
For, the ground there is hard.
Turn over the dirt,
The grass and the stones
And bury the bones
And bury the bones.

Jaime's breath quickened. He thought of the photographs in his coat pocket. He pulled them out and looked at them under the beam of his flashlight. He flipped through the pictures of gashes and broken bones until he came to another one of a person resting on a bed. It suddenly occurred to him that he recognized the bed. It was the same as every bed he had seen in the bedrooms that lined the winding hallways two stories beneath him. The pictures had been taken inside the house.

He flipped through them until he found another of a resting person and another and another. Each was posed the same, lying on their backs with their hands on their chest and their head on a pillow. These people weren't sleeping. They were dead.

His eyes widened. He looked at the letters scribbled in the bottom corner of one of the photographs and was struck by another chilling realization. He saw in his mind the small grove of trees at the side of the house. He could picture the candleholder nailed to each trunk and, above it, a set of initials carved into the wood.

Suddenly, it made sense. The grove was a graveyard. It was Edith's graveyard.

A chill ran down his spine. "What did she do to all of them?" he said out loud.

He thought of the tree near the front of the property, apart from the rest. That was where she had buried her Father. He was sure of it. But what about the smaller tree next to it?

His heart began to pound. In his mind's eye, he replayed the scene he had encountered when he arrived that evening. He could see Edith in her white working dress tearing at the ground with her shovel. The hole she was digging was too deep and too wide for gardening. She was digging another grave. He remembered the look on her face when she heard Jaime's feet brush the undergrowth near her.

All at once, adrenalin flooded through his body. Instinctively, he started to get up but, before he could, he heard the sound of creaking hinges. His head snapped up just in time to see the door to his room closing. He was shut inside. He jumped to his feet but, before he could reach the door, he heard a key being inserted into the keyhole and the sound of the door locking. He fumbled in his pocket for his own key and, reaching the door, frantically shoved it into the keyhole but it wouldn't turn. He twisted it as hard as he could in both directions but to no avail. He was trapped.

He pounded on the door then immediately wished he hadn't. Maybe Edith didn't realize he was in the room. If she had intentionally trapped him inside, then pounding on the door was useless. If she hadn't, then silence was his best protection. Nervously, he stood quiet and still and listened for the sound of footsteps approaching or the door unlocking. He heard neither.

Frustrated and scared, he hurried over to the window on the other side of the room. There was no way to open it. He pressed his forehead against it and looked down. Even if he could get through the window, it was a straight drop to the ground ten or fifteen feet below. On top of that, he was pretty sure it was too small for him to squeeze through.

He turned around and scanned the room for a way out, turning his head from left to right and back several times. There was nothing to be done. There was no way out. He stood numbly, not knowing what to do. Then, finally, he leaned his back against the wall and sunk to the floor. Sitting cross-legged, he gazed ahead absently.

The room was drafty. He was sure it would be quite cold within a couple of hours. There was no padding between the thin carpet he sat on and the hard, wooden floor beneath. It was uncomfortable and a little painful. He started to cry, which made him feel stupid and ashamed. *'Don't be scared!'* he scolded himself in his head. But, this time, he didn't think he could force the fear away.

Leaning his head against the wall behind him, he took a deep breath. As he did, he noticed his flashlight and the open journal lying on the floor next to him. He picked up the flashlight and weighed it in his hands. It was solid and made of metal. He gripped his fingers around it tightly and imagined yielding it like a club. He would use it to defend himself if he needed to.

He wiped the tears from his eyes and took another deep breath. Relaxing his grip on the flashlight, he forced himself to slow his breathing. Several minutes ticked by as he stared at the floor in front of him, trying to grapple with his situation and listening carefully for any evidence of Edith approaching. He heard nothing.

Finally, he looked at the journal again and his curiosity began to return. Edith might not be coming back tonight but sleep wasn't even a consideration. He picked the journal up, opened to the first page, and placed it in his lap. He turned his flashlight on and began to read.

1891

CHAPTER 9

Joseph's throat was dry and starting to burn. He kept his mouth closed, making sure to breathe through his nose, hoping that this would prevent it from drying out any further. The tiny particles of cotton fiber that saturated the air were beginning to take their toll on him, as they usually did by the end of the day. He tried not to breathe too deeply for fear of starting another coughing fit.

It had been a couple of hours since the candles had been lit around the mill to compensate for the falling darkness outside. It would probably be at least another hour until Mr. Hill directed the bell to be rung, signaling to everyone that it was time to go home. Joseph looked to the head of the rows where Mr. Hill liked to stand. He was a large man with jet-black, receding hair that sat on top of a high forehead. He always wore the same thing: brown trousers tucked into his boots, a brown vest, a white shirt, and a cravat around his neck. He was standing with his chin up, his feet spread at shoulder width, and his hands behind his back. He looked formal and official, like a watchful soldier guarding his post.

Joseph returned his attention to the two busy machines in front of him and the other three workers that he was in charge of. Together, the four-person team watched several long, skinny threads of cotton moving through the spinning mules and winding around spools. The young girl to his right reached over a few of the threads to one that had broken. Moving quickly and skillfully, she grabbed the two severed ends and rubbed them together between her thumb

97

and her ring-finger until they were intertwined as the thread continued moving toward the spool.

Joseph glanced at the two stubs on her hand where her index finger and middle finger used to be. He had been at the mill several months prior when an accident at one of the spinning mules had taken them. He remembered removing the crimson-soaked cotton from the machine before it was restarted and before everyone continued on with their work. He admired her for returning as quickly as she had although he knew she probably didn't have much of a choice. If she was like most others at the mill, she probably couldn't afford to go without work for more than a few days.

Joseph felt lucky that he had not joined the ranks of workers with injured or missing limbs and extremities. Another minder on his row in charge of supervising a team of 3 was missing an arm below the elbow. Abby told him that a girl on her floor had a chunk of hair ripped from her head when it got caught in a machine a few weeks back. The worst he had heard of was a small boy who had supposedly been killed when he was crushed by a machine he had crawled beneath to clean. He didn't know if that one was true but he hoped it was just a rumor. The thought made him cringe.

He looked back at the front of the room where Mr. Hill was. For some reason, he had taken an interest in Joseph recently and Joseph had come to realize that, in reality, his reputation as a demanding task master wasn't entirely warranted. It was true that he had a hot temper and a driving appetite for excellence but this was matched by his beaming pride in a job well done. Outside of the mill, he was generous and often jovial. His defining characteristic, though, was simply the size of his emotions. Whether it was cheer, ire or charity he was feeling at the moment, his feelings tended to bubble up and boil over.

Joseph and Hill met eyes from several feet apart. When they did, Mr. Hill briefly broke his military-like gaze and, with a subtle nod of his head, gestured to Joseph to meet him outside. Joseph watched him turn and walk out the door. He took one more look at the tightly wound strands of cotton running through the machine in front him before following.

Joseph descended one story down the narrow stairway to the ground level. He stepped outside where a brisk but gentle breeze against his damp skin nearly took his breath away. Mr. Hill, who was waiting outside by the door laughed at Joseph's visible reaction to the cold.

Joseph smiled a self-deprecating smile then looked back toward the mill. "Are you sure it's OK for me to leave my station?" he asked with genuine concern.

Hill shrugged cavalierly. "It'll be fine," he said. "We won't be long."

Joseph's concern was always the same and it was always met with the same response, which, to some, might have seemed out of character for Mr. Hill. However, Joseph had come to know him well enough that he was less and less surprised by the contradictions he observed in him.

Joseph opened his jaw wide. He laughed quietly when he noticed Hill doing the same thing. "It doesn't stop the ringing," he said.

"I know, but I always try." Hill replied. "I don't think you ever really get used to the deafening noise. I've been the Agent of this mill for more than five years now and I'm still not used to it."

Joseph nodded and looked over at his boss. Hill was large but the two were nearly identical in height. Where Mr. Hill was broad and barrel-chested, though, Joseph was more narrow and straight – although still stout and very strong.

They were physical opposites in several ways. Both men had dark hair but Hill's was thinning and wispy on top while Joseph's was thick and wavy. Mr. Hill was clean-shaven while Joseph's olive complexion was darkened by two or three days' worth of stubble. His soiled, thread-bare clothes stood in contrast to Hill's. Joseph wore a white, collared, working shirt with long sleeves rolled halfway up his forearms and canvas trousers, each which looked like rags compared to Hill's more formal and higher quality clothes.

Their temperaments were starkly different as well. Hill was a gathering storm, Joseph a still, summer night. Hill's strength was in his force of will, Joseph's was in his quiet steadiness. Impulse was a hallmark of Hill's character, restraint a hallmark of Joseph's.

Mr. Hill took a wad of chewing tobacco from the front pocket in his vest and pushed it in his mouth behind his cheek. He put his hand on Joseph's shoulder and said, "I like you, Joseph."

"Thank you, sir," Joseph said.

"I mean it," Hill continued, "you're a hard worker, dependable, never complain. You're a leader, too, and I don't think you even try to be. People just like you and you inspire their loyalty. And best of all, you're not Irish!" he said with a loud laugh.

Joseph silently shifted his eyes at this last comment hoping none of his Irish co-workers – many of whom he was friendly with – were near enough to hear. But Joseph and Hill were alone. Nobody dared leave his or her work station during working hours. Everyone knew exactly how expendable he or she was to the mill and everyone desperately needed the work.

"You're kind, Mr. Hill," Joseph said.

"Well, I'm not telling you this to be kind," Hill replied. "I'm telling you so you understand why I want to promote you."

Joseph looked up.

"That's right," Hill said. "I want you to be my supervisor of the spinning room. The mill is growing and I can't handle all the managerial tasks on my own anymore. I think it's time you get off the factory floor and start aiming for higher things. What do you say?"

Joseph's eyes widened with excitement. Still, with little emotion in his voice, he asked "what's the pay?"

Hill chuckled. "Plenty," he said. "Double what you're making now."

Joseph's eyes widened further. His wife worked one floor beneath him at the mill and made just a little more than half of Joseph's wage. This would change everything for them.

"I know you have a young family at home, Joseph," Mr. Hill continued. "You stay loyal to the mill and I'll make sure that family of yours is taken care of."

Joseph felt like he could cry. Mr. Hill wasn't offering his hand but Joseph took it anyway, held it in both of his, and shook it heartily. "Thank you, sir," he said. "Thank you so much. I won't let you down. I swear I won't."

Mr. Hill squeezed Joseph's shoulder and winked at him. He spit on the ground, black saliva landing just inches from both men's feet and splattering tiny specks of mud on their shoes. "I know you won't," he said. "That's why I chose you. Now let's get back inside before all those chickens in there start running the hen house."

Joseph was the first out the door when the quitting bell rang. He rushed down the stairs and onto the ground-level floor of the factory before most had left. He pushed his way through the stream of weary employees anxious to get home and found his wife. Before saying anything, he gave her a big hug, lifting her feet off the ground. Her fatigued face suddenly brightened and her hunched shoulders straightened.

"Well what's that about?" she asked with a smile.

"Maybe I just missed you," he said. "Don't you think a man should hug his wife at the end of the day?"

Abigail looked at him sideways. "I know you better than that, Mr. Fridman."

Joseph smiled. "Come on," he said. "Let's get away from this crowd. We'll talk outside."

As the two walked home on a muddy, narrow road, they talked about Joseph's conversation with Mr. Hill and all of its implications.

"You know what this means, Abby?" he asked. "You can stay home with Edith now. We won't have to leave her with Ms. Cummings anymore."

"Do you really think so?" she replied.

"Well...yeah. I mean, we won't be rich but even without you working, we'll be doing better than we are now. And we don't need to be rich, right? I know how much you hate leaving Edith every day and now you won't have to."

Abigail smiled but, despite her smile, her eyes quickly turned sad as her thoughts turned to their little girl waiting for them at home. "She's too young to be without her mom," she said with a tinge of guilt. "It breaks my heart to think that, at two and a half years old, she's spent more time being raised by Ms. Cummings than by me. I think Ms. Cummings should swap me. I'll take Edith during the day and she can deal with her at night. That child is such a loud sleeper!"

Joseph laughed. As he did, Abigail gasped with delight as a thought came to her.

"Joseph, do you think we'll be able to move? I mean, not out of Fall River obviously but into something nicer? Somewhere where Edith can actually sleep in a room of her own?"

Joseph furrowed his brow. "What about Ms. Cummings?" he asked. "Who would take her in?"

101

"I don't know," Abigail said. "There's probably someone who will – someone like us who needs help with the cooking and the kids. We'll do what we can to help her find a place, of course, but, honestly, we can't stay in these slums for Ms. Cummings. We've got to do what's best for our family."

A feeling of excitement began to stir in Joseph's chest as well as he thought about what Abigail was saying. A new place for his family, no more mill work for Abigail – he could barely believe his fortune. He felt Abigail slip her hand around his arm near his elbow. "I'm proud of you," she said. "You've earned this."

They walked the rest of the way in silence. After one year of courting and nearly four years of marriage, there were still times like these when Joseph marveled at his wife. The butterflies he used to feel had been replaced by something so deep and profound that, in moments like this, he could hardly wrap his mind around it. He wanted to put it into words but didn't know how so, instead, he just listened to the sound their feet made on the gravel and dirt.

When they got home, Edith was already asleep. A fire that Ms. Cummings had started in the small, brick fireplace crackled but the apartment was still drafty and cold. Joseph lit a candle and snuck into his room where Edith lay, wincing every time the floors creaked. When he reached the small bed that she and Abigail shared, he cast as little light over her as he could. She was sleeping on her stomach with a mess of black hair sticking out in every direction from the back of her head. Gently, he reached down and laid his hand on her back and felt it rising and falling. She stirred slightly but didn't wake. A warm feeling swelled in his chest. Then he did something he seldom did; he whispered a prayer. "Thank you, God," he said simply. "Thank you."

When Joseph woke up the next morning, the sun had not yet risen and the moon was still brightly shining. Almost immediately, his conversation with Mr. Hill from the day before popped into his mind and he felt something in his stomach that reminded him of birthdays when he was a kid. He was actually excited to get to work. He couldn't remember ever feeling that way before.

He rolled out of bed and set his feet on the cold floor. He had become an expert on rising slowly and moving across the floor without causing it to creak or making any other noise that might wake Edith or Abigail. Abigail would be up soon but Edith was usually still asleep when they left the apartment.

He started a fire in the fireplace and warmed his hands for a second before getting ready. Then he dressed and washed his face. By the time he crept toward the kitchen for a slice of bread, Abigail was awake and standing next to the fire. He stopped and kissed her on the forehead knowing how much she hated to be kissed on the mouth just after waking. "Good morning, beautiful," he whispered, rubbing her back to warm her. She smiled silently.

Before long, they were walking through a cold, dense fog toward the mill with their arms linked. "You're excited," Abigail said to him. "I can tell."

Joseph smiled broadly, "Abby, I feel like a little kid. I'm excited and nervous and I kind of feel like I might wet myself."

Abby laughed. "Please don't," she said. "I'd have to walk up ahead if you did."

Just then, the bell from the mill rang out, echoing off the homes and buildings around it. It was announcing the start of the work day. Joseph and Abigail could hear the shuffling of feet from others behind them as they picked up their pace. They were nearly to the front entrance, though, and felt no need to do likewise. Besides, Joseph was a supervisor now and Abigail's days at the mill were nearly finished. Literally, overnight, everything had changed.

When Joseph arrived, Mr. Hill was waiting outside of the front door for him. "Hello, Abigail," he said with a smile. "It's nice to see you."

"Thank you, Mr. Hill," Abby said politely. "It's nice to see you too." She stood on her tiptoes and kissed Joseph on the cheek. "Good luck today," she said. "I'll see you at closing."

Joseph watched her disappear into the mill.

"You'll be by my side all day today," Mr. Hill said, putting a hand on Joseph's shoulder. "I want you to be my shadow."

Joseph nodded to show he understood.

Hill began the day with a tour of the mill as if Joseph had never worked there before. It was useful though. He saw things he had never seen. They started on the first floor where Abby worked. Mr. Hill explained that the large room that spanned most of the first floor was called the "picking" room. The workers there used machines to clean the debris out of the cotton after it arrived in bales. Joseph already knew this from conversations with Abby but he just nodded politely and said the occasional "hmmm."

Next, Mr. Hill took Joseph to the room that housed the giant steam engine that powered the mill. The size and force of it were staggering. Joseph could feel the pumping and churning rhythm of it pulsing through the floorboards beneath his feet and deep in his chest. Mr. Hill didn't attempt to speak; the engine was too loud to be heard over. He did, however, point to a few parts including a large rod that set into motion a system of smaller rods, gears, and leather belts that ran over the heads of the workers on each floor and kept the machines running throughout the mill.

On the second floor, Mr. Hill walked Joseph up and down the rows, introducing him to each team manning a pair of spinning machines. Joseph already knew most of the people Hill introduced him to, which worked to his advantage. The people he worked with liked him and trusted him. He had gained a reputation among them as a quiet, strong, and nice man who was never afraid to do the right thing. Almost without exception, news of his promotion and his new status as the second-floor supervisor was met by his colleagues with warmth and well wishes.

The third floor was the weave room. Some of the cotton that had been spun into spools of thread on the second floor would be gathered and sold without further processing. Other spools, though, were transferred to the third floor where skilled workers wove it into sheets of fabric with the aid of large machines. Joseph watched in awe. There was something deeply satisfying about seeing the threads of cotton he stared at all day transformed into something so final and practical.

When the tour was completed, Hill took Joseph back to the second floor and had him stand next to him at the head of the rows of machines. Although Hill had supervisory responsibilities for the entire mill, he dedicated the day to Joseph's floor for his benefit. Joseph watched him all day as he barked orders to workers who were leaning on the machines or who hadn't noticed a thread slip from its place. He followed him up and down the rows and stood next to him as he nodded approval to requests for bathroom breaks.

When it began growing dark outside, Mr. Hill gave the order for the candles to be lit all through the building. Then, as had become his custom, he asked Joseph to step outside with him for a breath of fresh air. As they exited the building, Hill pushed a wad of tobacco inside his lip and Joseph shivered in the cold.

"Let's walk," Hill said. It'll keep us warm. They began strolling casually down the street in front of them. "So, what do you think?" Hill asked.

Joseph nodded his head. "It's good," he said. "I can do this. I won't let you down."

"I know you won't," Hill said.

The two stood in silence for a moment. Joseph looked up at the glowing moon while Mr. Hill spat tobacco juice. Joseph followed as Mr. Hill turned off of the road, bending into a path that circled the mill.

"Mr. Hill," Joseph said, breaking the silence between them. His tone was a little tentative. "My Abigail and I have a young child at home – as you know – and we would like Abby to be able to stay home with our daughter. With this new position, I think we'll have the money to allow for that but, of course, it means she'll have to quit her job here. I apologize for any inconvenience but I hope you'll understand."

"I do," Mr. Hill assured him. "She'll be missed but I understand. I meant what I said before; I want you to be able to take care of that family of yours."

Just then, in the distance, a frantic, piercing scream from inside the mill caught both men's attention. They paused and looked at each other for a brief moment before darting back toward the mill. They were several yards away when they heard a window burst on the first floor and saw bright orange flames pour out. Two other exploding windows followed immediately after the first. Joseph hurried his pace, pumping his legs as fast as he could.

He saw a steady stream of people rushing out of the building's only exit through a dark cloud of smoke. As he reached the crowd, he swiftly searched the faces for Abigail. When he didn't see her, he quickly began growing desperate, grabbing people by both their shoulders as they passed. "Have you seen my Abigail?" he asked several people. "She's this tall, brown hair, crooked smile." Some shook their heads but most just looked at him blankly.

"Abby!" he yelled loudly. "Abigail! Where are you?" He listened for a response but only heard a small chorus of others desperately searching for someone each of them had lost. Cries for help could be heard from inside the building. Someone in the crowd called out, "look! The fire's reached the second floor!"

With no more time to lose, Joseph hurried to the entrance. Just as he was about to step through the door, though, there was a loud crack and an enormous crashing sound inside. A searing wave of heat rushed out of the building, nearly pushing him backwards. He suddenly felt sick to his stomach and panicked all at once.

He dashed through the door and into the picking room. Fire blanketed the ceiling above him and a thin smoke clouded his sight. The heat was nearly unbearable but he pushed ahead. "Abby!" he yelled but his voice was drowned out by the rushing and crackling sounds of the flames. "Abby!" he tried again.

When he reached the middle of the room, he saw a devastating sight. A mountain of rubble filled the rest of the floor. Wooden beams, scraps, and large pieces of machines like the one he worked at on the second floor lay piled on top of each other. He looked up and saw a large, gaping space where the ceiling used to be. Half of the second floor had fallen. The half over his head still remained.

Without thinking, he rushed to the rubble and grabbed one of the beams entangled in the mess. It immediately seared and blistered his hand. He cried out in pain and pulled his hand away. Just then, he heard a loud cracking sound behind him. Instinctively, he ducked and shielded his head with his arms. Another part of the ceiling came crashing down, throwing glowing, hot fragments in every direction.

The heat was getting worse and he was feeling lightheaded. He spotted a blown-out window in the nearest wall and rushed over to it. He took his coat off and placed it on the window seal so he could put his hands down without burning them then he reached his head and shoulders out as far as he could, took a deep breath, and coughed hard. Slightly revived, he brought himself back inside the building and yelled for his wife again.

There was another crashing sound as even more rubble fell on top of the mound of scraps in front of him. Confused, he looked up and saw that the third floor was beginning to crumble now too. A hole had opened up in what used to be the second-floor ceiling.

He pushed himself against the empty window frame behind him as rubble continued to fall. Just then, a pair of hands grabbed him from outside of the window and forcefully pulled him out through the opening. A sharp piece of glass protruding from the frame cut into the back of his thigh as he was pulled past it. He yelled out and brought his hand to the gash as it began to bleed.

The next thing he knew, he was lying on the cold dirt. He looked up and saw Hill standing over him. Joseph scrambled to get back on his feet. "What are you doing?!" he yelled. "Abigail is still in there!"

Mr. Hill grabbed Joseph as he moved toward the window and held him while he struggled to get free.

"Do you want to get killed?" Mr. Hill said.

Just then, there was another large crashing sound as the rest of the first-floor ceiling caved, filling the entire picking room. The window Joseph had just come through was suddenly blocked by debris speckled in glowing embers and flames. He ran over to it and desperately yelled inside for Abigail but heard nothing in response. More crashing sounds resounded as the third floor continued to cave.

As he strained his ears, hoping to hear Abby call back to him, it suddenly occurred to him that *no one* was calling out from inside the building anymore. The other voices that had been calling for loved ones from inside were now silenced. He stepped back and looked up at the flames now dancing on the top of the building. The mill was quickly becoming a hollow, brick shell, thoroughly gutted by the fire. He sunk back to the ground and held his head in his hands in stunned devastation. He stared blankly at the dirt and gravel in front of him then felt Hill place a hand on his shoulder. He wanted to push it away.

The sound of fast approaching horse hooves got his attention. He turned his head to see a long, bright red fire wagon approaching with several men seated on it. Quickly, he popped up from where he was kneeling and ran to the wagon, waving his arms in the air. "Over here!" he cried. "Over here!"

The wagon sped past him, headed toward the mill's entrance. Joseph turned around and chased it. Before he reached it, it stopped and the men jumped off. Several grabbed buckets of water hanging from the sides and ran to different locations around the building's perimeter. Others turned their attention to a large contraption the wagon was carrying which shot a long stream of water from a large, steel tank.

Joseph reached the wagon while the men were still working to get the water stream started. He began yelling at anyone who he thought might pay attention. "Listen!" he yelled. "There are open windows along the side of the building over there." He was waving his arms toward the blown-out window he had come out of earlier. "It's a straight shot into the building."

Nobody was listening, though. Everyone seemed to have a role to play that consumed his attention.

"Please!" Joseph called out in desperation. He felt hot tears welling up in his eyes. "My wife's in there. You've gotta help her!"

Joseph felt a pair of hands grab his shoulders from behind. He turned around to see Mr. Hill again. The sympathy in his eyes made Joseph uncomfortable. Hill had surrendered to sadness but Joseph wasn't ready to.

"Come on, Joseph," he said. "Let's let these men do their job."

"Abby's in there, Mr. Hill," Joseph shot back, "and if you're not going to help me get her out then I don't need you here."

He turned back to the firemen. "Over here!" he yelled more forcefully. "Are you here to put out the fire or not?!" As if in response to his own question, Joseph suddenly realized that none of the men were actually working on the fire burning inside of the mill. The men on the wagon had got the stream of water flowing from the contraption and were using it to soak the branches of a large tree that stretched dangerously close toward the fire's heat. He scanned the grounds for the men with the buckets. Some were putting out small fires in shrubs and grass around the perimeter. Others had set their buckets down and were using axes and saws to cut down vegetation that grew close to the mill.

Soon, a few of the men jumped back on the fire wagon and left their spot near the mill's entrance. They drove to a small, one-story building near the mill and began soaking its roof, hoping to fire-proof it. As he stood staring at the scene, one of the men with an axe in one hand and a bucket in the other passed Joseph. Joseph grabbed him by his arms as he walked by.

"Wait!" he said, looking as frazzled and panicked as he felt, "aren't you guys going to do anything about the people inside the building? You've got to try and help them."

Irritated, the man pulled free of Joseph's grip. But then seeing the desperation on his face, he softened. A look of sympathy crossed his face. "I'm sorry, sir," he said, shaking his head. "There won't be anyone else to save. Anyone who survived the heat or the collapsing building would have suffocated by now. There's nothing we can do." He paused for a second then apologized one more time before moving on.

Joseph stood still and numb as the sounds of the mill's crumbling interior continued. Once again, Mr. Hill approached, more tentatively this time. He came to Joseph's side and stood next to him in silence. Without a word, both men watched as the life they knew burned to the ground.

Joseph stayed until the early morning hours when the last flame had died and the glowing embers had all been soaked. He found himself with a shovel in his hands, helping to dig at the mound of building scraps as bodies were pulled from ash and rubble. Abigail was among them. None of them were alive.

Mr. Hill stayed too. He did a round to see who had lingered, offering condolences as needed. Much of his time was spent, though, working next to Joseph, mostly in silence. When Abby was finally found, he said a few kind words and encouraged Joseph to go back to his apartment where his little girl was asleep. Joseph, finally defeated, nodded his weary head and turned for home.

CHAPTER 10

It was still dark outside when Joseph woke up. He rubbed his eyes and stumbled out of bed. Four months had dragged by since Abby's passing and he still awoke with a pit in his stomach every morning. Ms. Cummings and Edith were asleep in Joseph and Abby's old bedroom with the door closed. Joseph had asked Ms. Cummings to start sleeping there shortly after the night of the fire. He moved his pallet out of the apartment's only bedroom and arranged it across from the kitchen table where he now slept every night.

Clumsily, he made his way to the sink where he washed his face and put on several layers of clothing. His stomach growled and he looked at the remaining half of a stale loaf of bread on the kitchen table. It needed to last until he could get the money to buy another one and he didn't know when that would be. So, he left, the food for Edith and Ms. Cummings and walked out into the cold.

Outside, a thick layer of hard-packed snow covered the streets and sidewalks. There was an occasional, soft crunch beneath his feet as he passed over it. After several blocks of walking, he reached the docks and stopped at the end of a long line of shivering men. He breathed deeply through his nose and smelled the familiar smell of salt water, fish, and filth.

Soon, the line began to move, bringing a little life into the men.

"Long line today," the man standing next to Joseph said to him.

Joseph just shrugged his shoulders. He didn't feel like talking. He recognized the man from the mill and he was pretty sure the man recognized him but he didn't have anything to say. He didn't want to think about the mill and he didn't want to be seen by the dock workers fraternizing with others who had come from it. Both would cause trouble, as he had come to learn.

Another man came up behind them, joining the line. Joseph turned his head and the two met eyes briefly. He recognized this man, too, as one of the dock's regulars - someone, Joseph assumed, who had been coming here for work long before Joseph's shadow ever darkened the dock's weathered planks.

In a flash, the dock worker's eyes seemed to fill with disgust and disdain as he recognized Joseph and his companion as part of the group who had flocked to the docks after the mill burned down. This is how it always was. Every day was a slog, pushing through the scowls and snide remarks from the rest of the dock workers. Every day, they came ready for a turf war. Joseph wasn't interested in fighting for territory, though. He just wanted some money to buy some bread.

Up ahead was a short man with leathery skin, jet-black hair, and dark stubble on his face. He stood at the head of the line with a hardened expression, holding an opened, leather-bound book in his left hand and a pencil in his right. He was known around the docks as Mr. Knightly and he was part of the union that controlled the labor. Anyone who wanted to find work here had to pass through him. Every morning, he decided who had a job that day and who didn't.

The line was long and Joseph was near the back. It was moving quickly, though, which was a good sign. It meant that there was plenty of work.

Everyone who reached the front of the line was met with a critical glare from Mr. Knightly who looked him over, wrote something in his book, gave him his orders, and called out "next!" in his gruff and raspy way. He had no tolerance for questions or comments. Everyone was to take their orders and move on.

After the first ten or fifteen men passed through, Mr. Knightly paused at the next one in line who Joseph recognized as another colleague from the mill named Thomas. Mr. Knightly asked him his name then flipped back through the pages in his book. He stopped after turning a few pages, read something he had written before, and ordered Thomas to step aside and wait. Then he called for the next man up.

This pattern repeated itself nine or ten more times, whenever a former mill worker reached the front. So, when Joseph and the man in front of him were up, they weren't surprised to receive the same treatment. The last few men who had filtered in behind Joseph passed easily through. Then Mr. Knightly turned his attention to the small group of men waiting in the cold to be doled out their assignment.

"Wait here," Mr. Knightly commanded with his deep, crackly voice. He turned and walked away toward the ships where the loading and unloading of cargo had begun. Several minutes later he returned and curtly gave his orders. Nine of the men were directed to one end of the dock, Joseph and Thomas were directed to another, and the man who had been in front of Joseph in the line was left standing.

"Where should I go?" he asked hopefully.

"There's no work for you," Mr. Knightly replied coldly. "I don't care where you go as long as it's not on my docks."

Joseph and Thomas knew not to waste any time. As they walked to their assigned station, though, Joseph looked back at his former colleague they were leaving behind. The hollow, disheartened look of despair on his face was all too familiar to him. He felt bad for the man but, at the same time, he felt a tinge of relief that his own fortune was better.

When Joseph and Thomas got to their spot, they saw that the other men were already busy unloading wooden crates from a large ship. One of the men scoffed loudly when he saw them coming. "Sorry, ladies," he called out, "the spinning mill is that way" he said, gesturing with his head. "This work is for men." The others laughed loudly.

Thomas looked like he was about to say something so Joseph quickly and inconspicuously grabbed him tightly by the arm. "Just keep your mouth shut and get the job done," he said quietly. "Hard work will shut them up." Thomas shook his arm free of Joseph's grip. For a second, Joseph thought he was going to ignore his counsel but, to Joseph's relief, Thomas stayed quiet.

Joseph nodded his head as the two reached the crew. "Gentlemen," he said, greeting everyone at once. He stood at least a head taller than the rest of the men and had a stout frame, which quickly quieted some of the snickering among them. "How can we help?" he asked.

"You can go back home," one of the men said as he spat on the ground.

Joseph looked at him squarely and calmly. "Right," he said. "We'll start moving some crates." He looked at his companion, "come on, Thomas."

"Yeah, come on Thomas!" one of the men mocked as Thomas and Joseph walked past them to the ship. The others laughed.

Thomas and Joseph began grabbing crates and carrying them out to the stacks that had accumulated. Soon, the rest of the men returned to work and, after several minutes, things finally began to normalize. Thomas and Joseph kept their heads down and worked hard, giving way to the rhythm that was developing among the crew.

After a few hours, Mr. Knightly walked around to each station and told them they could stop for lunch. Thomas and Joseph sat down on a crate apart from the rest of the men. Joseph turned his face to the sun and closed his eyes while he rested his tired muscles. He was damp with sweat but the sun on his face felt good. It provided a nice balance to the cold, winter breeze coming off of the ocean.

"Did you bring lunch?" Thomas asked.

Joseph opened his eyes and shook his head, no.

Thomas reached out, holding a cooked potato in his hand. "Take it. I've got another in here," he said, holding up a paper sack with his other hand, which was clothed in a brown, ragged glove.

"Thank you," Joseph said, taking the potato. "I'm actually starving," he admitted.

They each took a bite of their potato. The food was cold and desperately needed salt but neither man was in a position to be picky.

Thomas looked over at the rest of the men who were sitting in a circle eating sandwiches and fruit. "Why do you think they hate us so much?" he asked.

Joseph didn't look up. He shrugged his shoulders and took another bite of his potato. He watched a seagull nearby searching the ground for scraps. "I suppose we're a threat," he said. "Work is hard to come by and we all have families to feed."

Thomas huffed. "Some more than others," he said, thinking of his wife and four children at home. He suddenly paused and looked

113

at Joseph, concerned he might have said something he shouldn't have. "Hey, I didn't mean...we're all really sorry about your wife."

Joseph's face hardened a little. "Thanks," he said tersely, hoping to put a quick end to the topic.

"I can't imagine what you've been going through."

"Look," Joseph said in a tone that was firm but not unkind, "I don't really want to talk about it, OK?"

"Sure," Thomas said, nodding his head. "Sorry, I didn't mean to..." he trailed off. There was a heavy silence between them.

"You shouldn't let them get under your skin," Joseph finally said, breaking the silence. "That's exactly what they want, you know."

Thomas looked at Joseph and furrowed his brow in confusion.

"The dock workers, I mean," Joseph said. "Don't let them get to you."

Thomas tightened his lips, frustrated just at the thought of the mistreatment he and others had endured since they began coming to the docks. "You're probably right," he said, "but I don't think I'm as patient as you."

Just then, their conversation was interrupted by the sound of approaching footsteps. The two looked up to see a few of the dock workers coming toward them.

"Are you girls done with your tea time?" the one at the head of the group said. It was the same one who had started the taunting earlier in the day.

Thomas's shoulders rose and fell as he took a deep breath, trying to summon his patience.

"What's wrong with you?" the man said, staring down Thomas. Thomas met his gaze and stared back. "Do you have something you want to say?" the dock worker asked.

"You need to learn to shut up and do your job," Thomas said. "You might actually get some work done if you could stay quiet for a few minutes."

The dock worker clenched his fists and stepped closer. Thomas sprung to his feet and stood an inch from him with his chest out and his chin high. Both men breathed heavily as they stared each other down.

Joseph was quickly on his feet, too. He came between the two men and tried to calm the tension. "Come on, everybody," he said, "we still have a job to do. Let's just get to it, OK?"

The dock worker turned his gaze to Joseph, looking at him with thick disdain. "This 'aint the cotton mill, son, and we're not a bunch of girls waiting to spin fabric. If you want to tell someone what to do, why don't you go home to your wife? Maybe you can help her with the house chores; that might be more suited for you."

Joseph felt a hot ball of anger rise up in his chest. He took a breath and pushed it down as he turned and stood so that he was chest to chest with the dock worker. The worker had to tilt his head back to meet Joseph's gaze, four or five inches above him.

"Do yourself a favor," Joseph said in as commanding and intimidating a cadence as Thomas had ever heard, "and never again let me hear you say a word about my wife."

The dock worker smiled half-heartedly, trying to mask his nerves. Joseph pushed his weight against him further until the man stumbled backward. The man caught himself awkwardly as he nearly fell to the ground. Unable to help himself, one of the man's companions snickered, which quickly wiped the smile from his face.

Figuring his point had been made, Joseph turned to leave. Before he could go, though, the man spoke up again, so angry now that his voice was quivering. "I know who you are," he said. "You're the one who couldn't save your wife in that fire. I heard you weren't man enough to go in after her."

In a flash, Joseph spun around and lunged at the man. Before anyone could react, Joseph had him pinned to the ground and began punching him in the face, one blow after another. Everyone tried breaking it up but there was nothing anyone could do. One of the other dock workers ran to get help while Thomas tried to pry Joseph away.

"Joseph! Stop!" Thomas yelled. "Get off him before someone gets the police!"

Soon, the dock worker who had fled came running back with Mr. Knightly at his side. "Break this up!" Mr. Knightly bellowed but Joseph didn't stop. He tried to get close but, when he did, Joseph inadvertently elbowed him in the face as he brought his arm back for another blow. Mr. Knightly stumbled backward and looked angry. Fortunately for him, he had dealt with this sort of thing before and had come prepared with a short, thick, wooden club. He lifted it up high and struck Joseph across the back of his head.

Joseph remained conscience but he felt like the ground was suddenly spinning and tilting toward him. He stumbled off of the dock worker who lay limp on the ground with blood smeared on his face.

"Get out of here!" Mr. Knightly yelled loudly. "Both of you! I don't ever want to see you on my docks again!"

Thomas helped Joseph to his feet, who soon regained his balance.

"This isn't our fault," Thomas said to Mr. Knightly passionately. "We're just trying to earn an honest wage."

Mr. Knightly didn't want to hear it, though. "Go!" he said, pointing his club in the direction he wanted the two to go. "And don't ever come back!"

"Come on," Joseph said to Thomas, pulling him away from the scene. Thomas resisted for a moment but knowing it was a lost cause, finally surrendered. The rest of the crew watched in satisfied silence as the two men left.

They walked for several minutes before either of them spoke. "There are other docks in town," Joseph finally said. "They're not as close as this one but we'll just have to leave earlier in the morning. Why don't we meet up at one of them tomorrow? We should be able to find work at another dock."

This was against his instincts. He preferred to do things alone these days. But, he felt guilty. He had just cost Thomas a job and he couldn't help but do something about it.

"I know," Thomas said, matter-of-factly. "You're right. I've actually heard that some of the men from the mill have found work at the dock just south of this one. Do you know the one I mean?"

Joseph nodded his head.

"We could meet at that one in the morning." Thomas said. Joseph agreed. They worked out the details and then parted ways.

When Joseph got home, Ms. Cummings was tending a fire in the fireplace. "Mr. Fridman," she said in surprise, "you're home early!"

"Work ended early today," he said flatly. "How's Edith?"

"She's napping right now. She's been an angel today, believe it or not. She ate like a child twice her size."

116

Joseph looked over at the table where he had left half a loaf of bread that morning. Most of it was gone.

Ms. Cummings noticed Joseph's gaze. "I think there's enough for the three of us this evening but we'll need more first thing tomorrow."

Joseph's stomach sunk and his chest tightened simultaneously. He managed to keep his expression and his tone even, though. "You and Edith eat tonight," he said. "I had a good lunch so you two can have my part in the morning. I'll bring some more home after work tomorrow." He forced a smile so Ms. Cummings wouldn't sense his growing anxiety.

"You're a good Father, Mr. Fridman."

Joseph smiled again. "I'm going to check on Edith. I'm awfully tired. I think I'll go to bed early tonight," he said. He walked into the room where Edith was sleeping and quietly closed the door. Approaching her bed, he saw that she was resting soundly. Then he walked over to the nearest wall and leaned his back against it.

All of the events of the day came rushing at him with incredible force. He put his head in his hands and slid down the wall until he was sitting on the ground. The darkness in the room gave him a small sense of refuge against the crushing realization of his situation. He wanted to wrap it around him like a thick blanket and hide.

Tomorrow he would meet Thomas at the southern dock and they would find work there. He kept telling himself this until he drifted off to sleep.

When the two men met the next morning, Joseph thought that Thomas looked as tired as he felt. They briefly exchanged words and then fell into the line. They had arrived promptly and were near the front. Being new here, they weren't accosted by any of the sneers or scowls they had come to expect at the other dock. These workers looked at them suspiciously but not with disdain.

When they reached the front of the line, the union leader who ran the dock asked their names. His head came up from his book at their response and his eyes narrowed as if the names sounded familiar. He searched through his notes, stopped on something, and then told the men there was no work for them.

Thomas looked at the long line behind them. "There has to be a mistake," he said. "There's no way the work's all taken. We were one of the first ones here!"

"Sorry, gentlemen, there's no work for you here," the union leader said.

Thomas and Joseph stared back in disbelief.

"Move along, please," the man directed.

"But..." Thomas began.

"I said, move along," he said, more emphatically this time.

Thomas and Joseph began to go. As they did, though, the union leader added, "By the way: there's no need for you to check any of the other docks." Thomas and Joseph stopped and turned to look at him. "There won't be any work for you at those either," he said. "Do you understand?"

Shocked, neither Thomas nor Joseph responded. The man called for the next person in line and they watched him hand out a work assignment and then another. Stunned, they watched for a moment longer before finally turning their backs defeated.

All of the feelings from the previous night came flooding back for Joseph as they walked away. His chest felt tight and his mind began to race.

"What are we going to do?" Thomas asked.

Joseph felt like being alone. He didn't want to be part of a "we."

"I don't know," he said, "but I've got some things I've got to do. I'm sorry this is happening. Maybe you need to go home to your family for a little bit and figure out your plan. I don't know but I need to go."

Thomas was surprised but he wasn't upset. He had an idea of the kind of burden Joseph was bearing. They parted ways and Joseph wandered aimlessly for a while. The pit in his stomach kept growing. Since the mill fire, this moment had been looming in the distance but, until now, he had managed to stave it off. He had no money and no food for his little girl and he didn't know how to change that. He was completely powerless.

He knew the mills weren't hiring but he visited several of them anyway. At each one, he was summarily turned away. Giving up on that idea, he decided to walk to a busy part of town where he often went to buy food. It was mid-afternoon and the sun was still high in the sky. He didn't have any hope of finding work this late in the day but, maybe if he went to where the people were, some kind of opportunity would present itself.

As he walked toward his destination, he found himself on a street he had never been down before. More than half of the block was taken up on one side by a large poorhouse. As he passed it, a rank smell of body odor and filth emanated from the open doors and windows. Several of its residents were loitering along the walkway. Joseph looked at them in disgust. They were greasy and dirty and ragged. Some had children lingering around their legs. An image flashed in his mind of him and Edith standing among them, looking just as ragged and desperate. He hurried on before his mind could run away with the thought any further.

When he reached the square he was aiming for, he slowed to a stop, unsure what to do next. At first, he just stood numbly and watched people passing. Then, making his way to an open market, he watched others buying fish, apples, and dried meats. The pit in his stomach deepened as he watched person after person taking coins from their pockets or purses and filling their bags with food. He was mesmerized by the simple act as if he hadn't witnessed it thousands of times before. He wondered how it was that he took it for granted for so long.

He noticed a man sitting against a building, holding out his hat and begging. He watched him for several minutes, studying his actions. He had passed plenty of beggars before but never took the time to appreciate their craft. He was surprised at how many people mindlessly dropped coins in his hat.

He thought about his empty pockets and his empty cupboards at home. He imagined the day arriving when he would have to watch Edith cry from hunger and it made him shudder. It felt unfair that this man might feed himself tonight while Joseph and his household went hungry. He looked at the faces of the people passing by and tried to picture himself stopping any one of them to ask for a handout. He didn't know what he would say; He couldn't formulate the words in his mind.

A clock tower rang out in the distance and Joseph realized that an hour had already gone by since he had arrived in the square. He had nothing to show for his time there. He couldn't believe he had wasted an entire hour. His chest felt even tighter than before and he suddenly began to feel panicked and desperate. Without thought, he stopped the next friendly face that he saw.

"Excuse me," he said.

The woman stopped. "Yes?"

Joseph stared at her blankly.

"Can I help you?" she pressed.

"Sorry," he said. "It's just...I." He couldn't bring himself to ask for a handout. "I'm sorry, it's nothing. I was mistaken."

The woman furrowed her brow in confusion and moved on.

Distraught and scared, he took a deep breath and shook his head. Unsure what to do, he followed the crowd past the tables of vendors selling their goods. As he approached one vendor selling bread, he noticed the round, sourdough loafs on one side were nearly spilling off of the table. One of them that his hand nearly brushed was hanging far over the table's edge. Without really thinking, he put his hand on it in order to reposition it so it wouldn't fall. As he did, he realized how easy it would be to take it.

He looked at the vendor who was busy helping a customer. A rush of adrenalin passed through him. He knew the opportunity wouldn't last so, without wasting any more time, he pulled the bread from the table and quickly tucked it into his jacket.

Immediately, his heart began to pound. He couldn't believe what he had done. He had never stolen anything in his life. He looked around to make sure nobody was watching him and suddenly felt self-conscious. Was he acting suspicious? Did he *look* like he was hiding something under his coat?

He quickly left the square, suddenly feeling very uncomfortable there, and hurried home. When he walked through the door, he still felt a little panicked but the panic soon gave way to a subtle sense of safety. It wasn't warm inside but it was warmer than it had been outside. Ms. Cummings sat on the rug near the fire with Edith, who smiled when she saw him and called out "Dad!".

Something strange happened, for the first time in weeks, it felt good to be home. He looked at his precious little girl who was welcoming him and felt a familiar warmth inside that, for the first time in a very long time, was not clouded by fear or anxiety. Feeling the large loaf of bread beneath his coat, he suddenly felt an assurance and confidence he hadn't felt since the mill fire. All at once, the bread and the means by which he obtained it sparked a new sense of hope in him. He was buoyed up by the feeling that he could provide for his daughter no matter what. Nothing was going to stop him. Whatever the circumstances, he was going to find a way.

He removed the bread and placed it on the table.

"Ooh," Ms. Cummings commented, "that's a nice loaf!"

Joseph smiled. He had expected to feel guilty but he didn't. He only felt relief.

CHAPTER 11

On Sunday, Joseph was back at the market, hoping to bring home a wedge of cheese or some dried beans for Edith and Ms. Cummings. He stood in the sun as people passed and thought he could feel a subtle warming of the air as though spring was in reach. Then, as he looked through the sea of faces in front of him, he suddenly noticed one that was familiar.

"Mr. Hill?" he called out.

Hill paused and, for a moment, scanned the crowd to see who had called his name. When he saw Joseph, his face brightened. "Joseph!" he said, covering the distance between them in just a few, long strides. "It's been too long, my friend. How are you?" he asked, as he took his hand and shook it heartily.

Hill was smiling but he looked tired and worn. Joseph hadn't seen him since the mill fire. He had dark circles under his eyes that hadn't been there before and his face was noticeably thinner.

"I'm good," Joseph responded politely. "How are you?"

Mr. Hill shrugged his shoulders. "Eh," he said, "it's tough to say." He laughed but it didn't seem like he was joking. Joseph looked back at him, noticeably concerned. Mr. Hill waved a hand across the air as if trying to brush Joseph's concern aside. "No, I'm fine, I'm completely fine. So, what are you doing for work these days?"

Joseph shifted his weight. "Oh, you know," he said, "day jobs. Just, whatever I can find. I've done some work at the docks and, just, other stuff here and there."

"At the docks?" Hill asked in surprise. "Why didn't you go to another mill?"

Joseph shrugged his shoulders. "There's no jobs at the mills," he said. "I've checked a hundred times. There are a lot more people than work and everyone's trying to get a mill job. You've got to know someone who's already working at one if you want to get hired."

"Sorry to hear that," Hill said. "I wish I could help."

"It is what it is I guess," Joseph said. "So, what about you? Where are you working?"

Mr. Hill shifted his weight like Joseph had done and glanced down at the ground. "Hm," he laughed quietly. "Nowhere now," he said. "After the fire, I found a job as a floor supervisor at another mill downtown. I thought it was going pretty well but I was let go a few weeks ago. The Agent's daughter got married and he gave my job to his new son-in-law. So, I got the boot."

Mr. Hill took a deep breath and blew it out. The weight on his shoulders was nearly visible. "It's tough not having work, Joseph," he admitted. "We have enough to live off for a while but it's hard not to get a little panicked every time an employer turns you down. And bread's not getting any cheaper!" he said with a little laugh as he held up the loaf he was holding in his hand.

Joseph nodded quietly. *'It is for me,'* he thought to himself.

A heavy silence settled over the two men and they let it linger for a moment.

"You say the docks are hiring?" Mr. Hill finally asked.

"It depends on the day," Joseph said, "and on whether the union boss likes you. Honestly, Mr. Hill, it's not a good situation for us. They don't like folks from the mills down there."

Mr. Hill took another deep breath and exhaled. He shook his head. "What are we going to do, Joseph?" he asked.

It was odd and a little uncomfortable to see Mr. Hill in this state. He seemed so vulnerable. But then something occurred to Joseph that quickly made him forget about the awkwardness. Hill had money and connections and Joseph needed both if he was ever going to improve his situation. Hill's desperation might be useful to him.

"We worked well together, didn't we, Mr. Hill?" Joseph said.

Hill nodded his head. "I think you were the best worker that came through that mill in all my time, Joseph. I was proud to work next to you."

"You were always good to me, sir. I was excited to learn from you. It's a shame it all ended before you were able to teach me more."

Joseph looked at Mr. Hill. His eyes were narrowed and peering into the distance as if he was deep in thought. Joseph pushed on. "Maybe we could find a way to do it again, Mr. Hill. I'm sure you know people – people who could employ us. We could work side by side like we used to. We could pick up right where we left off."

Hill's expression was unchanged. He continued peering into the distance, lost in his thoughts. Joseph wasn't sure he had heard him. "Mr. Hill?" he said.

Hill snapped out of it and looked at Joseph. He had a strange look in his eyes. "What was that you were saying, Joseph?"

"Well, I was just saying, you're a man with a lot of connections. Maybe we just need to reach out to them. We could..."

"No, not that," Hill interrupted. "You were talking about the mill, how I was beginning to train you. Joseph, I know everything there is to know about running a mill."

"That's true, sir," Joseph said, unsure where Mr. Hill was going with this.

"And you're as capable a mill worker as I've ever known. You're a great leader, too. The men and women who were working with us really respected you."

"Thank you, Mr. Hill."

"And you know," Hill continued, "I bet you anything a lot of them are still out of work just like you and I." Joseph stared back at him blankly. He didn't understand what that had to do with anything they had been talking about.

"Do you see what I'm saying, Joseph?" he said with excitement building in his voice.

"I'm sorry, sir," Joseph said, "I'm not following you."

"Joseph!" Hill exclaimed enthusiastically, "what's stopping us from doing it all ourselves? We have what it takes to run our own mill. I have the connections. I know the suppliers and how things operate. You know the inner workings – and what you don't know,

124

I'll teach you. We won't have any trouble finding workers. We could do it together, Joseph. I really think we could."

Joseph was taken aback. This wasn't at all what he had in mind. "Umm..." he said, filling the silence while he tried sorting through the doubts that that were inundating him.

"It wouldn't have to be a big operation," Mr. Hill continued. "We could hire pickers and weavers to work out of their homes if we wanted to. That might make it easier to get the project off the ground. There are a lot of things we could do to keep costs down."

Joseph nodded politely, still unsure how to respond.

"Joseph, trust me," Mr. Hill said, looking at him squarely, "this could work. There's room in the market for at least another 10, full-sized mills in this area. We'll do just fine. You'll make more money than you ever imagined."

This got Joseph's attention and, for a moment, pivoted his thoughts away from his skepticism and doubts. He looked at Mr. Hill and again saw a desperation in him he had never seen a shadow of before. Again, it occurred to him that this desperation – and even Mr. Hill's excitement – could work to his advantage. "I don't know," he began. "To be honest, I've been considering a move to Boston. I hear there's a lot of opportunity up there. I've gained a lot of mill experience over the years – as you know. So, I'm thinking I should be able to land a good job – maybe even a floor supervisor at one of the established operations up there. Then, who knows? Maybe I work my way up the chain. Really, the possibilities are endless. Things could get pretty comfortable for me and Edith."

"Joseph, I don't think you're hearing me," Hill retorted. "I'm offering you something bigger than floor supervisor. You wouldn't need to work your way up the chain with me; you'd be right there at the top from day one. You'd be my agent."

"You mean I'd be managing *all* of the workers?" Joseph asked.

"That's right. And you'd be compensated well for it."

Joseph folded his arms and shook his head as if deeply contemplating Mr. Hill's proposal. "So, you'd take care of all the behind-the-scenes work and I'd take care of everything else," he said.

Mr. Hill's demeanor changed slightly. "Well," he said, "maybe not *everything* but..."

"No, of course not," Joseph interrupted. "There would be times when we would need your expertise on the floor but, it seems to me that, if this is going to work, you can't be tied to the building. You need the freedom to be out meeting with your connections, using your expertise on the road. Somebody has got to meet with suppliers and investors and what not and I can't think of anyone better at that sort of thing than you. That's where we'll really need your skills, Mr. Hill."

Mr. Hill nodded his head. Joseph felt like Hill was beginning to see his vision.

"It's an interesting proposal, Mr. Hill. You've given me a lot to think about. I'm not sure what my answer is just yet but I can tell you this: if we were to move forward, then rest assured that I would be willing to step up into the role I'm most needed in. I could do that for you and for the operation. I have some things to learn but, with your training, in no time at all I think I could be ready to run the operations on the ground so you could be free to use all your talents and expertise on the more important stuff." Joseph looked at Hill who was subtly nodding his head now. "You might be right;" he continued, "with us working together as partners, we might really be able to build something special."

Mr. Hill raised an eyebrow. "Partners?" he asked.

"Whatever you want to call it is fine with me," Joseph said, trying to sound casual. "But, honestly, I couldn't be comfortable joining you unless I was contributing all I could. If we were to do this, I would give just as much to the venture as you would, Mr. Hill. You have my word."

It was quiet between the men while Mr. Hill digested Joseph's words. He peered at the ground in front of him while his excitement began giving way to contemplation.

"Recruitment's going to be tough," Joseph said, breaking the silence.

Mr. Hill looked up with a slight look of concern. "What do you mean?"

"Well," Joseph said, "people want work but they want to work for someone they believe can pay them. Our competition is well-established. It might be tough convincing anyone to come work for a brand new, unproven operation."

Hill shook his head. "I don't think that will be a problem. If we present ourselves as professionals, they won't question us."

"The desperate ones won't," Joseph said. "But we're not going to get off the ground by filling the floor with all the people that nobody else is willing to hire. We need a pool of good, experienced workers and we need to convince them to bring their talents to us."

"We have that already," Mr. Hill said with excitement again building in his voice. "We have a whole workforce at our disposal. Think of all the workers that were displaced when the mill burnt down. They're out there and they're probably still looking for steady work."

Joseph exhaled slowly. "It's a bit of a hard sale, Mr. Hill."

Hill wrinkled his brow. "What do you mean?" he asked.

"Those people lost a lot when that mill burned down. Some of us practically lost everything," Joseph said solemnly. "Now, I'm not saying it was your fault but, honestly, you're asking a lot if you expect them to forget about everything they lost last time they worked for you and to come to work again. You'd be asking them to just hope that something like that doesn't happen again."

"That's why I wouldn't be the one doing the asking," Mr. Hill said, looking back at Joseph meaningfully.

Joseph suppressed a smile he felt creeping up on him. This is exactly where he was hoping to lead Mr. Hill. He feigned a look of surprise as if he hadn't considered Mr. Hill's point. "I guess I was pretty friendly with a lot of the folks we were working with."

"You absolutely were, Joseph. And they liked you – they all did."

Joseph nodded. "Some of the ones I didn't know knew my wife and I'm sure they loved her like I do. They might be willing to listen to me based on that alone."

"That's right," Mr. Hill said. "I think they would. You suffered losses just like them – probably more than most. They'll respect that."

"I see what you're saying," Joseph said. "I'd certainly be willing to give it a shot. I guess if I do the recruiting and I can help them see that I'll be there running things on the floor, they might feel like they're coming back to work for one of their own."

Joseph paused and looked at Hill. "You're a smart man, Mr. Hill. I think I can see your vision and you're exactly right. This

127

really could work. The things we bring to the table complement each other perfectly."

"We need each other, Joseph. So, are you in?" Hill asked, extending his hand.

"As partners?" Joseph asked, looking at the outstretched hand in front of him.

Hill hesitated but only for a second before replying. "Yes, as partners."

Joseph grasped Hill's hand firmly and shook it. "I'm in," he said.

CHAPTER 12

Winter was stubborn until spring became aggressive. It rained for three straight weeks at the end of May. By the time the gray, gloomy clouds finally cleared, all the snow had been washed away and the sun began to brighten the colors pushing through the dirt.

Joseph and Mr. Hill had been busy all season, working feverishly on their new venture. Joseph had convinced Mr. Hill to get a loan to help push things along. Joseph was in no position to appeal to lenders but he knew Mr. Hill was. He had connections and a home he could use as collateral.

Mr. Hill's Father-in-Law owned several acres of abandoned farmland outside of town that had been passed down in his family for a couple of generations. He offered it to the two men at a decent price. Property in town proved difficult to secure and, the more they considered it, the more they liked the idea of getting away from the competitive bustle of Fall River so they decided to look into it. They visited it shortly after the spring showers had subsided. Joseph brought Edith along and Mr. Hill, who had no children, brought his wife, Emily.

When the sun was nearly at its peak in the domed sky, the party came to a clearing in the woods and their destination came into view. Emily gasped quietly. The earth descended gradually on all sides, gently sloping toward a spacious, flat range that was intersected by a rushing stream almost as big as a river. Purple flowers speckled the hills all around and a gradual breeze moved them like calm waves across the ocean.

The farmland sat nestled against the nearest hill. Wooden, ranch-like fencing marked its vast borders. A humble, wooden cabin stood near one corner of the property.

"I can't believe my Dad never brought us here," Emily marveled.

Joseph put his arm around Edith who was riding next to him in the horse-drawn wagon they were on. He was surprised by the rush of feelings that came over him. As clear as memory, he could see Edith in his mind's eye running along the brush below and growing into a young woman away from the crowded mill town several miles behind them. His feelings had a lightness to them he hadn't experienced since Abby's death.

"It's perfect," he said. He pointed to a spot below. "We don't need a mill town," he said. "We'll build our own. The mill could go there, next to the stream. The flow looks strong enough to power a waterwheel."

"A waterwheel?" Mr. Hill said, thoughtfully. "It would be cheaper than steam, I suppose," he pondered out loud. "It really is a good spot of land, Joseph," he said. "If we could convince those recruits of yours to follow us here, I think you're right. We won't bring our mill to the town; we'll bring the town to our mill!"

Emily laughed and rolled her eyes. "You are *such* a dreamer," she said to her husband. Then, pointing at Joseph, she said in a tone of mock agitation, "and you're not helping! You're supposed to be the one that brings him down to earth!"

"Oh, come on," Mr. Hill said. "Keep an open mind."

Edith, who had been playing with a small, wooden doll that she brought along for the ride, suddenly chimed in. "What's this place called, Daddy?"

Joseph, Emily, and Mr. Hill all looked at each other, each a little amused and each with wheels now turning in their heads. Before anyone else could answer, Joseph looked back down at his daughter. "Edith's Hollow," he said, with a wink. "I mean, if you approve," he said, looking back at Mr. Hill and Emily.

Mr. Hill smiled politely. "Of course," he said. "That's perfect."

Edith beamed in her seat. "Can we get closer?" she asked.

"Absolutely," said Joseph. The group coaxed their horses back to life and descended into the small valley below.

Joseph and Mr. Hill didn't waste any time. They raised the frame to the mill within two months and all their recruits were there to help. They built small homes near the mill for the workers which were shared by two families each. At Joseph's insistence, his home and Mr. Hill's home were each built among the others. Joseph's home was hardly distinguishable from anyone else's. The Hills', on the other hand, was a little larger and more extravagant than the rest.

A modest, company store was built at one end of the development. Mr. Hill, who planned on making frequent trips into Fall River, committed to keeping the store stocked with groceries and basic supplies. One of the mill workers that Joseph recruited had a cousin named Sam who had recently moved from Rhode Island after losing his job shucking clams in a factory. Sam was young and unmarried and easily excited by the idea of a new adventure. He readily accepted the offer to run the store.

Across from the store was built a small, white church with a steeple and a wooden cross at the top. Joseph wasn't much of a church-goer but Mr. Hill was. Regardless, Joseph agreed with Mr. Hill when he said that the community wasn't complete without a church. Joseph didn't know the first thing about recruiting a Christian preacher so the church was preacherless when it was built. The people gathered there on Sundays anyway.

When Mr. Hill was in town, he liked to stand at the pulpit and say a few words – which always were more or less the same about how pleased he was with the mill's success. Mr. Hill was usually away from Edith's Hollow on the weekends, though, leaving the group of church-goers to talk among themselves. Often, the conversation turned to the company store. John from the weaving room always asked if they were ever going to have bacon, noting that he hadn't eaten bacon since leaving Fall River. Someone would point out that the store was nearly out of sugar or string or some other item that seemed important. Sam, with his small, short frame and bright red hair, would stand and, in his polite, congenial way, take note of everyone's comments and promise John he would tell Mr. Hill again that they would like him to get bacon next time he brought supplies.

Everyone got so used to Sam standing in front of them in church that it was only a matter of time before he became their de-facto preacher. Whenever there was a lull between the church walls on Sunday from people running out of things to say or hymns to sing, everyone would look to Sam to stand and address them. And, when the day came that they expected him to talk about the bible instead of bread, he obliged in his polite, congenial way.

The small home nearest to the church housed Thomas Baines, his wife and four children. Joseph had never stopped feeling guilty for getting Thomas banned from the Fall River docks. So, when the plans for a new mill began to materialize, Thomas was the first person Joseph talked to about coming to work. At the time, Thomas was still taking any day jobs he could find so he enthusiastically accepted Joseph's offer.

Joseph became friendly with the Baines. Edith spent her days with them while Joseph worked. One Sunday evening, after enjoying a meal in their home, Joseph helped the Baines' oldest son, Tommy, with his chore of splitting logs outside. Tommy was quiet and small for his age due to a serious illness he had as a baby. He wasn't very strong but he took his chores seriously and he didn't complain.

When Joseph went back inside, he told Thomas how impressed he was with Tommy's soberness and resilience.

"He seems like a hard worker," Joseph said.

"He is," Thomas replied. "Honestly, I think he's already figured out his lot in life. He's never gonna be as big or strong as the other kids but, he knows how to put his head down and get a job done – better than most kids twice his size." Thomas nodded, unable to hide his pride. "He's a good kid," he said. "He really is."

Suddenly, an idea came to Joseph. "How do you think he would like a job?" he asked.

Thomas looked surprised. "Really?" he asked.

"Of course," Joseph said. "We could actually use someone just his size. You know how it is at the mill with the machines always getting jammed up. We could use his help crawling up under them and what not."

Thomas's expression changed to one of doubt and concern. "Hmm. I know what his mom would say to that. That can be risky."

"Well, that's not all he'd be doing of course," Joseph said. "There's a lot of odd jobs I'd keep him busy with. He'd learn his way around the mill pretty good. It's not a bad thing to learn so early on. I think he'd enjoy it."

Thomas raised his eyebrows, still considering the offer.

"I'm sure it wouldn't hurt to have a second income-earner, too," Joseph added.

"That's for sure," Thomas said.

"Well, you think about it. Talk to your wife. I'd love to have him, though. He'd definitely learn a thing or two."

Thomas nodded his head. "I'll think about it," he said. "I'll let you know."

Joseph and Edith said their goodbyes just a short time later. It was late when they got home and Joseph insisted that Edith go straight to bed. "Daddy," she said as he tucked her in, "can I come visit you at work tomorrow?"

"No," Joseph replied without hesitation. "I don't think that's a good idea, Edith."

"Why not?" she asked.

"Well, the mill can be a very dangerous place for children. Plus, it's loud and not very fun. Maybe I can take you there sometime after work when all the machines are turned off."

"But Dad, we've already done that before." Edith retorted. "I want to come visit you while you're working."

Joseph shook his head. "Sorry, sweetheart," he said. "It's just not safe - maybe one day when you're older." Edith frowned. Joseph rubbed her leg then bent over and kissed her on the forehead. "Now go to sleep," he said. "Sweet dreams. I'll see you in the morning."

It only took a day for the Baines to make their decision. They accepted Joseph's offer on Monday and Tommy began work on Tuesday. Joseph filled his day quickly. He had him check the water wheel for obstructions in the mornings, light the candles in the evenings, sweep the floors at night after everybody had gone home, and do just about any other miscellaneous thing that needed done.

Tommy was a reserved kid but his walls weren't impenetrable. Eventually, he began feeling comfortable around Joseph. "Maybe I'll have your job one day," he said to him one time while they were walking down the stairs between floors.

133

Joseph smiled. "If you keep working hard and listening to what I tell you," he said, "there will probably be twenty mills out there that would be happy to give you a job as a supervisor – once you're a little older, of course."

"That's not what I meant," Tommy replied. "I mean, give me a few years and I think I might have yours. I'm getting pretty good at my tasks and you're...you know...getting kind of old. I might have to have a talk with Mr. Hill about it sometime."

Confused and taken aback, Joseph stopped in the middle of the stairwell and turned to look at his young companion. Tommy couldn't hold back the smirk pushing at the corners of his mouth. Suddenly he snickered, unable to contain it.

Joseph laughed as well. "You better watch yourself, son." he said. "I'm not as old as you think. I'm sure I can still chase you down if I need to!"

At the end of each day, after everybody went home, Joseph stayed behind to walk each of the three floors, make sure things were in order for the next day, and lock up. Tommy stayed behind as well to sweep the floors while his dad headed home. When they were done, Joseph and Tommy would walk to the Baines together where Joseph picked up Edith.

One evening, Joseph was on the third floor inspecting some of the weavers' work when the bell echoed loudly off the walls, signaling that it was time to go home. Tommy rang the bell each evening at 7:30 sharp, just as Joseph had instructed him to do. As the workers shuffled through the doors, Joseph lingered at the top floor, closely eying a piece of material that he was holding in his hands. Earlier in the day, one of the weavers had come to him complaining about the poor quality of work that her colleague was doing. This particular weaver was infamous for stirring up trouble among her co-workers. Still, the cloth she brought with her as evidence did, in fact, give Joseph cause for concern.

After sifting through several pieces of material and, to his relief, not finding any others that were as bad as the one he had been shown, he stood and stretched his back. He was about to begin his nightly routine of walking the mill when it occurred to him that the building was still buzzing and rattling with the motion of its machinery. He furrowed his brow. Tommy always shut down the belt system that powered the machines just after ringing the closing bell. It was one of his jobs and he wasn't one to shirk an assignment.

Joseph casually jogged down the stairs to the second floor. "Tommy!" he called out, trying to yell over the sound of the machines. He didn't hear a response but the room was so loud that he wasn't surprised. He jogged down to the first floor, which was quieter, and stood at the head of the room, calling out Tommy's name again but got no response. "Weird," he said aloud to himself as he made his way to the giant turbine that was pumping power through the mill. He shut off the system of leather belts and with a sudden jolt, the building was quiet.

"Tommy," he called out again as he walked across the floor toward the stairs. He didn't expect to find him there so, again, he wasn't surprised when there was no response. He jogged back up to the second floor where he was sure his young friend would be.

"Hey, Tommy!" he shouted when he got there. "Are you here?" His voice echoed through the large room.

Again, he heard nothing in return. The silence began to concern him. "Tommy?" he repeated as he began walking down one of the isles of machines. Tommy had already begun putting out the candles as he finished his tasks so the building was even dimmer than usual. But, when Joseph had just about reached the halfway point in the isle he was walking down, he thought he saw something under the last machine in the row. He squinted and called Tommy's name as he picked up his pace.

A few steps closer and he was sure that the dark mass he was seeing was a body. He rushed over to the machine to find a horrifying scene. Tommy appeared lifeless. He had apparently squeezed and scooted his way into the narrow space between the floor and the machine's long, steel arm that rhythmically moved back and forth as it spun the thin threads of cotton. He was often sent under the machines to clear the accumulating fibers or fix a fraying string so navigating his way through these spaces was familiar to him.

His body was lying at a center point in the back where a system of jagged, metal gears kept the machine in motion. Joseph figured he had gone to fix a jam. It looked like he had reached into the system of gears – probably to remove an obstruction and, perhaps, not anticipating how fast the gears would begin to turn when they jolted back into action.

His left arm, all the way up to his elbow, was completely entangled in the machinery and there was a lot of blood. He had apparently, somehow, hit his head too because there was a large bump on his forehead that was split open.

Joseph's eyes grew wide as he felt his face go cold. For a brief moment, his feet froze to the floor. Images of the night of his wife's death began flashing through his mind. Without realizing it, he buried his fingers in his hair and began shaking his head. "No, no, no, no, no…" he said, quietly at first but growing louder and louder.

Then, something switched on inside of him and he sprung into action. "Tommy!" he yelled, sprinting over to the machine. He stretched his body to try and reach him but he could only touch his leg. He tapped it and shook it gently but there was no response. He jumped up and ran around to the back of the machine and quickly made his way to the gears. He could see Tommy's mangled hand and forearm twisted into the toothy wheels. Frantically, he began looking around for anything he could attack the machine with when, suddenly, he remembered a metal rod he knew was resting against a wall upstairs from a recent repair to one of the weaving machines.

He dashed upstairs and grabbed the rod then quickly returned. Without wasting any time, he started swinging it like a baseball bat. The sound of iron striking iron rang duly in his ears and the metal vibrated uncomfortably in his hands. After a few, short minutes, though, it was clear his technique wasn't getting him anywhere. So, acting decisively, he tried something else. He found an opening in the gears just big enough to allow him to wedge the rod behind one of the gears pressing into Tommy's flesh. With some effort, he forced the rod as far into the opening as it would go until it was sticking out at a 45° angle. Then, using the rod as a lever, he pushed against it as hard as he could to try and force the lower gear out. He expected to bend the gear enough to release Tommy's hand and arm but, to his surprise, the gear started to loosen from the bolt that was holding it.

Encouraged but tired, he took a break from pushing on the rod and, stepping back, he began to kick it as hard as he could. After four or five swift kicks, the bolt that fastened the gear in place was protruding out more than an inch. Joseph hurriedly knelt down and began unscrewing it with his hand. Soon it was out and, gently, he pulled the gear away from Tommy's mangled arm.

Suddenly, Tommy screamed. Joseph's immediate reaction was a rush of relief that the boy was alive. Then, darting around to the other side of the machine, he strained until he could grasp Tommy's ankle in his hand and pulled him out from under the contraption. Tommy screamed again but quickly passed back out. As he emerged from the machine, Joseph noticed that the bleeding had increased dramatically.

Each work station on the second floor always had at least one pair of scissors that could be used to cut fraying string. Joseph found the pair of scissors closest to him and cut several, long pieces of cotton thread off of the machine and twisted them into a makeshift rope which he wrapped around Tommy's arm above the wound. Kneeling next to the boy, he cinched the rope as tightly as he could and tied it off. The bleeding nearly stopped altogether.

Joseph placed his hands on his knees and took a deep breath, slowing down for the first time since discovering the accident. He looked past Tommy at the broken machine he had pulled him from. Again, his mind flashed back to the night of his wife's death. As he had done hundreds of times before and against his will, he pictured her pinned under a machine much like the one in front of him or under a pile of burning rubble. Somehow, it felt like it was all happening again and that he was being crushed beneath a mound of a different kind.

Tommy made a groaning noise and Joseph snapped out of his thoughts, returning to the urgency of the situation before him. His mind began to race. What would the other workers think when they found out what had happened? Like him, most of them had come to Edith's Hollow in the aftermath of the mill accident that killed his wife and many of them had lost loved ones too. This mill was supposed to be different. It was supposed to be a refuge. Looking at the horrendous scene of blood and twisted metal in front of him, it didn't seem any different at all. If anyone saw this scene, it would change everything.

He grabbed the scissors again and began cutting any cotton from the machine that was stained in blood. As he did, though, Tommy made another noise. Joseph looked over at his pale face. "What am I doing?" he thought to himself. "I need to get him help."

137

That prospect flooded his mind with additional complications, though. Where would he take him? He couldn't bring him to anyone local. Nobody else in Edith's Hollow could witness what he was seeing.

He picked Tommy up in his arms. He had to get him to Fall River. The hospital there would take care of him. Joseph sprinted to his house, which was closer to the mill than any others. He saddled a horse and climbed atop, hoisting Tommy up. Before he began to ride, though, it occurred to him that Edith and Tommy's family would begin wondering where they were soon. He couldn't leave without telling them; that could ruin everything. The whole town would likely be in an uproar by midnight if he left without any explanation.

"Ughh," Joseph grunted in frustration as he spurred his horse and turned it toward the Baines' home. "Come on!" he yelled, pushing his horse to a gallop.

When they reached the Baines', Joseph rode near their front door and yelled for Thomas without getting down from his horse. Thomas came running out, hearing the urgency in Joseph's voice.

"There's been an accident," Joseph exclaimed. "We need to get Tommy to Fall River – fast! I'll explain on the way. Go get your horse."

Thomas's wife, Sarah, came to the door with Edith and each of the Baines' children close behind.

"Sarah," Joseph said, "we'll take care of him. I promise. But we need to go. Please, watch after Edith until we're back."

Thomas was quickly at Joseph's side and the two men took off in a cloud of dust.

Thomas beat Joseph to the hospital by several yards. When Joseph rode up a few moments later, Thomas was off of his horse waiting for him. He reached up and asked for his boy then, gently but swiftly taking him from Joseph's arms, he held him close to his chest and rushed through the hospital doors. The entrance was empty and quiet but a few voices could be heard coming from hallways and from distant rooms.

"Help!" Thomas yelled loudly. "Somebody help!"

Two nurses quickly emerged.

"Please," Thomas pleaded as only a parent could, "there's been an accident. He needs help. He's barely breathing."

"Hurry, go find the doctor," one nurse said to the other. The younger of the two ran out the front doors Thomas had just entered through. She nearly knocked Joseph over who was coming in just at that moment. He narrowly managed to dodge her.

"Come with me," the other nurse said to Thomas. Thomas followed her to a room with an empty hospital bed and Joseph was right behind. She had Thomas lay his son on the bed while she began gathering bandages, a large bowl of water, and several other items that she placed on the table next to him. "Here," she said, "hold his arm up like this." She showed Thomas where to hold and how to elevate the arm.

"Is he going to be OK?" Thomas asked, his eyes red and swollen.

"We're going to do everything we can," she replied. "He looks like he's lost a lot of blood but he's alive."

Joseph stood motionless just inside the room's entrance. He didn't know what to say or do. The enormity of the situation was almost too much. "Thomas, I'm so sorry," he said. But Thomas didn't even seem to hear him. Joseph's apology was the last thing on his mind.

Soon the Dr. entered with the nurse who had run to get him and another nurse they had grabbed in the halls. He walked straight to the bed where Tommy lay. "What's the situation?" he asked the nurse who had begun tending to him.

"His arm looks beyond repair," she said, "and his pulse is really weak. I've begun cleaning the wounds."

"What happened?" the doctor asked.

Nobody answered.

"Joseph!" Thomas said.

Joseph, who was barely following what anyone was saying, realized that he was the only one who could answer the doctor's question. The ride from Edith's Hollow to Fall River had been so frantic that Joseph had only managed to tell Thomas that the injury was to Tommy's arm and that there had been a lot of blood. Now, with everybody looking at him, his mind raced, searching for an explanation that wouldn't implicate the mill.

"Sir, answer the question!" the doctor said impatiently.

"He was run over," Joseph blurted out. "He came with me to my house so we could load up the buggy with some firewood I

139

wanted to drop off at the mill before he went home for the night. But we were done with all our work inside," Joseph emphasized, looking at Thomas. "We were just dropping off wood. And, I'm not sure what happened. We hit some kind of bump while we were on our way and it flipped Tommy right out of the buggy and before I could get the horse to stop, we went right over him. I jumped out as fast as I could but he was already knocked out on the ground with his arm looking like that. I don't know if the horse stepped on him or his arm got caught up in the spokes or what but it looked pretty bad."

The doctor and the nurse kept working while Joseph gave his explanation. When he was done, Thomas was silently staring at him.

"I'm so sorry," Joseph said.

"Is there anything else they should know?" Thomas asked.

"No," Joseph said. "I unhitched the horse and tied that rope around his arm to try and stop the bleeding then we came as quickly as we could. That's all I can tell you. That's everything I know."

"OK," the doctor said, "you two will need to leave the room."

"No," Thomas said matter-of-factly. "I need to stay with my boy."

"Fine," the doctor said, not wanting to waste any time or energy on arguing. "But stay out of the way."

One of the nurses took Tommy's arm, relieving Thomas of his only job. He stepped back, giving the doctor and the nurses enough room to work. His back was still to Joseph. All of his focus was on the scene in front of him.

Joseph suddenly felt a little out of place so he stepped out into the hallway. He didn't go far, though. He leaned his back against the wall just outside of the door to Tommy's room and slid down to the ground until he was sitting. He was exhausted. He gazed at the opposite wall, letting a myriad of thoughts and emotions just pass through him.

The next thing he knew, Thomas was standing over him, shaking his shoulder. He opened his eyes. He had no idea how long he had been asleep but it was still dark outside and Thomas's demeanor had changed. He looked less wide-eyed and panicked.

Joseph quickly sprung to his feet. "What is it?" he said. "What's going on? Is he OK?"

Thomas took a deep breath and exhaled. He looked even more exhausted than Joseph felt. "He's alive," he said. "He's not out of the woods yet but he's resting. They had to take his arm." He began to choke up when he said this but he caught himself, took a breath, and tried again. "They had to take his arm," he repeated, more collected this time. "But it could have been worse. We still have our boy."

Joseph reached out and put his hand on Thomas's shoulder.

Thomas looked up at him. "Thank you, Joseph," he said.

This took Joseph utterly by surprise and made him want to shrink away.

"You were there to save him," Thomas continued. "Your swift action made all the difference, I'm sure."

A feeling of guilt sunk in Josephs gut like a bag of sand. He was the only reason Tommy had been at the mill, climbing under the machines to begin with. He was the reason all of the folks in Edith's Hollow were working in the mill. He couldn't respond. He didn't know what to say. Instead, he swallowed a lump in his throat and shook his head, squeezing Thomas' shoulder beneath his hand.

"Sarah must be beside herself with worry," Joseph said. "Why don't you stay here and I'll go back and let her know what is going on."

Thomas nodded his head. "That's probably best," he said.

Joseph left the hospital and rode home in a haze. The guilt in his gut only grew heavier with every mile. He didn't know what he was going to say to Sarah and, before he knew it, he was standing at her door.

Joseph stumbled over his words as he spoke with Tommy's mom. She was a flurry of emotion – anger, relief, despair. He hugged her and, reluctantly, she let him. When he and Edith left a few moments later, he wasn't exactly sure what he had said. Edith had been sleeping and rubbed her tired eyes as they walked away from the Baines'. Joseph held her in one of his arms and led his horse by a lead rope with the other hand. He turned from the road they were on before they reached home.

"Where are we going, Daddy?" Edith asked.

"Sorry, honey," he said. "We can't go home yet. We have a job to do before morning."

Joseph led his little girl and their horse down the path to the mill. If he was going to get the scene of the accident cleaned up before anyone else could see it, he needed to hurry. The sun would begin to rise in another hour or so. Fortunately, he had an extra set of hands to help.

CHAPTER 13

The sun shone brightly on the church lawn and a gentle breeze lightly shook the tall, dark green blades of grass. Outside, the weather was beautiful. Inside, it was a bit too warm, despite the fact that every door and window had been opened. Church goers sat politely in the pews while Sam preached his sermon but his words were background noise to their daydreams of the things they would do that afternoon as soon as church got out.

Then, something unexpected happened. Joseph walked through the door with Edith by his side and sat in an empty seat near the back. He tried slipping in quietly but the church was small and the wooden floor was creaky so, naturally, half of the congregation turned their heads to look when they heard someone enter. When they saw that it was Joseph, a subtle buzz swept across the room as neighbors whispered to each other – some even leaning across the aisle or over the pews – spreading the news. Joseph had never stepped foot in the church for a service and that fact was well known.

"Welcome, Mr. Fridman," Sam said, shattering any remaining hope he had for a low-profile entrance. "Thanks for joining us."

"Thanks, Sam," Joseph said as he settled into his seat. Sam was about to continue with his sermon but before he could get his next word out, Joseph interrupted. "Actually, Sam," he said with just a hint of hesitation in his voice, "do you mind if I say a few words?"

"Of course!" said Sam in a warm, accommodating way that came natural to him. He stepped aside and gestured to the open pulpit. "Please, it's all yours."

Joseph rose and made his way to the front. As he did, the room quietly buzzed once again. When he turned around to face the congregation, though, the same people who had been whispering to their neighbors were now shushing them. The room fell quieter than it had been since services began. One lady near the front nudged her husband firmly, who woke from his nap, assessed the situation, and promptly fell back asleep.

"Well," Joseph started, "you can probably guess that I don't do this sort of thing very often. It's not really in my nature, you might say. But there's something that's been weighing on my mind that I want to mention to you good people. And it's something that made me want to be here with you today and sit with you, and sing hymns with you, and I guess stand up and talk to you - which I wasn't really planning on doing."

"As I'm sure you all know by now, little Tommy Baines had a terrible accident earlier this week. I was there when it happened. In fact, I was the only one there. It was a terrible thing to witness. I wish it never would have happened. I wish to God it wouldn't have happened." At this, Joseph clinched his fists and tightened his jaw while he fought to push down his emotions. He paused for a moment. The room was deathly silent. "I haven't been part of that kind of a scene since the mill fire, which most of you were affected by as well," he continued. Heads nodded and a couple of them bowed. Again, he paused while the group silently shared a moment. People looked around, reciting in their minds who had lost what. The injuries and death toll didn't need to be recounted out loud.

"I hated that night," Joseph said. "We all did. And I know terrible accidents like Tommy's happen from time to time. But, I consider that young man my friend and, I've gotta tell you, being there with him that night brought me back and I didn't like it at all. I felt responsible." Then, his tone suddenly shifted to something less contemplative. "Now, his accident didn't happen at the mill - which I hope you all know," he said. "In fact, it really had very little to do with the mill. But, still, it brought me back to that night in Fall River and it made me think about all of you and how we all came here with a lot of hope. I think I'd be right to say that each of you, like me, felt like we were building something different when we came here."

Again, heads nodded. "Well, I haven't lost that vision," he said, sounding a little brighter. "This place is whatever we make it and we're going to make it different." More heads nodded and Joseph began to feel encouraged. "We're going to make it better than anything any of us left behind. Nobody should have to risk life or limb just to put a roof over their families' heads." A few voices from the congregation called out their approval. "And they won't have to in Edith's Hollow!" Joseph said enthusiastically. "Our mill will be the safest mill in Massachusetts! It'll be the safest in the country! We can make it better and we will. And I'm vowing to you right here, right now, that nobody who works there will ever have to come to work and worry about whether they or their children or their husbands or wives will come home at the end of the day…" some of the congregation broke out into applause, "…*with* all their limbs!" Joseph added, causing even more cheers and applause.

The congregation grew quiet again and Joseph once again grew solemn. He looked from face to face. Most of the people in the congregation were sitting in families with their spouses and children around them. "I don't want to lose another person," he said, more quietly and soberly than before. "And we don't have to." He paused. "We can do this," he said, sounding like he was convincing himself as much as his audience. "We've *got to* do this."

With that, he stepped down from the podium and took his seat.

When services were over, it seemed like everyone wanted to talk to Joseph. Most just wanted to shake his hand and thank him and some wanted to offer suggestions. A few had tears in their eyes as they told him how much this meant to them. It felt good.

As he and Edith walked home, though, the gravity of his promises began to sink in. The weight was heavy. But, any fears or doubts that he felt were equally matched by a sense of determination. He had meant what he said; He *had to* make his vision a reality. He *had to* make the mill as safe as humanly possible.

A couple days before his church-service speech, Joseph had ridden back up to Fall River to visit Tommy. It had only been twenty-four hours since Tommy's surgery and, as he hoped, he was there when Tommy woke up. With a little finagling, he was able to find a moment alone with him and he quickly took the opportunity to tell Tommy that, if anybody ever knew that his accident had happened in the mill, the mill would close down and Tommy's Dad would lose his job. He rehearsed with him the story about being thrown from Joseph's buggy and getting his arm run over. Tommy promised Joseph to never tell anyone their secret.

Tommy came home a few days later on Monday. That same day, Mr. Hill returned from a business trip and Joseph visited him in his home. He didn't spend much time on small talk. "I have something important I need to talk to you about," he said to his business partner shortly after sitting down.

Mr. Hill leaned back in his chair and folded his hands across his waist, preparing for whatever might be coming. "Go on," he said; "I'm listening."

"It's about the safety of our employees," Joseph began.

Mr. Hill's shoulders fell a little, relieved that the "important" thing Joseph wanted to talk with him about wasn't something he would have deemed more serious. "I suppose this has something to do with that Baines boy?" Mr. Hill interrupted. "It's terrible what happened to him."

"Well – yes – sort of," Joseph stumbled a bit. "I mean, his accident didn't actually happen *in* the mill or, really, while he was on the job but still, it brought back some bad memories. It got me thinking a lot about the accidents you see in a mill. You know what I'm talking about, I'm sure."

"Mmm hmm," Mr. Hill said, nodding his head.

"…And, I feel like there's more we can do to prevent those sorts of things from happening in our mill. I'm sure there has to be more we can do."

"So what do you have in mind?" Mr. Hill asked.

Joseph began the speech he had rehearsed in his mind, talking at length about making the mill a safer place to work. Hill mostly just nodded politely, giving the issue a little lip-service but without any urgency. Joseph didn't relent, though.

"I'm sorry, Mr. Hill," he finally said to him in a moment of frankness, "but you haven't experienced mill work the way the rest of us have. It's different when you are the one standing at the machine every day. All of those workers – myself included – know what it's like to come home one day after work with your whole life changed because of some unfortunate accident that happened to you or someone you love. And you get up and you go back to work the next morning because, what else are you going to do? But you never stop wondering when the next accident is going to happen and who it's going to happen to.

I know what I'm asking for probably isn't popular among mill owners. There might not be another mill in a hundred miles putting time and money into preventing accidents but who cares? We don't have to be like them. If we do this, it will mean everything to our workers. And you know what else? People will *want* to work for us – even if our wages aren't good."

Mr. Hill raised his eyebrows. Joseph finally had his attention.

"If we put a roof over their heads and give them a place to work that's safer than any other mill out there, we can pay them less and they'll stick around; I'm sure of it," Joseph added.

"Well," Mr. Hill started, sounding like he was deep in thought, "there is one thing we could do."

"What is it?" Joseph asked eagerly.

"I've heard of a couple of mills in Boston that have started using guards on their machines that are supposed to keep people from getting caught in them and what not. I suppose I could visit one and see what it's all about."

"Yes," Joseph said. "You should."

"This sort of thing costs money, though, Joseph. I really don't know if it's going to be feasible for us."

"Just look into it," Joseph urged. "Do it as a favor to me."

"Alright," Mr. Hill agreed. "I'll arrange a visit to Boston."

"This week?" Joseph pressed.

Hill chuckled. "You're a persistent little bugger when you want something, you know that?"

Joseph smiled but didn't break his gaze.

"Yes!" Mr. Hill said. "I'll go this week."

Joseph didn't wait on Hill. He started making changes right away. First, he adjusted the schedule. Early starts and late nights meant there were a lot of sleepy workers running a lot of powerful machinery. That didn't sit well with him. So, he pushed everyone's start time back by an hour. Then he got stricter about breaks. Nobody was allowed to skip theirs, no matter what. He knew Mr. Hill wouldn't agree with these changes so he made sure not to tell him.

A few weeks later, guards were installed on all the machines. "I'm actually impressed," Hill told Joseph when he returned from

Boston, sounding surprised. "Those guard things seem to really do what they're supposed to. But they're not cheap," he emphasized. Joseph insisted, though, offering to cover some of the cost out of his own pocket and suggesting that they cut back on supplies in the company store for the month to free up some funds.

Unsurprisingly, all these changes made Joseph popular – both at the mill and throughout the town. His policies had the exact effect he had hoped they would: people felt safe. They didn't wake up with anxiety when it was time to start work on Monday mornings and they didn't mind letting their children take jobs in the mill. There was hardly a day that passed without somebody in the street or at work stopping Joseph to thank him or to slap his back. Four months after the guards had been installed and the hours adjusted, there had not been a single accident and he couldn't be more proud.

Word spread. Workers wrote home to friends and family that the mill in Edith's Hollow was safer than any they had worked at and the hours were much better too. It began to gain a reputation through the region. When Mr. Hill was on business in Boston or Fall River, strangers would approach him, eager to tell him that they knew one of his employees and ask him if he was hiring. They not only wanted to work for him and Joseph, but they were willing to work for cheap.

The timing couldn't have been better. Just as the mill's popularity began to spread among the labor pool, Mr. Hill made a new connection that he was very excited about. One evening, he and his wife attended a dinner in Boston at a social club they were members of. It was the kind of thing the couple loved to be a part of. The men wore tuxedos, the women wore fancy dresses, and the tables were adorned with white linen and doily centerpieces.

The club was hosting Massachusetts Senator, Henry Dawes, as its special guest. Mr. and Mrs. Hill arrived early, as usual, and found only one other couple at their table when they were seated. They struck up a conversation right away. The pair was much younger than the Hills and a few other things quickly became apparent: they were friendly, ambitious, and earnest – all traits that Mr. Hill admired. On top of that, they kept referring to Senator Dawes as "Hank."

"Do you know the Senator personally?" Mrs. Hill asked.

148

"We do," the young woman replied. "Charles is a member of his staff," she said, gesturing to her husband.

Mr. Hill perked up. "Good for you," he said. "You must be a bright young man."

Charles straightened in his seat a little. "Oh, just lucky I suppose," he said.

"He's very bright," his wife interjected. "He has a college degree from Harvard University. He can tell you all about it. He's bright and he's a hard worker."

"A University man?" said Mr. Hill. "Good for you, indeed. Our country could use more young men like you. Do you think you'll stay in politics?"

"Well, it's hard to say. I mean, you know what Emerson said: *'Do not go where the path may lead, go instead where there is no path and leave a trail.'* He was a Harvard man, too, you know; I'm sure you're familiar with his works."

Mr. and Mrs. Hill each nodded, quietly hoping that they wouldn't be called on to demonstrate just how deep their knowledge of Emerson ran.

"We studied him quite a lot at Harvard," the young man continued. "I find politics interesting and, of course, a politician can exert a good deal of influence over his fellow man. But I suppose there's a level of irony in an individualist – which of course, I consider myself to be – in entering politics in order to help his fellow countrymen blaze a path of independence from the State. Am I right?" he said with a hearty laugh.

Mr. Hill joined the laughter although he wasn't entirely sure what he was laughing about.

"Well, there certainly is more than one way to make your own way in the world and to influence others while you're at it," Hill said.

"Yes, I couldn't agree more," the young man replied. "What is it that you do, Mr. Hill?"

"I'm in the textile industry. I own a mill south of here."

"Oh," the young man said, somewhat curtly. A brief, awkward pause followed. Clearly, the textile industry wasn't intellectually titillating enough for his musings.

"We can talk about my wife and I later, though. Tell me more about your time at Harvard," Mr. Hill said, quickly saving the conversation. "A Harvard education must be a fascinating experience. We would love to hear about it."

The young man's eyes lit up. "It is, indeed, a fascinating experience Mr. Hill. You know, I had an economics professor that had a theory about capitalism in America. Perhaps this will interest you."

The Hills listened while their young friend moved seamlessly through an array of scholarly theories and while his wife sat next to him, beaming with pride. The Hills, who were quite adept at navigating high society, smiled and encouraged and complimented until the young couple had warmed up quite nicely to their new friends. By the time dessert was served, the young couple had offered to introduce the Hills to Senator Dawes and the Hills, feeling they had won some sort of social game, happily accepted.

The Hills' conversation with the Senator couldn't have gone better. When Mr. Hill mentioned that he owned a cotton mill, Mr. Dawes perked up. He explained that he was good friends with an Army General who oversaw several of the outposts throughout the West and who was having trouble keeping his men in uniforms because of slow production from the mill their supplier was using. He offered to introduce Hill to the uniform supplier and Hill jumped at the opportunity. He and his wife stayed another three days in Boston while the meeting was arranged.

Hill toured the uniform supplier's facility, said all the right things, and knew all the right questions to ask. He was invited back the next day for a follow-up meeting and, by the time he left, he had secured a contract that doubled the mill's business overnight. That afternoon, he quickly penned Joseph a letter for speedy delivery before he began making preparations to return to Edith's Hollow. The letter simply said "New contract. This is big. I'll be back shortly to discuss. If anybody asks if we are hiring, the answer is Yes!"

Mr. Hill was right; the new contract *was* big and it brought with it a host of issues for Joseph to solve. The most pressing one was a dire need for more labor. It was all Joseph could think about for days. The mill needed to generate twice as much work but they couldn't afford to pay twice as much in wages. He thought about increasing hours but he just couldn't bring himself to do it.

Then, one morning, he woke up with an idea. The mill's reputation was growing and people wanted to work there. Surely, he could capitalize on that. Perhaps if he did even more to keep workers happy, he wouldn't have to pay them as much. He decided to try it out. He travelled to Fall River three times that week and, by the end of the week, had recruited enough new workers to nearly double the mill's workforce. Instead of promising them decent wages, though, he promised them a more comfortable life, and they accepted.

Then, he went to work making good on his word. He had extra housing built so that nobody had to share quarters if they didn't want to. He recruited a rancher to move to Edith's Hollow and then bought two milking cows and a dozen chickens so the mill's employees could pick up milk and eggs at any time for free. And, he established the first Wednesday in July as "Mill Day" where the mill closed at lunch time and the entire town was invited to a picnic with food and games. Suddenly, the mill was unlike anything its workers had ever experienced and recruits from all around jumped at the opportunity to come work for Joseph.

One of the new recruits had a brother who worked for a Boston newspaper that ran a story on the mill. The story was buried deep in the issue but it was noticed by Senator Dawes who took great pleasure in learning that the mill he had referred the army to was apparently worthy of high praise. The next week, he made a trip to Edith's Hollow where he toured the facility with Joseph and Mr. Hill and where the two men honored their Senator friend with a parade. At the end of the parade, the Senator gave a speech. He praised Joseph's leadership and, naturally, took some credit for the mill's success and the townspeople's happiness.

There was, however, a downside to all of this. With so much new business and a flood of new employees, the mill quickly began running out of space. One hot, summer afternoon, Joseph and Mr. Hill sat in Joseph's office and ran some numbers; They didn't like the results. They figured they would have to nearly double their number of machines to accommodate their growth and the only way to do that was to build a larger mill, which they didn't have the time or the money for. As they leaned back in their chairs and brainstormed solutions to their problem, Joseph had an idea.

"What if we create a night shift?" he proposed.

Mr. Hill raised his eyebrows. "Go on," he said.

"Well," Joseph explained, "we could bring on more employees in the space we already have if we have half of the work force working during the day and the other half working at night."

Mr. Hill nodded his head contemplatively. "Maybe," he said. "But we'd have to run the machines nearly nonstop. I don't like that. The strain on the equipment would be enormous."

"That's true," Joseph said. "The savings would be enormous, too, though – at least compared to the cost of building more space."

"Hmm," Hill said. "Maybe we need to sleep on it."

Joseph's solution wasn't perfect and Mr. Hill required some convincing but, after a few days of discussing it, they decided it was the best option they had. It was simple and cost-effective. Mr. Hill reluctantly conceded.

Judy Wilhelm was among the workers assigned to the nightshift. She was one of the original residents of Edith's Hollow still remaining along with her yappy Scottish Terrier whom she called Leonard after her late husband. She had been a weaver in the Fall River mill before it burned down. On the day of the fire, she happened to be home, sick with a terrible cough.

She was fortunate not to have lost anyone in the fire but, that was largely because she had nobody to lose. Her husband had died eight years before, when they were each 52, leaving her, for the first time in her life, in need of a job. She had never had children and had lost touch with her two sisters who each lived in different states. So, she bought a dog and found work at the mill. The dog barked incessantly but it was better than silence.

When Joseph asked her to come to Edith's Hollow, she couldn't see any reason not to. She took almost no convincing. For the second time in her life, she was in need of work and she wasn't inclined to turn down an offer.

Judy wasn't the friendly type. She liked to be where people were, she just didn't like to talk to them. She did, however, like to sound a frequent "hmph" of disapproval when somebody she was eavesdropping on said something she didn't like. She attended church each Sunday and sat on the front row in a corner where she was noticed but not bothered. She pursed her lips tightly through each service and promptly left at the end of the closing hymn.

Given her aversion to conversation, very few of her co-workers had ever spoken with her. So, when Joseph was awoken late one night by Emory Green pounding on his door, Emory was unable to tell him the name of the person who was, at that moment, lying on the mill floor, grasping at her face, and crying out in pain. He was, however, able to explain to Joseph that an overhead belt in the weaving room had snapped in half and the severed end that flew through the air with great speed forcefully struck one of the women.

Emory was eighteen years old along with his new bride, Eliza. He still had a few faint freckles and a slight gap between his front teeth. He had worked in a cotton mill since he was nine, which made him more experienced than some of his older colleagues. Joseph had recently appointed him as general supervisor of the night shift, but it had little to do with his experience. He wasn't a strong leader but he was loyal and eager to please. Joseph knew he would do whatever was asked of him.

Joseph quickly threw on some clothes and sprinted to the mill with Emory by his side. He had seen the thick leather belts that ran along the ceilings of cotton mills do serious harm to people and property when they broke. They didn't, however, usually break when they were as new as the belts in his mill. As he ran, he could hear in his head Mr. Hill's repeated warnings that running the mill day and night would cause this sort of thing to happen.

"Has anyone informed Mr. Hill of the accident?" he asked before the two men reached the mill.

"No," Emory said. "I was the only one sent to get somebody and I came directly to you."

"Good," Joseph said. "Make sure nobody goes to him." Then, realizing how his instructions must have sounded, he quickly added, "there's no need to wake him and his wife at this hour."

When they got to the mill, they climbed the stairs to the third floor to find Judy still on the ground with her face held tightly in her hands. A considerable crowd had gathered around her. Joseph acted decisively. He immediately walked to her and picked her up in his arms. "Get back to work!" he bellowed as he turned toward the exit. "And nobody wake Mr. Hill!" he added as he reached the stairwell.

Emory was standing in the doorway. Joseph addressed him before exiting. "Send home everyone that works on this floor," he said, "and find somebody to fix that belt. Even if you have to wake them up – it has to be done tonight. Nobody should be on this floor until that belt is fixed and all signs of the accident have been cleaned up."

Emory nodded vigorously. "Yes, sir," he said. "I'll get it done."

Judy was small and light. It wasn't difficult for Joseph to carry her to his house where he took her inside and set her gently on a chair. "You'll be OK, Judy," he said.

She couldn't be consoled. It was clear she was in immense pain and she was beginning to hyperventilate. "I can't see. I can't see!" she said several times.

"I'll make sure you're taken care of, Judy," Joseph said. "Please, try to calm down."

He went into another room and came out with a rag that he tore into strips. Just then, Edith emerged from the back, yawning and rubbing her eyes. "Oh, good," Joseph said when he saw her. "Sweetheart, go fetch me a bucket of water."

"What's going on, Daddy?" Edith asked.

"Ms. Judy Willhelm has had an accident. Please, I need some water right away."

"But, Da…" Edith began.

"Now! Edith," Joseph said more forcefully.

Edith left the house as Joseph kneeled down in front of Judy and examined her injury more closely. "Can you move your hands so I can see what's happened?" he asked. When she did, he was disappointed to see that things were worse than he had thought. She was bleeding badly out of one eye, which was swollen shut and discharging some kind of liquid in addition to the blood. He tried not to react. "We'll get you taken care of," he said as he used one of the strips he had torn to wipe the blood and fluid from around her eye.

"I can't see," she said again.

"I know," Joseph said as he got up. He went to his kitchen and found a bottle of whisky which he opened and held out. "Here," he said, "take a drink of this. It will help."

"I don't drink liquor," Judy said through her short, frantic breaths.

"Don't think of it as liquor; Think of it as medicine. It will dull the pain."

Judy wasn't in a state to object so she nodded her head. She had returned both of her hands to her injured eye but she reached out with one of them to take the bottle. She took a swig and handed it back to Joseph. "I'm going to wrap this around your head, over your eyes," he said, holding out one of the strips of cloth. "Maybe it will help the bleeding." Judy nodded again.

As he was tying the strip of cloth in the back of Judy's head, Edith returned grasping the handle of her bucket of water with both hands.

"Edith, bring that bucket over here," he said. She promptly obeyed. He dipped another strip of cloth in the water and cleaned the rest of the blood off of Judy's face. "I need to go prepare a horse to take Ms. Willhelm to Fall River," he said to Edith. "I'll be back in the morning. While I'm gone, I need you to clean up this blood," he gestured to some blood on the floor, "and then go to the mill and clean up the blood in the weaving room."

"Tonight?" Edith asked in shock.

"Yes, tonight. Right away, in fact."
"All by myself?"

"Edith, I don't have time to debate the matter. You'll clean up our floor then go to the mill and clean up the floor in the weaving room, do you understand?"

"Yes, Father," she said obediently.

"Find Emory Green when you get there. He can direct you to the spot."

With that, Joseph left the house. A moment later, he was lifting Judy up onto a horse which the two shared on the ride to the Fall River hospital. When they arrived, he sat on a wooden bench while Judy was tended to. He put his head in his hands and sighed heavily. He was frustrated that Judy's accident was witnessed by so many of the workers. It was going to be a black eye on the mill's reputation.

For a long time, he sat and stewed over how this was going to impact business and his own reputation and worried about how he was going to contain it. Anger started boiling up inside but there really was nobody to be angry at. So, it eventually settled into a general grumpiness as he drifted off to sleep.

The doctor couldn't do anything for Judy's eye. One of the nurses woke Joseph up and explained that Judy would have to wear a patch for the rest of her life. He shook his head in frustration. Any hope he had for an injury that the townspeople might quickly forget about vanished. He thanked the nurse, told her he would return later that day to pay the bill, and headed back to Edith's Hollow.

The day shift at the mill had already begun when he got back into town. Before stopping by work, though, he checked in on Edith who was just waking up when he arrived. As he came through the front door, she emerged from the back of the house, rubbing her eyes.

"Good morning, sweetheart," he said.

She puffed out her bottom lip into a frown and scowled back at him.

He dropped down to one knee and stretched out his arms. "Come here," he said. "Give me a hug."

She didn't move.

"You're mad about last night?"

She stared back coldly. "You shouldn't have made me go to the mill by myself. I didn't want to go."

"But you went, right?"

She folded her arms and refused to engage.

Joseph took a deep breath and exhaled. "Edith, I know you didn't want to go but, you're growing up now, and there are going to be lots of things you don't want to do that you're just going to have to do anyway. That's part of getting older."

She stared at the floor, her defiant frown only growing deeper.

"I'm sorry I had to leave you alone all night but Ms. Willhelm was very hurt and she needed somebody to tend to her. Did you clean up all the blood at the mill?"

Edith nodded her head silently.

"Did anybody help you?"

She nodded her head again.

"How many? Who were they?" he asked, sounding a bit urgent.

Edith shrugged her shoulders. "Just Mr. Emory Green," she said. "He didn't let anyone else help. He made the rest of them get to work."

"Good," Joseph said, relieved. "Good for him. Thank you for doing that, Edith. I'm proud of you."

She kept staring at the ground.

"Are you sure I can't have a hug?" he asked. She shook her head again. "OK," he said, giving up. He stood up from the floor. "Go ahead and get dressed, then, so I can drop you off at the Baines."

Edith huffed to make sure Joseph knew she was still angry. However, she enjoyed going to the Baines so she wasn't going to resist. She retreated back to her room and Joseph retreated to his to wash his face and change his clothes. He was exhausted but he didn't have time to rest.

After dropping Edith off, he went to the mill. He first headed up to the weaving room to see if there was any sign of the accident from the night before. He was pleased to see there wasn't. He stood under the belt that had broken and watched it moving until he saw the seam pass from where it had been repaired. The repair wasn't as clean and professional as he would have liked but it would have to do.

After checking in with each team to make sure things were running smoothly, he headed back home where he hitched up his wagon and drove it over to Judy's house. He parked the wagon around the back where it was less likely to be seen from passersby and then packed up all of her belongings. Although she had more than many of her fellow mill workers, her belongings were few enough that he was able to finish the job in a little more than an hour. The last thing he removed from the home was her yappy dog, Leonard, which he held on his lap on the way back to Fall River.

Before returning to the hospital, he spent some time driving around town until he found available, inexpensive housing. After settling on a place, he spoke with the landlord to secure a unit and told him he would be back shortly. Then he got Judy.

He waited until they were leaving the hospital before breaking the news to her. Once she saw all of her belongings in Joseph's

157

wagon, he had to tell her what was going on. "Judy," he said, "you're not coming back to Edith's Hollow."

She looked at him utterly confused. "Of course I am," she said.

Joseph shook his head. "The mill won't have you." The expression of disbelief on her face begged for an explanation. "It's not safe for the other workers," he added. "You're half blind now and those machines are dangerous. I just won't have it. I'm sorry."

Judy pursed her lips. "Then I'll find something else to do," she said. "There are plenty of services the folks of Edith's Hollow need. I'll get by. Let's stop this nonsense and take me back home, please."

"What home, Judy? Your house was owned by the mill. Where will you live?"

An expression of disbelief again flashed across her face but, when Joseph stood firm, it quickly changed into an expression of defeat. Her eyes grew wide and she shook her head. "But, what will I do?" she said, not really speaking to Joseph.

He had never seen Judy look so vulnerable. "I'm not going to leave you on the streets, Judy," he assured her. "I've found you a place to live here in Fall River and the mill will pay for it. Hop in the wagon and I'll take you there."

She looked at Joseph out of the corner of her eye, suspicious and unsure of his proposition. Still, she got in the wagon and the two drove to the housing Joseph had found. The unit was one of several in a house that had been converted into separate living quarters. It was dirty and dank and didn't have indoor plumbing. Judy looked around with her lip curled up on one side in disapproval.

"This place is awful," she said.

"But it's free," Joseph replied. "I'll make sure all the expenses are covered." She clearly wasn't impressed. "We'll also give you some money to live on each month."

"How much?"

"Twelve dollars."

"For what?" she asked.

Joseph furrowed his brow.

"I'm no fool, Mr. Fridman. You must want something in return."

"Well," Joseph said, sounding like somebody about to give a confession, "there is one thing. You would need to promise never to come back and never to tell anyone that you got your injury in our mill."

Judy's face lit up with understanding. "Oh, I see," she said. "So, this has nothing to do with you feeling bad for this little old lady, does it?"

"Judy, please..." Joseph started.

"No, no. I understand. Your mill has gained quite the reputation, hasn't it? I suppose you have, too. And you can't risk that. It wouldn't be good for business, would it?"

"Well..." Joseph started again, worried he was losing control of the situation.

"It's fine, Mr. Fridman," Judy interrupted. "I'll do it."

Joseph looked back at her, pleasantly surprised.

"But not if you're going to put me up in a dump like this and not for a measly twelve dollars a month."

Joseph's expression quickly fell. "This place isn't so bad," he contested.

"It's awful, Mr. Fridman. I won't live here. If you want my cooperation, find me something better."

Joseph sighed then surrendered. "Fine," he said. "Come with me. I have something in mind." He drove her to another apartment he had come across in his search earlier that day. This one was in a better part of town and was much cleaner with indoor plumbing.

"No," Judy said before they even went inside. "It's too small."

"Now you listen here," Joseph said, agitation rising. "I gave you a job and a place to live when you needed both. It's not my fault that you went off and got yourself injured but, now that you have, I'm offering to help you get by. I owe you nothing. Take my offer or leave it. This isn't a negotiation."

"What about your secret?" Judy asked. "You think I won't tell? Because I will."

"Go ahead and tell the world," Joseph said. "See if I care. It'll come down to your word against mine and who do you think people are going to believe? I've got powerful friends, Ms. Wilhelm. You do not want to go against me."

Judy stared at Joseph with narrowing eyes, her lips pressed tightly together, looking like she might be ready for a fight. Joseph stared back firmly.

"Fine," she finally said. "You win, Mr. Fridman." She picked up her dog which was lying at her feet, climbed down off of the wagon, and stood at the door of the apartment.

Joseph found the landlord and got the keys then let Judy and her dog inside. Not a single word was exchanged between them as Joseph unpacked all of her things from his wagon. When he was finished, he handed her the keys.

"I'll make sure you get $17.50 a month," he said.

She stared back coldly without responding.

"I'm not a bad person," Joseph said.

Judy huffed. "That's between you and God, Mr. Fridman. It was nice knowing you."

"Take care, Judy," he said as he turned towards the door and left.

CHAPTER 14

Judy Willhelm was promptly replaced by a small family with two young children who moved into her house a couple days after she had been moved out. Right after moving Judy into her new home, Joseph called on a few prospective employees that he selected from a list he kept. His third visit was to the Smiths who were anxious to find work and willing to work for low wages. Neither Mr. nor Mrs. Smith had ever worked in a mill before but they both were seeking employment. Joseph was pleased. In several ways, he felt like he had traded in Judy for higher value.

"Judy's just fine. Her injury looked far worse than it actually was," he told anybody who asked – and several who didn't. "At the end of the day, it was really just a nick. I think it frightened her more than anything. Funny thing, though: she got back to Fall River and started feeling like that's where she belonged more than Edith's Hollow. She thanked me for her time with us and asked if I wouldn't mind bringing her things to her and, of course, I obliged."

Over the years, Judy's dog and its incessant yapping had been the topic of conversation more than she had been. So, nobody dwelt on her departure. She was quickly erased from the town's memory.

A few weeks after the Smiths began work, Mr. Hill approached Joseph with some good news. He had just returned from a trip to Boston where he had visited with Senator Dawes. The Senator, who was happy with the experience he had had with the Edith's Hollow mill (and was also happy with the good publicity it had afforded him) offered to introduce Hill to a second military supplier who was looking for another mill it could offload some extra work onto. Hill enthusiastically agreed to the meeting and, even though it wasn't true, confirmed that they had capacity for more work. Within a few days, Mr. Hill had secured the contract.

Hill was too much a man of business to let anything stand in the way of embracing a good opportunity. He figured they would simply have to create the capacity they needed. When he and Joseph sat down to work out the details, they determined they would need to build an expansion to the mill and increase their labor force by 50%. Mr. Hill urged Joseph to increase everyone's hours in order to reduce the number of new hires. Joseph adamantly refused but, Mr. Hill was unrelenting. He felt sure that he was nearly maxed out on debt, which meant the mill would have to find ways to expand on a thin budget.

Finally, Joseph compromised. He said he would agree to a modest increase in hours, slightly reducing the need for new employees. Then, to appease Mr. Hill, he took things a step further. He identified several people on his list of recruits who he was sure would work for even lower wages than he was already offering. He also suggested that they save money by purchasing used machines instead of new ones for the expansion. Mr. Hill liked his ideas. So, with that, the two men went to work.

Joseph left the meeting with a nagging concern that he kept to himself. A new, un-experienced workforce combined with used machines running day and night was a recipe for accidents. Secretly, he began to prepare for the worst.

One Monday morning, when the day shift arrived, everyone was surprised and perplexed to see some unusual construction going on inside the mill. Joseph had ordered tall, physical barriers to be erected between every work station in every part of the mill, new and old. When the barriers were completed, each work station was enclosed on three sides with only the workers' backs exposed to open space. Joseph could walk down the aisles and see into each station but it was impossible for the workers to see what anyone else was doing.

Next, Joseph eliminated the use of teams, causing no small stir throughout the mill. Instead of three-person teams manning the machines, the workers would have to learn to do the job of three all at once and no more than one person would be allowed in a work station at a time. Emory Green, the night shift supervisor, voiced his concerns about this change to Joseph, which was entirely against Emory's nature.

"Honestly, Mr. Fridman, I just can't see how it's going to work," he said to Joseph while standing inside his office with the door closed behind him. Emory had stopped by near the end of the day shift to speak with his boss. "It just seems impossible. Take a spinning mule, for instance. You would have to mind the front end, while at the same time, watching for broken threads that need fixed. If you see one, you would have to rush over to it in a hurry before the severed ends become caught up in the machinery and then rush back to mind the front again."

"That's right," Joseph said matter-of-factly. "That's exactly how it's going to work. Don't worry, Emory. I promise you it can be done. It'll be fine. We're so used to things being done a certain way that we're convinced anything else is impossible. That's just not the case, though. We just need to change our mindset. I know this is a novel approach but that's what makes it so important. Think about it," he said enthusiastically, "we're going to revolutionize the way that mills are operated! And Emory, you're going to be part of it! Your role in all of this won't be forgotten."

Emory dutifully nodded his head and said, "I guess I hadn't really thought of it that way."

"You need to understand why we're doing all this, Emory,' Joseph continued. "These changes are being made out of deep concern for each employee's well-being. Isolated, blocked off work stations with one worker in each station will eliminate distractions and less distractions means more safety. It will also be good for the mind. We're creating little islands of serenity for each employee. They're going to love it."

"Oh, OK," Emory said. "I can see that."

"I knew you would," Joseph said. "Now, I need you to do something for me. I need you to help spread the vision, OK? If you hear workers complaining, explain to them why this is for their own good. Can you do that?"

Emory nodded his head.

Joseph stood up from behind his desk and stretched out his hand to Emory. "Good man." he said. "I appreciate you stopping by. I had actually been meaning to talk with you about this. You're a smart man; I knew you'd get it. You'll see, it's going to work out really well."

The two shook hands and exchanged some parting pleasantries while Joseph ushered Emory out the door.

The workers didn't love the changes quite the way Joseph had promised but most of them endured them. Two of the workers, however, were so upset that they quit. They were easily replaced but Joseph quickly recognized the need to do something to smooth things over. So, he raised everybody's wages. He was supposed to consult with Mr. Hill on any financial decisions but he knew Mr. Hill would say no so he moved forward without him. The higher wages did the trick. The grumbling quieted.

Joseph's final measure was to give strict orders to Emory that, if any accidents occurred, he was to follow a simple, two-step procedure. First, if the accident was witnessed by another worker, Emory was to take that worker to Joseph's office, make sure he or she stayed there for the time being, and lock the office door. Second, Emory was to come directly to Joseph without alerting anyone else of the accident. Again, Joseph explained, this was designed to reduce distractions for the other employees and encourage an atmosphere of peace and tranquility throughout the mill. Emory said he understood and that, really, it made a lot of sense.

Joseph didn't have to wait long to put his system to the test. In the middle of September, just as the leaves were beginning to turn, Emory came to Joseph's home early one morning with more bad news. As the night shift was nearing its end, Emory walked the floors of the mill and the grounds outside, as he was accustomed to doing each day. When he came to the water wheel, he thought he saw something bobbing and churning in the rushing waters that pushed the powerful wheel. He moved closer and, upon examination, recognized the lifeless body of Adam Tingey.

Adam was nearly 30 but, because he was neither very bright nor very skilled, he was tasked with several assignments that a person half his age could have performed. One of his jobs was to periodically check the water wheel for debris and obstructions. Joseph and Emory surmised that Adam must have been attempting to remove an object from the water when he fell in. When they pulled his body out, they discovered his coat was stuck in part of the machinery of the wheel, which helped explain why he hadn't escaped and why his body hadn't been pushed downstream.

Emory knew he was under strict orders to never speak of injuries at the mill to anybody. But nobody had ever died at the mill before so Joseph made sure to emphasize his orders again. "His poor wife," he said to his young supervisor. "What a tragedy it would be for her if this became fodder for town gossip. Let's honor Adam's memory and be kind to his wife by making sure this never gets out."

"Sure," said Emory, nodding his head. "That makes sense."

Joseph let Emory go home before loading Adam's body into his wagon which he then covered with a sheet. Adam didn't have any children which, at this moment, Joseph was glad for. Still, though, as he drove to the house where he knew Adam's wife was probably just waking up, the crushing feeling in his chest, cold sweat on his palms, and dark memories of his own wife's death all returned in a rush.

Joseph took a deep breath. He couldn't afford his feelings to overwhelm him. There were arrangements that needed tended to before the day shift began. When he got to Adam's house, he quickly composed himself and knocked on the front door. When Rachel answered, he kindly asked her if she would step outside. He told her there had been an accident at the mill that involved her husband and that she needed to come with him to Fall River.

Joseph waited until they were several miles outside of town before revealing everything to Adam's young bride. He pulled the wagon over and told her there was something more she needed to know. She screamed when he walked her to the back of the wagon, told her of her husband's death, and pulled down the part of the sheet that was covering Adam's face. He was grateful they were far enough out of town that nobody could hear her or see her sobbing.

He didn't tell her they had found Adam by the water wheel. Instead, he said that, during everybody's morning break, Emory saw Adam walk away from the mill along a path that followed the river. Emory figured he was just taking a walk. But, an hour after the break was over, when he still hadn't returned to the mill, Emory went looking for him and found him drowned in the river.

Joseph asked Rachel if she had family or anyone she could go to. She said her parents were in Rhode Island which was too far for Joseph and her to ride to. So, he told her he would pay for her to stay in a hotel for a few days so she could send for them and that, if she would let him know when they were arriving, he would return on the same day with her things.

When Rachel calmed down from her crying, she became wide-eyed and silent. She barely said a word the rest of the trip and only nodded when Joseph said anything to her. He felt terrible for her. When they arrived at the hotel, he asked for one of their nicest rooms, hoping to make her as comfortable as possible. Before dropping her off at her door, he repeated his instructions about sending for him to bring her things when she heard back from her parents and, again, she just nodded.

After leaving the hotel, Joseph turned to the business of Adam's body. He found a mortuary that he thought might take care of it for him but the owner asked a lot of questions and wanted some paperwork kept on file. So, he left and rode to the poorest part of town he knew of, knowing that things were done differently there. His instincts were correct. After asking around a bit, he learned of a nearby mortuary where you could also get your hair cut or your face shaved, which sounded exactly like the kind of place he was looking for.

The mortuary owner was happy to comply with Joseph's requests when he told him how much he would pay. The owner explained that there was a nearby cemetery that conducted mass burials every month where they disposed of people who had died in the poor houses or the prisons. They put them all in a mass grave with no coffins. He said he could arrange for Adam's body to be included in the next one and Joseph said that would be fine.

He rode back to Edith's Hollow with mixed feelings. He was relieved to have navigated another accident without any unwelcomed attention from the community. At the same time, though, he was beginning to worry. The accidents were starting to feel unwieldy. The cost of hospitals and lodging and mortuaries added up. If accidents kept happening, as he was sure they would, he didn't know how long the mill could keep up. He needed to find another way to deal with them, and soon.

Winter was cold with plenty of snow. There were two accidents in December and three in January. Each required hurried trips to Fall River, hospital bills, moving arrangements, and new recruits. Joseph's skill at concealing the accidents grew but so did his anxiety. Each incident taxed his time, energy, and emotions. They were expensive, too. Sometimes he paid the costs out of his own pocket, sometimes he paid them out of the mill's funds. But he couldn't shake the feeling that neither was sustainable.

The machines presented their own set of challenges. Sometimes a break led to an accident and sometimes an accident led to a break. Whatever the case, Joseph couldn't risk hiring locals to repair them. He couldn't afford the questions that would follow or the possibility of word getting back to Mr. Hill that his prediction was right; the strain of running the mill day and night was taking its toll. So, he fixed the damaged machines himself. He was amateur for sure, though, and, to his chagrin, the breaks he fixed often broke again.

February provided some relief with no injuries but March made up for it with five. The bright side was, by the end of winter, he had learned a few tricks about recruiting. He discovered that, if he bypassed Fall River for Boston, there were a lot of job seekers that suited his situation nicely. Boston had plenty of immigrants and transplants from out of state. The fewer connections they had, the better he felt about hiring them. Soon, nearly every new employee he hired was single with no family within 500 miles. It helped immensely with keeping the accidents under wraps.

The mill's new extension was finished in April and it was immediately at capacity. Business was booming. Joseph and Hill felt more confident than ever in their enterprise and they reaped the benefits. The Hills built a new home in a picturesque spot in the woods, quite a distance from the rest of the community. To them, it was a dream come true to have a secluded haven of luxury all their own. When Joseph learned of their plans, he was disappointed. To him, it sent the wrong message to everyone else. It felt elitist. But he had to admit, the Hills were usually gone anyway and Edith's Hollow was hardly the tiny, tight-knit community it had started out as.

The house was beautiful. It was surrounded by a short, brick wall topped with a black, wrought iron fence that matched the tall, double gates at the entrance of the estate. The gates' wrought iron was twisted into an intricate design of entangled branches like that of a lively vine. A lever that had been installed in the road outside of the gates caused them to swing open slowly when an approaching carriage ran over it. It felt a little like magic.

The house was tall and white and made mostly of brick. To Joseph, it was a mansion. He was in awe the first time he visited after its completion. The thick, oak front door opened to a large, spacious room with a stained wooden floor. In the center was a spiral staircase that wound its way up to an open, second floor with a running balcony that overlooked the ground level. There were a number of bedrooms upstairs for visitors. If you climbed the stairs, turned to your left, and rounded a corner, you would find yourself in a hallway lined, on one side, by a wall with windows that overlooked the front lawn.

Joseph stood and gaped out one of the windows to the grassy lawn below. He had never been somebody who dreamed of having fancy things but, to his surprise, he was completely enamored by the Hills' new home. He could picture himself living in it and he liked the way it felt. He could see himself standing at the top of the stairs of *his* house and welcoming guests. He could see Edith sitting in the grass in the yard playing with a doll.

It was so foreign to him to imagine any kind of luxury for him and Edith but, '*why?*' he wondered. Why couldn't they have a home like the Hills? Why shouldn't they?

The Hills showed Joseph and Edith around the entire house. When they were finished with the tour, they stayed and visited a while. As they did, Joseph's awe began to decay. By the time he and Edith finished their visit, a sharp feeling of irritation had begun to stir deep in his chest. The question in his mind was morphing from '*why not us?*' to '*why them?*' In her innocent way, Edith seemed to feel some of what he was feeling, too.

"Can we come back and visit again, sometime, Dad?" She said when they were only a few feet past the Hills' gate."

"Of course, sweetheart," Joseph said.

He kept stewing in his thoughts before Edith broke the silence again.

"Dad," she said, "why don't we have a staircase? I think that would be so fun to have one."

"Our house isn't big enough for a staircase," he replied. "To have a staircase, you have to have a 2nd floor and we don't."

"Why not?" she asked.

"That's just not how we built our house," he said, hoping to be done with the conversation so he could return to his thoughts.

"Yeah, but shouldn't we have one if the Hills have one? I mean, you're the boss of the mill too, just like Mr. Hill, aren't you?"

Joseph smiled a subtle smile. She was right. Until Edith said it for him, he couldn't quite put his finger on why he was so irritated. Edith cut to the center of it, though. Why should the Hills be the ones living like royalty in a mansion in the woods? Wasn't Joseph the one who was *really* responsible for the mill's success? He was the one who was up early every morning and stayed at the mill late until everybody had gone home. He was the one who understood what a mill worker wanted and he was the one who had created something that was unlike any mill any of their employees had ever experienced. He was the reason they were getting recognized by newspapers and senators. Meanwhile, the Hills were hardly even around.

Joseph nodded. "You're right, honey," he said to Edith. "I'm the boss, too. Maybe we *should* have a house like the Hills. Or maybe we should just have their house."

Edith laughed. Joseph didn't.

CHAPTER 15

July was stifling. It was rainier than usual, which brought with it a suffocating humidity that vexed everybody in town. It was a constant topic of conversation. Sam preached about it in church, shoppers at Sam's store talked about it as they placed summer squash, cheese wedges, and ears of corn into their baskets, and everybody complained about it at work. Joseph kept every window and door of the mill opened day and night to provide some relief but it barely seemed to help.

Joseph made three trips to Fall River in July – two of them because of injuries in the mill and one to pick up supplies. Each time, he was pleased to find the air a little dryer than in Edith's Hollow, which offered a bit of a silver lining to trips that were otherwise unpleasant. On his third trip, late in the month, he was met by an unwelcomed surprise at the hospital.

He had become pretty good at explaining away his frequent visits to the hospital staff. It took some craftiness – and a lot of lying – but he got by just fine. That all changed, though, one day late in July when he walked through the hospital's front doors and was greeted by a familiar face. Sitting at the front desk was Meredith Morrison, a woman for whom marriage had had the unfortunate effect of a name with sing-song alliteration. Meredith was the third cousin of Joseph's late wife. She and Joseph weren't close by any means but they certainly were well enough acquainted to recognize each other.

"Well hello, Joseph! What a pleasant surprise," she said as he entered the hospital.

Joseph winced when she said his name. He glanced around the room to see if anyone else was in ear shot. Fortunately, nobody was.

"Hi, Meredith. This is a surprise! How long have you been working here?"

"I just started. This is only my fourth day."

Joseph nodded his head. "Good for you," he said. His mind was racing. He had to get out of there quickly.

"I read all about you and that mill of yours in the newspaper article they did. Congratulations! It sounds like things are really going well for you."

Joseph winced again and glanced around. "Thank you," he said in a slightly hushed voice. "Yes, we're happy with the way things are going. You know, I wish I could stay and catch up but I'm actually in a big hurry. I'm headed back home but I thought I'd stop by to check on my friend really quick. Is Ivan McPherson still here?"

Ivan was the last person Joseph had brought to the hospital. He knew that Ivan's stay had ended a few days prior.

Meredith looked down at a book with large pages that lay open on her desk. She turned back a page and then another. "I don't see him in here," she said. "He must have been discharged. I can go ask one of the nurses if they know when he left."

"No, no," Joseph said quickly. "No need for that. I just thought I would check. I'll look in on him next time I'm back in town. It was really nice to see you. Like I said, I've got to run. I have some urgent business I need to tend to back home but I hope things go well for you here. Maybe we'll run into each other again."

"Yes," Meredith said. "It was nice seeing you, too. Have a safe journey.

Joseph walked back out to his buggy. Lying in the back of it on a pile of blood-stained blankets was Emily O'Connor, a middle-aged, Irish immigrant spinster who had been working at the mill for just over a year. Earlier in the day, she had dropped her scissors beneath the machine she was working at and attempted to retrieve them with her foot by getting on the ground and stretching her leg under the contraption. Her dress got caught up in the moving parts and soon she had a terrible gash across her thigh that cut all the way to the bone. It looked like the machine had nearly taken her leg off.

Joseph wrapped the wound tightly and gave her a good amount of hard liquor for the ride. At his request, she had drunk more than half the bottle before they left Edith's Hollow. Her screams had mostly stopped by the time they reached Fall River and she lay quite lethargic in the buggy.

Joseph climbed into the driver's seat and started back home. He didn't know what he was going to do when he got there but he felt an urgency to get out of Fall River as quickly as he could. Several minutes before reaching Edith's Hollow, he passed a trail that cut into the thick forest to his right. Joseph knew this trail. The Hills had recently blazed it for easy access to and from their property when leaving town or returning from the north.

Joseph stopped the buggy. He had an idea. He knew that the Hills were gone – as they often were – for an extended stay out of town. This time, they were on vacation. They had taken a train from Boston to a popular resort hotel in the town of White Sulphur Springs, West Virginia. They had only left a few days ago and Mr. Hill had told Joseph they expected to be gone for at least three weeks. He recognized the opportunity this provided him. He turned the buggy around and took the narrow road to the Hills' home.

When he arrived at the property, he entered and looked around. Although he knew nobody was there, he couldn't help but feel a little nervous. He wasn't sure what he would say if he was discovered. The squeaking sound the opening gates made as metal rubbed against metal seemed extra loud and so did the scraping sound of gravel beneath his buggy's wooden tires.

He followed the circular driveway that led visitors to the front door then stopped and got out. Just to be safe, he walked to the door and knocked loudly. He waited and listened. He couldn't hear any movement inside. Thirty seconds passed – then a minute, but there was only silence.

Emily groaned in the back of the buggy. Joseph knocked again and waited. Nobody came to the door and nothing moved. He grasped the dark, cast-iron knob and pushed the door open. "Hello?" he said, poking his head and shoulders inside. "Mr. Hill? … Anyone?" The house was quiet and empty. He stepped inside and took a few steps to the middle of the large, spacious room at the home's entrance. The sound of his shoes against the hard, wooden floors echoed off of the walls. He stopped, rested his hands on his hips, and gazed up at the balcony that ran along the second story. He turned his head and looked around, feeling a bit like a king in his castle.

Then, remembering why he was there, he went upstairs and surveyed the bedrooms. He was hoping to find one that was simple and unadorned but none of them were. So, instead, he chose the one that was furthest from the room he planned on sleeping in. He removed some of the nicer, unnecessary bedding from the bed and then went downstairs and got Emily.

Emily groaned loudly in pain when Joseph lifted her from the buggy and again with each step as he ascended the stairs. After gently laying her in her bed, he went downstairs to the kitchen. He returned with a glass of water along with an empty glass and a bottle of liquor he had found in a tall cabinet. He placed them each on the nightstand next to her. The glasses and bottle clanked and jingled dully against each other as he set them down. Emily opened her eyes and looked at Joseph with a level of consciousness she had not achieved since Joseph had taken her from the mill. She looked deeply confused.

Joseph stared back at her intently, wondering what she was thinking and hoping she would drift back into a daze.

"Mr. Fridman?" she said slowly.

Joseph nodded his head. "You're going to be alright, Emily," he said. "We're going to take care of you."

"Where am I?" she asked. "Is this a hospital?"

"Not exactly," Joseph said. "But you're going to be fine."

"But my leg – I need to go to a hospital." Panic began rising in Emily's voice and she started to sit up in her bed.

Joseph put his hand on her shoulder, pushing her back down to her pillow gently but firmly. "Shhhh," he said. "My Edith and I are going to take care of you. Your leg is going to heal. You're going to be alright."

"No," she protested. "I need a doctor." She was too weak to muster much of a fight.

"Shhhhh," Joseph said again as he unscrewed the lid from the bottle of liquor and filled the empty glass. "Here, drink this. It will help with the pain." He put the glass to her lips and tilted it up, leaving her without a choice. He kept it there until the liquid had been emptied. "There you go," he said, as he took the glass away and set it back on the nightstand.

The effect of the alcohol on Emily's petite frame was swift. She relaxed and took a deep breath.

"Now, try to get some more sleep," Joseph said. "It will help you heal. I'll come back and check on you in a little bit."

"Please find a doctor," Emily said sleepily as she turned her head to her side on her pillow and closed her eyes.

Joseph stepped quietly out of the room and gingerly closed the door. A list of things to do was growing in his head. Before he left the house, though, one thing was urgent. He searched inside and out until he found a long piece of twine. He was hoping for a length of rope but the twine would have to do. He then climbed the stairs back to Emily's room and tied one end of the twine around her doorknob. He stretched it tightly across the hallway and tied the other end to the banister that faced the door. The bedroom doors could not be locked from the outside but he was comfortable with his solution.

He drove back into town and went straight home to pick up Edith. He explained that he had some chores he needed her to get an early start on that afternoon. Then, he told her she needed to pack some of her things. "We'll be staying at Mr. Hill's place for the next week or so," he explained.

"Why?" she asked.

"I'll explain when we get there," he said. "Just pack your things."

Edith obeyed and soon she and her dad were on their way to the Hills' home. Joseph acted strange the whole ride. It had begun with him throwing a blanket over their luggage in the back of the buggy. When Edith asked him why he had done that, he again brushed her off and said he would explain later.

Each time they passed someone on the road, rather than greet them in his usual way, he ducked his head and pulled his hat down low over his brow. "Don't wave," he said to Edith quietly and urgently; "Don't say hi. I don't want to draw any attention."

"What's going on, Dad?" Edith asked.

"I promise, I'll explain everything when we get to the Hills'. Why don't you climb in the back with the luggage and pull the blanket over you?"

174

'Uh, Dad," Edith complained, "It's hot out and the back of the buggy is bumpy."

Joseph took a deep breath and exhaled then gazed down the road thoughtfully, judging the distance they had until they were out of town. They didn't have far to go. "Fine," he said. "But don't draw any unnecessary attention, OK?"

Edith wrinkled her brow. "OK," she said confused. "I guess."

"Just trust me," Joseph said. "It's for your own good."

When they got to the Hills', Joseph drove the buggy through the circular drive and stopped at the front door, just as he had done an hour or so before. He stared ahead for a brief moment, gathering his thoughts. Then, he turned and faced Edith.

"Somebody was injured very badly at the mill today," he said.

Edith's eyebrows came down in a look of deep concern. "Are they OK?" she asked. "Who was it?"

"It's nobody you know," Joseph said. "She got a really bad gash on her leg. It will take a long time to heal but she'll be OK. She won't be able to work at the mill again, though."

"But nobody gets injured at your mill, Dad – not since that elderly lady with the eye at least."

Joseph took a deep breath, his shoulders rising then falling. "Edith," he said, choosing his words carefully, "as you get older, you'll learn that right and wrong isn't so black and white. Sometimes, doing the right thing might actually mean doing something that *seems* wrong but you know you have a good reason for doing it."

Edith looked confused. "What are you talking about, Dad?" she asked.

"Never mind," he said. "We'll come back to that another time. I just need you to understand something. Sometimes your Father is going to ask you to keep secrets. If you love me, you'll do as I say. It's very very important that when I tell you to keep a secret, you keep it. If you don't, terrible things will happen. I could lose my job, the mill could close down. If that happened, everyone here would be out of work and parents wouldn't have any food for their children. Would you like to see that happen?"

Edith shook her head.

"No," Joseph said, "of course not. That's because you're a good girl Edith. You and I, together, will always do the right thing for the people of this town and we'll keep the secrets we need to keep. Right?"

"Right," Edith said, still confused and unsure of what she was agreeing to.

"OK, then," Joseph continued, "there's something you need to know. This is one of those secrets that it's very important for you to keep. The person who was injured in the mill is here at the Hills' home."

"Why?" Edith asked. "Shouldn't she be at a hospital?"

"No," Joseph said. "It's better for everybody if you and I take care of her here at the Hills' home."

"But, Dad," Edith objected, "I don't know how to take care of someone who is hurt."

"Edith," Joseph said firmly, "just do what I say. No questions."

Edith went quiet.

"The Hills are away on a trip and won't be back for a long time so you and I are going to stay here and take care of the woman who was hurt until she is well enough to be on her own. I think that will be a week or two. Until then, you are not to go anywhere or talk to anyone unless I tell you to. OK? Nobody knows about the injury and nobody knows that you and I are staying here and those are both very important secrets that you and I need to keep. OK?"

"OK," Edith said, skeptically.

"OK," Joseph repeated. He set down the reins that were still in his hands and wrapped them around a knob near his feet.

"Dad," Edith said before Joseph stood up, "what's her name?"

"What's whose name?" he asked.

"The woman that was injured at the mill. You said it was a girl, right?"

Joseph nodded his head. "Yes, it's a girl. Her name is Emily."

"That's a pretty name," Edith said.

Joseph hopped out of the buggy. "Let's get our stuff and bring it inside," he said.

As soon as they walked through the front door, Emily let out a groan of pain that could be heard throughout the house. Edith stopped in her tracks. The look on her face was a cross between worry and fear.

"Is she OK?" she asked.

"She's fine, Edith," he said. "People sometimes do that while their wounds are healing. You're going to need to get used to it."

Another, quieter groan came from Emily's room upstairs.

"Do you think she needs anything?" Edith asked.

"I'll take care of that," Joseph said. He turned to face Edith and got down on one knee so that he was at eye level with her. "Listen, I don't want you going up there. You are not to go in Emily's room. Do you understand?"

Edith nodded her head.

"You can sleep down here on a couch so you don't hear her as well. I'll tend to most of her needs."

Edith nodded her head again to show she understood. Joseph stood and Edith looked around. Despite her worry for Emily, she was excited to stay in the Hills' home. She began exploring the house and the grounds around it. There was so much to discover. The kitchen was large with pots and pans made of bright, shining copper hanging from one of the walls. There was a squatty oven made of thick, black iron with a pipe that ran through the ceiling where a circle of soot had formed. The cupboards were stocked with small towels and forks and knives and wooden spatulas. She played for more than an hour there and, before she was done, helped herself to a slice of bread that she cut from a loaf she found in a bread box.

There was a door near one end of the kitchen that Edith opened to find a damp, echoey darkness. The air coming through the open doorway was cold and stale. Curiously and cautiously, she poked her head as far into the empty space as she could without stepping into it. She could only see a foot or two in front of her but there was nothing there. "Hello?" she called out. She knew it was silly to think that anybody would be down in the cellar but the space felt so dark and creepy that she couldn't help herself. She waited but, when there was only silence, she closed the door and kept exploring.

Next, she moved outside where she stayed until dinner time. She explored the yard and the woods beyond. A stream ran a short distance from the house. She threw rocks into the water for a while then took her shoes off and splashed around in it.

When she finally returned to the Hills' house, she was tired. After dinner, Joseph found her some blankets which she used to make a bed on a couch. Obeying her Father's counsel, she settled down to sleep on the main floor rather than taking one of the rooms upstairs. It didn't make sleeping any easier, though. Emily groaned all through the night and Joseph's pacing footsteps could be heard in his room, through the hallway, and, occasionally, into Emily's room.

Edith tried burying her face into the couch and pressing her hands against her ears but nothing worked. The noise wasn't just irritating, it was disturbing and stressful. Even in the moments of silence, Edith couldn't stop thinking about Emily lying alone in her room suffering the way she was. She wished she could do something. She wished the suffering would stop.

When morning came, Joseph came downstairs dressed for the business of the day. His clothing was the only thing that looked presentable, though. He had bags under his eyes, a spot of hair on the side of his head was sticking up, and he wore an expression that looked anxious and disheveled.

"Good morning, Edith," he said flatly. "How did you sleep?"

Edith just shrugged her shoulders. She was sitting cross-legged on the couch she had slept on, running her hand along the blanket across her lap. There was plenty running through her head about the stranger upstairs groaning in pain all night and locked away in her room but she didn't know how to vocalize her thoughts for her Father nor did she know if she wanted to.

"I have to go back to Fall River this morning," he said. "You'll need to stay here alone. Are you going to be OK?"

Edith nodded her head silently. She probably had ten different questions for him but, for some reason, she was afraid to ask any of them. There was something about her Father's demeanor that told her she needed to tread lightly if she didn't want to anger him.

"Good," he said. "I trust this goes without saying but I'm going to repeat it anyway. You do not go upstairs while I am gone. Do you understand?"

Edith silently nodded her head again, still running her hand along her blanket like she was petting a dog.

"It's very important that you obey me on this."

"I will," Edith said.

"OK, then. I should be back around lunchtime or maybe shortly after. I won't linger. If anyone comes to the door – which I don't think they will – don't answer."

"I won't, Dad."

"Thank you, Edith," Joseph said as he turned to leave.

Just before he reached the door, Edith called out. "Father!" she said. She couldn't contain it.

He turned to look at her. "Yes?"

"Ummm…"she hesitated for a moment, fidgeting with a corner of the blanket she had picked up. "Shouldn't we have a doctor come see Emily?"

"No," Joseph said abruptly.

Edith was confused and it showed on her face.

Joseph softened his tone a little. "I appreciate your concern, honey. I'm concerned too. That's why I'm going to Fall River. I'm going to get her some medicine and look up a few things in a medical book at the library. It's going to be fine. I'll take care of her. The best thing you can do is let her rest. OK?"

Edith nodded her head. "OK. I'll see you when you get back."

She watched the door close as her dad left. Almost immediately after he was gone, her curiosity surged. She turned her head and looked at the stairs behind her – fighting the urge to climb them. She didn't last long. After a few minutes, she gave in. As she ascended the stairs, for some reason she couldn't explain, she felt the need to step gingerly, careful not to make any noise.

She wasn't sure what her plan was. When she reached the top, she tip-toed to Emily's door. Then, stretching out her neck, she quietly put her ear to it and held her breath in her lungs. Nothing. She couldn't hear anything from the other side. In fact, the entire house was silent except for the sound of a ticking clock coming from downstairs.

She stepped back and stared at the door, unsure what to do next. She looked at the string her dad had tied to the doorknob then followed it with her eyes across the hallway and to the banister where it was tied again. She stepped close to the banister and bent down to examine the knot. Then, almost instinctively, she brought her fingers to it and began to pick at it. It unraveled quite easily and, before she knew it, she was holding the untied end of the string in her hand.

Her heart began beating a little faster. She glanced over the banister to the floor below and to the front door. The door was closed and everything was still. She knew her dad must be miles away by now. So, without any more hesitation, she stepped to

Emily's door and turned the knob slowly. It made a little noise but not much. She gently pushed it open and poked her head inside.

When her eyes fell on Emily, she was startled to find Emily staring back at her. She gasped and quickly brought her head back out of the room, accidentally banging it on the door frame as she did. She stood outside of the partially opened door, rubbing the sore spot on her head.

"Hello?" Emily called out weakly.

Edith knew she couldn't leave now. Her curiosity and her sympathy swelled simultaneously. She stepped into the room, feeling a little sheepish.

"Hi," she said. "I'm Edith."

"Edith…" Emily repeated, then trailed off. Edith wasn't sure if she was talking to her or just repeating what she had heard. She had a dreamy look in her eyes, which were only half opened. Her skin was pale and her breathing was shallow and quick.

"I don't think I know where I am," she said. She shifted her eyes back and forth, looking disoriented. Edith stepped over to her side and took her hand. She was surprised by how cold it was. Emily turned her head and looked at her. Her lips were visibly dry.

"You need some water," Edith said. "I'll get you some. Are you hungry?"

Emily weakly nodded her head, still looking quite confused.

"OK. I'll be right back." Edith left and returned with a glass of water and a slice of bread. "Here you go," she said, setting them on the nightstand next to her. But Emily didn't say anything. She just stared ahead at nothing in particular. "Emily," Edith said, trying to get her attention, "I brought you some water. You should drink it." Emily blinked but otherwise didn't respond.

Edith bit her lip and looked around the room. She felt like she needed to do more to help but she didn't know what she could do. She picked the glass of water up from the nightstand and tried again. "I brought you this," she said, holding it in front of Emily's gaze.

"Water," Emily said, almost in a whisper.

"That's right," Edith said. "Here, I guess I'll just…" she trailed off as she uncomfortably brought the glass to Emily's lips. Emily took a long drink. "More," she said when Edith pulled the glass away. Edith returned the glass to her lips and she took another long drink, emptying the glass.

"Thank you," Emily said. Then she turned to look at Edith. She wrinkled her brow in confusion. "Are you a doctor?" she asked.

Edith giggled. "No," she said. "Girls aren't doctors. And I'm just a kid."

Emily didn't laugh. "My leg is hurt," she said. "It aches so bad. My whole side aches."

Edith looked down at where Emily's leg was. Most of the bedding had been pulled back and only a white, blood stained sheet covered her leg.

"Will you check it for me?" Emily asked.

Edith shook her head. "No thanks," she said.

"Maybe there's something you could do," Emily continued undeterred. "Or maybe you could get the doctor."

"But I'm not a nurse," Edith said. "This isn't…" she decided not to finish. *'Maybe she WANTS to believe she's at a hospital,'* she thought to herself.

"Please, just look," she said weakly.

Truthfully, Edith's curiosity was piqued and this wouldn't be the first wound she had seen so she knew she could manage it. "Well," she said, "I suppose I could take just a quick look." She stepped back to where Emily's leg was resting on the bed and gingerly took the end of the bed sheet between her two fingers. "I'll just pull this back, OK?"

Emily nodded her head.

Nervously, Edith pulled the sheet to expose Emily's wound. Part of the dried blood stuck a little as she pulled and Emily cried out, suddenly sounding much more awake and alert. "Sorry! Sorry!" Edith said putting the sheet back down.

Emily calmed down quickly. "It's OK. Keep going."

Edith took a deep breath and exhaled, picked the sheet up and began again. This time, she was a little more careful. Still, more dried blood stuck a little as she pulled. Emily winced and clenched her fists but contained herself.

Soon, the wound was fully exposed. When Edith saw it, she suddenly felt sick and lightheaded. It was the grossest thing she had ever seen. It was badly swollen and filled with yellow and greenish puss. Patchy, red streaks extended from it up and down her leg. It smelled bad too.

Edith quickly threw the sheet back over Emily's leg and backed away.

"Is it going to be OK?" Emily asked.

"Ummm...I'm not a doctor so I shouldn't guess."

"But how does it look?"

"It looks like it really hurts."

Emily smiled a little. "It really does," she said.

Edith returned to Emily's side and knelt down. Instinctively, she took her hand and caressed it. "You're going to be OK," she said. "My Dad went to get you some medicine. That's going to help. You should eat some of the bread I brought you. Maybe you won't feel so weak if you do."

Edith took the bread from the nightstand and held it out. "OK," Emily said. She took it in her hand and took a bite. "Thank you," she said to Edith. "You're kind."

Edith took Emily's hand again and stayed with her for a moment longer. After just eating half of the bread, Emily said she couldn't eat anymore. "I'll let you sleep, then," Edith said. "You look tired."

"I am," Emily said, closing her eyes.

Edith left the room, bringing the bread with her so there wouldn't be any evidence of her visit. She closed the door and tied the string as it had been before she entered. Emily slept until Joseph returned. Edith was outside in the yard when he rode up in his buggy. When he asked her if Emily had made any noise, Edith lied and said she couldn't be sure because she had spent the day outside.

Edith followed her dad inside and to the kitchen. He was carrying an armful of groceries and a few other things. He set everything down on the long, wooden table that filled the middle of the room. Edith noticed two small, glass bottles each with a cork on top. She tried reading the labels but didn't recognize the words. One read "Laudanum" and the other "Heroin."

"You got the medicine for Emily?" Edith said, gesturing to the bottles with her head.

"Yes," Joseph said. "Although, I'm a little concerned it won't be enough." He picked up one of the bottles and held it with his thumb on the bottom and his index finger on the top. It looked even smaller in his large hand. He eyed it skeptically. "The man at the pharmacy said the bottles are small because only a small dose is required but I'm not so sure. Emily's been in some real pain so I think I'll start with a strong dose and see what happens. I picked up some sleeping medicine for her too, which I think she'll appreciate." He pulled a third bottle from his pocket and set it on the table. "I think sleep will help her to heal."

Edith stared at the bottles of medicine while her dad started putting groceries away. "Is any of this stuff going to make her better?" she asked after a brief moment of silence. Joseph paused. He was surprised that Edith was still thinking about Emily.

"Edith," he said gravely, "Don't worry about Emily. She's going to be fine. I'll make sure of it."

Edith continued staring at the bottles. The image of Emily's swollen, discolored wound had returned to her mind and she couldn't get rid of it.

"OK, sweetie?" Joseph said.

"OK, Father," Edith said, finally looking up. She forced a smile and her Dad went back to putting groceries away.

As Edith made her bed on the couch, she worried that sleep would be difficult again that night. She didn't know how she would bear the stress of hearing Emily crying out again. As it turned out, though, her fears were unwarranted. The house was silent all night and Edith slept like a rock. When she woke up in the morning, she was surprised to see the sun coming through the windows. She sat up and stretched her arms over her head. *'The medicine must have worked,'* she thought to herself.

All at once, she noticed that her dad was in the room with her. He was standing near the entrance to the kitchen, his back to Edith, leaning on one hand which was pressed to the wall. His other hand was on his waist. His head was down. He was still and seemed to be gazing at the ground, deep in thought. Edith wondered how long he had been there.

"Dad?" she said.

"Mmmm?" he said, seeming a little startled to hear her. He snapped out of his gaze and lifted his head. He turned to look at Edith. "Oh, hi honey," he said. He looked even more stressed and disheveled than he had the previous morning. Edith was surprised considering how well the night had gone for her.

"Are you OK?" she asked. "I didn't hear Emily at all last night. Did you?"

He shook his head. "No," he said. "No, she was quiet all night." He still seemed to be wrapped up in his thoughts as he spoke.

"Well that's a good thing," Edith pressed a little.

Joseph settled into another gaze and nodded his head without saying anything else about it. "Hey, Edith, let's go somewhere today," he said. "Let's spend the day away from this house. There's a pond off the road about half way between here and Fall River. We can go there and fish and have a picnic; you can get in the water if you want. How does that sound?"

"That sounds fun!" Edith said. It had been a long time since she and her Dad had done anything fun together. She was genuinely excited. "We'll have to go home to get my bathing suit and our fishing rods."

"Hm," Joseph said, considering her point. "We'll just go into Fall River and pick up some things there."

"All the way to Fall River for a bathing suit and fishing rods?" Edith asked? "You just got back from there. Why don't we just go home really quick?"

"I need a new rod and, besides, it's part of the adventure." Joseph said. "It will be fun. Trust me."

Edith shrugged her shoulders. "OK. If you say so," she said.

The trip to Fall River was quick. They stayed just long enough to visit two stores where they found everything they needed. At the first store, they bought the bathing suit and fishing rods they had come for. At the second store, they bought food for a picnic and a shovel. Edith was confused by the shovel so she asked her dad about it after he threw it in the back of their buggy.

"It's just for work," he said. "I've been meaning to buy a new one to keep at the mill so I figured I would pick it up while we were here."

Edith couldn't figure out why a cotton mill would need a shovel but there was a lot she didn't understand about her Father's work so, she just let it go.

The rest of the day was fun. When Joseph and Edith arrived at the pond, the first thing they did was spread out a blanket and have lunch. They were both hungry. Then, they spent the rest of the afternoon in leisure. Joseph mostly fished and Edith mostly swam.

The water was chilly and, each time she got out, she would lie on the blanket, close her eyes, and let the bright sun warm her skin. She liked lying among the trees and the birds with her Father by her side. It felt good. It felt safe.

Joseph and Edith walked through the front door after arriving back at the Hills'. The house was quiet. Edith thought about Emily for the first time since leaving that morning.

"Do you think we should check on Emily, Dad?" she asked. "She's probably thirsty or hungry."

"I'll check on her," Joseph said. "You stay down here. Start bringing in our things from the buggy. Just leave everything downstairs."

Joseph was upstairs for a long time. When he returned, he said Emily was fine.

"She doesn't need any water or anything?" Edith asked.

"She's fine, Edith," he said sharply, raising his voice a little. "Stop worrying about her."

Edith didn't say anything and the silence that hung in the air pricked at Joseph's conscience.

"I'll bring her water later," he added in a softer tone. "She's sleeping right now."

The day had gone quickly. Joseph made dinner a little later than usual and the two sat at the Hills' table and ate. As they did, Joseph told Edith that he was going to bring Emily to a hospital the next day and leave her in the care of doctors and nurses. Edith was relieved. She couldn't figure out why he hadn't come to that conclusion earlier. It would mean yet another road trip for Joseph in consecutive days but she was silently grateful he was willing to do it.

He also told Edith he wanted her to sleep upstairs that night. "I'll trade sleeping arrangements with you," he said. "You can sleep in the Hills' bed where I've been sleeping and I'll sleep down here on the couch. I want to make sure you're getting some good sleep."

"I sleep fine on the couch," Edith assured him but Joseph insisted. His insistence took her by surprise but it sounded fun to sleep in the Hills' big fancy bed so she didn't put up a fight.

She wasn't disappointed by the bed. She could roll across it three full turns from one side to the other. The pillows and the comforter that was spread across the top of the bed were fluffy and cozy. She fell asleep quickly.

Late in the night, she was awoken by a noise in the hall. She opened her eyes and wrinkled her eyebrows. She could hear movement on the wooden floors. She wondered if her dad had come upstairs to check on Emily or maybe to give her more medicine. She decided to get up and peak out her door to see if she could glimpse what was going on. She got out of bed and tiptoed across the floor. She knew her dad would not be happy if he caught her spying so she was careful not to make any noise.

When she reached her door, it was already slightly ajar. Carefully, she pushed it open far enough to peak her head and shoulders through the opening. The hallway was empty but she could see that Emily's door was open. She hoped everything was OK.

Then, Joseph emerged from Emily's room. He was carrying something large in his arms and looked like he was trying to step carefully to avoid making any of the floor's wooden planks creak. Edith squinted, trying to figure out what it was that he was carrying. It was wrapped in a sheet and the size of...Edith almost gasped audibly but she stopped herself. He was carrying Emily's limp and lifeless body. She wanted to call out to her dad but something inside her told her it wasn't a good idea.

She ducked back into her room and sat on her bed and started to cry. She was so confused. What had happened to Emily and where was he taking her body? She needed to see more. She got up and went back to her doorway again and peaked into the hallway. It was empty now. Carefully, she came out of her room and moved down the hall, stepping gingerly. She got to the top of the stairs where she could see to the floor below.

She saw her dad, still holding Emily's sheet-wrapped body, open the front door. He picked up the shovel that was leaning against the door frame before exiting and closing the door behind him. *'That's the shovel he bought this morning,'* she thought to herself.

She went back to her room and got under her covers, pulling them over her head. She didn't want to think about what she had just seen but she couldn't quiet her brain. After several slow minutes passed, she pulled her head out of the covers and stared at the ceiling with questions swimming in her mind. Then, after what felt like a very long time, she heard rustling in the hallway again. She got back out of bed and snuck back over to her door, opened it carefully, and peaked out. Again, she was confused by what she saw. Her dad was coming out of Emily's room holding a small pile of bed sheets in both his arms. He disappeared down the hall.

Edith laid back down. She had even more questions now but, the longer she stared into the dark trying to sort through her thoughts, the heavier her eyes grew. Her pillow felt soft and inviting. She would try to figure all of this out in the morning. For now, she just wanted to sleep.

When Edith woke, pale, morning daylight was coming through her window. The house was quiet. A bird was whistling outside. She yawned and stretched her arms and legs before sitting up. She was hungry and wanted breakfast.

As she came downstairs, she could hear her dad breathing heavily like he often did when he slept. He was laid out on the couch, still fully dressed, clutching a blanket that he hadn't gotten around to spreading over himself. The couch was too small for him. One of his arms hung over the side and his hand rested on the floor. His boots, which were still on his feet, hung over the end. They were dirty with mud that was still wet in some places.

Edith stepped close to him. She could see he had worked through the night. Mud was spattered up his pant legs. His clothes and hair smelled of smoke.

He opened one eye like he sensed he was being watched. When he saw Edith standing next to him, he stretched. "How long have you been awake?" he asked, sounding exhausted.

"Just a few minutes," Edith said. She was dying to ask him about what she had seen in the night but decided to wait. She was sure it would come up soon and he would explain everything.

"How did you sleep?" he asked. His eyes were closed again.

"Umm, OK I guess. Except..." Edith hesitated, unsure how to bring up the thing that was pressing on her mind.

Joseph's eyes popped open. "Except what?" he asked intently, although trying to sound casual.

"Well, I thought I heard something in Emily's room," she said, testing the waters.

"You didn't go in there this morning, did you?" Joseph suddenly grew tense. His tone was ominous and a little threatening. It made Edith nervous. She realized she would need to be more cautious than she thought.

"No, I promise. I came right down stairs this morning. I just thought I heard something last night, that's all. Is everything alright?"

Joseph relaxed and closed his eyes again. "Yes, everything's fine. I just had to go into Emily's room and give her her medicine last night. She's OK. She's still sleeping."

Edith was stunned and utterly confused. *Still sleeping?* Why would he say that? She knew it couldn't be true. She stared at him in disbelief but he didn't see.

"In fact," Joseph continued, "I wanted to talk to you about Emily."

'This must be it,' Edith thought. Her dad's last comment didn't make any sense but now he was going to explain what had happened during the night.

"I'll be taking her to the hospital this morning. So, I'll need you to stay here without me again. I'll be gone a few hours. Is that OK?"

Edith was speechless. She continued to stare.

Joseph opened his eyes and looked at her. "Edith," he said. "Are you listening?

"Yes," she said mechanically and a little coldly. "That's OK."

She couldn't believe her Father was lying to her.

Breakfast was uncomfortable. Joseph and Edith sat across from each other and ate eggs and buttered toast. Joseph barely spoke and Edith hardly said a word. By the time they were finished, Edith's confusion had twisted into anger. Joseph was too preoccupied to notice, though. He was deep in thought all morning.

After breakfast, he asked her to play outside while he loaded the buggy. He told her he would be leaving soon. She obliged but watched him from a distance, shielded from his view. He loaded a blanket, his fishing rod, and a small basket; nothing else. Edith's anger swelled. Her face felt hot.

"Edith!" he called out, standing next to the buggy and searching the yard with his gaze.

Edith snuck out from her hiding place and stepped into her Father's view.

"There you are," he said. "I'm leaving. Come give me a hug."

He stepped away from the buggy to keep her from getting too near it and seeing its lack of contents. She walked over to him and stepped close so he could hug her. She didn't return the hug or say a word.

"Be safe," he said. I'll be back this afternoon.

Still, she didn't say anything. She watched him go in silence. When his buggy was gone from view, she went back inside and up to Emily's room. She didn't know what she expected to find there but there was nothing remarkable to see. Her Father must have cleaned and restored the room in the night. New sheets were on the bed and all signs of Emily were gone.

She went downstairs and back outside. The nighttime image of her dad picking up the shovel that was resting next to the front door as he walked outside flashed in her mind. Maybe she could find the spot of ground where he had dug. She searched for 10 or 15 minutes before noticing a grove of young nut trees to one side of the house. When she approached, she promptly spotted the freshly dug grave.

Quickly she walked over to it and knelt down next to it. She felt the freshly turned over soil with her hands. She felt like crying again. She knew that Emily was dead and that her Father was lying to her but seeing and touching her grave made it real in a whole new way.

She felt like she needed to do something. This anonymous grave that nobody would ever visit just didn't seem right. Emily was hardly cared for as she lay dying in her room and Edith couldn't bear the thought of her final resting place being treated with the same callousness.

She knew that whatever she did needed to be subtle. With the grave so near the Hills' home, she didn't want to draw attention to it. She didn't know what her dad might do if she revealed his secret or what the consequences to him might be. As angry as she was at him, she didn't want to find those things out.

She stood up, gathered some nearby wildflowers, and rested them against a tree that grew at the head of the grave. Then she had an idea. She went inside and returned with a sharp knife from the kitchen. *If Emily doesn't get a gravestone, at least she can have a tree*, she thought to herself. She carefully carved an "E" on the tree and circled it. It was simple but, at least in some small way, it meant Emily would be remembered.

Joseph started down the road that led to Fall River but he didn't go far. He turned off onto the small path that led to the pond he and Edith had visited just the day before. When he reached the water, he spread a blanket on the ground and took out his fishing pole and the basket of food he had packed. He laid down on his back in the sun and pulled his hat over his eyes, crossing his feet and resting his hands on his chest. The warmth of the sun relaxed him and he desperately needed to relax.

He closed his eyes, took a deep breath and exhaled. All things considered, he felt that the situation actually resolved quite nicely. It could have gone much worse. The mill kept its good name and Emily's fatal injuries were forever concealed. As it turned out, the Hills' secluded home could be extraordinarily useful for these sorts of things…if it weren't for the inconvenient fact that the Hills lived in it.

He took another deep breath and cleared his mind of anything he didn't have to think about. He'd spend the rest of the day fishing and unwinding. For now, though, he wanted to sleep.

CHAPTER 16

At the northernmost part of town, at the foot of the hills that circled Edith's Hollow stood an old, deteriorating cabin surrounded by the vestiges of an abandoned farm. The cabin was small and unadorned, unlike any home Mrs. Hill had ever lived in. Yet, she found herself drawn to it. She visited it two or three times a week and walked its grounds with a sense of reverence for her ancestors and the life they had built there. She pictured them with calloused hands and sore backs sitting at the fire or around the dinner table on hard, wooden benches, discussing their joys and sorrows of the day. Perhaps it was the stark contrast from her own life that drew her back to this place again and again.

When they first moved to Edith's Hollow, Mrs. Hill made her husband come with her every week to visit her ancestors' lot. But he felt no connection to it and soon began making excuses when she asked him to accompany her. So, she found herself going alone. Still wanting to share the experience, though, she decided to do something about it.

Mrs. Hill knew that the women of Edith's Hollow were not the high-society type. However, she also knew that they would appreciate a chance to get out of their homes and come together once in a while. So, she started a women's club and they met every Tuesday at her ancestors' cabin. At first, she envisioned the club as a literary society but she quickly learned that several of the women couldn't read. So, it became a place to socialize and for Mrs. Hill to lead discussions on social issues.

As it turned out, the women of Edith's Hollow had no shortage of opinions and there were plenty of things they were eager to see reformed right there in their growing community. Mrs. Hill, who was well-read and well-informed, elevated the conversation with stories and ideas. Some nights, the room was afire with the feeling of possibility. Mrs. Hill loved it.

Mr. Hill hated it. When Mrs. Hill had first told him of her plans to start a women's club, he was in full support. In theory, it sounded like a great idea. In practice, though, it was a terrible imposition on his contentment. Every Tuesday, Mrs. Hill came home charged up about a new issue she was ready to tackle. And, considering Mr. Hill's position of influence in the community, her expectations for him were annoyingly high.

There was also the matter of the cabin itself. Mrs. Hill was perpetually involved in a project to restore or beautify the place. That would have been fine with Mr. Hill except that she couldn't seem to leave him out of it. Everything required his labor or his money, and both prospects made him irritable.

Really, the heart of the problem was that Mrs. Hill was simply more invested in Edith's Hollow than Mr. Hill was. Mr. Hill appreciated the business opportunity the settlement provided him; He enjoyed his venture and the success he was having there. However, he didn't feel tied to the people or the place. He didn't have familial history there or a place to sit with like-minded people and discuss the future of the community. Instead, he had Joseph and the only future he ever discussed with Joseph was the future of the mill because, when it came to Edith's Hollow, that was his only concern.

Joseph knew all of this about Hill. Being quick to observe and slow to speak, he knew Hill better than Hill knew him. He knew about the women's club and how it grated on him. He knew he felt no passion for the community he had helped to build, only for the business that was done there. He knew that Hill was a man of status and a man of ego and that by feeding those two things, Joseph could persuade Hill to do unlikely things.

So, Joseph immediately recognized the opportunity quietly nestled in the events that unfolded on the evening of September 25th. At the invitation of Senator Dawes, Mr. Hill and Joseph had met him for dinner in Boston that evening. In the letter the Senator sent his dinner companions, he explained that he had taken great interest in the mill and Edith's Hollow ever since visiting the place and wanted an opportunity to catch up and discuss the needs of the community, the people, and the mill. Joseph thought this was very generous of the Senator and was happy for the opportunity.

On the ride to Boston, Mr. Hill, who was far more politically savvy than Joseph, treaded on some of Joseph's feelings of goodwill toward the Senator when he explained away the invitation they had received. "You know that elections are five months away, right?" he said to Joseph as their buggy wobbled up and down on a bumpy section of road.

"No," Joseph admitted. "I didn't realize that. And Senator Dawes is running for re-election?"

Hill nodded his head. He had a smug grin on his face, proud of himself for discerning the Senator's motives. "Edith's Hollow might be a small establishment but it's low hanging fruit for a politician. If the Senator can gain the vote of the entire community with a quick visit or two and an evening with the community's most prominent members, then why would he pass that up? It's a pretty good return for a small investment of time."

Joseph nodded. "I suppose it is," he said, a little disappointed.

"Don't get me wrong," Hill continued, "that doesn't mean he invited us to dinner so he could talk about himself. The Senator is smarter than that. In fact, it will probably be quite the opposite. He'll spend most of the evening probing us to learn what things are important to the community. A good politician is like a good salesman; they know they must first sniff out the need before they can convince you that they are the solution."

"Well, I hope you're right" Joseph said, "because Edith's Hollow has some needs I'd like to talk to him about. Even if he has ulterior motives, maybe he'll help us with a thing or two."

"We will see," Hill said.

Joseph was impressed with the accuracy of Hill's assessment. For the first hour, dinner went just as he had predicted. The Senator quizzed Joseph and Mr. Hill about the things that ailed the people of Edith's Hollow. He came off as earnest and sincere. He casually suggested that, perhaps, he could come visit the community as he had done before and address the issues that were on their minds.

Joseph, who, thanks to Mr. Hill, had some insight into the game that was being played, marveled at how well the Senator played it. However, Senator Dawes wasn't the only one whose skill was on display. Joseph also marveled at Mr. Hill. He was remarkably comfortable and clearly in his element. He seemed to know the right things to say at just the right times.

Joseph couldn't escape the feeling that Senator Dawes and Mr. Hill knew some set of unspoken rules to a gentlemen's dinner that Joseph couldn't even fathom. For most of the meal, he hardly said a word. He simply watched and nodded when he was expected to.

Things took a turn, though, after the main course had been cleared.

"This has been a nice evening," the Senator said to his companions as the waiter laid dessert spoons on the table. "Today's work has been mind-numbing and tomorrow will be the same. Thank you for giving me some respite."

"No, thank you, Senator." Hill replied. "It's been a great pleasure for us. I can't say how much we appreciate the invitation and the lovely meal. You've piqued my curiosity, though. I must ask, what has been so mind-numbing about your day?"

"Oh," the Senator said with a small chuckle. "I don't mean to sound so dreary about it. It's just that Governor Wolcott has asked for my help in appointing a new Secretary of the Commonwealth. The last gentleman resigned in the middle of his term so he needs another to fill the spot. He's drawn up a list of prospects a mile long and has asked if I would sit through interviews with him of each one while I am in town." Senator Dawes rolled his eyes at this. "It's made for a terrible day and tomorrow will be just as bad."

"Doesn't he have a friend or some political ally whose back he wants to scratch?" Mr. Hill asked.

Senator Dawes laughed. "Are you sure you've never worked in politics?"

Mr. Hill only laughed in reply.

"You're right, though," the Senator said. "It strikes me as a bit odd that he's having so much trouble finding the right person but he simply isn't enamored with any of the candidates. He's an attorney, you know. *That's* the problem. He analyzes to death every aspect of every person on that stupid list." Senator Dawes began to chuckle, sounding as if the alcohol he had been drinking through the evening was starting to take effect. "Those poor interviewees," he said, through his growing laughter. "He treats them like witnesses on the stand. You should see the look on their faces by the time he's done with them! I don't think any of them even *want* the job by then."

As the Senator rambled, Joseph noticed an expression on Mr. Hill's face he had seen before. His eyes had a glimmer of interest Joseph recognized. It wasn't so unlike the look he had years before when he and Joseph had sat together atop the ridge and looked over the land that would become Edith's Hollow.

"I think he's hoping I'll put him and all his candidates out of their misery and make the decision for him," Senator Dawes said. "Or, better yet, that I'll recommend one of my own people to him. I'm just not sure I know the right person for the job."

"What kind of person are you looking for?" Joseph asked. Joseph had spoken so few words that evening that both of the other men at the table looked a little surprised to hear his voice.

The Senator made a face like he was considering Joseph's question. "Well, political acumen is important, of course but so is leadership. He'll need to be a good leader – able to organize systems and people. He needs to be a Republican, too. The Secretary of the Commonwealth is only 3rd in line to the governor, you know, so Governor Wolcott will certainly want to appoint somebody from his own party."

"What about somebody from the private sector?" Joseph asked.

Senator Dawes made the same face as before, pondering Joseph's question. He nodded his head, "Yes, that's a possibility," he said. "The Governor has a strong business background himself. Not only is he a lawyer but he also served on corporate boards before being elected so he's actually quite keen on men who have risen through the ranks of business. Why? Do you have someone in mind?"

Joseph looked at Mr. Hill who still had the same, familiar glimmer of interest in his eyes. Hill didn't say anything, though, so Joseph followed his lead. "No," he replied. "But if I think of someone, I'll let you know."

"I appreciate that," the Senator said.

A short time later, the men decided it was time to retire for the evening. "Where are you gentlemen staying tonight?" The Senator asked as the three stood from their seats.

"We are in Hotel Touraine, over on Tremont Street," Mr. Hill replied.

The Senator nodded in recognition. "Not a bad hotel," he said. "Although, I always prefer to stay at Young's when I'm in Boston. You should visit it next time you're in town."

"Young's is magnificent," Mr. Hill said.

"You're familiar with it?" asked the Senator.

"Of course," Mr. Hill said. "I've dined there a few times and I've visited the billiard room once or twice."

"Well, it's a lovely place to stay. I'd recommend it. Anyway, thank you for a nice evening. I'll take into consideration the things we've discussed. And I'm serious about making another trip down to Edith's Hollow. I'll be in touch about that."

With that, the men said their goodbyes and parted ways.

Joseph and Hill rode together back to their hotel. Mr. Hill was in a good mood and had a lot to say. When Joseph was finally able to get a word in, he didn't waste any time.

"That's interesting what he said about the Secretary of Commonwealth position, isn't it?"

Mr. Hill raised his eyebrows. "How so?" he asked.

"Well, you know," Joseph pressed, "it seems like a really fascinating opportunity...for the right person." Joseph was looking at Hill out of the corners of his eyes.

"Are you interested in the position?" Mr. Hill asked, sounding a little surprised.

"No!" Joseph said emphatically, with a little laugh. "Not at all. I want nothing to do with politics. It sounds like what they need is someone who knows business *and* politics – someone who can navigate both worlds – a businessman who is comfortable rubbing shoulders with the politicians and playing their game. That definitely isn't me." Joseph paused and looked at Mr. Hill out of the corners of his eyes again. "But it is you," he added.

Mr. Hill quickly turned his head to look at Joseph. "What are you talking about?" he said. "We're running a mill. I couldn't possibly..."

"Mr. Hill," Joseph interrupted, "you're perfect for the position. Anyone can see that. I would be a bad friend and a bad business partner if I didn't point that out to you."

Mr. Hill laughed. "Well, that's nice of you to say. It would never work, though. The mill requires too much attention."

"I think you're wrong," Joseph persisted. "We could make it work. I already have Emory Green supervising the night shift. He's very competent. He could take on more responsibility, I could shift my role a bit, we would make do."

"If I didn't know better, I would think you were trying to get rid of me!" Mr. Hill said, laughing heartily.

Joseph smiled. "No, no, no. Of course not. I just want to support you, Mr. Hill. Like I said, I would be a bad friend and a bad business partner if I didn't recognize that this is a perfect opportunity for you. I'd hate to see you go but, worse than that, I'd hate to watch this pass you by – especially if I felt like it was me and the mill holding you back. Look, you've done your time in business – and you've done well for yourself. Maybe this is the next big thing for you. Maybe the best thing you can do for the mill is to make a name for yourself in politics. Think how much good you can do for our little community as a public servant just a couple seats away from the governorship."

The gleam of ambition returned to Mr. Hill's eyes as Joseph spoke. But then he began to shake his head. "No," he said. "I would be lying if I said it didn't appeal to me. There are just too many obstacles, though – starting with Mrs. Hill." He turned to look at Joseph and pointed a finger at his face, "Don't you ever tell her I said that."

"My lips are sealed," Joseph said.

"It's true, though," Mr. Hill continued. "I could certainly entertain moving into politics but Mrs. Hill has become quite fond of our lives in Edith's Hollow. She feels connected to the place." Mr. Hill laughed quietly and began shaking his head. "That stupid cabin," he said, almost like he was talking to himself.

"You mean the one where the women's club meets?"

Mr. Hill nodded his head. "That's the other thing. The women's club, the cabin, it's all connected for her. It gives her purpose, I suppose. Who would have thought it would mean so much to her?"

Joseph suddenly felt deflated. Mr. Hill was right. That would be a difficult obstacle to move passed. "Well," he said, "be that as it may, just know that you would have my support. We'd be just fine at the mill. Besides, I think it would make sense for you to keep an advisory role – and, of course, keep being paid a salary for it."

"I'm not sure that's allowed of a government official," Mr. Hill said.

"What are they going to do?" Joseph asked, "report us to the Secretary of the Commonwealth?"

Both men laughed. Neither said another word the rest of the way to the hotel. For the first time all evening, Mr. Hill was lost in his thoughts.

When Joseph got to his room, he immediately found a pen and paper and wrote a note to Senator Dawes:

Dear Senator,

Thank you for an enjoyable evening and, more importantly, for your commitment to doing good for the citizens of our State and for the people of Edith's Hollow. Your work has not gone unnoticed by our community.

During dinner, you mentioned a vacancy at the position of Secretary of the Commonwealth. Although he was too modest to say anything at the time, Mr. Hill is perfectly suited for the position. As you have seen, he is a brilliant man of business and possesses a remarkable gift for managing and influencing people. Although the people of Edith's Hollow would be sad to lose such a strong and beloved leader in the community, their gains would far outweigh their losses. They would gain an advocate and a voice at the highest levels of our State government and, I must say, they would be eternally grateful to the Senator who helped to make that happen.

After dinner, Mr. Hill divulged to me that he desires to enter public service and would be thrilled to accept the position of Secretary of the Commonwealth if it were offered him. However, this was all spoken in confidence so, for the sake of my friendship with Mr. Hill and in order to preserve his dignity, I ask with some urgency that you keep this letter a secret between you and me. If you and the Governor determine to speak with Mr. Hill regarding the vacancy at hand, please do not mention my part in suggesting his name.

Thank you again for your interest in our community. I hope the rest of your stay in Boston is pleasant.

Your Friend,
Joseph Fridman

Joseph walked his note to Young's Hotel and left it with the front desk, asking that it be delivered to the Senator right away.

Joseph was standing at a spinning mule, explaining to its operator a quicker way of mending severed cotton threads when Mr. Hill found him. Mr. Hill never came to the mill so Joseph immediately thought something serious had happened. The grave expression on Mr. Hill's face confirmed it.

"Can we go to your office?" he yelled above the noise of the machines.

Joseph nodded his head. "Of course," he said. He told the worker he would return later and then hurried to catch up with Mr. Hill who was already several steps away.

When they got to Joseph's office, they closed the door, which was extra thick and heavy, blocking out a fair portion of the sounds coming from the mill floor. They sat down in the two wooden chairs that faced Joseph's desk.

"What's going on?" Joseph asked, getting right to the point.

Mr. Hill took a deep breath and exhaled. "Last week at dinner, do you remember Senator Dawes mentioning that there was a vacancy the Governor was trying to fill in the State government?"

"Yes," Joseph said. His heart sped up a little. He knew where this was going. "Of course. Secretary of the Commonwealth – you and I spoke about it on our way to the hotel after our meeting."

"That's right," Hill said. "Well, a couple days after we returned from our trip, I received a letter from the Senator asking if I would return to Boston to meet with him and the Governor."

Joseph's eyes widened. "Good for you!" he said. "Are you going to go?"

"I already did – twice," Mr. Hill said, sounding a little uncharacteristically sheepish.

"Twice?" Joseph asked in surprise.

"The first meeting was with Senator Dawes and the Governor and it went quite well. The second meeting was yesterday. It was just the Governor and I."

"And?" Joseph asked. "How did that one go?"

"He offered me the position."

Joseph stood up from his chair. "You're kidding!" he exclaimed enthusiastically. "Congratulations!" he said, patting Mr. Hill on the back.

Hill remained sober. "I don't know if I can accept."

Joseph furrowed his brow. For a brief moment, he didn't know how to respond. "You *have to* accept," he finally said. "This is an opportunity of a lifetime. What are the odds that you'll ever get a chance like this again?"

"I know," Mr. Hill said, sounding tortured. "Believe me, I've thought about that. I was up all night, Joseph, considering every possible angle in my mind. It's just, we have a mill to run…"

"I told you," Joseph said, interrupting Mr. Hill, "you don't need to worry about the mill. We'll get by just fine."

Mr. Hill nodded his head. "I know," he said. "I trust that you will. The real problem, though, is still Mrs. Hill. She absolutely does not want to move from here."

"So you've already spoken with her about it?" Joseph asked.

"Yes," Hill said, "and it didn't go well." His shoulders drooped as he sunk in his chair.

An idea began to form in Joseph's mind. "You know what you need?" he asked. Mr. Hill looked up at him. "A drink," Joseph continued, "and a night out."

Mr. Hill flashed a small, insincere smile out of courtesy.

"I'm serious," Joseph said. "I've got a bottle of whisky at home waiting to be opened. Take the day to think things over but, tonight, we'll let go a little. I'll come pick you up at 9:00."

"I appreciate it, Joseph," Hill said, "but…"

"I won't let you say 'no.'" Joseph said, convincingly.

"Fine," Hill said. "I'll see you at 9:00."

Joseph got to Hill's house around 9:15. It was dark out and a little chilly. The earliest hints of autumn were beginning to appear in the late evenings. Mr. Hill climbed into Joseph's buggy in the empty seat next to him. "So, where are we going?" he asked. "Edith Hollow's famous tavern?" He was being sarcastic. Edith's Hollow didn't have a tavern.

"No," Joseph said, "the next best thing."

Hill was surprised when Joseph pulled up to his wife's family cabin. He chuckled. "Nice one, Fridman," he said. "How am I supposed to drink away my sorrows when they're staring me in the face?"

Joseph laughed. "Come on. It'll be therapeutic. We can kick some dirt on it or smash the bottle against it after we've emptied it."

"OK," Hill said, climbing down off of the buggy. "I'm game."

The men sat on the front steps of the cabin and talked and drank. Joseph drank quite a bit less than Hill but was careful not to let him notice. He repeated his case to Mr. Hill for taking the position in Boston but he didn't waste too much time trying to talk him into it. Instead he listened, asked questions, and kept pouring him whisky.

Hill was a gregarious drunk and, after a while, he was laughing heartily at just about everything. Suddenly, though, after a particularly long laughing spell, he became more serious. "I really hate this place," he said, looking over his shoulder at the cabin.

"I know you do," said Joseph.

"You see all these windows?" Hill said, gesturing generally towards the cabin. There were three windows in the south-facing side of the cabin where they sat. "Who do you think put the glass in those?"

"You did?" Joseph asked.

"Every last one of them all around the cabin. Took me two full weekends. I broke three panes and nearly sliced my finger off on the one you're standing next to because I didn't know what I was doing." Joseph, who was leaning against the wall near the front door glanced at the window that was right by him. "I'm not a window pane installer, Joseph – or a bricklayer or a carpenter or whatever else she has in mind for me next time something needs done here."

Hill shook his head in frustration. "You know, I didn't build all my wealth so I could get stuck in some nothing village in the middle of nowhere and work on projects for my wife the rest of my life." Hill stopped and looked at Joseph. "Sorry," he said, "I know you like it here."

Joseph had never heard Mr. Hill speak that way about Edith's Hollow. He shrugged his shoulders. "It's alright," he said. "You have bigger things to accomplish. There's no need to apologize for that. The only thing you should be sorry for is letting an opportunity to do something great pass you by."

Mr. Hill nodded his head. "You're right, Joseph," he said. He began laughing to himself. "She'll be so upset if I make her leave," he said. "You should hear her when she comes home from her stupid women meetings at this place. *'Why don't women vote? Why don't women own businesses? We're going to change everything! Women are going to change the world!'*" he said, mocking his wife. "But really, *I'm* the one who's supposed to change everything. *I'm* the one who she expects to do all the stuff she dreams up because – I don't know – I'm the only one who's ever accomplished anything in this meaningless place."

Joseph felt a sting of resentment at this but he let it go. He wanted to see where this was heading.

Hill began laughing to himself again. He sounded exasperated. "I really do hate this place," he said. He sat in silence on the front steps of the cabin for a moment. He seemed to be done.

Suddenly, without saying a word, Joseph lifted his arm and brought his elbow down hard on the window next to him. The glass shattered, showering pieces of glass on the floor that tinkled and crackled as they fell.

Mr. Hill's head snapped up. At first he looked shocked and angry and, for a second, Joseph regretted what he had done. But then Hill's shock melted into a smile. He began to laugh. At first it was low and quiet but his laughter quickly grew until he was roaring loudly.

"That's right!" he said. Hill picked up a rock near his feet, stood up, and threw it at another window. In his drunkenness, he stumbled a little and almost fell over. The rock missed.

"Try it again!" Joseph encouraged.

Hill picked up another rock and took aim, this time hitting his mark.

Joseph laughed loudly. "Nice one!" he said. "Let's burn this place down!" he called out.

Hill was amused. "Yeah! Burn it down!" he repeated, yelling it more loudly.

"Burn it down!" Joseph echoed.

"Burn it down!" Hill yelled again. He stumbled again, this time falling to the ground on his butt. He sat and laughed heartily for a while.

As the laughter from both men died, Joseph walked over to Hill and extended his hand. "Come on," he said. "We need to get you home."

Hill climbed into Joseph's buggy still laughing, stumbling, and swaying. He fell silent when the buggy began to move, though. By the time they reached his house, he was asleep with his chin in his chest and snoring loudly.

Joseph dropped Hill off and then drove straight back to the cabin the two men had just come from. He climbed down and tried entering through the door but it was locked. Stepping back, he began kicking it hard near the door knob. On his third try, the door frame splintered and the door swung open.

In the back of Joseph's buggy, he had loaded a bale of hay which had been covered by a blanket all evening. He took the hay from the buggy and carried it inside the cabin where he spread it all over the floor. Then, he took out a match he had been carrying in an inner coat pocket, struck it, and dropped it to the ground. The hay immediately exploded into flames.

Joseph exited quickly. He climbed back in his buggy and watched the fire spread. The drapes in the windows caught fire quickly. Soon, the walls followed. When Joseph was satisfied that the fire was well under way, he snapped his horse's reins and left.

The next day, the town buzzed about the fire. A volunteer fire crew mobilized after being notified in the middle of the night by somebody who noticed the flames. They weren't able to do much, though. The entire building was already engulfed when they arrived. The roof and all of the walls crumbled before the night was over.

Mr. Hill arrived at the mill unexpectedly early in the day and found Joseph. He looked disheveled and a little panicked. In all of his years of knowing him, Joseph had never seen Mr. Hill in anything that remotely resembled his current state. Before Hill could say anything, Joseph gestured toward the exit with his head. "Come on," he said. "Let's go outside."

As soon as they were out the door and away from anyone who might hear him, Mr. Hill spoke. "What did we do last night?" he said, getting right to the point.

"What do you mean?" Joseph asked.

"Joseph, my head is pounding and most of last night is a blur but I remember being at my wife's cabin, I remember some windows breaking, and I remember yelling some stuff. Please tell me this fire wasn't us."

Joseph took a deep breath and blew it out. "Well," he said, "it wasn't *us*; it was you. I was pretty drunk as well so it's a little fuzzy for me too but you got pretty angry at some point. You were going off on the women's club and on being stuck in Edith's Hollow. I think the fire was probably an accident. We had a candle burning on the front porch for some light and you knocked it over while you were ranting. One of the porch's floorboards caught but when I went to stomp it out, you stopped me. You said to just let it burn."

"And you listened!?" Hill said in frustration.

"I'm sorry, Mr. Hill," Joseph replied. "Neither of us were in our right minds. We had drunk a lot of whisky."

"What are we going to do?" Hill asked. "If my wife finds out…"

"Someone notified the fire department," Joseph interrupted. "Whoever that was saw the fire burning and they might have seen us leaving the scene."

Hill shook his head. "Maybe I should just tell her. If it's going to get back to her anyway…" he trailed off.

"It doesn't have to," Joseph said.

Mr. Hill shot him a look that was both confused and intrigued.

"Accept the Governor's offer. Move to Boston. But do it quickly before the gossip mill starts to churn."

Hill stared at the ground in front of him, considering Joseph's plan.

"I'll help wrap things up for you when you go. I assume you'll want to sell your house."

"The house?" Hill said. "I haven't even thought what we would do with the house if we move. Who around here would buy it? I don't know; it might be nice to have a place to get away to."

"Are you really going to vacation to Edith's Hollow?" Joseph asked. "That's a lot of money to keep tied up for a home you might never really visit. Besides, any time Mrs. Hill returns, you're running the risk of someone saying something to her about the fire."

Mr. Hill nodded.

"You know," Joseph said, as if an idea had just popped into his head, "the hospital in Fall River is named after some philanthropist – like most of the theaters in Boston or the library downtown. I always thought that was inspiring that someone would care enough about their community to give it a place for the people to go and learn, or a place to be healed."

Mr. Hill furrowed his brow. "What are you saying?" he asked.

"I'm saying, this is what the great politicians and philanthropists do. You said Mrs. Hill is always talking about making changes and doing good for Edith's Hollow. Well, Edith's Hollow needs a hospital. What better good could you do than to give them one?"

"I'm still not following you," Mr. Hill said. "What does this have to do with selling my house?"

"Your house could be our hospital. We'd convert it."

Hill began shaking his head.

"Wait," Joseph said. "Just listen. We could convert some of the space – maybe add a wing and call it the Hill Hospital. You wouldn't have to give it away, though. The mill will pay you for it as a charitable donation. Don't you think Mrs. Hill will feel better about leaving if she knows her departure is contributing to such a good cause?"

Hill's arms were folded and his gaze fixed in contemplation. "Maybe you could call it the Emily Hill Hospital, after her. She would like that."

Joseph nodded in agreement. "I've seen a lot of women and children get injured in Edith's Hollow that have to make the journey all the way to Fall River before they can get treatment. It's an awful sight. You two will really be making a difference."

Joseph was right. When Mr. Hill went home that day, he talked to his wife again about the public service position that had been offered him. He told her there was nothing in Edith's Hollow for them anymore and appealed to her fondness for high society. And, when he proposed to leave a hospital behind in her name, it was a bright spot for her in a dreary conversation. She wasn't entirely happy but, in the end, she agreed to go.

Joseph organized a large gathering to cheer the Hills and bid them farewell as they left. The next day, he and Edith moved their things into the Hills' home. When they were finished unpacking their last load from the buggy, Joseph climbed the stairs and, with his hands resting on the banister, looked down on the room beneath him.

Edith was sitting on a chair playing with a doll. A question had been weighing on her mind since her dad told her they were moving into the Hills' home. Lately, he had been so secretive and unpredictable, though, that she was afraid to ask him anything remotely prying. She never knew how he would react to things anymore. Still, this was important so she summoned her courage. "Dad" she called, looking up at him.

He looked down at her to show he was listening but he didn't say anything.

"Why are we here?" she asked. "I mean, why are we moving into this house."

"I thought you liked this home," he said.

"I do," Edith said. "It's just...you know...why?"

Joseph took a second to gather his thoughts. "You know the woman from the mill we brought here a little while ago?"

"Yes," Edith said. "Emily."

"That's right. Well, there's going to be more like her. People are going to keep getting hurt and now we have somewhere to bring them when they do."

Something about her Father's response made Edith very unsettled but she tried not to show it. "OK," she said, faking a small smile. Then, after thinking for a moment, she spoke up again. "So...is it going to be like a hospital?" she asked.

Joseph chuckled at Edith's question for quite a while. She furrowed her brow. She didn't understand what was funny.

"Some might call it that," he finally said. "But I wouldn't. For you and I, it's home now."

1974

CHAPTER 17

Jaime turned the page of the journal resting in his lap and read the final few lines of the entry:

> *Looking back now, that's when the worst of it really began. Maybe I should have found a way to put an end to it all back then. I was so young, though, and Father was so strong.*

He slid the book from his lap and placed it on the floor next to him. He needed a break from reading.

He rested his head against the wall behind him. Earlier in the day, the fear-stoked adrenalin that flooded his body made sleep seem impossible. Now, though, his eyelids were beginning to feel heavy. He closed his eyes and started to drift off. Then he felt something running up his leg. His eyes popped open to see a small, grey mouse resting on his knee. Instinctively, he jumped to his feet. To his surprise, the mouse didn't fall from his leg. Instead, it ran further up his thigh.

Jaime began frantically jumping and slapping at his leg. As he did, he stumbled backwards into the bookshelf that stood in the corner of the room. He hit it hard, creating a loud bang. The thin pane of glass in one of the bookcase doors he had previously left open rattled and a couple books fell from one of the shelves to the floor. He saw the mouse fall to the floor as well and scurry away. He relaxed, leaned his back against the bookshelf, and laughed at himself quietly.

His heart rate had just begun to slow back down when he thought he heard something in the hallway. He picked up his flashlight, walked over to the door and pressed his ear against it. He could hear rustling and muttering. It was Edith. He must have woken her. She sounded like she was walking down the hallway toward Jaime's room. The sounds of her footsteps and her voice were getting closer.

He tightened his grip on the weighty, metal flashlight in his hand. Soon, he could hear her right outside of his door. She was close enough now that he could hear what she was saying. *"Yes, Father, I'll take care of it. Yes, I know what to do if he's woken up. No, it won't be the first. You stay in bed. This won't take long."*

His heart began beating fast again. Edith tried turning the doorknob but it was still locked. He saw it move as she jiggled it. He brought the flashlight up close to his head and watched the knob carefully. Then, suddenly, she stopped moving it and went silent. Jaime pushed his ear against the door harder and waited to hear anything. In a moment, he heard rustling again but this time it was moving away from the door. It sounded like Edith was going back to her room.

Jaime could hear the muffled sound of Edith's door closing. He stood with his ear pressed against his door for another four or five minutes before relaxing his shoulders and walking back to the spot where he had left the journal. He picked it up and sat on the bed cross-legged. Any thought of sleep was gone once again. He placed the journal in front of him; it was still opened to the spot where he had left off. Fanning the remaining pages, he saw that there was still a lot left to read. So, skipping ahead several pages and stopping randomly, he began again.

1901

CHAPTER 18

Edith woke up to her Father shaking her. "Edith!" he said with quiet urgency, "why are you sleeping?!"

She rolled over onto her back and rubbed her eyes. "What time is it?" she asked sleepily.

"It's nearly midnight. You should have started an hour ago."

She breathed a tired sigh. "Ok, I'll get up."

"Now!" Joseph demanded, trying to keep his voice down.

It was the night of the harvest moon – Edith's least favorite night of the year. She normally didn't go to bed until the early morning hours, if at all, on this night but this year was different. She had barely slept the night before because she was tending to a guest most of the night. Her Father would not have been happy if he knew, which is why she wasn't telling him. His instructions were always the same: *give them their medicine, their food, and their water, then shut the door and lock it. Don't return until it's time for more medicine, no matter what. And don't linger. Our guests need their rest.*

Edith didn't always obey. This particular guest had just arrived earlier in the day and he was only 9 years old – a few years younger than she was. His right leg was broken badly. Joseph had attempted to set it but it still didn't look right to her and he was in a lot of pain. Edith snuck into his room after her Father had gone to bed. The young boy was sweating and tightly gripping his sheets when she entered. She did the only thing she knew to do; she gave him an injection from the small bottle labeled "heroin" that her Father told her to carry with her. Typically, extra doses were not given to guests unless they were screaming loud enough for others to hear but Edith couldn't bear to watch the boy suffer.

A moment after receiving the injection, the boy relaxed. *'This one's not going to die,'* Edith thought to herself. She had gotten in the habit of predicting which ones would live and which ones would die. She was quite good at it. Although, sometimes guests who seemed to only have minor injuries would surprise her by dying in their sleep a few days after arriving. She suspected that it had something to do with the medicine. Her Father demanded that each new guest be placed on regime of very large, daily doses which he said could be tapered off if they seemed to be getting better. The injections kept them quiet and made them easier to manage. Secretly, though, Edith had begun giving smaller doses in increased intervals and she noticed that more patients were surviving the first few days of their stay.

She sat down next to the boy lying in his bed and asked him his name. "Henry," he replied with a thick, Irish accent.

Edith reached out and touched his hand but he immediately pulled it away. He seemed nervous.

"I'll take care of you, Henry," she said. "You're going to be OK."

The boy didn't say anything.

"Do your parents live here in Edith's Hollow?" she asked.

Henry shook his head. "My Dad's dead and me mum still lives in Ireland. She sent me and my brother here to find work."

Edith nodded her head. That was no surprise. Most of the injured who came to their home these days had a similar story. Most of them were immigrants or outsiders without family. There were still a few of the original workers left from the early days but not many. These days, Joseph made it a point not to hire anyone who was already from town. That didn't go over well with the locals and it resulted in many of the original families leaving. Edith still remembered the day the Baines left Edith's Hollow. She was sad to see them go.

"Maybe tomorrow I can find you a pen and paper so you can write home to her," Edith offered.

"I don't know how to write," Henry said.

"Well, I can write," Edith said. "I'll help you."

"OK," the boy said, not really showing any emotion. He looked tired so Edith stopped trying to make conversation. She stayed with him, though, until she was sure he was asleep. It was late when she crawled into her own bed.

The next morning when she woke up, she immediately realized her mistake. She remembered that the harvest moon would rise that night and that she wouldn't have a chance to catch up on the sleep she had missed. So, hoping for a quick nap, she snuck off to her room around 8:00 in the evening. The next thing she knew, it was midnight and her Father was waking her.

Edith stretched her legs then sat up in her bed. Her Father was still standing over her, waiting to make sure she was following his directive. "Sorry," she said. "I'm coming."

"You gather the bedding and things; I'll start the fire."

As Edith got out of bed, familiar words sprung to her mind; *'First, to the attic where the cobwebs have massed. Dig through the remains of years that have passed.'* Three years prior, late in the summer, her Father had come to her one evening and handed her a piece of paper with a poem written on it. "What is it?" she asked.

"It's a poem to help you with your chores on harvest moon nights," he said. "I want you to memorize it." Then he quizzed her day after day until she knew it by heart. She thought it was clever. The poem did exactly what it was intended to do. Each year on the night of the harvest moon, she knew her tasks by simply repeating the poem to herself.

She made her way to a trap door in the ceiling that led to the attic and stood beneath it. She had to stretch to reach the rope that hung from the door. When she pulled on it firmly, the door opened and a wooden ladder slid down, beckoning her to climb. At the top of the ladder was an attic that was empty except for the stacks of bedding and used clothes that lay near the entrance.

Edith picked pieces from the two, unfolded piles to her left and dropped them to the floor below. Each item was stained with blood. She worked until the piles were gone. Then, she turned to her right where there were several neatly folded piles of unstained bedding. She took two blankets and a pillowcase off the top and climbed down the ladder.

She left the pile of stained bedding and clothes lying on the ground. There was no chance that anybody would come across them. Her Father was outside tending to the fire and, inside, every guest was sedated and locked away in their rooms. Even if somebody managed to get out, the chances of them reaching her were almost zero. Her Father had spent years constructing the "hospital wing" (as he liked to call it) in a way that carefully minimized the risk of guests encountering each other or finding their way out. A labyrinth of hallways and staircases intersected by waiting rooms and locked doors had proven quite effective.

Edith had become so familiar with the addition her Father built onto the front of the Hills' old home that she was sure she could find her way through the maze with her eyes closed if she needed to. She wouldn't want to, though. No matter how familiar they had become, the dimly lit halls always felt creepy to her. This was in no small part due to the way the cries and moans of the guests who lay injured in their rooms echoed all around. Her Father had hoped that by building twisting and turning corridors, he would keep the noise in each hallway from reaching the others. Instead, the opposite had happened. As one walked the halls, voices and other sounds would seem to come from everywhere and nowhere at once. Usually, it was impossible to identify their source.

Edith took solace in knowing that there were only two keys that would unlock the doors in the hospital wing; one belonged to her Father and one belonged to her. She kept hers with her at all times, tucked away safely in a pocket near her waist. Of course, this was for convenience as much as it was for comfort. One of her Father's strict rules was that every door in the hospital wing must remain locked at all times, including entrances, exits, guest-room doors, and doors connecting corridors. So, all day every day, Edith was constantly locking and unlocking doors. And, for extra precaution, one of her jobs was to walk every inch of the house each evening before going to bed to ensure every last door was locked, including her Father's and her own.

There were two guest rooms that had not been used for months due to the need for items of clean bedding and the stains on the walls that Edith had not been able to get clean. This happened from time to time. When it did, she saved the work for the harvest moon, as she had been told to do. Even in the busiest times, the hospital wing was never filled to capacity. There was always enough vacancy to leave some rooms unused until they could be properly cleaned.

Edith gathered a few supplies and made her way to the soiled rooms. She changed the bedding as needed and scrubbed the walls until all signs of the previous guests were gone. Then, carrying a large, wicker basket she had retrieved from a room near the kitchen, she returned to the pile of clothes and bedding she had left in the hallway upstairs. She stuffed both piles into the basket and carried it outside.

When she stepped out of the backdoor, every muscle in her body suddenly tightened against the cold. She immediately realized the mistake she had made of not putting on more layers of clothing. But she didn't have the time to go back.

Her Father was easy to find. He was deep in the woods but the fire he had built was large and bright. She could feel its warmth from several feet away as she approached. Relaxing her tense muscles, she savored the heat for a quick moment. When she reached her Father's side, she set down the heavy, wicker basket next to him.

"This is all of it?" he asked. The crackling fire reflected an orange light on his face, interrupted again and again by dancing shadows.

Edith nodded her head. "Yes," she said.

"OK. You know what to do, kiddo." He reached into the basket and pulled a thin, soiled sheet off the top which he wadded into a large ball and tossed onto the fire. Edith followed suit, grabbing a pair of pants that looked to be about her size and adding them to the flames. Without speaking a word between them, the two continued emptying the basket one piece at a time until they were all gone.

Joseph spoke again when he saw that the basket was empty. "Come on," he said, "let's go get the other stuff."

Edith shuttered quietly. This was her least favorite part of the night. "Did you finish the hole already?" she asked. "I can finish that up if you need me to while you get them," she offered.

Joseph shook his head. "I finished it earlier today," he said. "Besides, I need your help." He turned and walked back toward the house, stepping out of the fire's light into the darkness. Edith followed. She caught up a little before they reached their destination. Instead of going to the back door, which they usually used to enter the house, they went to the side of the house where a trap door led to the cellar.

215

Joseph bent down and unlocked the padlock securing the door, swung it open, and nodded toward the opening. "Go on," he said to Edith. Doing her best to suppress her misgivings, she stepped onto a rung near the top of the cold, steel ladder that descended into the cellar and began climbing down. Although surrounded by walls, the cellar was no warmer than the open air outside. When she reached the dirt floor at the bottom, she stepped aside and waited for her Father.

Joseph climbed down and walked over to a large wooden box sitting next to one of the walls. It was six or seven feet long and approximately four feet wide. The top had been removed and the wood was splintery and unfinished. "Help me with this," he said to Edith. Together, the two of them carried the box to a dark heap in the middle of the floor that was difficult to discern in the unlit cellar. Edith knew what it was, though, and it made her stomach churn.

As soon as they set the box down, Joseph began taking remains from the small pile of decayed bodies and putting them in the box. Edith just stared. "Come on," Joseph said when he noticed. "Don't just stand there."

Reluctantly, she reached down with both hands and grasped what was in front of her. She couldn't see exactly what she was grabbing but she felt it separate from another part it had been connected to. Almost immediately, she felt something moving on her hand. She looked down and, in the darkness, thought she could see something crawling. She screamed and dropped what she had picked up.

"It's just the maggots," her Father said. "Brush them off. They won't hurt you. It's not like you haven't done this before."

Edith calmed down, took a breath, and brushed the maggots off of her hand. "Just because I've done it before doesn't mean I have to like it," she said sulkily.

"Life's all about doing things we don't like, Edith. That's how we survive."

She took another deep breath and started again. The nearer they got to the bottom of the pile, the more decayed the bodies were. The last one was nearly just bones.

When they were finished, Joseph found the lid which he secured tightly to the box with some rope. "There are quite a few more than last year," he said. "This is going to be heavy for you. Go on and try to lift your end. Let's see how this goes."

Joseph lifted his side while Edith bent down and grasped the bottom corners near her feet. Her Father was right. The box was difficult for her to get off the ground but, with considerable effort, she pulled it up as high as her waist.

"I'll tell you what," he said, "set it down and go climb the ladder. I'll hoist one end up out of the cellar then I'll just need you to grab the rope that's wrapped around it and pull as hard as you can."

Edith hesitated. "Are you sure you can do that?" she asked skeptically.

Joseph smirked and winked. "Watch me," he said.

Edith smiled. "OK," she said. "Let's see what you can do." She climbed up the ladder and waited up top. She could hear her Father struggling as he picked up the wooden box. Then, with a loud grunt, one end of it appeared through the cellar-door opening and landed with a thud near Edith's feet.

"Pull," her dad called out in a strained voice.

Edith quickly grabbed the rope that was tied around the box and pulled as hard as she could. As she did, her dad pushed from the other side, climbing up the ladder once the angle of the box allowed. Edith marveled at his strength.

After a few minutes, the task was complete. Joseph let Edith rest for a minute before the two of them carried the box to the large hole he had dug near the grove of nut trees that grew near the side of their house. They set the box next to it then Joseph used his foot to tip it on its side, dumping the contents into the hole. He grabbed the box and shook it a little to make sure nothing was left in the bottom. Then, looking at Edith, he said, "I'll take this box back to the cellar. Fill in the hole and then you can be done for the night. The shovel is lying against that tree over there." He nodded in the direction of a tree at the front of the grove.

Edith recognized the tree. It was Emily's tree – the one she had carved an "E" in several years before in remembrance of the young woman who had died under their roof. Despite how young she had been and all the time that had passed, she still remembered that day vividly.

Edith nodded her head. "Yes, Father," she said.

He paused before leaving. "Are you going to do your little candle thing again this year?"

Edith nodded silently. Joseph rolled his eyes. "Well, I'm going to get some sleep. You need to do the same. There will be work to do tomorrow."

"I'll go right to bed when I'm done," Edith said. "I promise."

Joseph sighed a sigh of disapproval but didn't say anything else. Although neither Joseph nor Edith would ever say so, they both knew that, despite how strict and difficult Joseph could be, he didn't like telling Edith no. He picked up the box and headed toward the cellar side of the house.

Edith walked over to Emily's tree as her Father walked out of sight. Before picking up the shovel, she searched the tree trunk for the circled "E" which she quickly found. It grew a little further up the tree every year. She reached out and traced the carving with her finger. Back then, she couldn't have guessed that Emily would end up being only the first of many. She wondered what her younger self would have thought if she could have peaked into the future and seen her life as it was now. Surely it would have depressed her. There was no school or friends or any of the things other children got to experience. Her Father never brought her to town or, for that matter, permitted her to go anywhere or interact with anyone other than their guests in order to bring food and medicine or, occasionally, with her Father's night-crew supervisor, Emory Green when he came through their back door and sat with Joseph at the kitchen table to discuss mill business.

She grabbed the shovel and began scooping spadefuls of dirt into the hole her Father had dug. Her arms and back were accustomed to tasks like these and she finished quickly. She headed back to the house and, after putting the shovel away, went upstairs to her room.

In one of the bottom drawers of her dresser was a pocketknife, several small candleholders designed to be nailed to a wall, and a stack of photographs. Her Father had bought the candleholders for her after a fair amount of begging. The photographs were pictures she had taken herself with the box camera her Father had proudly brought home from Boston a few years prior. He handed it to Edith and explained that he wanted her to start taking pictures of their guests' injuries so they could try to diagnose them in the medical books he bought from a Boston bookstore.

After about a year of very little success with the medical books, Joseph lost his enthusiasm for trying to heal their guests. Instead, he focused his energies on minimizing their interference with his daily life and keeping any knowledge of them from leaking outside of the walls of his home. More and more, he shifted the burden of their care to Edith and expected her to keep them quiet, keep them locked in their rooms, and keep them a secret.

However, Edith had not given up on curing the injuries of those she tended to. Long after her Father's enthusiasm had waned, she was still taking pictures and, almost daily, comparing them to the pictures in her Father's books. She tried everything she could with the few resources she had and kept notes on what worked and what didn't.

As devastating as it was to lose guest after guest, she took some satisfaction in knowing that at least some had healed nicely under her care. Oddly, her Father seemed grumpy whenever he had to load a healed guest into his buggy and drive them away with their belongings. Edith didn't know where he took them but she never saw them again.

She discovered the camera was useful in another way, too. When a guest died, she had learned to take a picture of them and write their initials in the corner of their photograph. That helped her remember who they were.

Edith opened the drawer with the pictures and took the first seven off the top of the stack. She also grabbed her pocketknife and seven of the candleholders and put them in a gunny sack that she kept under her bed. Before going back outside, she loaded her sack with a hammer, nails, and a small box of matches. Then, heading back to the grove of trees by the freshly-filled grave next to her house, she got to work.

She took the pictures and the pocketknife from her sack. For each guest that had passed that year, she found an unmarked tree and carved his or her initials in it. Then, she nailed a candleholder above each new set of initials. Finally, she took out the box of matches and lit every candle in the grove, both from that year and years passed.

She stepped back and folded her arms tightly against her body in the cold. She laughed silently at herself for once again failing to put on anything warm before coming out into the night. The rows of tiny orange flames and dancing shadows mesmerized her. She thought of the guests she had lost that year, running their faces through her mind. Some she had barely come to know but others she had spent hours with next to their beds, holding their hands, and hoping something she had done for them would work.

She breathed a heavy sigh. Several minutes passed while she remained deep in her thoughts. Finally, she yawned and realized how tired she was. So, while the candles still burned, she went back to bed.

CHAPTER 19

Sam sat on a wooden chair behind the register with his legs stretched out and his nose in a book. It was a little after lunch time on a Wednesday and nobody was in the store but him. There was once a time when customers would trickle in all throughout the day but, these days, there weren't many families living in the mill-worker's homes with them. The mill houses were mostly occupied by single men and women and Irish immigrants who had come across the water alone and who often mistook Sam for an Irishman due to his bright, red hair.

As the demographics changed in Edith's Hollow, so did the foot traffic at the company store. The steady trickle had been replaced by a daily rush that began when the dayshift ended at the mill. In fact, for many, a stop at the store on their way home had become part of their daily routine, regardless of whether they had anything to buy. They would stand around the register and shoot the bull with Sam, who was hard not to like.

Sam was still preaching at the church every Sunday so he enjoyed any opportunity to gather ideas for his sermons. He kept a notebook under the counter which he would occasionally pull out and quickly scribble something on while the mill workers talked around him. Whenever someone cursed, everyone would pause briefly so they could apologize to Sam who would smile politely in return. He had given up on reminding them that he was only a preacher by default.

This time of day was always extremely slow. So, Sam was surprised when he heard the bell above the door ring as someone entered. He was even more surprised when he looked up from his book and saw someone that he didn't recognize. That rarely happened. The man was short with leathery skin, jet-black hair, and dark stubble on his face. "Hello," he said curtly with a deep, crackly voice.

Sam set down his book and stood up from his chair. "Hi," he said. "Can I help you with anything?"

The man walked straight to Sam. "I'm looking for the owner of the mill," he said, getting straight to the point.

"Mr. Fridman?" Sam asked.

"Yes, that's the one. Where can I find him?"

Sam hesitated. Something about this stranger made him uncomfortable. He wasn't sure he should be handing over information about anyone to him. "I'm sorry, sir," he said, shrugging his shoulders. "I don't know where he is. He hasn't been in the store at all today.

The man stared at Sam for a second, seeming skeptical. "I know how these small towns work," he said. "Everyone needs groceries and that means everyone comes to the general store and when they're here they talk. So, that means you know things. Don't mess with me, boy. I need to find Fridman. Where is he?"

Sam was taken aback. He was annoyed and a little intimidated at the same time. He was telling the truth, though. He really didn't know where Joseph was. "Honestly," he said, "I don't know. Have you tried the mill? That's usually where he is during the day."

The man scowled in disappointment. "He's not there; I already checked. I'm told his house is somewhere in these woods," he said, nodding in the general direction.

"That's right," Sam said. "But, I've never been there. I actually don't know anyone who has. Mr. Fridman likes his privacy and I hear his place can be tough to find if you don't know where you're going."

The stranger scowled again. He could see that Sam was telling the truth. He had nothing to offer. "Fine," he said gruffly. "If you see him, tell him Josiah Knightly is looking for him." He said his name as though Sam would recognize it.

"OK," Sam said, not seeming impressed.

Josiah reached in his pocket and pulled out a metal badge. He slapped it down on the counter in front of Sam for him to see. It was a six-pointed star made out of copper. In the middle it read "DEPUTY SHERIFF." "Maybe you mill people haven't heard yet but I'm the law here now," he said. "I've made my home in town so you'll be seeing plenty of me."

Sam picked up the badge and raised his eyebrows. "We've never had law enforcement around here," he said. "I guess it will be nice to have a public servant joining our community." He was being polite. Truthfully, he didn't see the need for the Sheriff's Office to keep a deputy at Edith's Hollow.

Josiah put his hands on the countertop that stood between him and Sam. "You know, the people in town don't trust you mill people. Why is that?"

Sam met Josiah's gaze. He resented how everyone who lived in the newer part of town referred to their section as "in town" as if the section around the mill was outside of town. He had been around when the mill *was* the town. If it wasn't for the mill and its workers, the town wouldn't exist.

"I don't know, Deputy. I guess that's something you'll have to look into," Sam said, handing the badge back.

"Oh don't worry, I intend to," Josiah said as he stuffed the badge back into his pocket. "And by the way, you can just call me Sheriff. It's easier to say, don't you think?"

Sam didn't reply. Josiah turned on his heel and walked out the door. Sam was close behind him. He stepped outside and tried to shake the irritation that had risen up inside of him from the Deputy's brief visit. He wasn't one to get upset easily but Josiah Knightly rubbed him the wrong way.

He stood in the sun and watched Josiah walk down the road. He looked to be heading to the juncture that led back to the new part of town. Over the years, the newcomers had carved a path off of the main road. The path bypassed the mill part of town and was trafficked so frequently that it quickly became the main thoroughfare. So, if somebody was travelling South from Boston or Fall River, unless they were careful not to miss the turn to the mill, the road would naturally lead them to the new part of Edith's Hollow.

From early on, suspicion had soured any hope of amity between the two groups of townspeople. Although, it had all begun innocent enough. Just three years prior, a couple moved into town, building a home away from the rest of the community. They wanted to move somewhere with room for a large farm. They had heard of Edith's Hollow and, when they visited, they fell in love with the land and with the untapped opportunity they saw in an underserved community.

They were the first people to move to town who didn't work for the mill in some capacity. Naturally, everyone was a little suspicious of them. However, the newcomers had a nice harvest that Fall and when they set up a booth near the church and began selling fresh fruits and vegetables that couldn't be bought at the company store, everyone put their suspicions on hold.

The townspeople probably could have gotten used to just one new family but the newcomers had friends and relatives. First, two of their adult children with families of their own built homes near them. Their son to one side helped his dad on the farm and tended to sick and injured animals. Their son-in-law to the other side was a carpenter and a barber.

The people in Edith's Hollow weren't accustomed to having services available to them. They had grown used to doing things for themselves, travelling to Fall River, or doing without. The sudden change was nice. A haircut from the barber up the road and a house call for an injured horse felt like luxuries. Their little town felt like it was blossoming.

The problem was, the newcomers prospered. So, word spread to their friends. Within the year, a small community had sprung up around them. Before long, the mill people needed the newcomers more than the newcomers needed them. And, soon it became clear that the newcomers preferred the company of each other over the poor and the immigrants that mostly made up the mill community.

There were only a couple miles of distance between the mill and the new part of town but the two sections felt completely distinct from each other. Still, the newcomers adopted the name "Edith's Hollow" and took it upon themselves to write a town charter. They applied to the state legislature for recognition without involving Joseph or anyone from his part of town. When recognition was granted, Joseph was furious but mostly just because he hadn't thought of writing a charter himself.

Sam was the closest thing the two groups had to an intermediary. His store kept a few things that even the newcomers couldn't get elsewhere and he was the only person conducting any kind of services on Sundays. Whatever he thought of the newcomers, he didn't feel right denying them groceries or God so he welcomed them to his store and to church.

When it became clear that the two groups could hardly sit in the same room together on Sunday mornings, though, Sam began conducting an extra session of church in the afternoons. It worked. The newcomers attended. And, by preaching to them, Sam came to know them. He still didn't like their smug attitude or the things they sometimes said but at least he knew them, which was more than could be said of anyone else from his side of town.

When Josiah Knightly was out of sight, Sam headed over to Emory Green's house. If anyone knew where Joseph was, he figured Emory would. He was right. In fact, when he knocked on Emory's door and asked if he knew where Joseph was, Emory invited him in where Joseph was sitting on a wooden rocking chair in the main room of Emory's house.

After some brief small talk, Sam told Joseph about his encounter with Josiah.

"What did you tell him?" Joseph asked.

"I told him the truth," Sam said. "I said I didn't know where you were. He asked how to get to your house but I explained to him that I've never been there so I didn't know for sure."

"Do you think he really is law enforcement?" Joseph asked.

Sam shrugged his shoulders. "He showed me his badge. I'd say he is."

"Thank you, Sam. You know, you're actually the third person today to tell me this fellow is looking for me. I guess I'll have to head over to that part of town and see what this is all about."

"Well, good luck with that, Mr. Fridman," Sam said. "I better get back to the store. The millworkers will be getting out soon."

Joseph pulled a pocket watch from his pocket. "Is it already that time?" he asked. "I better get going too, then."

The three men said their goodbyes and went their separate ways. Joseph went to the mill to take care of a couple things before the day shift ended. Then he went home to tell Edith he might be late and rode his horse to the new part of town. When he arrived, he could see activity at a small building he knew the townspeople sometimes used for meetings and gatherings. He tied up his horse and opened the door.

The room was full. A group of five sat at the front facing everyone else. He stepped inside and one of the women at the front stopped mid-sentence. "Can we help you, Mr. Fridman?" she asked.

Everyone turned in their seats to look at Joseph.

Joseph shook his head. "I don't intend to interrupt," he said. "You can go on."

The woman cleared her throat, seeming a little nervous and a little irritated at once. "This is an official meeting, Mr. Fridman. If there's nothing we can do for you, perhaps you should excuse yourself."

"What kind of meeting?" Joseph asked.

The woman huffed in irritation. The man next to her chimed in. "It's a town meeting," he said, looking like he was ready for a fight.

"You mean a meeting for the people of Edith's Hollow?" Joseph asked rhetorically.

Nobody responded.

"Good," he continued. "I'm in the right place. See, I'm a citizen of Edith's Hollow so I thought I'd come down and join your meeting." He took his hat off and sat down on the seat nearest him, making a few people in the row squirm uncomfortably. "You can continue," he said.

The woman at the front glared back at Joseph with pursed lips. "Go on, Camellia," a man a few seats down from her urged. "Just continue."

"Well...um...as I was saying" she kept glancing at Joseph as she regained her composure, "the final item of business tonight is the town book we've been discussing for weeks now. You'll recall, the idea was first raised by councilman Richards and it's received overwhelming support by everyone here. I'm proud to announce tonight that the book has formally begun." She pulled a large, leather-bound book out of the bag resting against her chair and held it up for everyone to see. "A Living History of Edith's Hollow," she said. The room applauded.

Out of the corner of his eye, Joseph noticed a man near the front on the opposite side of the room that kept looking back at him. He watched the back of his head until he turned to look at him again.

When he did, Joseph's eyes widened. He recognized his face. An image from several years before flashed in his mind of him and Thomas Baines being banished from the docks by a short, greasy man with a scowl on his face. In his right hand, he tightly gripped a fat, wooden club that he had used to strike Joseph across the back of his head.

Joseph's face suddenly became hot. He had never expected to see that man again – especially not here. He tightened his jaw and clenched his fist. He was half inclined to make him pay for all the trouble he had caused Joseph and Thomas and their families. But what was a union boss from the docks doing in Edith's Hollow?

Joseph didn't have to wait long to satisfy his curiosity. Before he knew it, the meeting was over and the small building began to clear. He waited in his seat, hoping for an empty room when he confronted the man. The man found him first, though.

Joseph was surprised when he heard his crackly voice. "So you're Joseph Fridman," he said.

He looked up and saw the man standing over him. Joseph stood, deliberately rolling back his shoulders and reaching his full height. "That's right," he said. "You found me. I've got to admit, I never expected to see you again."

Josiah furrowed his brow in confusion. It occurred to Joseph that the short, greasy man didn't know who he was.

"You don't remember me, do you?" Joseph asked.

"No, I don't" Josiah admitted.

"I worked on your docks years ago."

"You and hundreds of others, Fridman. I didn't make friends with the laborers."

"I didn't say we were friends," Joseph said. "You kicked me and my companion off of your docks one day and kept us from ever working in Fall River again. The guy that was with me had young kids at home. You nearly ruined his family."

Josiah's eyes lit up with recognition. "I *do* remember you," he said, sizing Joseph up. "And here you are, the king of the mill people. Good for you," he said sarcastically. "Once a mill rat always a mill rat, I guess," he snickered.

Joseph took a step closer and stared Josiah down. "I don't know why you're here," he said, "but I think it's time you leave my town."

"*Your* town?" Josiah laughed.

"That's right," Joseph said. "This is my town. I was here long before any of these people. I built this place out of nothing."

"Well, that might be," Josiah sneered, "but it's not yours anymore. In fact," he said, pulling his deputy sheriff's badge from his pocket, "I think this badge says this town is mine now."

Joseph furrowed his brow in confusion. "So you're the one that's been looking for me," he said.

"That's right."

"But…" Joseph began. A number of questions were running through his mind and he wasn't sure which one to start with.

Josiah interrupted. "I had to leave the docks and, let's just say, I had connections with the local law enforcement."

"So what do you want with me?" Joseph asked. Suddenly, he was nervous. Had someone found out about his dying workers and reported him?

"Well, Mr. Smith just up the road here had some nice new tools he bought in Fall River recently. Just a couple nights ago they went missing out of his barn. Everyone around here suspects one of your people did it."

Joseph scoffed. "We have better things to do then hang around your part of town," he said. "Trust me, it wasn't any of my workers."

"That's just it," Josiah said. "I don't trust you. And I don't trust any of those people you surround yourself with."

"Well then, I'll make this real easy for you. We'll stay on our side of town and you stay on your side. That should keep you out of any precarious situations, Deputy," Joseph said with contempt.

"Is that a threat, Fridman?" Josiah asked. "Absolutely" Joseph said, staring him in the eye.

"You better remember who you're talking to," Josiah said. "I'm keeping tabs on you, Fridman. You make one misstep and you better believe justice will be swift and unyielding."

"Thanks for the fancy speech, Knightly," Joseph said, tipping his hat. "Maybe you should go home and start working on your next one. I'm going to bed."

Joseph turned and walked away, leaving Josiah fuming. As he rode home, he felt a strange mix of relief and rising paranoia. He was relieved to learn that the only reason Josiah had been asking around about him was because of some frivolous accusation of petty theft. He didn't feel like he had much reason to relax, though. The last thing he wanted was an officer of the law watching him. Josiah Knightly was going to be trouble.

CHAPTER 20

Edith woke up with a flutter of excitement in her chest. She got out of bed and walked over to her window where the morning light was coming into her room. It looked clear and sunny outside. As far as she could tell, there weren't any clouds in the sky or any wind blowing the trees. She knew it would be a little cold out but, otherwise, the weather was exactly as she had hoped it would be.

The ocean was about 2 hours away on foot. Although, she had decided she would go on horseback, which would speed up the journey a little. She would likely be returning with a heavy load that she would rather not carry the whole way home.

When they had first come to Edith's Hollow, Joseph used to bring Edith with him on his journeys to the ocean almost every week. They had found a small cove that was difficult to reach and pretty well hidden. He set several lobster traps there and, over time, dug out a brine pond which he lined with clay that he found in the ground nearby. The pond trapped water from the tide and left behind salt as the sun evaporated the water. When the weather was dry and warm, the pond could yield a surprising amount of salt.

Edith's Father liked to say, "You're fortunate if you know how to make enough money to survive but you're more fortunate if you know how to survive without money." So, he taught her survival. He taught her to garden, hunt, trap, harvest honey, preserve food, build fires, and do many other things that freed them from dependence on anyone.

In recent years, though, Edith had become more and more confined to her house. The secluded cove on the ocean had become the only place her Father ever let her go but even those trips were rare. All month, she had been asking him if she could take one more trip there before winter came.

Joseph had seemed even more busy and preoccupied with his work than usual over the last few days. Edith had walked in on him several times pacing the floors and talking to himself underneath his breath. There seemed to be something happening at the mill that had him worried. Despite this, Edith persisted. She appealed to his practicality, urging him to check the traps and harvest the salt at the cove before the first snow so the resources wouldn't go to waste.

Her tactics worked. He finally gave in and, as she had hoped, he told her she would have to go without him. She had only gone to the ocean alone twice before. Each time had been like a dream come true. Joseph gave her strict instructions just as he had done on previous occasions; "go directly to the cove and come directly back, stay on the path, and don't talk to anyone." Edith eagerly agreed.

She had spent a day preparing for her journey and now she was ready to go. Joseph helped her load a few things onto her horse and reminded her of his instructions before she left. She promised again to obey and rode away, tightening her coat around her against a subtle but sharp breeze that was blowing. The sun was at her back, casting long, morning shadows as far as she could see.

The trail was blanketed in red and yellow leaves that rustled and crunched beneath her horse's hooves. The trees all around were ablaze with fall colors. A tiny thrill tingled inside of her and, for a moment, her world felt full of hope and possibilities. She sighed, wishing desperately she could hold on to this moment forever.

She could smell the salt water and feel it on her skin as she got close to the ocean. Once she could hear the tide slapping the rocks and sand, she turned off the trail. She rode several feet to the head of a steep drop off that led to the small cove she and her Father had privately claimed as their own. After tying her horse to a familiar tree, she unloaded a rake, a bucket, and a large gunny sack and carefully made her way down the rocks to a half-moon shaped plot of dry sand below.

The beach was small. Late in the evening, the tide would rise until the water reached the rocks Edith had climbed down and the beach disappeared. At the southern end of the cove, the rocks descended to a low bench that sat a few feet above the beach. This is where Joseph had prepared the brine pond. It was just low enough for the water to reach at high tide but high enough that salt deposits wouldn't be washed away if you raked them to the edges.

Edith wanted to relax and enjoy the beach but she had work to do first. She poured out the few food items she was carrying in her gunny sack and filled the sack with salt she harvested from the brine pond. Then she checked the lobster traps. To her delight, two of the traps each had a lobster in them. She filled her bucket half full with seawater and then dumped the lobster into it.

Then she took off her shoes, sat down just beyond the tide's reach, stretched out her legs, and pushed her heals into the soft, cool sand. She smiled. She couldn't think of another time she had felt this good. She ate lunch while she watched the ocean waves lapping over each other. She hoped to catch a glimpse of some kind of ocean life but all she saw was birds landing on the water's surface.

After lunch, using her gunny sack of salt as a pillow, she lay on her back and watched the clouds. The sounds of the sea nearly put her to sleep. Then, after several minutes, she decided it was time to get up and explore. She walked with her feet in the water and picked up seashells. Most of them, she threw into the water, tossing them as far as she could, but she kept a few of the prettiest ones, storing them in her pockets.

When she grew bored of finding shells, she knew it was time to go home. Her heart sank at the thought. She felt like she could stay at the beach all day but her Father would be angry if she was gone too long. He would worry that she had stopped and talked to someone contrary to his strict instructions.

She stood at the edge of the water and breathed the damp air deeply while the ocean breeze blew wisps of her hair all about. Then she sighed and turned around to gather up her things. When she did, she gasped out loud. A man was standing at the bottom of the rocks watching her.

Instinctively, Edith picked up a large stick and held it at her side, gripping it tightly. She didn't know what she would do with it but it made her feel a little safer.

The man held out his hands. "I'm sorry," he said. "I didn't mean to startle you." He was yelling so he could be heard over the ocean. "I was walking along the cliffs and I saw your horse. This spot is steep and rocky so I just wanted to check to make sure everything was OK."

Edith didn't say anything, creating a gap of silence between them filled only by the sounds of the tide and the seagull calls.

"Are you OK?" the man asked.

Edith nodded her head. Her Father hadn't explained how she was supposed to avoid speaking with anyone if they spoke to her first.

The man stepped a little closer. "Are you here alone? Where are your parents?"

Edith tightened her grip on her stick and raised it slightly. But as the man's face came into better view, to her relief, she realized that she recognized him. "I know you," she said.

He wrinkled his brow.

"You're the preacher from church."

"That's right," he said, still looking confused.

"I went to your church once – a long time ago – with my Father."

"Who's your Father?" he asked.

"I don't think I'm supposed to tell you," Edith said.

The man smiled at this, amused at the childishness of it. "Well, my name is Sam," he said, "but perhaps you knew that."

Edith shook her head.

"Is your Father here with you?" Sam asked. "I'd like to say hi to him if he is."

Edith shook her head again. When she did, she could see that Sam seemed concerned. She loosened her grip on her stick. She was used to reading faces and she felt like this was one she could trust.

"My Father is Joseph Fridman," she said.

Suddenly, Sam looked shocked. "Mr. Fridman?" he asked. "I didn't know that Mr. Fridman had children."

"Just me," Edith said.

"I've never seen you around town." Sam replied.

"I don't go to town."

"Never?"

"No. Never. I'm not supposed to."

"What about school? You go to school, don't you?"

Edith shook her head, no.

Sam furrowed his brow again in confusion and concern. "You don't go to school?" he said, taking a step closer. "Does your Father know you're here, at this beach?"

She nodded her head, yes. "Sometimes he lets me come here but nowhere else."

"Edith," Sam said, sounding very grave, "Are you OK?"

Now Edith furrowed her brow. "Yes," she said. "What do you mean?"

"I mean, does your Dad…ummm…are you, well, safe at your house?"

"Yes, of course. My Father's there. He makes sure I'm safe."

"And he doesn't hurt you?"

"My Father?" she said in surprise. "No, of course not! He would never hurt me. He gets mad at me sometimes – maybe a lot. But he would never hurt me."

Sam nodded his head, a little relieved. "Does he tell you you can't leave?" he asked.

"Well, yes but…" Edith trailed off. She knew her Father wouldn't be at all happy about this conversation. "I think I need to go," she said, abruptly. "It's a long ride back home. I should get started before it gets late."

"Sure. I understand," Sam said. "Let me help you with your things, though."

"Oh, I can get them," Edith said. It was too late, though. Sam had already picked up the bag of salt and was walking over to the lobster bucket. "These things are heavy," he said. "You were going to carry them all by yourself?"

Edith shrugged her shoulders. "It's not that bad," she said, picking up the rake she had brought to harvest the salt.

Sam scrambled up the rocks behind Edith as best he could, carrying the load. When he got near the top, Edith reached down. "Here," she said. "I'll take those." He handed each item up and was surprised at how well she was able to heft them. She had already begun loading the bag of salt into a saddle bag when he climbed over the last rock to the top.

"What are you going to do with that bucket?" he asked.

"Just carry it," Edith said. "I've done it before."

"Doesn't it get heavy or awkward?"

234

"Ummm…yeah," she admitted. "It kind of does. But I can do it." She began untying her horse.

"I'll tell you what," Sam said, as he began untying his horse too which was close to Edith's, "I'm headed back the same direction as you are. Why don't you let me carry that bucket for you until we get to your house?"

"Really?" Edith said.

"Yes, really. I'd be happy to."

"Well, OK. But, Mr. Sam."

Sam laughed. "Just Sam is fine."

Edith corrected herself. "Sam," she said, sounding suddenly serious, "you can ride with me but it's really important that you don't come to my house. You need to go a different way before we get there."

"Why is that?" he asked.

"Please," Edith said. "Just do it. Promise me you will."

Sam looked back at her for a moment wondering what could be going on in the walls of her home and trying to decide what to say. "Fine," he finally said, crossing his finger over his heart. "I promise."

Edith enjoyed having Sam with her on the ride back home. He was very kind. It was nice to talk to someone who wasn't drugged or lying injured in a bed.

About half a mile before reaching her home, she told Sam it was time for her to go a different direction. "Are you sure I can't take this the rest of the way for you?" he asked as he handed her the bucket of lobster and seawater.

Edith shook her head vigorously. "No, you definitely cannot. Thank you, though. It was very nice of you to ride with me."

"It was my pleasure," Sam said. "Be safe. And, if you ever need anything, you can usually find me at the store in town."

"Thank you," Edith said again.

Sam watched her as she rode away, trying to discern the path to her house. She never looked back to see him peering at her until she was out of sight. When she got home, her Father was outside, working in the front yard. She breathed a sigh of relief that she had left Sam behind when she did.

"Welcome back, kiddo," Joseph said. He looked at the bucket she was balancing on her saddle horn. "It looks like we got some lobster."

"Just two, but they're big ones," she said.

"Good," Joseph said, walking toward the gate to meet her as she came through. When he got to her, he took the lead rope and led her horse to a small pin. "Everything went OK?" he asked as he helped her down.

"Yes," Edith said. "The beach was so nice. It was a little cold, but I was OK with that. I found these shells…" she started to reach into her pocket but Joseph interrupted.

"Did you see anyone?" he asked.

"No, Father."

"You didn't pass anyone on the trail or along the shore?"

"No. Not a soul."

"Good." He handed her the bag of salt and the bucket with the lobster. "Bring these things inside and put on a pot of boiling water. I have some more work to do out here so I'll be in in a while. I'm glad you're home safe."

"Yes, Father," she said. "Me too."

CHAPTER 21

Edith heard knocking downstairs. She opened her eyes and lifted her head off her pillow, listening carefully. It was the middle of the night - perhaps she had just dreamed it. Then she heard it again. She got out of bed, walked over to her door, and opened it slightly. Her dad had come out of his room and was passing hers.

"Father!" she whispered loudly.

He didn't stop. "Go back to bed, Edith," he said. "It's nothing."

She was too curious to go back to bed, though. She waited until she heard her Father descend the stairs and then she came out into the hallway. Stepping gingerly, she crept down the hallway and down the stairs. She heard her dad in the kitchen, opening the back door. He spoke with someone briefly and then lit one of the kitchen lanterns.

She snuck closer until she was close enough to hear what was being said. She recognized the voice of the visitor. It was Emory Green, the night shift supervisor at the mill. Both men sounded exasperated.

"Another one?" Joseph said in disbelief.

"It's just like the others," Emory said. "all the parts seem to be moving the way they should but the lines of thread along the bottom become all loose and tangled up until the machine is completely unusable."

"Did you shut everything down so you could try and fix it?" Joseph asked.

237

"No," Emory said. "That proved to be a waste of time with the others that have done this so I didn't want to stop everybody else's production."

"Good," Joseph said. "I agree. Let's not put the whole mill on hold for one machine that we're not going to know how to fix anyway."

"So, what do you want to do?" Emory asked.

"Just send the worker home, I guess," Joseph said, sounding frustrated.

Emory sighed heavily.

"This is the fifth one this month," Joseph said. "The *fifth*," he repeated. "We can't sustain that kind of loss of production. We *have to* get this figured out."

"Did that guy from Boston write you back yet?" Emory asked. "The one who works on machines like ours?"

"He can't come until next month," Joseph said.

"Next month?!," Emory exclaimed.

"Yes, and even assuming he can diagnose the problem, he said it could take a week or more to get the parts and fix it."

"Isn't there anyone else who can come sooner?"

Joseph shook his head. "The machines we use are old. There aren't a lot of people who work on them."

"Well..." Emory said, sighing heavily again.

"If we don't get production up, we're not going to be able to fill either of the military's orders this month."

"How are they going to take that?" Emory asked.

"I don't know," Joseph said. "There's a lot of competition out there so, I just don't know."

The conversation sounded like it might be winding down so Edith decided to leave before she got caught. She snuck back upstairs and to her bedroom. *'So THAT is what Father has been worrying about,'* she thought to herself as she crawled into bed. All the times she had caught him pacing the floors and talking to himself recently now made sense. She fell asleep hoping things would improve at the mill for her Father's sake.

Unfortunately, things didn't improve. Two weeks passed and Joseph's stress kept rising. Edith could see it in almost everything he did. He was more withdrawn and quicker to snap. Emory was visiting the house for hushed meetings more than ever before. When

238

the end of the month passed and the look of worry on her Father's face still hadn't faded, Edith figured that the mill had not filled the military's order she had overheard her Father and Emory talking about.

A few days later, she was at the bottom of the stairs picking up a pile of dirty rags she had accidentally tipped out of a laundry basket when she heard her Father come home. He walked through the back door and sighed heavily. When he came around the corner, he didn't even acknowledge Edith sitting in front of him. Instead, he threw a folded piece of paper down on a table near the stairs, shaking his head in frustration, and then walked past her as he climbed the stairs without saying a word.

Edith's restraint only lasted about half a minute. As soon as she heard her Father's bedroom door close, she stood up and walked over to the table to examine the paper he had put down. When she unfolded it, she recognized it right away to be a Western Union telegram. It said it was from the office of Senator Henry Dawes and it was addressed to her Father. She read on:

> The Senator is apprised that the recent textile orders of two Army battalions were unfulfilled. As of this writing, the problem has not been remedied. These contract breaches concern the Senator and reflect poorly on him and you. The Senator will be visiting your facility this Thursday to ensure your operation continues to meet his standards for referral.

Edith laid the telegram back down. She knew enough about her Father's business to understand that, if he lost his contracts with the Army, the mill would be in serious trouble. Thursday was just two days away. Judging by the pit in her own stomach, she could only imagine how her Father was feeling. But, knowing there was nothing she could do, she decided to get back to work. Ever since the machines had begun having problems, injuries at the mill had increased. Edith and her Father were up to 9 guests in their hospital wing and it was time for Edith to give them their doses of medicine.

Before she could begin her work, though, a noise caught her attention. It sounded like someone knocking on a door. She stood still and listened intently then heard it again. It was coming from the front of the house. It was so rare to have a visitor knocking on their front door that Edith's stomach churned a little with a mix of apprehension and excitement. Her Father wouldn't want her speaking with their visitor but she had to at least see who it was. Her curiosity wouldn't allow her to do anything less.

Rather than winding her way through the hospital wing, she knew she could reach the front door more quickly if she slipped out the back and walked around the house. So, that's what she did. She stopped when she reached the front corner of the house and only poked her head out so she wouldn't be seen. But, when she looked around the corner, there was nobody there.

Confused, she came out from where she was standing and walked to the door. As she got closer, she could see that it was ajar. "Hello?" she called as she walked inside cautiously. A familiar voice responded.

"Edith?" he said.

The house seemed dark when coming in out of the sun but her eyes quickly adjusted. When they did, she saw Sam standing at the end of the hall. "Mr. Sam!" she exclaimed in hushed urgency. "What are you doing here?"

"Edith, there you are," he said. "Sorry for walking in but I knocked and nobody came. Does this hall lead anywhere?" he asked, looking confused by the seemingly dead-end corridor he was standing in.

"Why are you here?" Edith repeated, sounding frustrated and worried.

"I wanted to speak with your Father. Is he home?"

"You can't," Edith said. "I told you not to come here. You need to leave. He can't know you're here."

"Why not?" Sam pressed. "Edith, I have to be honest with you. I'm concerned that you're not safe here."

"You don't understand, Mr. Sam. *You're* not safe here."

"Edith, this isn't normal," Sam said. Before he could say anything more, though, a door that blended into the wall behind Sam opened and Joseph stepped through it. He was taken aback when he saw the scene in the hallway.

"Sam?" Joseph said. "What are you doing here? Edith, what's going on?" his anger was rising. He closed the door behind him.

"Mr. Fridman, hello," Sam said, hoping to calm him down. "I was just telling your daughter, I came here to speak with you. Edith didn't know I was coming. She didn't have anything to do with this."

Joseph furrowed his brow in suspicion. "Of course she didn't," he said. "How would she know you were coming?"

"She didn't," Sam reiterated. "I just…"

Joseph interrupted. "Edith, leave us," he ordered.

"But, Father…" Edith began.

"Leave us!" Joseph thundered, startling Edith and Sam.

"Mr. Fridman," Sam said, holding out his hands. "There's no reason to get upset." Edith was already walking past both men toward the door her Father had come through. When she opened it, she was horrified by what happened. An unmistakable groan of pain, loud and clear, resonated from the corridors below.

Edith froze and looked at her Father. Panic flashed across his face but his expression quickly hardened back into anger. The suffering person below groaned loudly again.

"What was that?" Sam asked.

In a flash, Joseph pounced on Sam, turned him around, and pinned his head against Joseph's chest with Joseph's forearm firmly against Sam's neck.

"Father, no!" Edith cried but Joseph ignored her.

Sam struggled, kicking his feet, pulling at Joseph's arms, and swatting at his head. It wasn't any use, though. Joseph was bigger and stronger than Sam and he wouldn't be deterred. Edith tried her best as well. She pulled at Joseph's shirt and begged him to stop but to no avail.

Soon, Sam's body went limp and Joseph lowered it to the ground.

"Is he dead?" Edith asked, stunned. She wiped away a tear running down her cheek.

"No, of course not," Joseph said matter-of-factly. "Help me get him downstairs." He lifted Sam from his armpits and picked the upper half of his body off the ground. Edith stared without moving a muscle or saying a word.

"Edith, snap out of it," Joseph said. "I need your help. You're not doing him any good by leaving him lying on the floor."

"OK," she said numbly. Reluctantly, she picked up Sam's feet and followed her Father through the camouflaged door at the end of

241

the hallway and down the stairs to the corridors of the hospital wing. "What are we going to do with him?" she asked tentatively.

"We're going to make him comfortable," Joseph replied. "In here," he said as he turned toward a door in the hallway. "Nobody's in this one, right?"

Edith nodded her head.

"Put his feet down and unlock this door."

Edith did as she was asked. She swung the door open and Joseph dragged Sam into the room. He hoisted him onto the neatly-made bed. "OK, bring your medicine over here," he said to Edith.

"What?" she asked, reflexively.

"The medicine, Edith. Come on!" Joseph said impatiently. "He's going to wake up soon."

"But he's not injured," Edith said. "He doesn't need medicine."

"Do not argue with me, Edith," Joseph said sternly. "Bring the medicine over."

Just then, Sam began to stir. Joseph grabbed his arms and held them down.

"Now!" Joseph demanded.

Sam opened his eyes. He looked confused.

Edith nervously fumbled in her pockets for the small vial of liquid and a syringe. She filled the syringe and walked over to Sam, still hesitating. Sam began to become more coherent. "What's going on?" he asked as he began to struggle.

Edith stood frozen at his side for a moment with the needle in hand.

"Edith!" Joseph urged again.

She took a deep breath and shoved the needle into Sam's arm which was restrained under Joseph's strong hand. She pushed a large dose of the slightly murky liquid into his vein then quickly pulled the needle out. When she was done, she spun around and walked quickly out of the room. She stopped a few feet outside of the door and stared at the carpeted ground. She couldn't remember ever feeling so angry.

Joseph came out of the room a moment later. He closed the door behind him and locked it. Edith's back was to him. He turned to her and placed a hand on her shoulder. "You did good," he began to say.

"I don't want to talk," Edith said coldly. She dropped the empty syringe on the floor and walked away. She passed through the winding hallways and stairs until she reached her bedroom. When she got there, she stepped inside, closed the door, sat on her bed and cried – but only for a second.

She took a deep breath and willed the tears to stop. Her anger was still pulsing deep inside her chest. She thought about everything that had just happened. She could hear her Father's voice in her head ordering her to give Sam the medicine. She replayed it again and again in her mind, feeling the anger swell until it filled her body. It felt better than sadness. It erased the feeling of helplessness.

She heard a knock at her door. Before she could say anything, the door opened and her Father poked his head in. "We need to talk," he said.

"I don't want to," Edith said.

Joseph ignored her. He came inside and sat next to her on her bed. "Are you OK?" he asked.

"No," she said.

Joseph paused. "Look, kiddo. Nobody's perfect. OK? I know I'm not. But there are some things I have to do for you and me so I just do them. That's how you survive. You just do the things that have to be done, no matter how hard."

Edith remained silent with a scowl on her face. Her body was tense.

Joseph paused again, searching for the right words. "I know your life isn't fair, Edith. You're asked to do a lot of things a kid your age never should have to do."

Edith shifted her weight. She wasn't used to hearing her Father talk like this. She was interested in what he had to say but she tried not to show it.

"And I don't tell you enough," he continued, "but I am so incredibly proud of you. When hard things come your way, you don't complain and you don't give up. You're a lot like your mom was. I'm sure she's proud of you too."

Tears came to Edith's eyes and she quickly wiped them away. Joseph put his arm around her and squeezed her in half a hug.

"Dad," Edith said, "we have to let Sam go. We can't keep him locked up."

"No," Joseph said, suddenly sounding cold and immovable. "If Sam gets out, we'll be ruined. I will not let that happen."

"But we can't leave him down there forever."

"We're done talking about it, Edith." He stood from the bed. "I have work to do and so do you. Don't linger in here." He kissed her on top of the head and walked out the door.

She took another deep breath and stood from her bed. Her Father was right; she had a lot of work to get to. Before leaving, though, she wanted to sort out what she was feeling inside. Her emotions were mixed up and confusing and it felt like something big was trying to push through. *'He has to be stopped,'* she thought to herself. The thought took her by surprise. It made her feel suddenly scared and empowered, lonely and hopeful all at once.

She thought about all their guests locked in their rooms downstairs. Face after face flashed through her mind of people she had tended to, bodies she had buried, and candles she had burned on crisp autumn nights year after year. This had been her life for so long now that, even though it felt wrong and miserable, it also felt comfortable. Her Father loved her, even if he wasn't good at showing it and he and her would always take care of each other. Plus, someday there would be another trip to the ocean and she could endure until then.

Then she thought about Sam again. "No," she said out loud. Anger and fear aside, she simply knew what needed to be done. She couldn't stand by and do nothing anymore. Her Father needed to be stopped. She didn't know how yet, but she was going to put an end to all of this.

CHAPTER 22

    Joseph arrived at the mill an hour before starting time. The cotton fibers in the air had still not settled from the work of the night crew and the machines were still warm from use. The sound of his feet on the floor's worn, wooden planks echoed around the empty building. It was normal for him to arrive before everyone else but he usually wasn't this early. Today, though, the Senator would be visiting the mill and Joseph wanted to make sure everything was in order. Besides, he hadn't been able to sleep all night anticipating the events of the coming day.

    After walking each section of the mill, he returned to the bottom floor. At one end of the building was a lever that brought together a system of gears connected to the churning water wheel on the other side of the wall. He pulled hard on the lever and with a loud noise, the mill came to life. A large, tall piston in front of him began to spin and the leather belts overhead began to turn.

    Joseph went back upstairs to the second floor where the spinning mules were. The night before, Emory had reported to him that eleven of the fifty machines were down. That number had remained steady for a week, which was a very small piece of good news considering that, in the prior weeks, new machines were breaking daily. He walked past each station, counting in his head the ones that were not working. One of the oddities about the problem they were having was that, machines that had run just fine hours before during the night shift would suddenly stop working when they were turned on for the day shift and vice-versa.

    When Joseph finished, he had counted thirteen inoperable machines. "That can't be right," he said to himself. He went to his office and found a pencil and a small notepad. He walked the floor again, this time keeping a written tally of the machines. At the end, he counted the marks he had made. Again, he counted thirteen broken machines. A pit grew in his stomach.

He felt like throwing something but, before he could react, he heard someone enter the room. "Hello!" the person called loudly above the noise of the machines and belts. Confused and surprised, Joseph walked out of the aisle he was in and looked toward the room's entranceway. When he saw who it was that had entered, it soured his mood even further.

"What are you doing here?" he called back to Josiah Knightly who was standing in the doorway.

"I have something for you," he said.

Joseph wanted to yell at him to come give it to him but he knew it would be quieter and easier to talk just outside the entryway Josiah was standing in. So, he gave in and walked over to the short, squatty man who was waiting for him. When he reached him, he said "in here," and kept walking past him to the stairwell behind him. There, the noise of the mill was muted a little but not much.

"What do you want?" Joseph asked as Josiah joined him. He was still speaking loudly so he could be heard.

"Don't worry, I'm not here to ask you for a play date," Josiah said. "I'm here on assignment. The town voted and they want me to bring you this," Josiah held out a large book he was holding in both hands.

Joseph stared at the book without taking it. "What is it?" he asked.

"Some book they've put together about the history of Edith's Hollow." Josiah shrugged his shoulders, "it's important to them," he said, "and when I'm given an assignment, I follow it so here."

Joseph still didn't take the book. "What am I supposed to do with it?"

"They want you to display it. They've been putting it out in different places around town so people could...I don't know...appreciate it, I guess. It's just for a few days. With the Senator coming to town, they figured it was important to have in the mill for his visit."

Joseph was taken aback, "how did you know about the Senator?"

"Take the book, Fridman," Josiah said irritably. "I'm getting tired of holding it." Joseph took the book, still waiting for an answer to his question.

"How did you know?" Joseph repeated.

"Because I know things, Fridman. I spent twenty years with the union so I've got connections. Anyway, here's what you're going to do; I brought a little podium with me to place on the first floor near the entrance. You're going to put the book on the podium and keep it there so the Senator's sure to see it. A couple of the townspeople from the council will be here to stand with it."

Joseph started shaking his head. "No, no, no. Nobody's coming into my mill uninvited. Look, I'm running a business here, not a museum. Take this back," he said, holding out the book. "They'll have to find somewhere else to display it."

"That's not gonna happen, Fridman," Josiah said sternly. "You know, when I got here this morning, I noticed at least three violations of town ordinances in your operation. Maybe I need to spend a week here so I can observe things a little more closely and see what other violations need addressed. Each one is a fine, you know?"

Joseph rolled his eyes. "Fine, deputy. I'll put the book out. But it's just for a few days and then I'm bringing it back to the council myself if I have to."

"Whatever you say, Fridman," Josiah said dismissively. "Just make sure nothing happens to it while it's here or else there will be consequences. I'll go get the podium I brought and set it where it needs to go." He turned and walked down the stairs. Joseph shook his head while he watched him go.

The morning went by far too quickly. Joseph's employees began trickling in a little before 7:00 and, before he knew it, it was almost 11:00 and the Senator was arriving. Joseph saw his carriage coming down the road from the second-story window he had been peering out of nervously for the last twenty minutes. He went downstairs to greet him, feeling completely underprepared.

Two members of the town council from the other side of Edith's Hollow were standing by their book near the mill's entrance. One was to each side of it. They both stood tall with their shoulders back, ready for their guest. Joseph grimaced when he saw them. He walked past them on his way out the door and made sure to grunt loud enough for them to take note of his disapproval.

He made it out the front door in time to watch the Senator's carriage pulling in. The wooden wheels made a scraping noise against the packed dirt and a small cloud of dust rose as the carriage slowed to a stop. The driver hopped down from his seat and opened a door on the side which the Senator climbed out of. He was wearing a black suit with a matching vest and shining, polished shoes. Joseph squirmed uncomfortably in his worn, dirty boots. He wished Mr. Hill was there with him.

"Hello, Joseph. It's nice to see you again," Senator Dawes said, extending his hand.

Joseph took it and shook firmly. "It's good to see you, too," he said. "Thank you for taking the time to visit."

The Senator chuckled. "Well, don't thank me yet. This might not be pleasant."

Joseph nodded his head. "In that case," he said, "maybe it's not so good to see you after all."

The Senator laughed heartily and slapped Joseph on the back. "I've always appreciated honesty," he said. "Growing up, my Father always told me, 'say what you mean and mean what you say.'"

They passed through the front door as Senator Dawes continued talking about his dad. However, as soon as he was noticed by the two town council members who had been standing by their book like sentinels, they sprang into action, interrupting his story.

"You know, he was so blunt that..." the Senator had begun.

"Senator Dawes," one of the council members said enthusiastically, "we are so honored to welcome you to our humble town."

The Senator eyed the councilwoman out of the sides of his eyes, irritated that he had been interrupted. "Yes," he said dismissively. "Thank you. I'm glad to be here." Turning his attention back to Joseph, he started again; "He was so blunt," he said before he was promptly interrupted again.

"...Senator, did you know that we've begun planning for a library in Edith's Hollow which will make it the only town of its size in Massachusetts with a fully functioning public library?" chimed in the other councilman.

"Great. Thank you," Senator Dawes said, not even glancing in the councilman's direction or trying to sound sincere. He opened his mouth to begin talking to Joseph but before he could even get a word out, he was interrupted again.

"Senator, we've compiled this book that we think you will find interesting," the councilwoman said.

Senator Dawes finally turned with his full attention to the council members. "You're wrong," he said.

Both council members paused in stunned silence.

"I won't find it interesting," the Senator continued. "I am here to tend to business. I will tend to mine, you tend to yours. Good day."

Joseph smiled discretely as the two men walked away. *'Whatever else happens today, at least I got to witness that,'* he thought to himself.

Joseph's joy was short lived, though. As soon as he and the Senator reached the second floor of the mill, things started to go downhill. Near the front of the first row of machines were two, side by side, that were inoperable.

"What's going on with those machines?" the Senator asked. "Why are they not running?"

"Well, Senator," Joseph said uncomfortably, "we've had some trouble with our equipment recently."

"Trouble? What do you mean, 'trouble?'"

"We've...uh...had some of the machines break. To be honest, we kind of had a little wave of machines breaking all around the same time. But we're working on it. We'll have them all running again right away."

"When?" the Senator asked.

Joseph was caught off guard. "Excuse me?" he said.

"When will all of your machines be up and running again? Do you have a date?"

"Well...umm...no....not yet. But we have a guy coming down from Boston to look at them tomorrow."

"To look at them? So, you don't even know what the problem is yet? How long has this been going on? How many machines are shut down?"

"A few, sir," Joseph said. "There are…ummm…I think ten not operating right now." The actual number was thirteen but Joseph couldn't bring himself to say it.

"*Ten*?! No wonder you're not filling your orders. When is this going to be fixed, Joseph?" the Senator pressed.

"Right away, sir. I promise you; we're dedicating all of our resources to it."

"Why would *ten* of your machines break in a month's time?"

"We don't know, Senator. It's been very odd. Honestly, we are just as perplexed about it as you are."

"Well I hope that's not true, Joseph. I'm not in the business of running a mill. If you don't know any more about this stuff than me, then that's a problem."

"That's not what I meant, sir," Joseph said. "I just meant that it's been very odd – even to my best men. I've worked in the mill business most of my life and I haven't seen this before. But we will get it fixed and soon. I assure you."

Senator Dawes, who had become quite worked up, took a deep breath and exhaled. "Can we go in your office for a moment?" he asked in a calmer tone. "It's loud out here."

"Of course," Joseph said. "This way."

When the two men got to the office, Joseph shut the door behind them, muffling the noise of the mill a little. "Would you like to sit down?" He invited.

"Joseph," the Senator began, taking the seat closest to him, "I'll level with you. I like you. I really do. This operation that you and Hill built has always impressed me. You probably have the lowest injury rate and the highest morale of any other mill in the State. You're doing something right. But the fact is, if you're not producing your product the way your clients need you to, then all that other stuff is useless."

"You're right, sir." Joseph began.

"Let me finish," the Senator continued. "Now I know I'm not your client but I put my neck on the line for you when I told the Army they should start using your mill. So, I'm invested in your performance. I've worked hard to earn the Army's trust over the years and I can't afford to let that trust sour. So, here's what I'm going to do. I'll give you one week to get this mess sorted out. If you don't have these machines up and running in a week, then I'm going to recommend to the Army that they cancel their contract."

Joseph's heart sunk. One week wasn't enough time. The truth was, the guy out of Boson they had engaged to come work on the machines wouldn't even arrive for another week. "Sir," he said, sounding a little desperate, "I'm doing my best here. I've never had anything like this happen before. Can't you help me out a little? Give us *two* weeks. I think we can fix things in two."

"I *am* helping you, Joseph. I'm giving you a week. That's a courtesy I wouldn't extend to most. Get it fixed." With that, the Senator abruptly left Joseph's office and closed the door behind him.

Joseph sat down and sunk into his chair. He put his head in his hands and felt all the weight of his sudden circumstances bearing down on top of him. He didn't know what he was going to do. He didn't feel like being at the mill, though. So, he decided to go see Emory. Maybe they could come up with some ideas if they talked through this together.

It was just a few minutes past noon so Joseph knew that Emory would still be sleeping. He felt bad waking him but this was urgent. When he knocked on the door, Emory's wife answered. She had her dark, brown hair pulled back tightly into a bun and she was carrying their only child on her hip.

"Hello, Rebecca," Joseph said. "Can I come in?"

"Of course, Mr. Fridman," the young woman said. "Emory's asleep, though. He is usually not awake for another three or four hours."

"I know," Joseph said. "I'm going to need you to wake him, please. There's an urgent matter I need to discuss with him."

"Is everything OK?" she asked.

"Maybe not. We'll see. I'm hoping your husband can help. Will you get him?"

"Yes, of course," she said, turning to walk to the back of the house. When she returned a few minutes later, Emory was with her. He was rubbing tired eyes.

"Sorry to wake you, Emory," Joseph said. "Is there somewhere we can talk?"

"How about we step outside?"

"That will work."

251

A biting, late-autumn breeze blew across Emory's front porch where Joseph and Emory sat on wooden chairs. Joseph hardly noticed it. He was too consumed with other things. He told Emory about the Senator's visit and the 1-week deadline he had given them. He lamented over the impossibility of the task and how the mill might not survive if the army cancelled its contracts. Emory mostly just nodded his head empathetically.

"Here's what we're going to do," Joseph said after he had finally talked himself into a moment of resolve, "I need you to go to Boston and find our machine guy. See if you can talk him into coming any earlier. We'll pay him double if we need to. Tell him it's urgent and we need him right away."

"OK," Emory said, sounding a little shell shocked. Joseph had never given him an assignment like this before. "When do I need to go?"

"Well, if you leave right away, you can get there in time to find a hotel, which would allow you to find our man first thing in the morning."

"So, leave now?" Emory asked, wide-eyed.

"Yes," Joseph said, decisively, "as soon as you can. I'm sorry I can't go instead. Normally, I would but, under the circumstances, there are too many preparations I need to begin making here and I don't want to delay them." Joseph firmly grabbed his young friend's knee and looked him in the eye. "You'll do fine, Emory. I trust you."

"Thank you, sir," Emory said. "I'll leave right away."

Emory returned the next day late in the afternoon. Joseph was in his study when Edith came and told him that he had just arrived. He eagerly got up and walked to the kitchen to greet him at their usual meeting place around the kitchen table. Emory was already seated. An object was sitting on the table in front of him that looked a little like a long, metal comb with several fine, metal teeth.

"Welcome back," Joseph said as he entered the room.

Emory began to get up from his chair but Joseph waved his hand. "You're fine. Just stay seated," he said. "I'm anxious to hear how things went." Joseph took a seat at the table. "What is that?" he asked, motioning at the object on the table.

"I'll get to that," Emory said. "We might have an interesting situation on our hands."

"Go on," Joseph said. "Did the machinist say he could come any earlier?" Neither man was interested in wasting any time on small talk.

Emory shook his head. "No, he didn't."

Joseph's heart sunk in disappointment.

"Let me explain our visit, though" Emory said. "You'll want to hear this. First thing this morning, I left the hotel and went to the address you gave me for the machine shop. The door was locked and there were no signs of life so I waited for the machinist to arrive. I waited three hours! I began to get nervous that he wasn't going to come at all and that my trip was going to be a complete waste. Fortunately, he arrived a little before noon. He said he had been on a job all morning."

Joseph nodded, quietly wishing Emory would get to the point with a few less details.

Emory continued. "When I explained who I was, he invited me into his shop – which was a dimly lit, cramped little place with machine parts everywhere. I told him about our predicament. He was sympathetic but he said he simply couldn't come any earlier. He has back to back jobs up and down the eastern states for the next several weeks. He's in very high demand."

"That makes sense," Joseph said. "He was the only one I could find that still works on spinning mules as old as ours. Apparently, we're not alone."

"Right," Emory said. "Before I left, though, he asked me to explain the problem we were having. So, I told him how the yarn on some of our mules was getting all loose and tangled up. That's when he pulled this out." Emory held up the long, metal object sitting on the table. "He called it a faller bar. He said it might be the source of the problem and told me I should check the machines that were down to see if the faller bars were loose or had broken teeth or something. He said he only had three in the shop with him at the time but that I could take this one with me and if we discovered that this part was the problem, we could write him or send him a telegram and he would try to bring more when he came."

"So?" Joseph said eagerly. "Have you been to the mill? Did you check the machines?"

"Yes. I stopped by before coming here. You're not going to believe this, Joseph,"

253

"What?!" Joseph asked, losing patience with Emory's pace. "What did you find?"

"I went to all the broken mules and checked in the spot where the machinist told me the faller bar would be. The first one I checked, I couldn't find it. Of course, I thought that was weird but I figured I just wasn't familiar enough with the different parts of the machine. So, I moved to another one of the broken mules hoping for better luck but, still, I couldn't find the dumb bar. So, then I went to one of the mules that was working and, wouldn't you know, I found the faller bar no problem."

Joseph furrowed his brow.

Emory saw Joseph's reaction and nodded his head. "Joseph, I went back and checked every single broken mule and guess what I found." He held up the long, metal bar with comb-like teeth, "none of them had a faller bar. The part is *missing* from EVERY...LAST...ONE." The last three words he said with slow, dramatic, emphasis.

"*Missing?*" Joseph said. "How can that be? You're sure they weren't there?"

"I'm positive," Emory said. "I checked each one two or three times. I couldn't believe it at first, either."

"Well then someone has to be removing them, right?" Joseph said. "Someone is sabotaging us."

Emory nodded his head. "It's the only possible explanation."

"We need to find them," Joseph said, his face suddenly turning red. "I'll kill whoever is doing this to us."

Emory was a little startled by Joseph's sudden change in tone. He wanted to believe that Joseph was only speaking rhetorically when he used the word 'kill' but, truthfully, he wasn't entirely sure.

"We'll find him, Joseph," he said. "What he's doing is illegal, you know. We can turn him over to the law and they'll put him away."

Joseph huffed. "We're not getting that joke of a deputy sheriff involved. So, unless you've got a police officer up your sleeve, we're going to have to take care of this ourselves. Besides, we're starting tonight. We don't have time to wait on the law."

Joseph looked at Emory and saw dark circles under his eyes. Over the last 48 hours, Joseph had woken him from his sleep, denied him of his normal schedule, and made him travel to Boston and back. "I'll tell you what," he said, "you go home to your wife tonight. I'll take your usual shift. I want to look at this faller bar situation for myself and, if we're lucky, our saboteur just might show up after everyone else has gone home."

"What are you going to do? Hide out?" Emory asked.

"Yes. Exactly. When the night shift is finished, I'm going to shut the place down like everyone has gone home and then I'll wait."

Emory nodded his head. "Good luck," he said, not sure how else to respond. Joseph didn't even seem to hear Emory, though. He looked consumed in his thoughts.

"Hey, Joseph," Emory said a little hesitantly as a thought came to him that he couldn't help but bring up. "What if we can't find the guy? What if too much time passes and we still don't have the machines all working? Do we have a backup plan?"

Joseph breathed deeply and sighed as he exhaled. "Well," he said thoughtfully, "we *do* have fire insurance."

Emory chuckled at Joseph's response but Joseph didn't crack a smile. Again, Emory hoped that Joseph wasn't being serious but, truthfully, he couldn't be sure.

Edith snuck away up to her room. Neither Joseph nor Emory had noticed her eavesdropping on their conversation but she had heard the whole thing. She saw the faller bars that Emory showed to her Father. She heard her Father say he would kill whoever was sabotaging his machines and that he would burn the mill down if he had to. Unlike Emory, she didn't wonder whether he was joking – she was sure he wasn't.

When she got to her room, her heart was racing. A plan was forming in her head; It was time to act. Her Father would be gone all night and he would be alone at the mill after the night shift finished. She knew what she needed to do. She trembled as she thought through her plan.

She sat on her bed and tried to calm down but the nervous energy wouldn't stop pulsing through her. She tried holding her hands in her lap but she couldn't keep them still. She thought through the plan again and nodded her head feeling like it was going to work. Then, hoping it might relax her, she walked over to the bookcase next to her bed. She had filled the shelves with medical books and a few works of fiction. From the bottom shelf, she pulled out her journal and found a pencil in one of the drawers.

"Father needs to be stopped," she wrote. "He will be alone at the mill tonight. I know what to do. I know how I will end this."

1974

CHAPTER 23

Jaime's eyes widened as he read the last line on the page of the journal sitting in his lap. *'It's true,'* he thought to himself. *'She really did kill him.'* He wanted to read more but he had come to the end. Oddly, the rest of the pages in the journal had been ripped out. With his thumb, he brushed the jagged page fragments still stuck to the spine. He wished he knew what they said.

He looked over at the window in the wall. The night sky seemed to be brightening a little. His eyelids felt so heavy. *'I can't believe she killed him,'* he thought to himself as he laid down on the bed he had been sitting on and stared out the window.

The next thing he knew, he was abruptly awakened by the sound of a doorknob jiggling. His body jolted unwittingly and his eyes sprung open. It took him a moment to remember where he was and gather his senses. Morning sunlight was shining through the window. He looked at the door where he could hear a key being inserted and the lock being released. Then he saw the doorknob turning. He jumped off of the bed he was on and then stood still, trying not to make any noise.

The door swung open and Edith stood in the entry, her unseeing eyes scanning the room. She must have heard something or sensed Jaime's presence. Neither of them made a sound. Edith stretched her head into the room and listened carefully but Jaime did not dare move a muscle. She seemed to stand at the entrance for an eternity while the heavy, fragile silence hung between them.

Finally, she backed out of the room but still didn't leave. Adrenaline was rushing through Jaime's body. As much as he wanted to stand still and play it safe, he was afraid he might not get another chance to escape. Once Edith decided to leave, she might close the door and lock it again.

As quietly as he could, Jaime moved swiftly to the exit. It wasn't quiet enough. Before he could walk through the doorway, Edith tilted her head like she had heard something and took half a step forward. She got so close to Jaime that he could feel the heat from her body. He stiffened his muscles and leaned away from her, trying to maintain silence.

Suddenly, with surprising speed and accuracy, she snatched Jaime's wrist. Her strength was incredible, especially for a woman her age. She squeezed his arm tightly until it hurt. He froze, watching her carefully. He wasn't sure he could escape her grip even if he tried.

"Why do you haunt me?" she asked. "I hear your footsteps through the halls and in the woods. Why do you follow me?" The sternness in her voice teetered on anger.

Jaime didn't respond. He wasn't sure if she was talking to him or to voices in her head. He hoped that if he just stayed silent, this would pass.

"I have to make it stop," she said.

His heart began beating even harder than it had been. *'What is she going to do?'* he wondered.

Just then, her demeanor suddenly and inexplicably changed. Her stony expression drastically softened. When she spoke, she sounded pensive and sad. "Which one are you?" she asked. "What did I do to you? Have you come to take me with you, away from this world? I'm ready to go."

She let go of his wrist. Jaime thought about running but he stopped himself. Despite everything else he was feeling, he felt sorry for her.

As Edith dropped her hand, it brushed the edge of the journal Jaime was still holding. She paused and examined it with her fingers until she recognized what it was. Her demeanor abruptly shifted again. She furrowed her brow and looked like she had just woken from a dream. "Who are you?" she asked. This time, though, she seemed to have gathered her senses and Jaime was sure she was talking to him and not to some figure in her mind.

"I'm Jaime," he said, a little falteringly.

She stared past him. The wheels in her head seemed to be turning.

"I'm sorry if I've bothered you," he said. "I've been coming here and...I guess...I thought that maybe I was helping you."

She still looked to be deep in thought. "Did you read the journal?" she asked.

Jaime hesitated. He suddenly felt embarrassed that he had read it.

Swiftly and unexpectedly, Edith grabbed his wrist again, even tighter than before. Jaime tried to pull away but he couldn't. "Did you read it?" she asked intensely.

Jaime was frightened. "Yes," he confessed.

"All of it?"

He nodded his head nervously but quickly remembered she couldn't see him. "Yes," he said again.

She looked down at the ground considering a new thought. "Then there is something I must do," she said, almost as if she was speaking to herself. She stepped into the room, gently pushing Jaime to step backwards. Without turning around, she closed the door behind her.

"Are you going to hurt me?" Jaime asked.

All at once, Edith's eyes softened so deeply that it looked like she might cry. "No, no, no, my dear," she said earnestly. "I'm not going to hurt you." She let go of his wrist, seeming mildly startled, as if she had forgotten she was holding it. She lowered her hand a little, taking Jaime's in both of hers. "I've spent my entire life alone, Jaime, regretting those I have hurt." She paused, staring just past him with her sightless eyes. "I don't want to hurt anybody," she said.

She let go of his hands and chuckled quietly. "I'm sorry for my ways," she said. "You must find me very odd."

Jaime shook his head politely but Edith, of course, didn't see.

"I'm not at all accustomed to visitors, you know? And – well," she said, gesturing to her head, "my mind has been broken for many years. Perhaps you've noticed."

"Ummm..." Jaime hesitated.

"Of course you've noticed, Jaime," Edith said, taking his hand again and patting it. "You're very polite."

She walked past him and drew out a necklace that was around her neck but had been hidden beneath her clothing. "Wait right, there," she said. "I have something for you." A small key hung from the end of the necklace. She held it in her hand and knelt next to a short bedstand that stood on the opposite side of the bed from the bookshelf where the journal had been.

Feeling more courageous now, Jaime asked a question that was burning in his mind. "But what about the grave?" he said. The question sounded awkward as it escaped his lips and he immediately wished he could take it back.

Edith paused. Her back was to him but she straightened and turned her head to the side just enough that he was able to see her profile. All at once, she realized what he was talking about and began to chuckle again. "You mean the one in the front yard beneath the fruit tree? You thought I was going to bury you in it?"

"I don't know," Jaime said, shrugging his shoulders.

"I'm sorry," she said, still chuckling. "I suppose I shouldn't laugh." She cleared her throat. "That isn't for you, my dear."

"But it *is* a grave?" he pressed.

Edith sighed. "Yes. It is a grave."

"Then who is it for?" he asked. The answer occurred to him, though, before he had even finished asking the question.

"I am very old, Jaime. And, when I go, I would like to lie next to my Father. He is resting in the grave next to mine."

She turned her head back toward the nightstand and bent over to unlock the drawer in front of her. When she stood up, she was holding a small stack of paper which she rolled up in her hands. She walked back to Jaime and held the rolled pages out to him. "Take these," she said.

"What are they?" he asked.

"They are the missing pages from the journal you read. This completes the story."

He reached out and grabbed the roll but Edith didn't let go.

"Jaime," she said, sounding like what she was about to say was important, "I was so young and my Father was foolish and afraid. But there was so much good in him. And as for me -" she paused a moment, "I am not a bad person, Jaime. Please do not judge us too harshly."

"I won't," Jaime said as Edith released her grip on the pages. "I promise."

"And one more thing," she said. "Keep it a secret. The town doesn't need to know."

"OK," Jaime agreed. Then, hesitating a little, he spoke again. "So, I can go?" he asked.

"Of course you can go" she said, sounding surprised and a little amused by his question. "But I hope you'll be back."

Jaime nodded. "Thank you, Edith."

He wound his way through the maze of hallways and stairs that led to the front door then stepped outside into a chilly, autumn morning. As he walked home through the woods, he remembered that it was Halloween day. He suddenly felt nervous and a little sick as he replayed the events of the last few days in his mind. He had promised Mark and the guys that he would take them to Edith's house that night, prove to them that she was a murderer, and lock Karen inside as a prank.

He squeezed the rolled-up journal pages in his hand and felt a tiny wave of relief. Edith had given him exactly what he needed. He was sure these pages had the evidence he was looking for. A thought occurred to him. He could bring the guys to Edith's house that night and show them the rooms and the pictures of dead and injured bodies he had found in the dresser drawer. Then he would pull out the pages he was carrying and read to them his evidence. They would eat it up. It would be there best Halloween night ever and it would all be because of him.

Then his thoughts turned to Karen. With Jaime's knowledge of the house, it would be pretty easy to lose her in the hallways that led to the front door. He was sure he could get all the guys out and lock the door behind them while she was still searching for an exit. But getting her to come with them would be the hard part. How would he convince her to come to the house that night?

He was mulling over this question when he got home. His mom was still gone on her work trip so the house was empty. He didn't expect her until later that day. School had already started but the temptation to read the final journal pages Edith had given him was overwhelming. It was even stronger than his desire to lie down and sleep.

He went into his room to grab his backpack but he looked at the pages in his hand before setting them down. *There aren't that many*, he rationalized in his mind. *If I read fast, I'll still make it to most of school.* He decided not to fight it. He went into the front room, sat down on a chair, and began to read.

1901

Edith sat on the edge of her bed in her room as it grew dark outside. She had no intention of sleeping. Her Father was already gone for the night and now she was just waiting for it to get later. She was nervous and wanted to make sure she had the cover of night. In her lap sat a note she had penned earlier that evening. Now, she just needed the streets to be cleared and people to be asleep in their homes for her plan to work.

Well after midnight, she folded up her note and tucked it into her pocket. Finally, she stood, paced the floor while she went over the details of her plan one last time in her head, then she walked out of her door and made her way to the room where Sam was being kept. She unlocked his door with the brass key she kept with her at all times and opened it slowly. She had skipped his medicine that night so she half expected him to be awake waiting to pounce on her. In fact, she had skipped everybody's medicine that night. In her estimation, enough time had passed that the effects of the previous doses should have worn off. She wasn't sure how each of the guests would react as they emerged from their medicinal haze to fully grasp the fact that they were being kept prisoner in her home. She knew she might be in danger but she didn't care. She had to move forward with her plan.

Sam wasn't awake, waiting to pounce. He was snoring gently on his bed. Nervously, she walked over to him and placed a hand on his arm. "Mr. Sam!" she whispered loudly, shaking him a little. He moved but didn't wake. "Mr. Sam!" she said again, shaking him harder. This time he opened his eyes and, for a moment, seemed disoriented. When he saw Edith, though, he quickly came to.

"Edith!" he said, sitting up in his bed. "What are you doing? Are you alright?"

"Mr. Sam, it's time," she said. "My Father is gone and I am letting you go."

Sam looked at the open door and then back at Edith.

"Where is your dad? How long will he be gone?"

"He's watching the night crew. He'll be gone until morning – maybe longer. This is your chance to get away."

To Edith's surprise, Sam wasn't rushing out of bed. Instead, the wheels in his head were turning and he looked concerned. "What is he going to do when he discovers you let me go?"

265

"Don't worry about that, I have a plan," Edith said, starting to feel impatient. "I am letting everyone go tonight. But you need to go so I have time. Please hurry."

"Wait," Sam said resolutely. "Please, sit down. Explain your plan to me. Who are the others? How many are there? I want to help."

Edith shook her head. "No. I don't have time to explain. I can do this on my own. I don't want anybody else involved. Just get up and go home – *please*. She begged."

"Edith," Sam said, reaching out and taking her by the hand, "explain your plan to me. I am not going until you do. I want to help."

Edith sighed. She felt like she could trust Sam and she believed him when he said he wasn't going to leave until she complied. So, she gave in. "OK," she said, sitting down on the side of his bed. "I'll explain it but I can't take too long."

"We'll act quickly," Sam assured her. "Go on. Start by explaining who else is locked up in these halls."

"They're my Father's workers," she explained. "You're actually the first guest we've had who isn't one of his workers."

"Guest?" Sam repeated.

"Well – yes. That's what Father calls them. When one of his workers gets injured, he brings them here."

"But I thought nobody ever got injured at the mill. That's what it's known for. It has a reputation."

Edith shook her head. "No. People get injured and then they come here. But nobody knows about them except for me...and, I guess, you now."

"And what happens to them?" Sam asked in disbelief. "How long are they here? Surely you get them medical help, right?"

Edith shook her head again. "I give them medicine and I try to help them but they just stay here in their rooms until...well, some of them get better and my Father takes them away and I don't know what happens to them after that."

"And the ones that don't get better?"

"We bury them every year on the night of the harvest moon."

Sam's jaw dropped. "You just let them die?" he asked.

Edith's eyes watered. "I try not to, Mr. Sam. I swear! I try to help them."

"No, no, Edith. It's OK," he said assuredly. "I don't blame you. I just had no idea the secrets your Father was keeping in here. But then again, I suppose nobody did."

"So, you see why I have to stop him." Edith said.

Sam nodded. "What's your plan, then?"

"Well, I'm going to go to Mr. Knightly's office…" she began.

"The Sheriff?" Sam interrupted.

"Yes. I've heard my Father talk about him. I'll go to his office and I'll leave this note on his door." From her pocket, she pulled the note she had folded up and tucked away. "I wrote it anonymously. It says that there's something illegal going on at Joseph Fridman's home and that he's keeping people there against their will. I'll put the note on Mr. Knightly's door for him to see in the morning when he starts his day. After that, I'll ride back home and, in the morning, I'll wait outside somewhere where I can't be seen. As soon as I see Mr. Knightly coming, I'll ride straight to the mill where my Father is. He'll be angry to see me out of the house but I'll tell him that the Sheriff showed up unexpectedly and I snuck out the back to come find him. I'll say that he came in and discovered our guests and that we have to leave. Then we'll go," she said, as if it was simple. "We'll leave this place for good."

"And what if they find you?" Sam asked.

"Who?"

"The police. They're not going to just let you go."

Edith paused and stared at the ground. She hadn't considered this possibility.

"Like it or not, Edith, you've been part of this. If the police catch up with you, they might put both of you away for a really long time. Or, they'll throw your Father in prison and put you in an orphanage. Either way, it doesn't end up good for you, Edith."

Frustration suddenly welled up inside of her. Why was Sam trying to stop her? Couldn't he see what needed to be done? "I don't care," Edith said. "This has got to stop."

"But, Edith, think about what you are doing. Are you ready to be all alone? Because that's what being a hero like this is going to lead to."

"I don't care," she said again. "Something has to be done for these people. How can I possibly stand by and do nothing?"

"I'm not saying to do nothing," Sam said. "But I think we can do this in a way that protects you. Let me help."

"No," Edith said, shaking her head once again. "I don't want anybody else to get involved. I have to do this by myself."

"No, you don't," Sam insisted. "Listen, I can help you. How long would it take your Father to notice if everyone is gone from these rooms?"

Edith shrugged her shoulders. "Probably a couple of days," she said. "He hardly ever goes in any of the rooms. That's my job. But he'd eventually notice how quiet things are."

"Perfect," Sam said. "That gives us enough time. You and I will get everyone out of here tonight – right now – before your Father returns. Then, tomorrow, just pretend like everything is normal. I'll take the injured up north to get them help but I'll make sure not to raise any suspicion so we don't get the police involved just yet. Then, I'll come back for you. When your Father leaves the house again, you'll come with me and we'll take you to my place. While you are there safe, *I'll* go get the Sheriff. Nobody will have to know that you were part of this. You can stay with me, Edith. We'll tell everyone you're my niece and that you've come to stay."

"But what will happen to my Dad?" Edith asked. Her eyes looked sad and worried.

"You're Father has done terrible things…" Sam started.

"I know," Edith interrupted. "But *he's* not terrible. He's still my Father, Mr. Sam."

Sam breathed deeply and sighed. "I know." He said. "There's no easy answer here, Edith. But you are right; this has to end. And I am not going to let you suffer for your Father's sins. We can't protect him from suffering the consequences of the things he has done and we shouldn't try. But we can keep you safe. It's the only way, Edith."

Again, she sensed a determination in Sam that she knew she wasn't going to be able to defeat. Now that he knew everything, she couldn't untangle him from the situation. He wouldn't let her. "OK," she said. "We'll do it your way."

"Good," he said, getting up from his bed. "Where is your Father's buggy?"

Together, Sam and Edith moved each of the injured from their rooms to Joseph's horse-drawn buggy. It took a long time. Several of them groaned loudly and even screamed in pain as they were moved. A couple of them barely woke up even though their dose of medicine had long worn off. Sam and Edith did their best to make them as comfortable as possible, packing blankets and pillows around them.

When everyone was loaded, Sam climbed into the driver's seat and took the reins in his hands. "Remember the plan," he said to Edith. "I'll return as soon as I can and then we'll get you somewhere safe. Until then, just pretend like nothing has changed."

Edith nodded her head. "But, Mr. Sam," she said. "If something goes wrong…"

"It won't," he tried assuring her.

"I know…but just in case it does, I'd like to be able to go to the Sheriff…you know, for protection."

"But Edith, you know what will happen if you get the Sheriff involved. We talked about this."

"It's just for my protection – just in case. If I have to go to him, I'll do like you said and pretend like I wasn't involved in any of this and I was trapped in this house just like the rest of them."

Sam couldn't argue with the wisdom of having a backup plan. "OK," he said. "Sure. That will be our back up plan."

"Yes but, how do I get to the Sheriff's office?" she asked.

"Do you know how to get to the church?"

"Yes," she said. It had been several years since she and her Father had moved from their house near the mill but she was confident she could still find her way back to town.

"Well, if you're standing at the church, just head down the road away from the mill and you'll come to a T. Take a left and that will eventually take you to the new part of town. Once you're there, I suppose you'll just have to ask around. I've never been to the Sheriff's office myself. I'm sure the building is marked with a sign or something. It probably won't be hard to find."

"OK," Edith said. "Thank you. Thank you for everything. Good luck."

"You too," Sam said. "I won't be long." He whipped the horses' reins and rode away.

Edith watched Sam go until he was out of sight then she went to work. She didn't have any intention of waiting for him. She went back inside and wrote one more note:

269

Mr. Sam,

When you read this, we will already be gone. Please do not try to find us. I am sorry I lied to you but I do not want you or anybody else to be burdened by this mess that we created. We will be fine. Thank you so much for your kindness. It has meant so very much to me.

She made her way to the front door and tacked her note to the front of it. Then, she locked the door and began to walk toward town. Sam and her Father had taken their only horses so she would have to go on foot.

After several minutes of walking, she could see the mill in the distance. As she got closer, she could see warm candlelight glowing in the windows and could hear the churning of the belts and machines. She stopped and admired it for a moment. She could see shadows dancing on the windows. She was surprised to feel a thrill in her chest just to witness the bustling scene and be that close to other people.

She began walking again but she was in no hurry. She passed rows of darkened homes along the silent streets and stopped occasionally to admire them. She pictured herself sleeping inside and wondered what life was like for the people there.

She passed the church and remembered when she had gone there with her Father on a Sunday long before. She missed those times when he was more kind. She continued on until reaching a T in the road just as Sam had said she would. Turning left, she continued down an empty road lined on both sides by wild trees and shrubs. The road seemed to stretch on forever until, finally, she saw homes and small buildings in the distance. When she reached the new part of town, it only took her a moment to find the Sheriff's office. It was one of the first buildings she came upon. It was a small, square building with white walls and a large, gold, sheriff's star painted above the door.

She stopped and examined the building for a moment then reached into her pocket and took out her note but quickly realized she didn't have a way of fastening it to the door. She searched the surface for a tack or a small nail but to no avail. She tried folding the note and stuffing it a few different ways and in a few different places but wasn't satisfied with any of them. She was worried it would blow away or be overlooked.

Finally, she tried the doorknob on the off-chance that it might be unlocked. To her delight, it was. She looked behind her to make sure nobody was watching then opened the door further and crept inside. Although she was quite sure the building was empty, she felt jumpy. She tiptoed to the Sheriff's desk and walked around to the back of it, deciding that she should leave her note on his chair. When she pulled the chair out, though, something caught her eye. Under the desk was a tin bucket holding several tall bars with metal, comb-like teeth. She recognized the faller bars. They were just like the one Emory Green had brought to show her Father when he explained that missing faller bars were the reason the mill's machines kept breaking.

She furrowed her brow in confusion. *'Why would Mr. Knightly have a bucket full of faller bars?'* She wondered to herself. Then, all at once, she understood. Mr. Knightly was the one who had been sabotaging the mill. Her heart began to race when she realized the significance of her discovery. She knew of her Father's distaste for the deputy. She was afraid to think what he might do if he found this out.

She looked at the clock ticking loudly on the deputy's desk. She was startled when she saw the time. It was already 4:30. The events of the night had made it go by too quickly. In just 30 minutes, the night shift at the mill would be over. Perhaps Mr. Knightly would be striking again. If he did, Joseph was going to be waiting for him.

Edith suddenly felt sick to her stomach. She was still holding the note in her hand but knew she couldn't leave it now. She couldn't trust Mr. Knightly. She folded it back up and returned it to her pocket. She didn't know what she was going to do but she felt an urgency to get back home. Even if she walked fast, she knew she wouldn't get back to her part of town before 5:00.

She left the Sheriff's office in a hurry and began walking briskly down the dirt road, back in the direction from which she had come. Fortunately, it was still dark outside and the houses she passed were quiet and still. When she reached the part of the road that was lined only by wilderness, she was still walking swiftly but her legs were beginning to tire. She slowed down to give her muscles a break. She was tired – mentally and physically – and, instead of returning to her faster pace, she continued to slow down. Her plan had been disrupted and, for the first time since concocting it, doubt began to erode her determination.

It felt like a long time had passed when she finally reached the T in the road that led back home. When she got to it, she noticed something alarming. Thick, grey smoke was billowing from the mill a little ways ahead. An occasional flicker of orange light reflected against it. She thought of her Father and she thought of Mr. Knightly and she immediately began to run as quickly as she could toward the flames. Just before she reached the mill, though, she came to a sudden stop, not wanting to be seen by anybody. She didn't know what had started the fire and who might be nearby.

Hiding in the shadows, she creeped closer until she could feel the warmth of the growing flames. They had not yet reached the roof or the outside of the building but they could be seen through the windows. She saw someone tall standing outside of the burning building with his back towards her. She took a few steps closer and realized it was her Father. Springing from her hiding place, she called out to him in panic, shock, and anger.

"Father!"

Joseph was startled to hear Edith's voice. He spun around. "Edith! What are you doing here?! Go back home, now!"

Edith continued toward him entirely undeterred. "What's happening?! What are you doing?!"

"Edith," he said, roughly taking her in his hands by the shoulders, "go home! You cannot be here!"

Suddenly, a voice from inside the building called out loudly and distinctly. "Help!"

Joseph looked at Edith. She saw fear in his eyes. He released her from his grip.

"What have you done?" she asked. She might not have spoken so boldly but she couldn't keep the words from escaping her lips.

"Go home, Edith," Joseph said again, sounding a little more desperate this time.

She looked at him again, sizing up her chances, then dashed toward the building. She only managed a single stride before Joseph grabbed her again. Just then, one of the windows on the third floor busted from the heat and flames. Edith and Joseph both looked up when they heard the noise. The flames licked the branches of a nearby tree, catching them on fire. Joseph sprang into action.

"Look for a bucket or an axe," he ordered Edith as he ran toward the tree.

Edith ignored his instructions. She knew this might be her only chance. Again, she sprinted toward the burning mill, this time unnoticed by her Father. She grabbed the doorknob which was warm but not too hot to hold. She tried turning it but it was locked. She shook vigorously but to no avail.

She ran around to the side of the building which was lined with windows. Frantically searching the ground, she found a large rock and threw it through the window. There were no flames nearby but thick smoke billowed out and into Edith's face. She coughed, turned her head away from the smoke, and took a deep breath. Then, without any more hesitation, she climbed through the window and dropped to the floor on the other side.

The air was a little clearer near the ground so, instead of standing up, she decided to stay low and crawl. The problem was, she could barely see anything. She could hear flames crackling around her but, fortunately, they weren't close enough to make the heat unbearable. The room was very warm, though.

She called out Mr. Knightly's name then stopped and listened but he didn't respond. She called for him again then paused. Just when she was sure he again wasn't going to answer, she heard the faint sound of a weak cough. "I'm coming!" she cried out. She began crawling as quickly as she could toward the sound she had heard.

She bumped into the deputy without even seeing him. There was a very subtle breeze drifting across the spot where he was lying making the air a little more breathable. Edith felt around until she found Mr. Knightly's legs. She turned her back to him and lifted his feet beneath her armpits then spun him around until she was facing the breeze. Then, like pulling a handcart, she dragged him across the floor by his legs. She couldn't see what was ahead but she hoped that walking toward the cooler air would lead them out of the burning building.

She was right. In fact, the open door that was bringing in the clean air was much closer than she could even have hoped for. She reached it with just 7 or 8 strides. When she stepped out of the building into the open air, she took a deep, gasping breath. She pulled Mr. Knightly to a safe distance then kneeled over him and put her hand near his nose to see if he was breathing. She sighed in relief when she felt the warm, humid feel of him exhaling. His breathing was shallow but it was constant.

She looked down and noticed that he was hugging something tightly against his chest. It was a large, leather-bound book. The title read "A Living History of Edith's Hollow."

She leaned back on her hands and relaxed a little. Her own breathing was still heavy and fast. As she tried to slow it down, it suddenly dawned on her that she was sitting near where she had found her Father just moments before but now he was nowhere to be seen. She looked back toward the open door her and Mr. Knightly had exited through. It was the same door that she had tried opening earlier but hadn't been able to because it was locked.

She jumped to her feet and ran to the open door, realizing that her Father must have unlocked it and come into the mill looking for her. She cupped her hands and called into the fire and smoke. "Father! Father!" Nobody called back. "Father!" she tried again. Still nothing.

Edith knew this scene would be all too familiar to her dad and that he would search for her until he dropped if he had to. She ran around to the side of the building again and called into the broken window she had crawled through before. "Father!" There was no response. She ran along the row of windows searching for any sign of where he might be but all she could see was thick smoke. She stepped back and looked up to the second floor. She could see that the flames had reached that level but, still, there were no signs of life.

Searching the ground like she had before, she found another big rock and threw it through the last window in the long row. She called through this one but, again, to no avail. Then she ran again – all the way around the building, calling out for him. Desperately, she peered through windows and broke a few others. Some small part of her was hoping that he wasn't inside the mill at all and that she would find him somewhere on the grounds.

When she returned to her starting point, she knew she only had one option left so she dashed back into the building. The air had grown even hotter and more suffocating than before. She dropped

274

to the ground where the smoke was a little thinner and stayed close to the wall as she crawled and yelled for her Father. Each time she reached one of the windows she had broken, she briefly stuck her head outside and breathed the fresh air. She only made it about halfway around the floor's perimeter when she was blocked from going any further by large, scorching flames.

She crawled back the way she had come, moving more quickly this time. When she reached the door, she stepped outside, put her hands on her knees, and caught her breath, coughing as she did. '*He must have gone to the second floor,*' she thought to herself. So, without wasting another moment, she hurried back inside and headed up the stairs. As she climbed, the conditions became nearly unbearable. The smoke became thicker and the air became hotter. Her eyes and her lungs burned.

She made it to the top of the stairs and only took a couple of steps before tripping over something large lying on the floor. She tumbled to the ground. Then, rising to her hands and knees, she turned around and felt the ground around her to find what she had tripped over. As she had suspected, it was her Father. He wasn't moving and his lips were blue.

Her heart sunk. She had seen the look on his face all too many times in the people she had cared for in her home. Hastily, she grabbed him under his arms and hoisted the upper half of his body up then dragged him down the stairs and out the exit. She again gasped when she stepped into the fresh air.

Mr. Knightly was still lying on the ground where she had left him but he was beginning to stir. She laid her Father down next to him and knelt over him. She put her hand to his nose and mouth but couldn't feel any breath. Desperately, she began to shake him.

"Wake up!" she said. "Wake up!" but he showed no signs of life.

Just then, she heard voices. She turned her head and saw a small group of people coming up the road. They were running toward the mill. Somebody must have noticed the fire. No doubt, a crowd would soon gather. Edith jumped to her feet. Her first instinct was to grab her Father and take him with her but she immediately realized that was impossible. She had come on foot and she couldn't drag him all the way home. So, instead, she ran out of sight and waited in the shadows to see what was going to happen.

When the group reached the mill, they sprang into action, shouting orders at each other. "We need buckets!" "Someone should cut down that tree!" "Go wake up the town!" Nobody even noticed the two bodies lying on the ground. Edith wanted to shout at them but, instead, she waited and watched.

Soon, the group was joined by more. The crowd began to swell quickly. Some were frantically trying to control the fire while several others just watched. Finally, someone noticed Joseph and the deputy. "Over here!" someone yelled. "These two need help! I think they were in the building when it burned."

Mr. Knightly sat up, still clutching the book. He looked confused. Joseph continued to lie next to him motionless.

"It's Sheriff Knightly!" a tall man with dark hair said. Edith assumed it was someone from the new part of town. From things she had heard her Father say, she didn't think most people from her part of town would recognize the deputy, much less refer to him as 'Sheriff Knightly.'

"Look!" a woman next to the tall man exclaimed, "he saved our town history book from the fire!" The two rushed over to the deputy's side. "I think he saved that man, too," Edith heard the woman say. A few other people joined them. Someone helped the Sheriff to his feet while a couple others tended to Joseph.

"That's Mr. Fridman!" someone else from the crowd said. That got the attention of others who also gathered around Joseph.

"I don't think he made it," Edith heard someone say. "He's not breathing and I can't feel his heart."

Edith began to cry silently from her hiding place. She knew her Father was probably dead by the time she dragged him out of the mill but hearing someone say it suddenly made it seem more real. She wanted to run but she didn't want to leave him.

"What should we do with him?" another onlooker asked.

"Take him to the morgue" Mr. Knightly said, chiming in. He seemed to have his senses about him again.

"We don't have a morgue," one of the mill workers said.

"We do in our part of town," someone else responded.

"Take him to the morgue," Mr. Knightly repeated, matter-of-factly. "You can figure it out from there. We can't leave him on the street," he said, gruffly.

Edith discreetly searched the grounds until she found where her Father had tied up his horse. Fortunately, it was behind the mill and she was able to retrieve it without being seen. She led it back to a place in the shadows where she could watch the night's events unfold. When they took her Father, she wanted to be ready to follow.

It was several minutes before Mr. Knightly's directions were followed. The fire was still burning wildly and, from Edith's vantage point, everything seemed chaotic. New people kept arriving to witness the scene and to help. It took quite some time for a succinct, organized effort to control the fire to finally emerge. However, to Edith, it all seemed to happen in a haze. She was tired and her emotions felt strangely dull other than the constant urge to cry.

When a dark, horse-drawn hearse with black curtains arrived, Edith eyed it curiously. The driver stopped near Joseph's body, got down, and with the help of another, picked the body up and laid it in the carriage, which was entirely enclosed by windows and wood. A surge of energy suddenly shot through Edith. She watched the hearse drive away and waited until it was far ahead and then she followed, carefully keeping herself concealed at a safe distance. When it stopped at the morgue, she found another hiding spot. She was close enough that she could see the driver yawn as he pulled the hearse around the back. She expected it to take him several minutes to bring her Father's body inside and tend to it but, to her surprise, just a moment later, the driver emerged on horseback and rode away, yawning widely again as he did.

Edith looked around. The streets were empty for the time being. The sun was coming up, though, and the homes were beginning to come alive with lights in the windows and smoke in the chimneys. She knew she needed to act fast. She rode up to the morgue and around the back where the hearse was parked. She got off her horse and peered into one of the hearse's windows. As she suspected, her Father's body was still inside. The driver had simply left it there.

She looked around again. An idea had formed in her head and she knew this might be her only chance to pull it off. The streets were still empty so, as quickly as she could move, she hitched her own horse to the hearse. Then, she opened the hearse's door and, with some effort, removed the long coat her Father had been wearing and put it on. She climbed up on the driver's seat and pulled the coat's collar up high to cover her face. Then, with a flick of the reins, she rode away.

Her heart was racing as she drove through the streets, pushing her horse to keep a quick pace. Although it only took a few minutes to reach the edge of the new part of town, it felt like an eternity. She held the reins tightly in her sweating hands, hoping desperately not to be seen. When she finally reached the empty part of the road that led to her part of town, she exhaled in relief. She had made it without encountering a soul.

She turned off of the road and into the woods and rode the rest of the way home under the cover of trees, shadows, and shrubs. The protection and peace of mind were worth the extra time and effort it took to drag the hearse over unplowed land. When she got home, she rode through the cast-iron gate that protected the property and parked.

Much like she had watched the driver do before her, she yawned widely and got down, leaving her Father's body where it was. She needed some rest. She went around the back of the house and walked inside then paused. Everything was so quiet. Everything had changed so quickly. A rush of emotion came over her as she looked around the empty room and felt as though this was the first moment of a new life. The feelings were so conflicting that they only increased her desire to sleep. She didn't have the energy to sort them out.

She went upstairs and took a long nap. When she woke up, she didn't allow herself to linger in her bed. She had chores to do so she got up and got started on them. She could hear her Father's voice in her head telling her, "this is how we survive." And he was right. If she didn't stack the firewood and harvest the winter squash then nobody would. So, she went to work. It felt good to keep her mind and her hands busy.

She spent most of the next day digging a deep grave for her Father. She pulled the wooden box from the cellar they had used each year to move the bodies of those who had passed and laid it in the hole. She buried him under a young pear tree near the wall in the front of the property. When she was finished returning the dirt to the earth, she fastened a small candle holder to the tree and lit a candle that burned all night. She cried one last time, promised herself she was finished with that nonsense, and then went back to bed.

It only took a couple of days for the rumor mill to spin out of control. The mill workers and their families cared most about two indisputable facts: the mill had burned beyond repair and Mr. Fridman was nowhere to be found. The question of how these two things occurred was up for debate but there were plenty of theories. Most agreed, though, that Mr. Fridman had abandoned them.

The morning of the fire, after the flames had been put out but while the charred remains of the building were still smoldering, a small group of men ventured out to the Fridman home. Nobody was there. Edith, at that very moment, was slowly steering a horse-drawn hearse carrying her Father's body over the rough ground of the overgrown woods. The men knocked on the doors and the windows but everything was locked and nobody answered.

One of the men noticed Edith's note to Sam on the front door and called for the others to gather around. He read the first few lines out loud:

When you read this, we will already be gone. Please do not try to find us. I am sorry I lied to you but I do not want you or anybody else to be burdened by this mess that we created.

That was all the evidence they needed to confirm their suspicions. They took the note with them and headed back to break the news to the community.

Sam arrived a full day after the fire had been put out. His trip had been prolonged when a nurse at the Fall River hospital said they didn't have enough room to accept all of the injured people that were in his party. He immediately proceeded to Boston and returned home as soon as he was able. When he got to Edith's Hollow, he found a town in commotion. More than half of the community had already begun packing up their things to leave. Most of them couldn't afford to waste any time without earning a wage.

Sam asked several people what was going on and he heard several versions of the same story: the mill had mysteriously caught fire and Mr. Fridman had fled. When he happened to stop one of the men who had visited the Fridman home after the fire, the man told Sam he had something for him then he ducked into his home and returned with Edith's note. "We found this nailed to Mr. Fridman's front door," he said. "I didn't realize you knew the boss so well. Do you know why he fled?"

Sam shook his head while he read the note. "No," he said. "I don't but I wish I did."

When he finished reading the note, he felt crushed. *Why didn't she just wait for me?* He thought. He immediately developed his own theory of the night's events. He figured Edith must have moved ahead with her plan despite Sam urging her not to. However, it wasn't enough for Mr. Fridman to flee town quietly. In a fit of rage and panic, he must have burned down the mill as he left. It was his final assertion of control over the community.

Sam shook his head as he walked to his home. "What a shame," he kept saying to himself. "What a shame."

Within a week, the entire mill community had left. Sam was the last to go. He stopped at the church before leaving town. The morning sun cast an orange hue through the building. He stood at the pulpit and looked out over the empty pews. Then, silently, he said a prayer for Edith and left never to return.

Meanwhile, Edith was walking among the grove of trees where the bodies of her deceased guests rested beneath her feet. She hugged a large, wicker basket to her waist with one arm and searched the ground for fallen nuts. She would spend the morning making nut butter and the afternoon cleaning out the wood-burning stove in the kitchen. It would be a day full of chores, just like every other day.

1974

Jaime looked up from the journal pages he held in his hands. "Wow," he said out loud. Edith had long been interesting to him but now she seemed like more than just a mystery to solve. He suddenly felt a sense of reverence for her.

There was one more page with just three, short paragraphs on it. They looked as though they had been written long after the entries on the prior page. The handwriting was shakier and harder to read. They weren't dated, though, so Jaime didn't know exactly when they had been penned or whether they had each been penned on the same day.

> *Is the world outside as bleak and hollow as it is within these walls? Is there a world outside of my mind? I can hardly distinguish what comes from inside and what comes from without anymore.*

> *I am endlessly haunted by twin demons, pain and loneliness. Each time I see them, they are larger and stronger than before. Only, I cannot tell whether they feast on each other or whether they feast on me. Whatever the answer, this I know: they will never stop feasting.*

> *The harvest moon was last night. I lit the candles and watched the glowing lights. I would like to tell the deceased that they are not forgotten. I hope they know. It brings me peace to think they might.*

Just then, Jaime heard the distant sound of the school bell ringing announcing lunch time. He jumped up from where he was sitting. "Shoot!" he said. He had already missed half the school day. He didn't know how he would explain that to his mom and he didn't want to risk getting grounded on Halloween night.

He tucked Edith's journal pages away in the top drawer of his dresser. Then he changed his clothes as quickly as he could, brushed his teeth, grabbed his backpack, and ran to school. When he arrived, there was a large crowd gathered in the courtyard for the school's Halloween costume contest. He found Mark, Danny, and Joe, told them he had slept in, and exchanged some small talk. Danny and Mark both kept saying how stupid the costume contest was but they stuck around anyway, stretching their necks to see over the crowd whenever there was a loud reaction to someone's costume. Most of the participants were elementary students. The only older kids who had dressed up were a couple really brave ones and a handful of really awkward ones.

"Why didn't your girlfriend wear her costume?" Danny said to Jaime, gesturing toward Karen with his head. She was several feet away, standing by herself, watching the contest. Jaime got a pit in his stomach when he saw her, thinking again about how he had promised the guys that he'd lead her to Edith's house that night and lock her inside. The thought of it made him feel sick. Truthfully, he was relieved to see she hadn't worn her costume. It was weird and old-timey, a lot like the dress Edith wore around her house every evening. It would only have invited more insults from the guys.

Mark laughed at Danny's joke and Jaime smiled half-heartedly but he was very much not amused. Jaime shrugged. "You could go ask her yourself if you weren't so afraid of talking to girls," he said.

Mark laughed even louder at this. Danny's face turned red. "Are you going to get her to come to the woods tonight, or what?" he asked, deflecting the attention back to Jaime. "You're not going to wuss out on us, are you?"

Jaime hesitated. Even he was surprised by what he said next. "Actually..." he began; his palms started to sweat and his heart began beating faster. He could feel Mark, Danny, and Joe all staring at him, trying to anticipate how he was going to finish his sentence. He wanted to shrink into a ball and disappear but he just couldn't fight the guilty feeling in his gut any more. Plus, moving forward with the prank would mean bringing them to Edith and he couldn't imagine what they would do or who they would tell once that happened. "I'm not so sure about the prank tonight," he finally said.

"What!" Mark exclaimed, sounding irate. "You're kidding me, right?! You've got to be kidding."

Jaime wanted to back down but he couldn't. Instead, he dug in. "It's just...I have something I need to tell you." He took a deep breath.

"What is it?" Joe asked, anxiously.

"Yeah, spit it out," Danny said.

"I lied about the lady in the house," Jaime said. "I made it all up. There's nobody there. It's just an empty, old house in the woods."

"I knew it," Danny said. He was seething.

"We were all right about you from the beginning, Jaime," Mark said, coldly. "You're just a stupid little pansy that we never should have become friends with. I can't believe this! I can't believe you would do this to our Halloween."

Mark looked like he was ready to hit Jaime. Jaime straightened his back and met his gaze. He didn't know what to say but he wasn't going to cower.

"Well we could still do a prank, right?" said Joe. "Just because there's no one living in that house doesn't mean we can't do a prank."

"We're doing a prank on Karen," Danny said. "You're coming up with one for us or else," he said to Jaime, pointing a finger at him threateningly.

"Guys, look at her," Jaime said, growing bolder. "Come on, do you really need to be such jerks? Have you ever even tried talking to her like a normal person?"

"Oh, so now you're going to start defending her?" Danny said.

"Danny's right," Mark chimed in. "You better still have a prank for us tonight."

Jaime shook his head. "I don't think we should," he said.

"Come on!" Mark exclaimed, exasperated and upset.

"Think about what you're doing," Danny said. "Are you ready to have no friends? Because that's what being a hero like this is going to lead to."

Jaime looked at Danny. "What did you say?" he asked.

"You heard me," Danny said.

Danny's words were familiar and it only took Jaime a brief moment to realize why. He remembered a passage in Edith's journal about how Sam had tried talking her out of her plan to stop her Father. Danny's words sounded a lot like Sam's. Suddenly, he had an idea.

"Wait," Jaime said. "I've got it."

"Got what?" Mark asked, sounding annoyed.

"We can still pull off a prank," Jaime said. "I know exactly how we'll do it."

Just then, the bell rang signaling the end of the lunch period. Everyone in the courtyard began to disburse.

"You better mean that," Mark said to Jaime as the group began heading back to their classroom.

"I promise," Jaime said convincingly. "You'll get your prank. I know exactly what to do. Just meet me at the house in the woods a little before 9:00. I'll do everything else."

"What about Karen?" Danny asked.

"Don't worry," Jaime said. "She'll be with me."

CHAPTER 24

When school got out, Ms. Spencer asked Jaime to stay behind. After all the other students had left, she scolded him for being late and asked him what his excuse was. He said he wasn't feeling well that morning which technically was true considering that, when the morning had come, he was exhausted and scared. When Ms. Spencer was sure she had driven her point home, she let him go.

Jaime went straight to Karen's after leaving school. She was surprised when she saw him standing at her door. He said an awkward hello and then apologized as profusely and sincerely as he knew how for not being a good friend. His apology was clunky and incoherent at times but it was clear that he really was sorry. Luckily for him, Karen was quick to forgive by nature and she made no exception for Jaime.

When all the apologizing and forgiving was complete, Jaime asked Karen to come out with him that night. "I can't tell you a lot of details," he said. "I want to keep them a surprise but I promise it will be fun. It will be the best Halloween ever. You won't regret it.

Karen was skeptical and hesitant at first but Jaime wouldn't stop trying to convince her. "OK," she finally agreed after a while. "I'll come."

"Awesome!" he said. "I'll come by and get you at 8:00. Oh, and make sure you wear your costume."

"Of course," Karen said. "It's Halloween."

After leaving Karen's, Jaime returned home where his mom was waiting for him. "There you are!" she said when he came in the door. She wrapped him in a big hug. "You survived the night alright without me?"

Jaime shrugged his shoulders. "It wasn't that bad," he said.

She squeezed his cheek, knowing it would drive him nuts. "Look at my Jaime Bear getting all grown up."

He gently pushed her hand away. "Mom, Stop!"

She laughed. "What are your plans tonight?" she asked.

"Umm, me and some friends are gonna get together around 8:00. I think we're just going to – you know – go around town and see some stuff."

His mom raised an eyebrow. "Go around town and see some stuff?" She said. "Honey, I'm not stupid. I teach teenagers for a living."

Jaime smiled. "What?" he said.

"Look, you don't have to tell me what you're doing if you don't want to just promise me you won't get yourself into any trouble."

"I promise," Jaime said.

"OK. Now go do your homework. I need to start making dinner."

Jaime went to his room, dropped his backpack and collapsed on his bed. His pillow felt so perfectly soft beneath his head. He was asleep in no time and didn't wake up until his mom came in to let him know it was time to eat.

When Jaime arrived at Edith's house that night, Mark, Danny, and Joe were already waiting for him outside of the perimeter wall. He stopped in the path near the hidden lever in the ground that opened the tall, wrought-iron gate. "Where's Karen?" Danny asked.

"She's coming" Jaime assured him. "She's just a little ways behind me."

"So, what's the plan?" Joe asked.

Jaime looked at his watch. It was 8:55. "Let's go in and I'll show you," he said.

"In the house?" Mark asked, sounding surprised and maybe even a little scared.

"Just inside the yard should do," Jaime said. "Go on," he urged them.

The guys turned to scramble through the opening created by the broken half of the double gate. When Jaime was sure they weren't looking, he stomped on the lever near his foot. With a creaky, piercing sound, the half of the gate that still worked opened slowly. Mark, Danny, and Joe all stopped, suddenly becoming motionless.

"Holy crap," Joe said.

"Did you see that?" Mark asked.

"Whoa," Jaime said as he caught up to them. "Did that gate just open on its own?"

Nobody moved for a moment. Everyone was frozen in their tracks. "Come on," Jaime urged them. "Let's just keep going."

Nobody wanted to be the one to wimp out so they all pushed ahead. As they walked through the opening, Joe began to chuckle at the tension. "Are you guys gonna run away again like last time?" he said, laughing as he spoke.

"Shut up, Joe," Danny said. He was in no mood for joking. "You ran just like the rest of us."

Just then, the screech owl that lived in one of the trees on the property made a loud, eerie noise that sounded more human than animal. Jaime smiled to himself at the perfect timing. Again, everyone stopped cold in their tracks. Wide eyed, Mark, Danny, and Joe searched the night's darkness for the source of the sound but they didn't see anything. Jaime, who had walked to the lever that closed the gate, took the opportunity to step on it without the guys seeing him.

"Guys..." Jaime said as the gate began to swing closed. The other three looked back.

"I'm out of here!" Joe said.

Jaime stood in his way and held up his hands. "No, no, no," he said. "Come on, let's just do this."

Mark and Danny looked like they were ready to go too but they wouldn't admit it. "Yeah," Mark said. "Let's do this.'

"This better not be dumb," Danny said. He seemed to be getting angrier as things got scarier. "This prank better be good, Jaime."

"It will be. Come on; over here," he said, walking toward the old hearse parked near the driveway and motioning for the others to join him.

"By the hearse?" Mark asked.

The screech owl called out again, sounding like the painful moan of someone needing help.

Danny turned his head from side to side searching for the source of the noise. "This is so stupid," he said.

"Yes, by the hearse," Jaime said. "It's a good hiding place."

"There's no way I'm getting in that thing," Joe said.

"You don't have to," Jaime said. "We're just getting behind it."

"Come on, Danny," Mark said. It seemed like he was actually just trying to convince himself to move, though.

Jaime looked at his watch as the group scrambled behind the hearse. '*8:59*,' he thought to himself. '*Perfect.*'

"Now what?" Danny said, impatiently.

They were crouching down with a clear view of the front door to Edith's house and the 2nd story window just above it.

"OK," Jaime said, "when Karen comes through those gates..." he stopped suddenly, staring at the house with his mouth open.

"What?" Mark asked.

Jaime pointed and the other three guys looked to see what had stolen his attention. Edith was right on time. Just as she did every night at 9:00, she stood in the 2nd story window with a candle-lit lantern in her hand, looking out into the night with her sightless eyes. The moon was bright that night, illuminating her wispy, white dress even more than usual. She was ghostly and perfect.

Jaime couldn't tell who ran first but, with the frenzied sound of hands and feet scraping on the dirt, Joe and Danny found their footing and took off. Mark was right behind them. Jaime jumped up to chase after them. He caught up with them at the gate as they frantically pushed their way through the tight opening.

"Go!" Danny yelled impatiently at Joe who was in front.

In the chaos, Joe ran in the wrong direction when he got through the gate, following a small walking path into the woods and missing the main trail entirely. Danny followed him.

"No, this way!" Jaime called, pointing in the right direction, but Mark was the only one who heard him. With only the slightest hesitation, Mark glanced in the direction the other two had gone and then ran down the path Jaime was pointing to. Jaime followed him.

The trail took a blind turn around some trees that jutted out. Mark rounded the bend at full speed with Jaime right at his feet. Suddenly, Mark screamed a high-pitched scream, skidded to a stop and hunkered down in fetal position as if protecting himself from some sort of inevitable blow. Karen was standing in the middle of the path draped in her Halloween costume: an old, white dress with a wispy veil that flowed down her back. She held an old-fashioned, candle-lit lantern in her hand. To Jaime's disappointment, she was wearing a jacket too, which made the whole thing a little less authentic. He had tried to convince her to take it off when he asked her to wait where she was for his return several minutes earlier. Fortunately, it was unzipped, revealing as much of the creepy, old dress as possible. Plus, Mark had been so frightened at the sight that he didn't seem to notice the jacket nor did he recognize Karen.

Seeing Mark's reaction, Jaime couldn't hold back. He burst into laughter. Mark lifted his head – a little tentatively - and looked at Jaime, confused. Karen was confused too. But Jaime kept laughing. He couldn't help himself.

Mark looked at Karen and realized it was her and not a ghost standing in front of him. His mind couldn't make sense of what he was seeing. "But -" he said, then looked behind him, down the path toward Edith's house. "You were…" he looked back at Karen. "How did you..?"

Mark straightened from his crouch. As he did, Karen, Jaime, and he all noticed at the same time a large wet spot near the crotch of his pants. Jaime couldn't believe it. Mark had wet himself.

A series of expressions flashed across Mark's face, quickly turning from embarrassment to anger. Just then, Joe and Danny's voices could be heard a short distance away. They had apparently discovered their mistake and were walking towards the trail that the other three stood on. Before Mark could say anything, Karen took off her jacket. She shivered in the cold as she did.

"Here," she said, holding it out to Mark. "Tie this around your waist. Nobody else needs to know. Right, Jaime?" she said, looking over at Jaime sternly.

Jaime's laughter slowed to a stop. He nodded his head.

Mark looked a little unsure but he took the jacket and tied it around his waist before Danny and Joe got any closer.

"I'm sorry," Karen said as he did. "I didn't know that I was supposed to scare you. I wouldn't have done it if I knew that." Her sincerity was plain and undeniable. Mark didn't know how to react. Danny and Joe reached them before he had to respond, though.

"There you guys are," Joe said.

"What's she doing here?" Danny asked, coldly.

Mark looked at Karen and then at Danny, trying to wrap his head around all that had just occurred. "It's cool," he finally said to Danny. "She's hanging out with us tonight."

Danny furrowed his brow. "What?!" he said, sharply. "Wait, is this…" he trailed off. He was sure this had to be part of the prank and he was worried he had just blown it.

Mark shook his head. "No, it's not," he said, reading Danny's thoughts. "There's no prank. She's with us tonight, OK?"

Danny huffed. "No, that's not OK. What are you talking about?"

Mark looked at Karen. "Don't worry about it" he said. "He'll get over it."

"Have you lost your mind?" Danny said to Mark.

"Shut up," Mark said back. "Come on guys. Let's head back to town."

Danny was stunned. "Speak for yourself," he said. "I can find something more fun than hanging around with you losers."

"Fine. Go." Mark said.

Danny shook his head in disbelief. "Are you kidding me, man? Seriously. What is going on?"

"I'm dead serious," Mark said. "If you don't want to hang out with us – with *all* of us – then you should go."

Danny huffed again. "You guys are a bunch of idiots," he said. "I can't believe this. Come on Joe."

Joe didn't move, though. He just shrugged his shoulders. "I'm good," he said. "I'll hang out with these guys."

Danny rolled his eyes, turned around, and walked away fuming.

Mark looked at Karen, still not sure what to say. "Sorry," he muttered.

Karen shrugged. "I wouldn't expect anything less…from any of you really."

"I know," Mark said, glancing down at the ground. "Even if you had known you were coming to scare me tonight, I totally would have deserved it," he said.

Karen nodded her head. "I know. You absolutely would have."

"Sorry," he muttered again. He took the jacket from around his waist and handed it to her. "You should put this back on."

"Thanks," Karen said, accepting the gesture. "Let's head back," she said. "Maybe there's still time to do some Trick or Treating. It's a full moon tonight so maybe the extra light will make it seem not so late." The group started walking down the path back towards town. "In fact," Karen continued, "it's actually a harvest moon tonight. Did you know…"

Jaime interrupted. "Wait," he said, "tonight's the harvest moon?"

"Uh-huh," Karen said, nodding her head. "You know what that means?"

"Sort of," Jaime said. "I need to go back to the house."

The others looked at him quizzically. "I just…umm, I left something that I need to get."

He looked at Karen, wondering if she would be OK without him. She seemed to understand because she nodded her head subtly and gestured with her hand for him to go.

"I'll catch up," Jaime said. "Just go on without me."

"OK," Mark said. "What were you saying, Karen?" he asked as they continued down the path.

When Jaime reached Edith's house, he found a place in the shadows to hide in her front yard while he waited. He listened to the screech owl and watched the stars while the moon rose higher in the night sky. If it was the night of the harvest moon, that meant Edith would be lighting the candles. Jaime was curious to watch and, in a weird way, wanted to share the moment with her.

She finally emerged from the house after nearly an hour had passed. Her flowing white dress made her shuffle less pronounced. When she reached her personal graveyard among the trees, she struck a match and lit the first candle which she then used to light the rest. Soon, the grove was glowing softly and dancing with long, quivering shadows.

Even knowing that Edith was as mortal as he was and that her house wasn't really inhabited by ghosts, the scene in front of him was hauntingly eerie. Jaime couldn't look away. Edith looked majestic, sad, frail, and creepy all at once. A cold breeze kept lifting the delicate hem of her dress and her white, wiry hair, all of which subtly radiated a silver hue in the light of the full moon.

After moving through the rows of trees and lighting every candle, she turned from the grove and walked to her Father's grave, lighting his candle last. Then she walked slowly through the shadows and light. She looked nearly like she was floating as she walked in and out of the darkness, visiting each grave again. When she was done, she drifted back to her house and turned in for the night. Jaime stayed for a moment longer after Edith left and watched the candles glow.

The next day was Saturday. Jaime thought he might make it back to Edith's in the afternoon but his mom had different plans. She had a list of chores for him to do including helping her box up their summer clothes and getting the Christmas decorations down from the cellar. When all of that was done, she insisted they take a drive together to look at the last of the fall colors outside of town before they disappeared.

On Sunday, Jaime woke up late and had nothing to do. After eating breakfast and getting ready for the day, he told his mom he was going to a friend's house. He took the folded pages from Edith's journal from his top drawer and tucked them into his coat then began the long walk into the woods. Before even arriving at Edith's house, this visit felt different than the others. For the first time, he wouldn't be a silent intruder. He would talk with her and ask her questions about the things she had written.

When he reached her home, he went around the back and knocked on the door. He thought Edith would be more likely to hear him here and the back door was less cumbersome for her to get to. She didn't hear him, though. He knocked again, more loudly this time. Still, she didn't come.

He fished out the key he was carrying in his pocket and let himself in. He opened the door slowly at first and called for Edith but she didn't respond. The house was quiet – even more so than usual. "Edith!" he called again.

She wasn't in the kitchen or the large room at the bottom of the stairs. Jaime supposed she could be out in the woods but she usually didn't lock the door when she left the house to check traps or gather wood. He climbed the stairs to the second story, calling her name again as he did. When he reached the top, he made his way down the hall and could see Edith's door slightly ajar. He knocked on it, not wanting to be too intrusive. It opened a little further and he could see her lying on her bed.

She was wearing her evening dress, which, by now, she normally would have changed out of for the day. And, it was unusual for her to take a nap this early. "Edith," he said. She didn't budge. He walked to her side cautiously and slowly, placing a hand on her arm when he reached her. "Edith," he said again, much quieter this time. Still, she remained completely still. He shook her a little and then felt her wrist. There was no pulse.

He suddenly lifted his hands and backed away a step. He had never seen a dead body, let alone touched one. It made him uncomfortable; He didn't know what to do. He took a half step forward and poked at her arm. She didn't seem stiff or very cold.

For a second, he thought about running back to town and getting his mom or a doctor or the police. It seemed like someone should be there besides him. Somehow, though, that didn't feel right. This home and the yard outside were Edith's sanctuary and the least he could do for her was keep it undisturbed. The thought of others entering felt like a violation of something sacred. It felt like betrayal.

He walked back out to the hallway and peered out one of the windows that overlooked the front yard. He could see the grave Edith had dug next to her Father's. He remembered what she had said to him about her final wishes and, suddenly, he knew what he needed to do. Searching through the house, he found a few things that he would need which he gathered into a tin bucket. Then he went to the cellar and retrieved the shovel he knew would be there and, finally, to the grave where he set everything down on the dirt. Edith must have been working on the grave for days; it was quite deep now.

Returning to her bedside, he again felt apprehensive. Wanting to provide this final service for her, though, he willed himself forward. Gently, he folded her hands over her chest and carefully wrapped her in the blanket she was lying on. To his surprise, a lump rose in his throat as he did. He swallowed hard and slid his arms under her neck and under her knees then lifted. It took a great deal of strength for him. Although thin, Edith was solid and heavier than she looked. Holding her wrapped body tightly against him, he carefully walked down the stairs and out to the yard. Twice he had to set her down and rest.

When he finally reached Edith's grave, he laid her next to it, breathed heavily, and stretched his strained arms. Not wanting to simply roll her into the hole, he gripped the blanket as tightly as he could and carefully lowered her into the ground. Finally, he took the journal pages from his jacket. He knew that, without them, nobody in Edith's Hollow would ever believe the things he had discovered. He wasn't sure he wanted them to know, though, and he knew Edith didn't. So, he laid them on top of her body then turned to the mound of dirt she had accumulated and, with his shovel, returned it to the earth.

When the job was finished, Jaime rubbed his sore and blistering hands. He turned to the bucket he had brought and took out a small candle holder with a candle in it and nailed it to the tree with the hammer and nails he had found in Edith's kitchen. Then he took a box of matches from the bucket and lit the candle.

He watched the candle burn for a moment before returning the things he had borrowed to the house. He went back to Edith's room and straightened the sheets on her bed. As he did, a note lying on her bedstand caught his eye. He picked it up and began to read. The handwriting was shaky and uneven but the words were legible:

Jaime,

If you're reading this, it is because you've chosen to return and I think that means you are kind. Kindness means the world to someone like me. Some time ago, I broke a dish in my kitchen. I thought it was my last. But, curiously, I later found another in a spot where I know it had not been before. I thought it was the ghosts. However, I have considered it further and I believe it was probably you. I am glad I have left the world feeling like you were a friend.

He wiped a tear from his eyes and put the note in his pocket. He was curious to see that, beneath it was lying a long strip of paper with a familiar poem on it which he also folded and put in his pocket.

Before leaving the house, he found a knife and one more nail to bring with him. Then, with the key that he carried, he took several minutes to walk the halls, making sure to close and lock every door to every room, including the front door which he exited through. As he re-emerged to the yard, the sun was beginning to sink but the candle at Edith's grave was still flickering.

Walking over to the place where she was buried, he took out the knife he had found and carved the initials "EF" in the tree. Then, he took the poem from his pocket and fastened it in place below the burning candle with the nail he had brought. The paper made a noise as it flapped gently in the wind. Holding it down with his finger, he silently read the final few lines to himself:

Turn over the dirt,
The grass and the stones
And bury the bones
And bury the bones.

EPILOGUE

The morning sun was shining through the car window as Jaime and his mom pulled away from their house in Edith's Hollow. All their belongings were stuffed into the rear of their station wagon and in a hard-shell carrier that sat atop of the vehicle. Jaime wasn't sure where it was coming from but the sun had somehow created a prism on the cloth-lined ceiling above him. He watched it sway and bounce with the car's motion.

The weather was warming up and there was a hint of humidity in the air. All around, things were blossoming and blooming. Jaime knew that, when they arrived back in Arizona in a few days, it was going to look brown and baren compared to the green all around them.

"Are you going to miss it here?" his mom asked as they passed a sign that said 'Leaving Edith's Hollow.'

"A little," Jaime said. "It wasn't as good as home but there are definitely some things I liked about it."

His mom nodded her head. "I'm sorry we have to move again," she said.

"It's OK, mom," he assured her. "Things happen."

They rode in silence for a while until reaching the woods. The thick trees blocked nearly all of the sun's light.

"These woods still creep me out," his mom said as they entered the dark, thick cluster of trees, shrubs, ferns, and moss. "Are they scary to you?" she asked.

Jaime shrugged his shoulders. "Not really," he said. "I mean, they were kind of scary to me at first but I got used to them I guess."

"Well, I didn't," she said. "You must be braver than me."

To their left, Jaime caught a passing glimpse of a trail that met the road and continued deep into the forest. He had been watching for it. He thought about Edith's house somewhere among those trees, far out of sight. His mom was right; in his mind's eye he imagined walking that trail alone until he was surrounded by shadows and he couldn't deny that it sent a bit of a chill down his spine.

"Mom," he said, a little tentatively, "do you think it's ever OK to be scared?"

She was quiet while she pondered his question. "Well," she finally said, "I think fear is a part of life and we've got to learn to live in harmony with it."

Jaime nodded his head.

"Then again," she continued after a moment, "I suppose there are some things we should try our best *not* to be afraid of."

"Yeah, I think so too," Jaime said.

After several moments of silence, his mom spoke up again. "I think a lot of people are afraid of people or information that challenges what they are used to. It's not comfortable so they'd rather just push it away."

"Do you think that's why the school fired you?" Jamie asked, "because we were outsiders?"

"Technically, I wasn't fired," she said with a smile, pretending to be offended. "They just declined to renew my contract for next year. But, yes, I think that's basically what it boiled down to. The principal said I understand history but I don't understand *their* history. I think what he really was saying is that they prefer to keep insiders in and outsiders out."

Jaime suddenly felt bad for his mom, which was a feeling he wasn't used to. "I think you're a great teacher," he said.

"Thank you, Jaime!" she replied, genuinely sounding touched by his compliment. "You've never seen me teach, though," she added with a smile and a little laugh.

"Well, that's true," he admitted. "But I know what you're like and I'm sure you're really good."

"That's sweet of you, Jaime Bear," she said.

They rode in silence for a moment longer. Jaime was debating something in his head before deciding to speak again. "You know," he said, "those other teachers and stuff don't know as much as they think they do."

His mom raised her eyebrows, amused and a little curious. "Is that right?" she asked.

Jaime nodded. "I bet none of them could tell you why their town is called Edith's Hollow."

"Actually, I think you're right about that," she said. "I asked that question when we first arrived and nobody seemed to know the answer. That's interesting, Jaime. What makes you bring that up?"

"I'm just saying, I wouldn't take anything they say about your teaching personal. They don't know what they're talking about."

"I appreciate that," she said. "Thank you," she said again.

Jaime wasn't done, though. "Plus," he added, "I know why it's called Edith's Hollow."

"Oh, is that right?" his mom said, sounding amused again.

"No, I'm serious. I really do know," he said.

The smile melted from her face. "OK, now I'm curious," she said. "So, what's the story?"

"Well," Jaime said, "it starts with a little girl…"

Made in the USA
Las Vegas, NV
08 October 2023

78729612R00177